the

sunset
sisters

the

sunset
sisters

CECILIA LYRA

bookouture

Published by Bookouture in 2020

An imprint of Storyfire Ltd.
Carmelite House
50 Victoria Embankment
London EC4Y 0DZ

www.bookouture.com

ISBN: 978-1-83888-802-2
eBook ISBN: 978-1-83888-801-5

For Bruno

AUTHOR'S NOTE

This is not the story of my life. But it is a book about two sisters who, as children, forge a bond so strong that they decide to put each other before everyone else, including their parents.

And that is the story of my sister and me.

PROLOGUE

Julie

Nineteen years ago

At sunrise, I feel my eyes flutter open. It's here—it's finally here. My thirteenth birthday.

I prop myself on my elbows as I sweep my gaze across the room. It looks the same as it did yesterday morning: cool and tidy, a soft amber glow filtering through the blinds. Cassie asleep to my left. Slowly, I sit up and kneel over to the window. I lift one of the slats with my index finger.

"Is it time?" Cassie's voice is slow and groggy.

I nod, making a wave with my hand, thrilled that she's awake. "Come on."

Cassie stumbles over to my bed and flings her long arms around me. "Happy Birthday, Jul," she whispers in my ear. My face is buried in her thick, red mane. "*Thirteen.* My sister is an old lady."

"Hurry up, OK?" It's what I tell her every year on my birthday. I usually don't like it, being a different age than Cassie for two whole weeks. I wish we'd been born on the exact same day, like twins. But today I don't mind. I've been dreaming about turning thirteen for as long as I can remember. It's a big deal—I'm a teenager now.

"Yeah, yeah." Cassie releases me and begins pulling the blinds open. "Wow," she says, under her breath. I follow her gaze towards the orange-red sphere rising in the distance. The effect is magical, like the sun is defying gravity. "You were right. It's *beautiful*." She leans forward so that her nose is glued to the window.

"Told you," I singsong. Cassie is usually asleep at sunrise.

We're quiet for a moment, both of us hypnotized by the view.

"Do you regret it," she begins, her voice low. "Not traveling with our father and your mom?"

I frown. "Are you kidding me?" Where is this coming from?

"This is nice, but..." She turns to face me. "It's not Paris."

"I wouldn't trade it for the world." It's true: I don't take Montauk for granted. I know how lucky I am to spend summers with my sister and grandmother. Three years ago, I didn't have them in my life. Cassie didn't even know I existed.

"Let's promise we'll always come here for the summer," she says, her eyes wide and resolute. Cassie loves making plans. "Even when we're adults."

"Sounds good to me." I don't point out that she's giving up a lot more than I am. Daddy didn't invite her along on his trip with Sophie (obviously). But I'm sure her mom would agree to send her anywhere in the world. Whenever, wherever. They can afford it.

She extends her pinkie. "Summer together, forever."

"Summer together forever," I repeat, locking my little finger in hers.

CHAPTER ONE

Cassie

Monday, June 18th

The lawyer is a lot younger than I expected.

Over the phone, I pictured an older man because, really, who would name their child *Norman* these days? I wonder whether he was picked on as a boy. And whether his wife feels silly crying out his name when they're in bed. Because that's another thing I've noticed: Norman-the-lawyer—surely just fresh out of law school, with those baby cheeks and rosy complexion—wears a wedding band.

This is a new habit. As a young girl, I promised myself I would never walk down the aisle, and so I've spent the greater part of my life barely acknowledging left hands.

What's that saying about making life laugh by telling it your plans?

It's my saying, too. I share it with my patients all the time: *Never say never* and *Be careful what you wish for.* Clichés, but fitting ones—sentiments I tap into to remind my patients not to close themselves off, to face the future with an open mind. And yet here I am: thirty-one years old, unmarried, yes, and in love with a man who couldn't make me his wife even if I wanted him to.

Which I don't. I really don't.

But it is ironic.

"Your sister should be here any minute now," Norman says, sensing my impatience.

I nod as I scan the conference room: oval-shaped table, wood-paneled walls, identical leather-bound tomes neatly lined on a built-in bookshelf to the far left. The space is generic and elegant, not unlike Norman-the-lawyer, who is wearing a sharp, navy-blue suit, probably Italian. Not that I can tell.

Julie would know. Her mother read her *Posh* articles in lieu of bedtime stories. Julie's indoctrination on All Things Designer probably began in the womb. And she is her mother's daughter, after all. The apple never falls far from the tree.

That's a saying I don't use with my patients. Instead, I encourage them to forge their own identities, to break free from the stereotypes of their childhoods. *You can't change the past, but you can write your own story from here on*, I say.

Ha! If they could see me now, they'd find a new therapist.

"Ms. Meyers, I hope you don't mind me saying so, but my wife is a huge fan. She watches your show every week. And she's read your book twice."

I'm about to tell Norman-the-lawyer that it isn't *my* show when I hear the sound of a door opening behind me.

"I'm so sorry to be late."

That voice. It's been over a decade, but I'd recognize it anywhere.

I don't turn around. I want to, but it's important to keep my cool. Part of me is hoping that she's gained weight, or at least developed an adult acne problem.

"Ms. Meyers!" Norman exclaims. Why is he using her maiden name? "So glad to see you."

I resist the urge to roll my eyes as I watch Norman all but drool over her. He has forgotten all about me. Probably just forgot about his wife, too. The familiar tug of jealousy drums inside my chest. I'm betting he wishes that I'd been the one to arrive late. Story of my life.

"Please, call me Julie," she says.

I take note of this: she hasn't changed her galling habit of pronouncing her name with a soft *j*, in the French fashion.

"Hello, Cassie," she says, turning to me.

I give her a slight nod but nothing else.

She is unchanged: slim and petite, with cheekbones that could cause a paper cut, a heart-shaped face, and pouty lips. But her look is different: instead of the colorful, funky outfits she wore as a teenager, she is donned in an elegant, asymmetrical black-and-white pencil skirt, white silk blouse, and black stilettos. I can't help but wonder if Nana saw this transformation. They shared the same fashion sense—Julie began dressing like Nana on the very first summer they met. Nana would've been disappointed to see Julie in clothes that are so...unoriginal.

"How are you?" she asks, still looking at me.

I wonder what will happen if I answer truthfully.

I take a deep breath and focus on the fact that, while I do have to be in the same room as Julie, at least our father isn't here. Apparently, even Nana thought that would be too cruel.

"Should we get started?" I ask, turning to Norman.

"Yes, of course," Norman continues, composing himself. "As discussed on the phone, our firm handled your grandmother's affairs and she requested that you both be present during the reading of the will. Her final wishes were quite straightforward." Norman opens a cream-colored folder and clears his throat. "*I, Bernadette Patricia Meyers, being of sound mind, declare this to be my Last Will and Testament...* "

I feel a soreness in my throat as I listen to the officious legalese that sounds nothing like my spirited, creative grandmother. This is my first time at a reading of a will—my mom died without one.

Thinking of my mother sends a shiver down my spine. "Your father's bastard child" is what she called Julie when she was being nice. When she was sober.

I am aware of Norman's voice in the background, but my mind is too restless to process his words. "*I hope they keep the house in the family, but they are free to sell it as they see fit and share the proceeds from the sale equally, provided that the conditions herein are fulfilled.*"

Norman puts down the folder, his eyes fixed on Julie. It's like I'm not even in the room. I should have remembered this—and not only because she's gorgeous. All my life I've wanted to have her magnetism, her charisma—the invisible stuff that made her so irresistible to everyone, even to our father. She was the beautiful daughter: sophisticated, exotic, fun. I was the plain one: sensible and levelheaded.

I will myself to pay attention, but I must have a faraway look on my face because Norman narrows his gaze in my direction and speaks in a low, clipped voice. "In summary, she's leaving you the house and all her money if you both spend thirty consecutive days there this summer."

"Together," Julie whispers.

Wait…what?

"Yes." Norman nods.

The words Norman read only a few minutes ago begin to sink in. A wave of panic hits me. Julie and I are required to spend one month in the Montauk house?

"Is this a joke?" I blurt out.

"No." Norman's tone is sober. "These are your grandmother's last wishes."

"But is this even legal?" I say. "Making two people spend time together like that?" Surely, this kind of thing only happens in cheesy romcoms.

"It's perfectly legal, I assure you."

"What happens if one of us refuses?" I ask, leaning forward in my seat.

"Yes, what if one of us refuses?"

I roll my eyes. New look, still the same parrot of a girl.

"I have plans for this summer," Julie adds, her voice still barely above a whisper.

"If one or both of you refuse the conditions, the money goes to a charity that your grandmother wished to remain confidential," Norman says. "I strongly urge you to accept her conditions. The house in Montauk should be worth a significant sum of money."

And Nana realized this, which is why she decided to use it as leverage.

"What should we do?" Julie's head whips in my direction. She looks bewildered, lost. Like an actor who's forgotten their lines on opening night.

I remind myself that I am a trained psychologist—keeping my cool during stressful situations is a huge part of my job.

"We need to think about it." I say, still looking at Norman. "How long do we have to decide?"

"By June 25th," he answers.

"All right," I say. That gives us a week. "We'll get back to you then."

As I am leaving the offices of Katz & Kline, I retrieve my cell phone from my bag. Five missed calls and one new voicemail, all from the same number. I am about to listen to the recorded message when another call from the same number comes through. I answer on the first ring.

"Is this Cassie Meyers?"

"Yes," I say.

"Mrs. Meyers, my name is Melissa Thompson. I'm calling from Massachusetts General Hospital. We need you to come in right away, ma'am. Your husband has just checked into the Intensive Care Unit. He may have had a heart attack."

"My husband?"

"Is this Daniel O'Riley's wife?"

A pause. "Yes. Yes, that's me," I lie. "I'll be right there."

CHAPTER TWO

Julie

Monday, June 18th

It's coronation day, and the princess is late.

No, that won't work. Coronations are happy occasions.

It is the day of the great unveiling of the Queen Mother's last wishes, words that were carved in stone and will soon be presented to the entire kingdom, but mostly to the princess, who is running late because...

Well, because traffic in Boston sucks, that's why.

OK, so this story needs work. They all do at first.

I open a new Note on my phone and write the general premise of the tale. I'll have fun with it later.

Normally, I'd text Patrick a quick *I love you*, but not today. Not after last night.

The driver tells me I've reached my destination: a mirrored-glass high-rise in the Financial District. I silently pray that none of Patrick's friends work here because I make a run for it, thanking the driver, and scuttling inside. Very unladylike.

As I step out of the elevator, I take a moment to steady my breathing before introducing myself to a sleepy-eyed receptionist. My Louboutin heels click on the marble floors as I am escorted down a corridor lined with conference rooms. I know which one I'm headed to before the receptionist reaches for the door handle.

I recognize her red leonine hair through the frosted glass walls. My legs turn watery.

My sister.

The Fire Princess has porcelain skin and a red mane made of solar flare, gamma rays, and meteorites. The Sky Princess hasn't seen her in fourteen years.

(Watching her counsel people on TV for a few minutes every week does not count.)

"I'm so sorry to be late," I say, entering the room.

The lawyer shakes my hand and introduces himself, but I don't catch his name.

Cassie doesn't even bother to acknowledge my presence. Her hair looks different—on *East Coast Coffee* she always has it up in a bun, but it's untamed now, curly and free. I can tell she doesn't like her haircut by the way she's holding herself. I want to tell her to get a Brazilian Blowout—it does wonders for frizzy hair—but, of course, I don't. She's wearing dark jeans, a crisp, white dress shirt, and ballet flats. I wonder if she still hasn't gotten over her insecurity about her height. She would look stunning in heels. She definitely has the legs for it.

In my stories, the Fire Princess has a closet full of heels.

"Hello, Cassie," I say. Maybe all I need to do is extend an olive branch. Show her that I want to be civil.

Nothing.

"How are you?" I continue.

"Should we get started?" she asks the lawyer.

I wonder if she would've spoken to me if we'd run into each other in the waiting area. I chide myself again for my tardiness. I've never been punctual, but I've gotten so much worse, probably because it's a habit of mine that Patrick doesn't mind—a rarity. "Only Americans believe in punctuality," Patrick says when we're out. "The French consider it terribly unfashionable to be precisely on time." Patrick loves accentuating my European eccentricities.

I must look ridiculous staring at Cassie while the lawyer reads Nana's will. Her neck is stiff, as if she is purposefully avoiding returning my gaze. What did I expect?

The legal jargon is tedious, but one line stands out.

"*The condition that I ask of my granddaughters is that they spend a final month in the Montauk house in the summer following my passing, just the two of them,*" he reads.

Oh, Nana. Is this your plan? Do you really think it'll work? Or is this your way of getting me to leave Patrick, if only for a month? You've never liked him.

Like me, Nana was heartbroken that Cassie and I had become estranged. She had promised that she would find a way to make us reconnect, even if it was the last thing she ever did. I believed her. But seeing Cassie now—sensing the mercilessness of her resentment after all this time—makes me think that some things can't be fixed. I can't even begin to imagine how she'd feel towards me if she knew the full story. Nana did—but she took my secret to the grave.

Cassie is now asking the lawyer—what is his name? Really, they should wear name tags—if we can think this over.

I make sure to chime in, claiming to be busy. I can't be the loser with no plans, not when she's clearly unhappy about our predicament. Still, I feel a flicker of hope. She's not saying no to Nana's request—a small miracle. Cassie isn't shy about turning people down.

My therapist once suggested that I fell in love with Patrick because he reminded me of Cassie. I met Patrick shortly after Cassie and I had our falling out. Her absence had left a void in my life, a space I looked to fill with someone who instinctively takes charge, someone with a Type-A personality. Patrick made me quit going to therapy after that.

I used to think that meeting Patrick was kismet, but after last night I wonder if we got married too quickly. Was I really in love with him or was it just the *idea* of him?

I shouldn't be thinking about this, not now. I need to focus on the lawyer and Cassie and on Nana's crazy plan. Today is not the day to dwell on recent doubts surrounding my marriage.

I ignore the voice in my mind telling me they're not recent.

CHAPTER THREE

Cassie

Tuesday, June 19th

Daniel is an idiot. I make it a point to tell him as much now.

"Is this any way to treat your boyfriend after he's had a heart attack?" he asks.

I bring my index finger to my mouth and let out a low, shushing sound. "No talking, doctor's orders. And you didn't have a heart attack. You suffered something called unstable angina."

"I'm too young to have something that sounds so ominous." He holds on to the bed's side rails and sits up. His face is sunken and ashen, but his brown eyes are bright, luminous. Eyes of the man I love.

"You heard the doctor. It can happen at any age, even thirty-eight. It's no joke, which is why you need to rest. So no talking. Just listen."

"Yes, ma'am."

"As I was saying…you're an idiot. An idiot for not taking proper care of yourself. For working too hard. And for eating way too much clam chowder. From now on, I'm putting you on a healthy diet."

I try to steady my breathing as I prop myself on the edge of his bed. It isn't easy for me to be here, inside a hospital, especially given that I spent the night. Usually, I'd stave off my anxiety by focusing on my breath and noting my surroundings, but today that won't work. The bleach-like scent of the room. The sterile whiteness the walls. The humming of unfamiliar machines. This space will always be a trigger for me.

"All I need is you."

"You have me. I'm here."

"Thank you. For being here." He squeezes my hand.

"Thank you for telling the doctors I'm your wife. They wouldn't have let me in otherwise."

"I'm just grateful they didn't recognize you."

I roll my eyes. "It's not like I'm famous." And then, because I know that a hospital is probably filled with people watching daytime TV, I add, "It's the hairstyle." Although, of course, it's a lot more than that. It's the makeup and wardrobe—and a dozen other television tricks that make me look so different in real life. But mostly it's the hair.

"I like it like this." He runs his fingers through my wild mane. "Reminds me of Leo the Lion from Angie's favorite goodnight story."

A knot forms in my throat. If Sam and Angie were in town, I wouldn't be able to be here. They don't know about me. Obviously.

"Do you need me to call Bella?"

He shakes his head. "You know my sister. She won't be able to keep her big mouth shut. I don't want to scare them. Let them enjoy their summer break." He lifts a finger in the air. "What's that?"

I cock my head to the side. I can hear it, too. A loud, thundering voice coming from the halls.

"Daniel O'Riley. I'm looking for Daniel O'Riley. Where is his room?"

It's a voice I know well—authoritative, emphatic. One I would almost admire if I didn't know better, if I hadn't treated her for months.

Tatiana is here. Daniel's wife.

"I should go," I whisper.

"You're not going anywhere."

I look at my boyfriend, lying on a hospital bed, dressed in a generic white gown. His usual larger-than-life presence, brought by his muscular, squared-shoulders and imposing height, seems strangely fragile.

"You're supposed to be avoiding stress," I say.

"I'll handle her, Cass. I need you here—"

"You!" Tatiana shouts as she opens the door to the private room where Daniel and I have been since last night. "You seriously brought *her* here?"

"Tatiana, please lower your voice," Daniel says. He's wincing. Is it annoyance or could he be in pain?

"What the hell is she doing here?" She waves her arms frantically. Her tone is still loud. Louder, if that's even possible. "This isn't what we agreed on."

"Excuse me." A short, red-haired nurse holding a clipboard walks in, her freckled forehead scrunched up in a frown. "Ladies, this is a place with sick people in need of rest, including this gentleman right here." She points to Daniel. "Now whatever is going on here, take it outside."

"Excuse *me*, but I'm his wife!" Tatiana takes a step in the nurse's direction. "I have every right to be here."

"Not if you're causing a disturbance. Now, do I have to call security?"

I search the nurse's eyes for a flicker of recognition, but I see none. I'm actually thankful I didn't manage to sleep last night— who can sleep in a hospital?—since the dark circles under my eyes help keep me incognito.

"Come on, Tatiana." I gesture to the door.

Tatiana hesitates for a moment, darting her eyes between the nurse and Daniel. Finally she lets out a heavy sigh and follows me out the door. I'm surprised—I thought she'd put up more of a fight.

I lead the way, taking us to the hospital cafeteria. It smells of stale bagels and bad coffee.

"What's wrong with you, Cassie?" she asks, giving me a once-over. I'm grateful she's no longer yelling. "Do you know how inappropriate it is for you to be here?"

I meet her gaze. I can practically hear her judgmental thoughts as she takes in my wrinkled, day-old clothes, no doubt wondering what Daniel sees in me. Tatiana—who did not spend the night on the world's most uncomfortable foldout bed—is wearing a perfectly ironed V-cut purple dress and a long string of pearls. Her white-blond hair is pulled up in a stylish high ponytail and her skin is poreless and dewy. She looks like she always does: buffed and polished and perfect. Next to her, I look like an awkward, gangly giant.

"You want to talk about *inappropriate*?" I say. "Your husband had a heart attack yesterday and you didn't come to see him until today." I'm being unfair, choosing the more ominous term. Does she know enough to pick up on this?

If so, she doesn't let on. Instead, Tatiana looks like she's been slapped. Good.

"What business is it of yours? You're not our therapist anymore, Cassie."

"I'm not here as your therapist."

"No, you're here as his whore." A sneer.

"Call me whatever you want, Tatiana." I pause, crossing my arms over my chest. I know my measured tone is enervating. "We both know that if you cared about him, you would've been here yesterday."

"I don't have to explain myself to you." Her lips curl into a half smile. "And you better watch it. Have you forgotten what I know? Have you forgotten that I can *destroy* your precious little career? How many books do you think you'll sell once word gets out that TV's *Cassie the Couples' Counselor* ruined my marriage?"

I haven't forgotten. This isn't the first time she's threatened me.

"You know that's not what happened." I sound cool and in control, which is the opposite of how I feel.

"Were you not our counselor?" She takes a step closer. Even though she's wearing eight-inch heels, I'm still taller than she is.

"Daniel and I were never involved when—"

"Good luck getting people to believe that." Her tone is unremorseful. Defiant.

"You're right." A pause. I register the surprise in her eyes. "I *was* your counselor. Which is why I know you won't say a word. Because that would mean people would talk— and you can't have that."

She presses her lips into a thin line. From the outside, we probably look like two women engaged in a staredown. This isn't what I want, to be arguing with another woman over a man. This has never been what I wanted.

I gather my thoughts. I know what I need to do.

"Tell me you love him," I say in a slow, deliberate tone. I am thankful the cafeteria is empty. The last thing I need is to have someone record this and post it online.

"What?" she asks, confused.

"Tell me you love him. Tell me you want to be with him. Tell me you want to make your marriage work, and I'll walk away. You'll never see me again."

A stretch of silence. For a moment, I wonder if she'll prove me wrong.

I hold my breath. The thought of never seeing Daniel again is enough to send cracks through the surface of my heart. The pull I feel towards him is intense, magnetic. So powerful, it aches. What we have is once-in-a-lifetime: I know I'll never love anyone like I love Daniel.

But I also know this: I'm not bluffing. I really will walk away. If Tatiana loves him—truly loves him—I won't stand in the way of their marriage. No matter how much it hurts.

But Tatiana says nothing. She continues to stare me down with her imperious gaze.

"Do you even care about him?" I ask. An underlying sense of relief settles in me.

"I'll tell you what I *do* care about, Cassie." She takes a step forward. "I don't want *you* to have him."

I take a deep breath. Her words sting, though I'm not sure why. I've known how she feels for a long time now.

"You need help, Tatiana. I'm sorry I couldn't give it to you."

I turn on my heel and leave.

My heart hammers inside my chest as I hurry back to Daniel's room. I'm annoyed at myself for allowing Tatiana to take up so much of my time with him. What if he's had another angina? Or worse—an actual heart attack?

A thought leaps to the front of my mind, one that's been stirring inside my brain since I first saw Daniel in the hospital.

What if I lost him before ever really having him?

CHAPTER FOUR

Julie

Sunday, June 24th

I run a quick body scan in front of my closet's floor-length mirror: hair (down), eyelashes (brushed, no loose ones), breath (minty), nails (no chips), outfit (cream linen jumpsuit), shoes (patent leather ballet flats, one of the two pairs I only wear indoors). All good.

Patrick doesn't look up when I walk in. He's sitting in his favorite espresso-brown, distressed leather armchair, tapping on his iPad. Classical music floats softly from the built-in speakers. A tune I don't recognize, possibly Vivaldi. At the bar cart, I fix him a Scotch, making sure to get it exactly right: two fingers, neat, served in a crystal-cut glass.

I place the Scotch on the antique wood table to his right. I remember to use a coaster. Still no eye contact.

I take two steps back.

"We should have a baby," I say.

This catches his attention. He looks up and meets my gaze.

I wrap my arms around my waist. A reflexive gesture.

"This again?" His tone is sharp. An exhale. "Is this because of your grandmother?"

"No." I clear my throat and move closer to him, just an inch. "This is because I want a baby."

The Sky Princess is resolute: she wants an heir to the throne. The king is reluctant, but the princess will not be dissuaded. She has procured a rare potion from a sharp-toothed fairy, an elixir that will instantly put the king in a good mood while she persuades him to grant her wish.

The magical potion is—obviously—the Scotch. Alcohol is the closest thing the real world has to magic potions.

"Asked and answered, Julie," he says. I hate it when he gets all lawyerly on me. "You knew I didn't want any more kids when we got married."

He had told me two days before our wedding. Two days.

"And you knew I wanted kids," I say.

"We have Nate," he replies.

I perch on the couch to his left, purposefully crossing my legs at the ankle, like a proper lady. I can't afford to do anything to displease him today. (There are many things that displease Patrick.) I catch a glimpse of his iPad's screen. *The Economist.* No surprise there. It's Sunday evening. Patrick is a creature of habit.

"Nate is *your* son," I say. "And I love him, I do. But he lives in LA with his mom. We're lucky if we see him once a year for, what, a week?" Last time, it had been for five days. Two years ago. "Last week was Father's Day and he wasn't even here."

"I didn't see you flying across the country to spend the day with your father."

At this, I wince. Patrick knows I would've loved nothing more than to have spent the day with my dad, that I would've gladly have made the trip to Seattle for the weekend. "That was the day of the benefit dinner," I say. It's why I chose today to have this conversation with him yet again: it's been one whole week since he acted like a monster. I'm hoping that by now he feels remorse. Enough remorse to mollify his stubbornness.

But he doesn't seem the least bit moved. "I've done the baby thing." Patrick's tone isn't cruel, but it is indifferent. "I don't want to do it again." Does he know he's breaking my heart?

"Don't you want us to be a family?"

I've asked him this question more times than I can count. And every time the words leave my mouth, I feel a flicker of hope. I think to myself, *Maybe today he'll say yes.* Instead, he reminds me, once again, that I knew what I was getting into when I married him. My heart shrinks.

Patrick isn't wrong: he did tell me he didn't want kids. I was surprised—*shocked* is probably a more accurate description—and I did consider calling off the wedding. But I didn't do that because, in my heart, I didn't believe him. I had faith that, in time, he'd change his mind. I wasn't in a hurry: I was twenty-two when we got married. I had time to strengthen our bond, to persuade him.

Except, of course, it's been nine years since that conversation. And in this almost-decade, I've learned to be exactly the woman he wants me to be. I've learned to live by his rules. I use the perfume he picked out for me (Dolce & Gabbana Light Blue), wear outfits he approves of (classic cuts in neutral colors), and greet him with a quiet smile when he gets home from work (not being home is not an option; being chatty is annoying). I put on makeup right after I wash my face in the morning, but not lipstick—especially not red lipstick (red lipstick is for prostitutes and drag queens). I get a manicure every week and every week I choose the same color: bubble bath by OPI (before I met Patrick, I used to bite my nails). I only hum on occasion, even when I have a song stuck in my head—and I *never* whistle (whistling is for sailors and drunks). I even switched shampoos to please him (Patrick is very sensitive to smells). It sounds like a lot. And it is a lot. But the truth is that I'm happy to do all these things, I really am. Patrick knows what he likes, what he wants. And I'm flexible. I'm happy to adapt, to compromise.

Except on this: I want a baby.

Which is why over the past nine years I've brought up having a baby at least once every six months or so—more since I turned thirty. And he hasn't changed his mind.

I feel myself escaping—my mind is searching for comfort, trying to get back to my fairy tale. But I anchor it to this moment. I can't run. Not today.

"What if we left it up to fate?" I offer him a coy smile. "I'll go off the pill. We'll see what happens." I hold my breath and visualize him saying yes.

The king feels his steely resolve melting away.

"I'm not having this conversation again, Julie." There's a finality to his tone.

That is so *not* what the king would say! He would take the princess in his arms and make a baby with her right there on the spot.

Well, probably not *on the spot* since fairy tales are rated PG.

"A baby would do us good," I continue. "It would bond us together forever." And who knows? It might even encourage him to come home early every once in a while. To step outside his comfort zone—his miniscule comfort zone.

Patrick is a lawyer specializing in litigation. He deals with demanding, high-profile cases. When we first got married, I had a mental image of what our evenings would look like: the two of us sitting at the dining table, trading stories over a delicious meal, laughing. I did my part—I learned to make his favorite dishes, I told jokes. But Patrick gave me nothing in return except for low hums and one-word answers. At first, I reasoned that my mistake was asking him about work, so I tried steering the conversation towards current events or a funny story about one of my friends—but that failed as well. When I pressed him, he explained that he felt tired after a long day at work. His job was taxing, draining.

I asked him if there was anything I could do to help him de-stress. He gave me a list. A long one. Eventually, we fell into a routine. I greet him at the door in the evenings. I take his coat and put his shoes away. He changes out of his suit and goes into the living room, where he sits on his armchair to read. I fix him a Scotch, bring him a bowl of almonds, and give him a neck massage. After exactly ten minutes, I leave to check on dinner. We sit down to eat, in what he refers to as a companionable silence, exactly forty minutes after he gets home from work. I try not to complain—everyone is different, and Patrick is affectionate in his own way. But I do wish we were closer.

Sometimes I wonder if it's our age difference: Patrick is forty-eight, I'm thirty-one. But, mostly, I just think it's how he's wired. He's precise in his habits and forthcoming about his expectations. Yes, this makes him difficult. But, if you think about it, underlying his rigidity is actually a wonderful quality: knowing what you want, not being afraid to ask for it. Janette disagrees—she says his behavior is rooted in a need for control. But what does she know? She's not married. And it's not like I would know, either. Sophie and my dad weren't husband and wife. I don't have a marriage to emulate. And even though Patrick is like me in this respect—neither of us grew up in a conventional, two-parent household—he has been married before. True, they got divorced—but it's safe to assume he knows the rules of the game better than I do.

What we have isn't perfect, but perfection is not the goal in a marriage. Cassie says this all the time on her show. Patrick is handsome, a good provider, and he's never given me a reason to doubt his fidelity.

I should not be complaining.

Except, I do want a baby.

I didn't know Patrick when Nate was younger, but I can't imagine him being this rigid in a house with an infant. It simply isn't possible. I'm confident that if we have a baby, Patrick's unyielding ways will dissolve into a distant memory. And I, of course, will have found my calling. I've always loved children. I babysat from the ages of twelve to seventeen, and not just because we needed the money.

Also, last week's incident at the benefit dinner would've unfolded in an entirely different way if I were the mother of Patrick's child. He would've been worried about me instead.

"And do you know what it'll do to your body?" Patrick pauses, exhaling. "You'll be bloated and irrational."

I quickly realize that while I've been daydreaming, he's begun listing his Reasons Not to Have Kids. I've heard them before, more times than I care to remember. They begin with him discussing the effect pregnancy has on a woman's body and end with him comparing kids to walking shackles that strip a couple of their spontaneity. A dramatic soliloquy for a man who is supposed to be rational. And who doesn't have a spontaneous bone in his body.

"If we're not having a baby, then I'm going to the Hamptons for the summer," I say, interrupting his monologue. Patrick does not appreciate interruptions.

"Because of that silly provision?" He places his iPad on the side table, his own personal sign of full-blown annoyance. "I told you we'd fight it in court."

"I don't want to fight it. If I'm not going to be a mother, then I have to at least try to be a sister again."

"Half-sister," he points out.

I wince. Nana never allowed us to use that word, *half*.

"Why would you want to associate yourself with a woman who encourages people to air their dirty laundry on television?"

"She's a therapist. She *counsels* people."

"She hates you for no reason."

I bite my lip. Patrick doesn't know my secret. I almost told him during our honeymoon, but something made me hold back. Something other than fear and shame.

"She doesn't *hate* me," I say softly. *Does she?* "Besides, staying here feels like a waste of time. You work 24/7, even during the summer. If we could at least do something, just the two of us—"

"What's going on with you?" he interrupts me. "First you embarrass me at the benefit and now you're thinking of leaving?"

I feel the surge of tears. "That was an accident. You're the one who should be embarrassed by the…by your—" I stumble over my own words. Why does this always happen to me?

"Darling, listen to yourself." He looks at me with an expression that I can only describe as pitying. "It doesn't make any sense for you to go. You're confused. It's understandable, you've just lost your grandmother. But I know best. You want to stay here with me. You don't want to go to the Hamptons."

Patrick's tone is calm and self-assured. So much so that for a moment I wonder if he isn't right. Maybe I do want to stay here. Maybe I don't want to go to the Hamptons with Cassie.

But then a memory unfurls in my mind's eye: me, at the age of nine. My mother walking into my bedroom, telling me that I was going to spend the summer with my half-sister and my grandmother, two people I'd never met. My heart couldn't decide whether to feel terrified or ecstatic.

Which was exactly how I'd felt at the lawyer's office on Monday.

I haven't felt that sort of intensity in a very long time.

"This was obviously important to my grandmother, or she wouldn't have drawn up a will," I say. "Cassie is my sister. I know we haven't spoken in a long time, but she's still my family." *And I want to spend time with her,* I think to myself. Nana isn't the only one who held on to hope for so many years. I also want to believe that Cassie and I can find our way back to each other. I have to believe it.

"Your grandmother was obviously senile, Julie." Patrick exhales. "Cassie doesn't want you in her life. Why would you want to share a house with someone who's just going to ignore you?" He looks at me as though I'm insane to even consider going. And to him, I probably am—he never got along with his half-brothers.

But at this, I feel a spike of annoyance. For such an intelligent man, Patrick can be remarkably blind to his own faults. "Why wouldn't I?" I give him a pointed look. "I'm used to it by now."

He stares back at me, mouth agape. It's strangely satisfying, seeing him at a loss for words. Usually, I'm the inarticulate one.

Maybe his behavior at the benefit was the last straw or maybe it's the fact that I actually rendered Patrick speechless, but before he can think of something else to say, I get up, grab my purse, and leave our apartment.

I'm in the marbled lobby, trying to ignore the ache in my chest when I hear my phone ringing inside my bag. My heart leaps in excitement—Patrick is calling to apologize—but an unfamiliar number flashes on the screen.

"Hello?" I cringe when I hear my own voice: tentative, sniffling.

"Hi, Julie." A pause. "It's me."

My heart stops. "Hey, um, hi."

"Norman gave me your number," Cassie begins. Who the heck is Norman? "I'm calling because of the will."

I wince. She's going to challenge it, just like Patrick said we should. And I just told him I was going to Montauk.

"I'm going," she says.

I blink once, then twice. Then it's like my eyelashes are replaced by a hummingbird's wings. It's a sign. The sign I've been waiting for.

"I know you have plans for the summer," she begins, and I feel my brow furrow. What is she talking about? Then I remember what I said at the lawyer's office. Norman. That's who Norman is.

"I can cancel them," I say quickly. Too quickly. "I mean, it'll be a hassle, but I think it's important that we go. For Nana."

Am I being too loud? Patrick often chides me for being too loud. The doorman is staring at me. I quickly step out of the building. It's still light outside, the orange skies kissing the treetops in Boston Common. I look up and send Nana a smile. She's watching me—I'm sure of it.

"So, you'll let him know you're going? We have until tomorrow to get back to him."

I say, "Yes," at the same time she says, "Or I could just tell him if you want. I have to call him, anyway."

"You tell him," I decide. I amble down Beacon Street. Maybe I'll go into the park for a walk.

"All right then. I'll drive over on Wednesday." Her tone is flat.

I want to tell her that we should go together. We do live in the same city, after all. I want to ask her why that is, why she never moved away after Katherine's death. There's a lot I want to ask her, actually. And tell her. But there isn't any room for anything beyond polite scheduling matters. Our exchange is stiff, awkward. Nothing like the intimate shorthand we once shared. How did we end up this way? A dumb question. I know how, of course.

"OK, I'll do the same," I say. A white lie: there's no way I'm driving for over five hours.

We say our goodbyes. She is curt—this is Cassie, after all—but civil.

By the time I make my way through the park's wrought-iron gate, I notice that the knot in my chest has been replaced by an altogether different feeling.

Hope.

CHAPTER FIVE

Cassie

Tuesday, June 26th

I think they call it *muscle memory*, the reason why I still know the way to Nana's house after all these years. I make a right on Old Montauk Highway, taking in the picturesque horizon—the backdrop of my childhood. The happy bits, anyway.

My first recollection of the Hamptons dates back to when I was four or five years old. It isn't a particularly remarkable memory: Nana and I chasing seagulls in front of the house, back when my parents still summered here.

It was Gramps who taught me that Montauk is a hamlet in East Hampton located at the very tip of the South Fork in Long Island. Even as a young child I could list its main attractions, pointing out the historical significance of each one. My favorite: the lighthouse. The oldest one in America, around for over two hundred years, and still used to navigate ships in and out on the tip of Long Island. I spent countless hours mesmerized by Gramps' tales of this place. My mom seemed to think I was indulging him. "How polite of you to pretend to be interested in your grandfather's stories, Cassie," she'd tell me. She never understood that listening to Gramps was a treat.

The story I heard most often was of the origins of the house itself, or the "summer cottage", as my parents referred to it.

Gramps had bought it for Nana back when real estate on the island was still affordable. She dreamt of a home on the beach. My grandparents took pride in noting that the house turned out to be a great investment—property values soared in the 1970s and 1980s, when the Hamptons became the go-to summer destination for Manhattan's elite. But what had always stuck with me was that Gramps had actually *bought a house* to please his wife. This made sense. This was what husbands and wives were supposed to do for each other: small and large gestures to make the other person happy. In fact, my favorite thing about Montauk was just being around Gramps and Nana. They were an exceptionally happy couple, full of inside jokes and non-verbal communication. So very different from my parents.

Julie may not be my favorite person in the world, but it saddens me to think that she never got to meet Gramps. She missed out on so much. She never got to giggle as he plucked a coin from behind her ear. Never saw him shoo the wild turkeys that would, on occasion, make their way onto the backyard with surprising speed. Never watched him trace Sagittarius with his fingers in the summer sky or listened to him tell ghost stories as he roasted s'mores over a campfire. I know she would've loved him because he was kind and funny and patient. And I know he would've loved her because everyone loves Julie.

I'm thankful when I hear Daniel's ringtone. I don't want my mind on Julie.

"Hey, you," I say.

"Babe, are you still driving?"

"That's why you're on speaker."

"I thought you'd be there by now."

"Traffic," I say. "I can't complain. It'll be so much worse next week." After the Fourth of July, everyone and their mother will be in the Hamptons. Not that I can blame them, I think, glancing at the endless blue of ocean and sky. There are a few boats at a distance and, of course, the lighthouse up ahead. So beautiful, it looks like a painting. Gosh, I love this place.

"I can't believe I have to wait until Friday to see you."

"You're definitely coming?"

"Absolutely."

"OK. I told you the girls are coming for brunch on Sunday, right?"

"You mentioned I wasn't invited."

"It's *ladies'* brunch. They're driving all the way to the Hamptons just to see me." Christina and Rachel offered to come as soon as I told them about the will. I won't lie: I nearly choked with gratitude. I have no idea how I'd get through the month without my friends, even with Daniel driving over on weekends.

"Fine, I'll learn to share you," he teases. "I have to go back to work. I just wanted to hear your voice. Text me when you get there."

"Will do. Love you," I say, and we hang up.

Just three more days until I ask him. I am less than thrilled about being stuck in the same house as Julie for a month—but even I have to admit I need a breather from my life in Boston. Especially after the decision I've made. I wonder what the girls will say when I tell them. Rachel will be supportive—when is she not?—but I'm not so sure about Christina.

A few minutes later, I pull into Nana's driveway. The Montauk house is a two-story dwelling made of whitewashed wood and gray-shingled roof. It's literally on the beach, complete with an oversized sun porch that, from the look of it, seems to have been newly furnished.

As I step out of the car, the salt-heavy wind floods my senses, taking me back in time. To that first summer with Julie, right before our tenth birthdays.

I saw Julie before she saw me.

She and Sophie were standing on Nana's driveway, talking. Julie had her back to me. I couldn't stop staring at her hair: long, shiny, and dark. It made me hate my frizzy bird's nest even more. Her skin was a pretty olive color that made me think of honey. She was smaller than me, too: shorter, with delicate wrists and ankles.

She didn't look like my sister. At least not until she turned around.

When she did, I saw them. Her eyes, identical to mine. To Nana's.

Sophie didn't go in the house. I don't know if she wasn't invited or if she chose not to. What I do know is that the animosity between her and Nana was impossible to miss. This did not surprise me at all.

"Our eyes are the same," Julie said, once we were inside. "Just like our dad."

Our dad.

She wasn't wrong—he was *our* father. But it was such a strange thing to hear.

I shake myself out of the memory. I haven't even stepped inside Nana's house and already I'm being haunted by ghosts of the past. I can't allow this to happen. I need to stay strong.

I dig inside my purse for the keys given to me by Norman-the-lawyer. Unlocking the front door is enough to make my heart swell with recognition and longing.

Once I'm inside, I scan the familiar living room: wicker furniture, beaded cabinet doors, rocking chair. And the pièce de résistance: the farmhouse dining table, seating for twelve. Nana's pet piece of furniture, though I never understood why—it's too big. A place frozen in time. It isn't as dusty as expected. In fact, it doesn't smell like it's been closed for the past three weeks, waiting for Julie and me to learn about Nana's will.

I wonder, for the hundredth time, why Nana didn't want a funeral. If she had, would I have attended? It would have meant seeing my father. I think back to the last time I saw my grandmother: four years ago, when she came to Boston to take care of paperwork (perhaps her will). We had brunch at Finale: hash browns, pancakes, eggs Benedict. At the time, I was all but starving myself, but that day I ate like a normal person (maybe even a normal, *hungry* person). I had planned on telling her I was on a diet once we met at the restaurant, but seeing her, hugging her, had brought back my appetite, if only for a few hours. Nana was the one person in my life who always made me feel better. I had been afraid that she'd make me feel guilty for refusing to come to Montauk, but she never did. She understood—she always understood. Nana's response to everything was compassion. Which is why her final wishes are so confusing to me.

I take slow steps as I survey the first floor. The yellow L-shaped couch. The wooden rocking chair. And, of course, the granite island on the kitchen—Nana's last addition to the house, at least that I know of. I get a mental image of Nana kneading dough, her face spotted in flour. I see her bending over to fill Sebastian's bowl with wet food. Every object in this house, every surface, every corner, holds a piece of her.

"Hello there."

I turn on my heel—really, I give a small jump—to see a tall, tanned man by the door. He has a strong jaw, an athletic build, and hazel eyes. He's wearing blue jeans and a simple white T-shirt that says "Holly's" in orange and black. He's remarkably attractive.

"I'm sorry, I didn't mean to startle you," he says, smiling. His dimples are boyish.

"Who are you?"

"Where are my manners?" He sticks out his hand. "Sorry, I'm Craig. Bertie's next-door neighbor. Your neighbor now, I guess."

"I'm her granddaughter." I shake his hand.

"Bertie used to talk about you and your sister all the time." He looks me over—I'm wearing a plain, white summer dress and flats. "You're not Julie."

Of course he knows I'm not Julie. Nana probably showed him pictures of us, and his eyes popped out of their sockets when he saw Julie's long legs and pouty lips. I know this because that's everyone's reaction to seeing a picture of Julie. What annoys me is that while I may not be beautiful, I can certainly be pretty, particularly when I'm dressed up and my hair is tamed. But no amount of grooming will ever make me the pretty sister. Not when my competition is Julie.

"I'm Cassie."

"So is your sister here as well?" He looks behind me.

Five minutes into my mandatory vacation and this guy, this virtual stranger, is already asking for Julie. Well, he'll have to wait. She isn't supposed to get here until tomorrow.

"I don't think so, no."

There's a beat. I know I'm being curt, and I don't care. I resent his presence in my grandmother's house. Being here is difficult enough without having to deal with a nosy outsider. It's why I came a day early: I wanted a day by myself to get my bearings, process my emotions without interruptions.

"I'm happy you both agreed to come," he says. I must have given him a funny look because he continues, "Bertie told me about the will."

"She did?" I narrow my eyes.

"Yeah, I didn't think she would go through with it, though…" I follow his gaze as he stares at Nana's rocking chair. I wonder if he's thinking of her.

"Were you with her, when she…?" I let my voice trail off, unable to finish my sentence.

"No, it happened at night. Mrs. Bunsen found her the next day. They were supposed to go to the club." A pause. "We spent a lot of time together, though. I helped her around the house. I kept telling her to get a nurse, at least for the night, but you know Bertie."

"Stubborn."

"I was going to say *proud*, but, yeah, that sounds about right." A sad smile.

"How was she doing?" I ask, feeling guilty that a complete stranger knows more about my grandmother's final years than me. "I mean, physically. She said she was fine, but then this happened…"

I didn't shut Nana out completely, like I did my father and Julie, but I didn't make much of an effort to see her, either. I didn't blame her for what happened, but Nana rarely left the island and the memories of this place were just too much for me. We had regular phone calls, but other than the brunch at Finale four years ago, the last time I saw her was when she came into town for Julie's wedding—though, of course, she didn't tell me that's why she was in town, maybe because I never got an invitation (not that I wanted one). That was nine years ago.

"She looked well. She had her routine, tending to her plants when it was warm enough, meditating on the porch…I always thought it was impressive how she could sit down on the floor and get up all by herself at her age. My kids kept her pretty busy, too. They call her Nana Bertie…or called her, I guess." He looks down. "Plus, she had her friends. A group of four or five of them went to the Yacht Club for lunch every other Saturday and I know they played cards at least twice a week, though Bertie said it was less." A low chuckle. "And she met with Mandy weekly. If I'm not mistaken, it was Mandy who helped her come up with her… plan. You know, to bring you and your sister here."

"I'm sorry, who's Mandy?"

"Her therapist. Her grandmother is—"

"Nana had a therapist?" How could I not have known about this?

"Holistic therapist," he explains.

A chip falls into place. "Do you mean her *psychic*?"

He laughs. "That's the one."

"At least now I know who to blame for all this."

"Anyway, I've never seen her sick or anything. She was fragile because of her age, but that's about it. It was very unexpected. We were all surprised."

"Yeah," I say, looking at my canvas flats. I should have visited. Occasional phone calls just aren't enough.

I wonder how often Julie came to visit Nana. Part of me wishes I hadn't changed the subject every time Nana brought up Julie's name.

"It would've meant a lot to her that you two are giving this a chance."

"Hmm," is all I answer. I'm not about to open up to a guy I just met, even if he claims to have been close to Nana.

"Do you have bags in the car? I could give you a hand."

"No, thank you. I'm good."

"All right. Well, like I said, I live next door." He gestures to the left with his thumb. "So if you need anything, just holler. Most evenings I'm at Holly's. Do you know it? About five minutes from the Lobster Roll. It's not from your day, but it's a great diner."

"No, sorry," I answer. I'm feeling bad for having dismissed him as a Julie groupie. She isn't even here and he's being really nice.

"We serve the best crab legs in all of Southampton. Maybe you and Julie could stop by. I'd love to meet her."

Never mind. I was right the first time.

"Sure, I'll let her know." A lie. Julie may be the pretty sister, but I'm the smart one. I'm not about to send Julie off to meet some random guy at a bar.

"It was great meeting you. I've been looking forward to it," he says.

Yeah, right. I'm not the sister he wanted to meet.

CHAPTER SIX

Julie

Wednesday, June 27th

There's something wrong with the Hampton Jitney.

This isn't my first ride. I've been on them countless times as a girl, but back then they weren't quite so…bumpy. And were they always this full? I can't remember. What I do remember is that I used to love the ride here. I spent every second inside the bus reveling in the thrilling anticipation of spending *two whole months* with my grandmother and my sister. I'd practically jump from the window when I saw Cassie and Nana waiting for me. Cassie would be as close to the jitney's parking spot as possible, ready to secure my purple unicorn bag so that we could get in Nana's car and drive off, blasting *Summer Nights* on her CD player, singing along with gusto. Neither of us were very good singers, but what we lacked in talent we made up for in enthusiasm.

I don't know if I realized this at the time, but we were such happy girls. At least when we were together.

Of course, today there won't be anyone waiting for me. I should've hired a driver, but I didn't want to give Patrick an opportunity to remark on my expensive habits. He enjoys it a little too much. The subtext is not lost on me: he's reminding me of what I owe him. I wouldn't have gotten used to the finer things in life if he hadn't married me. Hence, the jitney. The bumpy jitney.

I fully regret my choice of transportation the moment I arrive. The taxi line looks like an improvised street conga. Schlepping to Main Street and finding a cab isn't an option—I have too many suitcases.

"Do you need help with that?" I look to my side to see a cheerful-looking man in his fifties wearing wrinkly linen clothes in summer pastels. "I can bring those over to your car."

"Oh, no thank you," I say. "I'm taking a cab."

He looks at the line and grimaces. "Ouch, sorry." He points to a group of people who are waving at him from a parking spot. "My family came to pick me up. I'd offer to give you a ride, but our car is full."

"Oh, don't worry about it," I say.

"Isn't there anyone you can call?"

I look down at my impractical wedge heels. "I'm actually the first one in my party to arrive." A lie. The law office called me yesterday to let me know that Cassie had arrived a day early. They didn't tell me why, but I'm hoping it's because she's actually looking forward to our mandatory month together. A girl can dream.

"Oh, well then, you'll do a good deed and pick them up when they get here."

I nod, thank him again, and say goodbye.

One hour later (I repeat—one *hour*), I am standing in front of Nana's house.

"Hello, Julie," Cassie says, opening the door.

I shouldn't have rung the doorbell. This is my house, too.

"Hi," is all I say back.

Cassie is holding a stack of what looks like old magazines. She catches me eyeing them. "I'm clearing some of Nana's old things. I'm staying in her room."

The unilaterality of her decision annoys me. I don't complain, though. She was the first one here. Besides, I wouldn't be able to sleep in Nana's room.

"I'll go put my things in our old room then," I say.

In response, she purses her lips and turns around.

I leave my tote bag on the dining table and haul my luggage up to my room. I stop midway up the stairs, catching a whiff of old wood, ocean breeze, and something else I can't quite pinpoint. It's so…Nana. It's been three years since my last visit. I've missed this place so very much.

My eyes examine the picture frames hung on the wall. So many of them are of Cassie and me. The two of us singing 'Happy Birthday' to ourselves, paddleboarding at the Yacht Club, grinning with ice cream cones in hand, swimming on the beach. I find the one we took of our identical eyes—emerald green with dark lashes—by flipping the camera, a makeshift selfie of the time. A haunting image.

"Something's ringing," I hear Cassie say. I jump when I see her walking over to the dining table, where my iPhone's screen is flashing with a familiar ringtone.

I can picture Sophie's face popping up. My mother is the only person who calls me on FaceTime.

"I got it!" I yell and sprint to pick it up.

Cassie gives me a funny look for about two seconds, and then walks out to the porch.

I bow my head and jog up to my room, phone in hand.

"I had to see it for myself," Sophie's eyes dart frantically as I take the call.

I adjust my earphones, drawing a deep breath. "Hello to you, too, Sophie."

"Don't *hello* me." I watch her light up a cigarette. "I had to hear you moved out from your husband."

My skin burns with irritation. I should've known Patrick would call her. "I didn't move out."

Sophie cranes her neck. "Is that not your grandmother's house I see?" She pinches her lips when she says *grandmother*.

I wonder if Sophie has a good enough idea of the house to know that I'm inside our old room. *Our*—Cassie's and mine. It looks like my childhood: striped blue-and-white wallpaper, slanted ceiling, twin beds with matching quilts. On our first night together, Cassie gave me the bed next to the window and took the one closest to the door. I assumed Nana had put her up to it, making her give me the bed that overlooked the ocean. I remember glancing out the window, pretending like I was aboard a cruise ship. From my bed it was all blue—blue water, blue skies. Not a speck of land.

"I'm only here for a month." I take a seat on my bed. "I told you about the will."

"The will! Such a ridiculous American custom," Sophie scoffs.

I stifle a laugh. Is she under the impression that the French don't leave wills?

"Patrick said he can take care of it. You won't lose the house."

"I *want* to be here."

"After everything I've done for you, this is how you repay me?"

This is the turn all our conversations take. It doesn't matter that I'm discussing *my* life. Sophie can make anything about herself.

"This is something I have to do for me."

A stretch of silence. Sophie eyes me suspiciously. I understand why: I'm quiet, unruffled. This is unusual—Sophie is an expert at ruffling my feathers. I meet her gaze. With her flawless, creamy skin, cocoa-colored hair and leonine golden eyes, Sophie is a beauty. Right now, she looks like a painting of a woman considering her next move.

"Is this about that girl?" she asks. *That girl*: it's what Sophie began calling Cassie, ever since she and I became friends.

"No."

"But she is there, is she not?" Sophie takes a puff of her cigarette.

"Yes."

"So it is a coincidence that you're willing to throw away your marriage now that you have a chance to play make-believe sister with her again? Do I need to remind you of all she has cost us?" She pronounces "us" as if it had a z. Her French accent is still strong even after thirty-five years in the United States—and I know this is by choice.

"Sophie, what *she* cost *us*?" I bring my voice down to a whisper. Sound carries through these walls. "Cassie lost her *mother*."

"Katherine was *folle*!" Sophie retorts. "Like the Americans say, batshit crazy!"

"Enough, Sophie."

"She is the reason you never had the family you wanted."

"I said *enough*."

A sharp exhale from Sophie. "Look, Julie. I know it's not her fault. But she is still the *raison*. You have a good life back here. A good husband, a beautiful home." She moves her hands in the air, a maestro conducting a symphony, waving her cigarette with precision.

"I've told you before…Patrick doesn't want to have children with me," I say, my voice cracking. I've dreamed of a family since I was a little girl. Surely, Sophie remembers this. Understands this.

I look away from the camera, my eyes landing on the chest of drawers that stands between the two beds. Specifically, on the frame that sits atop it: a photo of Cassie and me, taken when we were in our teens. I wonder if she's seen it. If she cares. If Nana were here, she'd find a way to get Cassie to talk to me. I'd give anything to have Nana here with me. With us.

"How many times do I have to tell you: men don't know what they want," Sophie says. "It's your job to know for them. Just get pregnant. You shouldn't have any trouble doing that. I did teach you how to seduce a man."

Ew.

"I'm not doing that." This is something I've told her before. More than once.

What is that saying about insanity being repeating the same thing over and over again, expecting different results? Whoever said it missed the point entirely. The *cause* of insanity is listening to one's mother say that same thing over and over again, expecting different results.

"You think it's better to leave him?" Her tone is accusatory, belligerent.

"I'm not *leaving* him. It's only a month."

"By the time you get back, he will have someone else, Julie. Men can't stay by themselves, especially not a man like Patrick."

I raise my eyebrows. "You mean rich?"

"I mean a man who can give a woman all that he has given you. All that we never had. Do you know how hard I had to work so you could go to a nice school and have nice things?"

Maybe it's my imagination, but I catch her glancing wistfully behind me. I realize I never considered how Sophie would feel about me inheriting Nana's house. Does it hurt her to know that this place is now legally mine—but it's never been hers, not even by association? I've never summered here with Katherine, but I'm positive she felt perfectly at home at her mother-in-law's house. Katherine was family. It's one of the many differences between a wife and a mistress.

I hate that word. *Mistress.* On the surface, it sounds sexy, in a forbidden sort of way. But that's only when it's used in the abstract. In context, its connotation is always dirty, taboo. Immoral.

"At least you had your career," I say, thinking of *Posh*, the fashion magazine where Sophie has worked since I was nine years old. Before that, she had two jobs: hostess at a French restaurant on Newbury Street and unlicensed "esthéticienne". "I feel like I have nothing." I raise my hands to inspect my nails. I feel a prick of anxiety when I see that I have a chip on my left pinkie. I'll have to book an appointment today. But then I realize that Patrick isn't here. I don't have to get a manicure at all. Or I could get a manicure and paint my nails whatever color I want. Bronze. Coral. Even red.

"You have a husband. You have a ring on your finger and a document that says he is yours. A career can evaporate in a second," she pauses for effect, snapping her fingers, "but this is binding."

"This is important to me," I say. Cassie is important to me. I absentmindedly begin picking at my chipped pinkie. It's oddly comforting.

"Fine, suit yourself. But there's something you should know about that girl." Sophie's lips curl into a knowing smile. "After all, it's awfully convenient that she didn't have plans for the summer, don't you think? Why do you think that is?"

"Maybe she also wants to—"

"Rumor has it she is seeing a married man."

Wait. What?

"How do you—"

"Sources at *Posh*." Her tone drops a register. "You know that after she wrote that little book, she became...*quasi*-famous."

"She became a lot more than that," I say.

"That's debatable." I watch as Sophie wrinkles her nose. Cassie's success is something of a sore subject for my mother. "People talk. And that's what they're saying."

"Even if it's true, what does that have to do with me?" I stare at my pinkie, now polish-free. I pull at my cuticles.

"Julie, don't you see? She is going on this little vacation because she has *no life*. That show of hers doesn't come back until the fall, she isn't married, and if this story is true, she is about to lose her career. I'll bet her boyfriend is summering with his wife just like Stephan did with his in that very house."

"It's really none of my business, Sophie." I ignore my spinning mind. "Or yours."

"Do I have to spell everything out for you? You've always been the better daughter, Julie, charming and fun and not the least bit boring, a product of love and not some sham marriage. And yet you used to hero-worship that plain girl with horrible posture who always had her nose stuck in a book! And now you're leaving your husband to try to be friends with her again. And don't tell me that's not the reason why you're there. Patrick has been Patrick for years now and all of a sudden you decide to leave? *Quelle coincidence!*"

"You don't know what you're talking about." I bring my pinkie to my mouth and suck on it.

"You're making a mistake, Julie. Staying there will only remind you of everything she took from you." Her words sound like more than a warning—they sound like a curse.

"That's enough, Sophie," I say. "This. Isn't. About. You."

I hang up before she can say anything else.

I reach for the frame on top of the dresser, grazing the glass with my newly naked pinkie. The picture of Cassie and me was taken inside this very room, on my bed. Cassie is sitting cross-legged and I'm standing behind her, propped on my knees, both of us grinning widely. I remember Nana holding the camera, calling out "Say, *summer*," before snapping the moment into eternity. We were so young. At the time, I thought we were so mature, so grown-up. We've never looked alike, but we're identical in our glee. We were so close. So hopeful and happy.

That was before.

CHAPTER SEVEN

Cassie

Wednesday, June 27th

Julie is here.

She arrived about an hour ago, lugging Louis Vuitton suitcases—such a cliché—wearing a white, midi-length halter dress with a waist belt and strappy, wedge heels. I wish her presence didn't unnerve me, but it does.

It doesn't help that she's treating me like some fragile doll. Frankly, it's insulting.

Her mother called her as soon as she arrived—an image of Sophie flooded her phone's screen—and Julie practically dove on top of it like a deranged gymnast. I nearly confronted her about it. I pictured looking her in the eye and saying, "Do you think I can't handle seeing the woman who killed my own mother?" Losing a parent makes you tough. Not that she'd know—she still has a mother and a father. I have neither. But I didn't say anything, not even when she came down from her room, humming in her stupid, carefree way.

"Can I…?" She's in the kitchen, pointing to the selection of fruits I bought yesterday at the farmers' market. Bananas, mangoes, pears. All of the berries.

"Help yourself."

"I feel like I should pay you for half the groceries."

"It's fine."

She doesn't respond. Good. Her attempts at chitchat are both pointless and unnerving. Except the silence isn't that peaceful, either. From my spot on the couch, I can hear the roar of the ocean, the gentle tick-tock of the antique wall clock, the faraway squawks of birds. Nana used to be able to tell birds by their song. All that's missing is Nana whistling in the kitchen while she cooks. I knew that coming here wouldn't be easy, but I underestimated how deeply I'd feel her absence. Missing a loved one in their home is a particularly torturous form of grief.

"Do we have to call the lawyer?" Julie asks. She is standing behind the granite island, holding a half-eaten apple in her hand.

I rub the back of my neck. "Why would we?"

"To, um, let him know we're here?" She shuffles her feet. I wonder if she's feeling uncomfortable inside her own house. This is, after all, *our* house now.

"We're good," I say. "The GPS is supposed to be working."

"What GPS?"

"Check your email. Norman sent a waiver. It allows the firm to track our phones, so they know we're here. All you need to do is download an app." I don't add that the email also includes a breakdown of our house rules. It's straightforward stuff: we must stay here until July 28th. No sleeping elsewhere, not even for an evening. No overnight guests. No exceptions. Who knew Nana had a jailor's soul?

"Oh." Julie looks, for reasons that I can't begin to comprehend, confused.

"It's entirely up to you if you want to do it or not. They still reserve the right to come by unannounced to check on us." Come to think of it, the firm will probably come by multiple times. Anything to rack up billable hours.

"I'm downloading it now." She holds up her device.

I don't bother replying.

"It's a little weird, being here without her." I watch as her eyes survey the room. "Everything reminds me of her—do you feel it, too?"

Of course I do. But I'm not about to agree. I'm here to secure my inheritance—*not* to connect with her. I love Nana, but she doesn't get to play puppetmaster. Not again.

A memory floats up. Me at the age of nine, on the day Gramps died. The day I found out about Julie. My mom walked into my room and told me to pack a bag—we were heading to Montauk. Her announcement didn't make sense—it was April, and it wasn't a holiday or anything—but Nana's house was my happy place, so I wasn't about to complain. It wasn't until I saw my father sitting by the kitchen table with his face buried in his hands, the *Boston Globe* and a cup of coffee untouched in front of him, that I realized that something was really wrong. I remember thinking, *My parents are finally getting a divorce.* I felt scared—but mostly I felt relieved.

But then my father pulled me into a hug and began to cry. He told me Gramps was dead—a heart attack—and that we had to go over to be with Nana and help her with the arrangements. I agreed, even though I had no idea what that meant.

On the way over, my mom asked me if I wanted a tissue. "It's OK to cry, darling," she had said, from the passenger's seat. To an untrained ear, her voice would have sounded merely concerned, but there was a slight slur to her words. I could tell. I was trained.

By the time we arrived in Montauk, I was exhausted. I also hadn't shed a single tear. I knew that I should be crying. My mom kept saying it was OK to cry, which obviously meant that it was strange that I wasn't. I had just lost my only grandfather (my mom's parents died when she was just a teenager). But I felt nothing. Not grief or sadness, or anything else for that matter. I was numb.

But when I walked inside the house and saw Nana, I crumpled. She was trying to be brave—I could tell. She was sitting in

Gramps' leather armchair: straight back, stiff mouth, sunken cheeks. Sebastian was curled up in her lap, purring softly, while Nana rested a hand on his soft, tiger-striped fur. Gone were her bright, cheerful outfits—she was wearing a formal and unflattering black dress and a string of pearls. And her eyes—the green eyes that were mine as well—were pained, broken. Nana had never looked young to me, but that was the first day I thought of her as old.

When she saw my father, she shuffled over to him and buried her head in his chest. They cried together for the longest time. I could make out some of the things she was saying, but not all of it.

"It was so sudden, Stephan. It could happen to any of us," was what stuck with me.

Looking back, I wonder if I picked up on something else in Nana's eyes. It would explain why that memory is seared into my brain, why the grief only hit me when I arrived at the Montauk house and saw her, and not before. Memory is a tricky thing. We all edit our past, knowingly or not. We add and remove details. We fill in gaps. It isn't dishonest— it's survival. We need to believe that there is a point to our suffering, that life isn't just chaos and randomness. I like to think that I saw a steely determination in Nana's eyes, an unshakable resolve to finally tell me the truth.

Because that's what she did.

Two days later, after the wake and the funeral, Nana pulled me into her room to tell me a secret. "You have a sister," she said. She was holding a mug of tea, untouched.

I was nine years old, almost ten. A child. Children aren't supposed to be cynical. But I was. I had to be.

"You're confused, Nana," I said, shaking my head.

The words were familiar to me: *you're confused*. They were the words I used on my mom after she drank too much and stopped making sense. *Sleep it off*, I'd instruct her. When that didn't work, when she was too worked up or paranoid, I gave her what she wanted: my presence. I'd pretend to listen to her rants while reciting a song in my head. Theme songs were the easiest. Their repetitiveness was simple, catchy. I loved my mom very much. I worried about her every day of my life. But I also resented how much she needed me, resented her frailty.

"I'm not confused, my dear." Nana's tone was firm, sober. She didn't sound like a muddled, grieving widow. "Though I appreciate your concern."

"Is…is my mom pregnant?" A horrifying thought.

"No. She's your sister on your father's side. She's your age. Her name is Julie," Nana pronounced the name with a soft *j*—the first time I'd ever heard it like that. "It's like Julie in English, but with a French accent. Her mother is French."

"I have a half-sister…?" I thought of Nicole and Claire, the twins in my class who had an older half-brother named Derek. All I knew about Derek was that he went to a different school because his mom lived on the other side of town.

"A sister, full stop," Nana said. "It doesn't matter that you don't share a mother. There will be no halves in this family. Not anymore. Not on my watch."

A sister.

I couldn't make sense of what Nana was saying.

"Your Gramps died before he had a chance to meet her," Nana continued. Her eyes brimmed with tears. "But I'm not going to let that happen to me. Or to you, if you decide you want to meet her."

"I have a sister." Not a question this time. My tone was now trusting, believing. A chip in my cynic's armor.

A secret sister. It felt dramatic, impossible—the sort of thing that happened to other people. I was Cassie Meyers: plain, ordinary. The only thing that was different about me, the thing that set me apart from the other kids in my school, was that my parents didn't love each other. I was sure of that even back then.

They hid it from the world, in the same way that my father hid his temper and my mother hid her drinking, but I was never spared. I knew—and I was expected to keep their secrets. To maintain the blissful suburban façade they so masterfully cultivated. On our street, we were the respectable Meyers: banker dad, stay-at-home mom, studious daughter. We mowed our lawn. We greeted our neighbors by name. We went to church on Sundays. People had no idea what went on in my house.

"You do," Nana said. "Your parents think you're too young to understand. I don't agree."

I've told this story to a handful of people in my life. Their reactions are divided into two camps. Some expect me to have felt blessed, thrilled. Others assume I felt jealous and threatened. They're both wrong. Once the shock wore out, I felt sorry for Julie. I didn't know her, but I knew this: we had the same father. And that meant she went through the same things I did. I knew what he did to my mom was wrong, even back then, before I had the language to describe my father's actions. Gaslighting. Threats. Abuse. There was another girl in the world who felt just as terrified and powerless as I did.

Nana's revelation hurt my mom—she felt humiliated, exposed by her mother-in-law. Julie had been kept a secret from me at her insistence. Once we were back in Boston, her drinking worsened. I began noticing empty bottles of Old Forrester and Jack Daniel's on the carpeted floor next to her bed. She started taking pills, too—tiny tablets that turned her into a shadow, a ghost.

I decided I didn't want to have anything to do with Julie. I was curious, of course. Not just about Julie, but about her mother, too. Who was this mysterious French woman who had been involved with my father, who had birthed his child? How did she react to my father's outbursts? Did she fight back? Did she offer Julie protection? Did she drink a lot, too? I wanted answers, I did. But I feared what it would do to my mom. If I'm being honest,

I feared what it would do to me, too. What if I liked Julie? She would be one more person to worry about, one more person I'd feel obligated to protect. Which is why I declined Nana's invitation to meet her. I said no to my grandmother, probably for the first time in my life.

Except Nana did get what she wanted.

Twenty-two summers ago, less than three months after Gramps died, I did meet Julie. I grew to love her. We became close, inseparable. We became what Nana wanted us to be: sisters.

But that was then, and this is now.

I glance at Julie still standing in the kitchen, still holding the half-eaten apple, still waiting for me to reply. Her expression is eager, expectant. Not unlike the first summer we spent here. But this time I'm not giving in.

Of course everything here reminds me of Nana. But admitting as much is pointless. As is Nana's attempt at manipulation. I know my grandmother. It's possible—likely, even—that she meant well by bringing us here. But her plan is misguided, unrealistic.

It's been too long, too much has happened.

Julie and I are entirely different people. With entirely different lives.

And no one, not even Nana, could expect me to forget why that is.

CHAPTER EIGHT

Julie

Wednesday, June 27th

This isn't what I expected. Not that I know what I expected, not really.

The Sky Princess is prepared for battle. To thwart the Fire Princess's venomous tongue, she has brought with her a toad that can swallow insults and spit out flowers. To combat deathly stares, she has an army of honeybees capable of turning evil eyes into candied treats. But none of her weapons can fight off indifference.

It stings, Cassie's indifference. It reminds me of Patrick's warning: *Why would you want to share a house with someone who's just going to ignore you?*

I take out Nana's bamboo cutting board—third drawer to my right—and begin slicing a banana. Once I'm done with that, I peel a mango. Nana used to love fruit salads.

"Would you like some?" I hold up identical mason jars filled with bright cubes of fruit. I've made two, my gesture says. One for you, one for me.

"No, thank you," Cassie says, and my heart deflates. But I tell myself to look on the bright side: at least she answered this time. Semi-politely, too.

I sit at the dining table. My usual spot: facing the stairs. Nana, Cassie, and I must've shared dozens of meals here. Possibly hundreds. Maybe I should make one of our favorites for dinner. Shrimp gumbo. Seared tuna and corn on the cob. Watermelon and cod tacos. Maybe even the sun-dried pasta that Nana prepared for my very first meal here. I could buy beer—Patrick isn't here to protest. I could even drink it straight from the bottle. I'll have to take a cab to the grocery store; Cassie isn't likely to drive me. But it's not like I have anything else to do. And I do enjoy cooking.

To pass the time, I reach for my phone to scroll through social media. I catch a glimpse of my left hand. I've now managed to peel off the polish from all five fingers. If Patrick and I have a video call, I'll have to make sure to hide my hands. Speaking of Patrick: he hasn't called, hasn't texted. It's odd. Usually, when I'm out with friends (the plural form is wishful thinking: it's just Janette), he texts at least half a dozen times. I sigh, thinking that he's probably punishing me with silence.

I come across an Instagram post from Sophie: an artsy, black-and-white picture of the Boston skyline. Sophie posts the most random things on her feed.

I take a peek at Cassie through the corner of my eye. She's on the couch, her laptop propped on the armrest. She doesn't look like someone who's dating a married man. Which is a silly thought, I know. What *would* that look like after all?

Instinctively, I run my unkempt hand through the seashell necklace hanging from my neck. Earlier today, I found it in the nightstand drawer, along with a pair of socks and a Rubik's Cube. I don't know where the sock and the cube came from, but the necklace used to be mine. Still is mine, I guess. Nana and I made it together on my first summer here. I'm not sure why I put it on—it looks a little ridiculous with my Reiss dress—but I like how it feels, hanging close to my heart.

My phone buzzes. A text from Janette.

It's official! I'm coming to see you on Sat!

My thumbs quickly text a reply. *YAY! I CAN'T WAIT!*

Another ping. *OMG, is she that bad?*

It feels disloyal to say yes, so instead I reply: *I'm just happy you're coming. I miss you.*

"I wanted to ask you something," Cassie says. "I know we're not allowed to have people sleep over—"

I slam my phone face down on the table. An unthinking, instinctive move. A stupid one, too. It would be impossible for Cassie to read my messages all the way from the couch.

"Sorry," I blurt out. I don't know why I'm apologizing.

Cassie arches her left eyebrow, flicking her eyes towards my phone. She looks annoyed. "A friend of mine is coming for the weekend and I was wondering if you'd mind—on Saturday—"

"My friend is coming on Saturday, too." It's official. I've lost control over the words that come out of my mouth.

"That's nice." Her tone is impatient. "Would you mind if I used the house for dinner on Saturday? I'd like to talk to him, and it would be best if we were alone."

My ears prick up: a Saturday-night dinner with a friend—a male friend. And they need to be alone. Could it be the married man? I picture Cassie and a tall, dark stranger meeting in a corner table in a dimly lit restaurant for a secret rendezvous. They'd never find a secluded spot in Montauk, not in the summer.

Cassie clears her throat. "Julie?"

"Sorry, I was...daydreaming." I smile. "Yes. That's fine. I'll make myself scarce."

This is progress, I decide. We're not bonding, but we are making arrangements. Peacefully, like roommates. Roommates often become friends.

I bring a forkful of salad—a grape and a slice of banana—to my mouth, chewing happily.

"Is he your boyfriend?" I bring my hand to my mouth, feeling my cheeks redden. I wasn't supposed to ask that out loud.

Cassie blinks once, then twice. The moment lengthens. I am convinced she won't answer my question, but then she says, "Yes." A second later, she returns her gaze to her computer.

I bite my tongue to keep from asking more. Sophie is many things, but she is seldom misinformed. It'll be refreshing to set her straight. *You see, Sophie*, I imagine myself telling her, *Cassie has a proper* boyfriend. Since this conversation is taking place in my imagination, I can even call her *Maman*—something I haven't done since I was seven years old.

"What will people think if you call me *Maman*? I'm much too young, *ma petite*!"

Maybe I'll call her *Maman* just this once. Serves her right for believing silly rumors about Cassie—of course she'd never date a married man.

But then it hits me: Sophie used to refer to my dad as her boyfriend, too.

She didn't do it to protect me—Sophie has never believed in sugarcoating things, least of all her relationship with my dad. As a child, I knew my dad had another family: a wife and daughter, my half-sister. For years, I imagined a half-girl: with only one arm, one leg, and half a body. Her image haunted me—I was glad she lived in a different house.

I remember the day I asked my dad if my half-sister lived in a half-house. My dad had been amused, chuckling as he explained to me that a half-sister meant that we shared only one parent, not two. Then he told me that my half-sister's mother was his wife.

"We're married," he said. "Do you know what being married means?"

"I do." I nodded eagerly, pleased to know the answer. "It means you're with someone because you have to be. Not because you want to be."

Daddy laughed, tipping his head back in delight. "That's a clever way to look at it."

Sophie had been the one to explain it to me like that. But I kept that to myself. I wanted him to think I was clever all on my own. He often said I was beautiful and sweet. *Like a princess*, he'd say. But he'd never called me clever before.

Back then, *wife* and *girlfriend* were just words. Equal and uncomplicated titles. In my mind, my dad having a wife and a girlfriend was tantamount to someone having two crayons: one yellow and one orange. It would be a few years before I realized that *girlfriend* was a lesser crayon than *wife*—and also that *girlfriend* wasn't the right word for my mother. Not according to the people in my school, anyway.

I was three when Sophie enrolled me at the Lycée International de Boston, in Sommerville, Massachusetts. The school was both expensive (twenty-thousand-dollar tuition) and impractical (forty minutes by car, one hour and a half by T), but Sophie refused to enroll me at the public school in Jamaica Plain, where we lived. On paper, she was like many of our neighbors: an immigrant single mother working two jobs. But Sophie considered our largely Hispanic, working-class neighborhood to be beneath her. *We're not like them, Julie. We're Europeans*, she'd say. The Lycée was a French school, and Sophie wanted me to have a French education. She promised I'd fit in there.

Except I didn't. The overwhelming majority of the kids at my school were wealthy. Some more than others—but *all* of them led privileged lives. I was the exception. But that wasn't what sealed my fate as an outsider among my peers. It was a conversation I had when I was five.

The assignment was simple. Draw a picture of your family and show it to the class.

"And remember," Ms. Monique had said, "every family is unique, so you'll all have different people to draw."

I drew Sophie and me inside our house and my dad inside his car, waving at us. His car was facing away from the house, which Ms. Monique thought was curious. I explained that he was driving to his other family.

"What do you mean, *other family*?" The question came from Mrs. Pierce, a volunteer mom. A bitter, nosy woman—not that I knew that at the time.

"My mom is my dad's girlfriend," I explained. "And he also has a wife. I have a half-sister, but she's a whole person."

Mrs. Pierce pulled me aside later that day. "What's your half-sister like, Julie?"

"I don't know," I told her. "I've never met her."

"Why not?" Mrs. Pierce pressed.

I shrugged. "Daddy says we're not supposed to know each other. But she's very different from me." What I didn't add is that I was Dad's favorite daughter—his sweet, beautiful girl, as he often said. It felt like showing off.

In a matter of days, the PTA moms—all avid volunteers at school—had dug up the details on Sophie and my dad. An ongoing affair with a married man. A secret family. His wife had no idea. After that, the gossip spread like wildfire.

"You've seen her around, haven't you?"

"The French one. Snobby. Thinks she's better than everyone else."

"She calls herself his *girlfriend*, can you believe it?"

"I heard she got knocked up so he'd leave his wife."

"Her own daughter told us. That poor thing is going to have some major daddy issues."

"She'll probably grow up to be just like her mother. We all become our parents."

On paper, the Lycée was diverse. It attracted kids from all over the globe—it was called the International School of Boston, after all. I was hardly the only one from a single-parent household. But I was the only one whose mother was *the other woman*—those words were always whispered, and for the longest time I was confused, thinking, *What other woman?* The day I understood their meaning was the day I understood why I was such an easy target for my classmates. Kids learn from their parents. They repeat what they hear. The teasing was cruel, relentless.

"Doesn't it bother you that your dad has a *real* family?"

"My mom says your mom has no self-respect. She's pathetic."

"I heard she's a homewrecker."

"I heard she's a slut."

Sophie thought nothing of it. To her, bullying was an American affliction—like wearing sweatpants outside the house or refrigerating butter. "You have to toughen up, *ma petite*. People won't always be nice to you. Especially plain-looking American girls. They'll hate you for being more beautiful and stylish than them."

This didn't add up. The popular girls at school were beautiful. Prettier than me: skinny, with long, silky blond hair and pretty blue eyes. I was skinny, too, but my hair was as dark as a clear, starless sky. If being beautiful was the problem, why didn't anyone pick on them?

I often wonder if things would've been different if we had been rich. Dad helped pay for school and he'd often take us out to a nice dinner, but for the most part we lived on my mom's income, which meant that I didn't have nice things like my classmates. Their lives seemed to be a steady stream of gifts and celebrations: new clothes and toys, trips abroad, lavish parties. I had to save lunch money for months to buy a pair of designer jeans. I didn't want just any denim, I needed the ones my classmates had, in part because I still hadn't met Nana—she was the one who helped me develop a personal style. But even after my summers in Montauk, I grew up coveting designer-brand items. The two interlocked Cs. An embarrassment of LVs. The mirror-imaged Fs. I didn't understand why we couldn't afford the kind of life that surrounded me, day in and day out. Or I did—but it never stopped bothering me.

As I grew older, I became more restless. I didn't voice my thoughts to Sophie—I had already picked up on the fact that she wouldn't listen—but, privately, I seethed. I resented her. Why didn't she marry my dad? Why did she stay with him even though he had another wife? Why should he get to travel to the Hamptons in the summer with his wife and other daughter when Sophie and I didn't have enough money to go to a cheap B&B? Why did it fall on me to help balance our checkbook and sort the bills? This was work meant for adults. I understood it was too much for Sophie to handle on her own. But that's why people got married, wasn't it? To share the workload. To let their kids be just that: kids.

In college, I became someone else. On the outside, anyway. I still wasn't able to afford prohibitive luxuries, but I had new friends. Ones who weren't wealthy jerks. And I never told them that my mom was the other woman. In fact, I seldom mentioned Sophie. And when I mentioned marriage, it was in the context of my own, future marriage. I made no secret of the fact that it was my dream: to get married and start a family. I kept a scrapbook with cutouts from bridal magazines. My friends teased me. They compared me to Charlotte, from *Sex and the City*.

We're only eighteen, Julie. We're way too young to be dreaming of our wedding day. I can only imagine what they'd say if they knew about the fairy tales I conjured up in my mind. I didn't mind the teasing. It was all in good fun. I laughed along, but, deep down, I knew I was right to focus on having a proper family. My friends could afford to be casual, to be flippant about their romantic futures. They had no idea what it was like, growing up as the daughter of the other woman. To be the family on the side.

Cassie knows. I've told her. All of it.

So if this *boyfriend* of hers really is a married man, then I hope she's not planning on getting pregnant. No child deserves that kind of life.

CHAPTER NINE

Cassie

Saturday, June 30th

"I want you to leave Tatiana," I say, facing the kitchen wall.

Too direct. Also, I'm not sure I should say her name. Would *your wife* sound better?

"Daniel, we need to talk," I try again.

No—unacceptable.

I snap the blender top shut. I'd be breaking my own rule. It's something I've said quite often on the show: Never begin a conversation with "we need to talk". You're already talking, so it's both redundant and unnerving.

"Daniel, I feel like it's time for you to leave your wife." *I feel?* Does that sound sensitive or narcissistic, like I'm making it all about me?

I turn on the blender. The sound is strangely comforting—strident, almost angry.

"Daniel, we can't be together if you're married."

Is that better or worse? I can't tell.

I detach the pitcher from the base, find a glass, and pour myself a fruit smoothie. I have no desire to share this house with Julie—it's why I've gone out of my way to avoid her—but being here without her is almost worse. It's strange, being alone in Nana's house. Familiar, but incomplete. Like walking without feet.

Twenty minutes ago, Julie announced that she was off to meet her friend Janette at a restaurant on Main Street. I stared at her, wondering what she wanted me to do with the unsolicited bit of information. After she left, it hit me: maybe she expected me to drive her there. Too bad. I'm not her chauffeur. She should have her own car. We're not kids anymore.

"Daniel, I know I told you I would never consider getting married, but I've changed my mind. I think you should leave your wife and we should be together."

Now I'm basically proposing to him. Great.

How am I supposed to have this conversation with Daniel if I can't manage it with myself? For all my training as a therapist, all my years of experience, the rights words often escape me when it comes to dealing with my own life. It's more than a little frustrating.

I consider how far I've come since Daniel and I started seeing each other. I never liked the fact that Daniel was married, and I *really* didn't like the fact that he and Tatiana had been patients of mine. At the same time, knowing that he was taken (it had been over a year since I'd treated him and Tatiana, but I knew they were still together) had made things easier. I didn't want to get married. I didn't even want to fall in love. Bearing witness to my parents' marriage was trauma enough for me.

But life had other plans.

Before I realized it, I had fallen for Daniel. For a while, I assumed my heart was playing tricks on me. That his unavailability was serving as an aphrodisiac. I tried staying away. Ending things. But it was impossible. I had become what I feared: a woman in love.

I still am. Daniel isn't just my boyfriend. He's my best friend. My partner. The first person I call when anything—good or bad—happens. He's the one I talk to every night before I go to sleep. He makes me feel safe and seen. Not just accepted, but adored. We share a connection that is different than anything I've ever experienced, beyond what I thought was possible. It isn't merely physical or emotional. It's visceral.

Seeing him at the hospital changed everything. That was a watershed moment for me, a turning point. That's when it hit me: I don't just love him—I want to be with him. For real. Which is why I'm initiating tonight's conversation. I could wait—for him to bring it up, for Tatiana to fall in love with someone else. But patience has never been my strong suit. And it isn't one I encourage my clients to cultivate, either.

I take a sip of my smoothie and go back to my imaginary conversation.

Practice makes perfect.

Daniel and I are on the porch, curled up on the oversized canopy daybed. Our view is perfect: a chilled bottle of 2011 Pouilly-Fuissé against the blue backdrop of the Atlantic Ocean. I should be relaxed. Instead, I'm nervous. Agitated.

"Where's your sister tonight?" he asks, stuffing fries into his mouth. He arrived earlier with sandwiches from the Lobster Roll—my favorite—but I could only manage a few bites.

"*Julie*," I begin, my eyes a warning, "is having lunch with a friend."

"She has friends on the island?"

"From Boston, I think." I really don't want to be talking about Julie right now.

Daniel takes the final bite of his sandwich, chews it slowly. "And where are you?"

I feel my forehead crease. "What do you mean?"

"I feel like you're not here." He strokes my hair. "Is it the house?"

We've talked about it already. About how weird it is for me to be here. Daniel and I talk about everything—from the mundane to the deep. Since his arrival, we've covered his health (he continues to follow his cardiologist's recommendations), my strategy with Julie (to ignore her), Norman-the-lawyer's annoying check-up calls (one so far, but I'm sure there'll be more), his kids (Angie and Sam are having a great time at Auntie Bella's house), his work (Preston quit—good news; we don't like him because he's taken credit for Daniel's work), and, of course, the house. As in: how much it reminds me of Nana, how much I miss her.

"I like having you here," I say. "It's like you're finally meeting Nana. The next best thing, anyway." I should have visited her. Should've been a better granddaughter.

"I wish I'd met her."

He leans in to give me a kiss. Slow, at first. But then intense, hungry. I wrap my leg around him, feeling my skin tingling. Heat floods my body. I'm about to suggest that we go inside—but then I pull away.

"What is it?" he asks. His tone is soft, concerned.

This is it. I'm going to ask him to leave his wife. I can feel my heartbeat pulsating on my fingertips. I'm hopeful, which means I'm also terrified—with me, optimism is always weighed down by fear.

"We've been seeing each other for over a year now. And it's been wonderful—"

"Are you…breaking up with me?" His tone drops a register.

"Of course not," I say. I nearly laugh. The idea of breaking up with Daniel is preposterous.

His chest deflates. "You had me worried." He's smiling now—pleased, relieved. It's touching, seeing his spike of fear at the idea of losing me. I should feel confident, buoyed. I don't, though. I'm now even more afraid.

"It's sort of the opposite of that."

He cocks his head to the side.

"I want us to be together," I continue. "For real." I sit up, holding my breath.

"Do you mean…?" he asks, focusing his gaze on mine. The sky is now painted in hues of red and pink.

"I want you to get a divorce and be with me." A clear delivery. I'm proud of myself.

"I didn't know you wanted that."

"I didn't, either. Not until now."

Daniel knows about my childhood—all of it. My dad's family across town. My mom's substance abuse problem. He even knows about the fights, about how helpless I felt having to watch my dad terrorize my mom. He's the only person in my life who does. Well, him and Julie.

"Are you saying you'd be open to something more…" Daniel pauses. "Permanent?"

I nod, sheepishly. I feel my mouth stretching into a smile. I shouldn't be celebrating, not yet. But I can see how excited he looks—I know we're on the same page.

He leans in and gives me another kiss. "You've made me so happy."

"I'm asking you to give up a lot," I say, looking into his eyes. I am thinking of Angie. He knows this. There is no need to point it out.

Angie isn't Daniel's biological daughter, a fact that she is not aware of. This, more than anything, is what's so tricky about our situation: Tatiana has made it clear that she'll tell Angie the truth if Daniel leaves her. I know this because she issued this threat in my presence. I was their therapist, after all.

I began seeing Daniel and Tatiana in early January of 2017. Their problems were not uncommon. Tatiana blamed Daniel for being a workaholic, which left her feeling isolated and lonely, especially after Sam was born ("I'm all alone in that big house with no one to talk to!"). Daniel depicted Tatiana as someone who was image-obsessed and materialistic ("How is it possible I'm making six figures and we don't have any savings?"). In our first session, I assured them that the challenges they faced were by no means insurmountable, as long as they were willing to do the work: on themselves and on their relationship. They said they were, which is how I became their counselor.

At first, they both seemed to be making progress. Daniel made an effort to be home at a decent hour. Tatiana began spending time with Sam at the park, not the mall. They spent more time together as a family—tobogganing, ice-skating, cooking dinners.

And then the bill for Tatiana's credit card arrived.

I remember that session with perfect clarity. Daniel sitting on the couch with his forehead resting on his hand, fuming. Tatiana on the other end, lips pursed, arms crossed. Daniel was telling her that they'd only be able to make the minimum payment. They couldn't afford to cover the entire bill. Tatiana dismissed his concern. "I already told you. My parents will pay for it." But Daniel was proud—he didn't want to rely on his in-laws.

I asked Tatiana why she had lied about her shopping hiatus. It was the first time that I'd considered that maybe she had a real problem—an addiction, perhaps. And that's when she broke the news: she was pregnant, two months along. "I had to buy things for the baby," she said.

Daniel was over the moon. He forgot all about the credit card bill.

Six months later, Angie was born. Daniel and Tatiana skipped several sessions. I didn't think anything of it—they had a toddler and a newborn. They were understandably busy, likely overwhelmed. When they did come, it became clear that they were slipping back into their old habits. Workaholic. Shopaholic. At this point, I suggested they try individual counseling as well. It had become clear to me that they both had compulsive personalities—an issue that went beyond their marriage.

Then everything changed.

One day, Daniel walked into my office without his wife. He looked shell-shocked, defeated. I could tell he'd been crying. For a moment, I imagined the worst—I usually did, after my mother. But then Daniel explained that Tatiana had left him. "She's been having an affair with her Pilates instructor," he said. "She says Angie is his. I should've known. She was born one month before her due date, but she didn't look premature. And now she wants full custody of both my kids." Daniel left before the session was over. If Tatiana wasn't coming, he didn't want to be there.

Three weeks later, they both came in for a session. By then, the DNA test had proved that Angie wasn't Daniel's biological daughter. Tatiana had ended things with the Pilates instructor. She no longer wanted a divorce. Except Daniel was still hurt, too hurt to take her back. He could forgive Tatiana for cheating, but not for threatening to take his kids from him. He was there to find a way to be civil with her. "You'll always be the mother of my children," he'd said. In his heart, Angie was his.

My heart went out to Tatiana. She'd made a mistake. An awful one. But she seemed to regret her actions. And I'd seen couples overcome infidelity before. I encouraged them to continue coming to therapy. I hoped they'd make things work. As it turned out, my optimism was unfounded. Weeks later, Daniel announced that he'd filed for divorce. He wanted them to be friends for the sake of the children.

I knew Tatiana wouldn't take this well. Rejection was a huge trigger for her. But I couldn't have predicted her reaction, not even if I'd been treating them for years. If I close my eyes, I can see it in front of me: Tatiana's newly narrowed stare, the way her lips curled ever so slightly, the subtle lift of her eyebrows. It was an eerie, frightening thing to watch. She looked menacing. She spoke in a paused, deliberate way. "If you leave me, I'll sue for full custody and you'll never see Angie again. I'll tell her—and the judge—that you're not her real dad. Don't test me, Daniel. You have no idea what I'm capable of." He tried to reason with her, to explain that their marriage was over. But she wouldn't budge.

"You are not leaving me, do you hear me? You will not do this to me. I will not be humiliated by you."

She looked like what she was: a woman both desperate and cunning. Tatiana is highly intelligent—but, sadly, also highly insecure. She saw the divorce as a defeat. And losing wasn't an option. Not for her.

Frankly, I was relieved when they never came back for another session.

I didn't think I'd see them again. Not until Daniel and I ran into each other, almost one year after that last session. I had no idea that the man who used to be nothing more than a patient of mine would turn out to be the love of my life.

But he did.

Now, as he caresses my hands, I'm reminded of all he stands to lose if we decide to be together. I don't like the idea of hurting Tatiana (and not just because she's more than a little scary), but the idea of hurting Angie is unthinkable. I might not have a relationship with her, but she's Daniel's child. That's enough to make me love her.

"I'll find a way to explain this to Angie," Daniel says. "I'm her dad. I'll always be her dad." A pause, he lowers his voice, "I'm not the only one with something to lose. What about your career?"

It's a fair question. Marriage counselors aren't supposed to tear couples apart. I know that's not what I've done, but people won't see it that way. And perception is reality.

"I'll quit the show." It's something I've been considering for a while, anyway. The spotlight isn't for me. Private practice, writing books—these are the things I love. Being on *East Coast Coffee* has been great for my career, but I'm not an on-camera person.

"What about your patients?"

"Claudia will think of something."

It's why I have a publicist on retainer, after all. To manage my image, to make sure that my brand—I do *not* like this word—is protected. Years ago, I resisted the idea of hiring a publicist—I wasn't a celebrity, after all. But after my book—*What All Happily Married Couples Have in Common*—became a bestseller, I received more interview requests than my agent could handle. Claudia won me over with her efficiency—she is petite and delicate but has the lungs of an opera singer and the bark of an army general. She's surprisingly down-to-earth for someone who trades in image.

"This is the best news." Daniel beams at me with bright, expectant eyes.

"Are you sure?" I say. "You don't want to think about it?" I had anticipated that he would. For Angie's sake.

"I've always been sure," he says. "I've always known that it was you. I never left Tatiana because…" His voice trails off.

"Because of Angie." I squeeze his arm.

He nods. "You were dead set against marriage. And I was afraid of losing my daughter." A pause. "I still am. But we'll find a way. If you're in, I'm in."

"I'm in."

CHAPTER TEN

Julie

Saturday, June 30th

Janette eats like a teenager with the munchies. It's refreshing.

"Do you think it's true?" Janette slurps her milkshake. She whips her head around, trying to flag a server.

"I don't know."

The server comes by—a tall, squared-jawed boy with large ears and an endearing smile. Janette orders another strawberry shake. I envy her metabolism.

We're at The Catch, a local spot unknown to most of the summer people. I picked it because both the food and the atmosphere are unpretentious—and inexpensive. If I had taken Janette to Paola's or Le Bilboquet, she would've balked at the prices. I wouldn't have blamed her.

"If it is, she's a hypocrite." Her tone is firm, self-assured. Janette is a stranger to insecurity.

"I don't know about that." I feel a spike of defensiveness. Janette means well. She's protective of me. Loyal. But I don't like it when anyone says anything negative about Cassie. We're still sisters—even if we no longer have a relationship.

I reach over and grab a fry from Janette's plate. She returns the gesture with a subtle lift of her eyebrows.

"Isn't her entire job, you know, helping couples stay married?" Janette says. She pushes her plate forward.

"It's probably not even true." My words lack confidence. Sophie has been texting me nonstop about Cassie and her alleged relationship with a married man. She seems sure of herself. Sophie is seldom wrong.

I peer out at Erie Avenue. The cars parked outside are on the older side, weathered. All of them have Montauk license plates. Not a Porsche or a Ferrari in sight. We're supposed to grab ice cream at The Fudge Company after this. It'll be an entirely different scene on Main Street.

I take another fry. They taste so good: salty and greasy and gloriously unhealthy. Much better than the Caesar salad I'm having, dressing on the side. Why did I even order this? It's like a part of my brain forgets that Patrick isn't here.

The server brings Janette her milkshake. She thanks him with her winning smile—the least intimidating thing about her. Janette is a lawyer—a public defender. She is all confidence and strength and confrontation. Arguing with her is downright scary. But when she smiles, she becomes gentler, softer. We've been friends since college, bonding over the fact that we were both there on a scholarship.

"You could find out," Janette says. And then, after I take yet another fry. "You could also order your own side of fries."

"I can't imagine Cassie doing something like that. She was always so…" I pause, searching for the right word.

"Uptight? Self-righteous? The bearer of a stick up her ass?"

As commander of the Captain of the Guards, Janette has sworn an oath to protect the Sky Princess from any foe—no matter how formidable. Commander Janette slays offenders with her words: her oratory powers can turn any enemy into Calacatta marble. The kingdom is now filled with beautiful statues of past adversaries.

"Responsible," I say. "And for the record: all those words were used to describe *you* back in school."

A sly smile from Janette. She is proud of her reputation. She should be.

"You're right," I begin. "Let's get more fries."

Janette beams.

"You didn't tell me: are you going to do it?" she asks, after she flags the waiter and requests an extra-large side of French fries.

For a moment, I'm not sure I follow. But then I understand—she's referring to Sophie's ludicrous request. "Of course not." I lower my voice. "I could never *spy on Cassie*."

"You know, this might be in your best interest." She pauses for a moment. "You could use it to jumpstart your career as a journalist."

I stare at her for a moment. "You can't be serious."

"You keep saying you want to go back to work."

"Start working." An important distinction. I've held many jobs— babysitter, barista, bartender, all while attending school full-time—but I've never had a career.

For years, this didn't bother me. In fact, it felt thrilling.

Growing up, all I wanted was for Sophie to be a stay-at-home mom like so many of the mothers at our school who occupied their days with facials and leisurely lunches. These women would eagerly await their children's arrival from school. They were happy to fix them snacks and help out with homework. Sophie had very little time for me. The school bus would drop me off to an empty apartment—I had my own key and I knew I wasn't supposed to go outside or turn on the stove or let anyone in. Sophie worked because she had to: we needed the money. The idea that someone would *choose* to spend eight hours a day under fluorescent lights was baffling to me. Having time to kill felt like the epitome of luxury.

But now that it's my reality, I find that I am, quite frankly, bored. Other than cooking dinner every evening, I try to keep busy with my grooming rituals (daily massages, twice weekly blowouts, weekly manicures) and making sure that our apartment is up to Patrick's standards (we have a cleaning lady, but she's constantly moving things around). A career would give me purpose. It might lessen the yearning I have for a child.

"So why not take advantage of your celebrity sister?" Janette asks.

Celebrity sister. It's an accurate characterization—Cassie *is* a celebrity. She isn't movie-star famous or anything. Most people know her as Cassie the Couples' Counselor since that's her name on the show. But it's odd to think of her as a famous person. Maybe because it isn't something she ever aspired to be, at least not as a child.

It's ironic, the turns that our lives have taken.

As a young girl, Cassie had two goals in life: to become a psychologist and to never get married. She held a fascination for issues of mental health—a dark hobby for a young teenager, but an understandable one, given her mom's history. Cassie wanted to help people through talk therapy—not pills. As for marriage, she rejected it on principle, deeming it unnatural and toxic. It's strange to think that she did stay true to her goals—she is a psychologist and she isn't married—but she *does* make a living helping other couples achieve their happily ever after.

My goals were entirely different. I was determined to do what Sophie couldn't: find a husband. An old-fashioned dream, I know. But I didn't care. I wanted a ring on my finger. A certificate of marriage. A proper family. I didn't spend any time daydreaming about having a job. My dreams were always about being a wife, a homemaker.

I don't need to be a psychologist like Cassie to understand how our aspirations stem from the same place: our dad. Cassie and I have the same dad—but we shared him in two very different ways. Our home lives were entirely different. She had stability, the sense of permanence that comes from having married parents, even if she did often remark on the loveless nature of their union. I was kept a secret—Dad showed up sporadically, but at least he was with us by choice. Our shared experience molded Cassie and me in opposite ways. What she ran from, I ran towards.

"There are worse ways," Janette says, interrupting my reverie. "You're a good writer. Writing this article could give you your big break."

"Sophie asked me to spy on Cassie. Not write an article about her." Sophie isn't a writer—she works in the magazine's marketing and publicity department—but she's hoping to bring this information to the editorial team. According to her, it would be a scoop. I obviously told her no.

Janette lets out a loud breath. "That's how negotiations start. You tell her you'll get the dirt on Cassie but only if you can write the article yourself. And if *Posh* isn't interested, then you can sell it to *Vogue* or *Harper's Bazaar*. Or even *US Weekly* or *People*. There's no shortage of periodicals looking for gossip. Don't you want your name on a byline?"

"Not like this." It feels wrong. And it would destroy Cassie. "Besides, I've never wanted to be a journalist." The only writing I've ever been interested in is fiction. Janette knows this.

"You hear about it all the time, authors who get book deals because of an article gone viral," Janette says. "And don't people have a right to know that America's sweetheart marriage counselor is dating a married man? They buy her books, watch her show. Trust her advice. She's a public figure. That makes her fair game."

"She's my sister."

"You'd be doing her a favor."

I frown. "How on earth—?"

"If this is true," Janette continues, "it's bound to get out, sooner or later. But if you break the news, you can make her look sympathetic. You can spin it in her favor."

"The other woman always looks bad."

"But you can make sure the damage is minimal," Janette says. "Besides, why should you care what she thinks? This is someone who stopped speaking to you for no good reason."

I shift on my seat. *No good reason* is wildly untrue—but I can't fault Janette for her mischaracterization. She doesn't know the truth about Katherine's death. It's my burden to bear.

"Also," Janette continues, "and I can't believe I'm saying this, because I'm not a fan of Patrick's, but your mom is right. You being here could potentially jeopardize your marriage. Patrick gets jealous when you spend the day with me. I can't imagine he's OK with you spending the month away from him."

"It's his choice not to come."

Janette frowns. "I thought you weren't allowed overnight guests?"

"He could get a hotel. Or come for the day, like you."

She gives me a pitying look. "You know he won't do that." What she doesn't say reverberates loud and clear: Janette is willing to come for the day when Patrick isn't. Janette loves me more than Patrick does.

"I know." A pause. "Sophie says he'll leave me if I stay here."

"You're eating fries and you haven't checked your phone since we got here." Her tone drops a register. "I'd forgotten what it was like, having an uninterrupted meal with you."

I feel my shoulders sagging. "He hasn't been texting me. No calls, either."

She nods quietly. "It says a lot that you're still here. I know how committed you are to making your marriage work."

"Right now, I'm not sure I care about my marriage."

"I'm sorry, what?" Janette cranes her neck. "What am I missing here?"

I bite my lip. Janette doesn't know about what happened at the benefit. I was too embarrassed to tell her after it happened.

Besides, Janette already has too many reasons to dislike Patrick. But I'm keeping too many secrets as it is. I need to tell her— anyone, really—*something*.

"Remember the benefit I went to at the MFA?" I ask.

She nods. "I think so? Wasn't it only a few days after your grandmother died?"

"That's right." Not to be dramatic, but I felt like death. I'd never lost anyone before. "Well, something happened."

Janette leans in. It feels good, having her full attention.

My mind takes me back to that day, the day I found out Nana had died.

The first stage of grief is supposed to be denial. But I skipped it altogether.

After Mrs. Bunsen called me to tell me that Nana was gone, I broke down in tears. It felt like I was trying to purge a sickness living inside me. Tears streamed down my face. My chest felt constricted. I had trouble breathing. I worried that I was having a panic attack. That my heart was actually—physically—broken.

I called Patrick to ask him to come home early. He said he'd try, but he didn't make it home until 7 p.m. By then, I'd been feeling so crummy that I took two Xanax. Months before, Sophie had given me a few pills when I confessed to struggling with insomnia. I hadn't taken any because I associated them with Katherine. She used to be addicted to them. But that day I didn't care. I didn't even think about it, to be honest. When he walked through the door, I was fast asleep in the living room. I woke up with Patrick standing next to me.

"What's this?" He held up an empty pint of Häagen-Dazs in my hand. Chocolate Midnight Cookies—an old favorite, though that day it tasted like salty cardboard.

I slowly sat up, my mind muddled because of the pills.

According to Patrick, I struggled to finish a sentence. All I remember is feeling exhausted. I remember Patrick asking me where I'd gotten the ice cream. He looked concerned, which made sense. It was probably the first time he saw me eating ice cream since we'd gotten married, or sleeping during the day.

"Bought it." I didn't say it was my second pint. Food eased the pain.

I went back to sleep. It was better this way. If I was awake, I'd cry. Knowing Patrick was home soothed me. As a girl, I didn't always have my dad around. But as a woman, my husband came home to me every evening. It felt steady, reassuring.

I tried to reach my dad, but all I got was his voicemail. I knew he'd broken up with his girlfriend a while back (Clara? Clarisse? I never got around to meeting her) and I didn't like the idea of him being alone after losing his mother.

I felt sad, of course—but mostly I felt guilty. I hadn't seen Nana in so long. After I got married, I stopped spending whole summers with her in Montauk. An understandable change—Patrick never took time off work, and I couldn't spend weeks apart from him. That's not how our marriage works. Still, for the first few years, I had made it a point to visit Nana for a few days, always during the week. But soon our social calendars became too busy—or rather Patrick's did. It seemed like every week there was a fundraiser, a book launch, an exhibit. Patrick sees these gatherings as networking opportunities, which I suppose they are. But he also takes it to an extreme: everything is about career advancement to him. He's the most ambitious person I know. And I wanted to support him—good wives are supportive. And so I cut back on my days in Montauk. Eventually, I stopped going altogether.

Before I knew it, three years had gone by. Nana and I spoke often on the phone, but when she passed away, I hadn't seen her in three years. Three years.

How had I let that happen?

The guilt was crushing, overwhelming. It felt like drowning. The pills helped, but only because they made me sleep longer. I hoped I'd dream about Nana, but I never did.

In that moment, I would've given anything to have another summer with my grandmother. Or even a day, an hour. Anything. I wanted to call Cassie. She was the only person who would be able to understand what I was going through. Hearing her voice would somehow make it better, mend the hole in my heart. But, of course, that was impossible. And that just made me hurt more. Eat more. Sleep more.

The call from the lawyer's office came the next day. I was expected to go in for the reading of Nana's will. Both Cassie and me—when I heard that bit, it felt like there was a flock of birds trapped inside my chest. I'd get to see Cassie. We'd be in the same room together for the first time in fourteen years! The meeting was set up for the following week. Now, I was guilt-ridden and anxious. My fairy tales just weren't enough anymore. And I had no energy to exercise. So I walked to Convenience City and stocked up on junk food: pints of ice cream, candy, cans of condensed milk—I was hoping to recreate the dessert Nana used to make. For the record, I failed. I drank the condensed milk straight from the can.

Four days later, Patrick pointed out, not unkindly, that I had gained weight.

"It's all the ice cream," he said, eyeing the spoon I had in my mouth at that very moment. "Lately, it feels like all you do is eat and sleep."

"I just lost my grandmother," I said.

"That's no excuse for stuffing your face and napping all day." His tone was affectless, but the disapproval was written across his face.

His words stung. Not because they were untrue: I had gained weight, and I was sleeping a lot more than usual. Still, I felt he was being unreasonable. These were unusual circumstances: I was hurting, grieving. It's not like I did this sort of thing all the time. Back in school, I'd often indulge in a midday nap or a bag of Doritos. But ever since we moved in together, I'd slowly phased out of these habits. Patrick has never been shy about criticizing what he perceives as unhealthy behavior. And I have always been eager to please him. But right then, I didn't care about staying healthy. I didn't care about my weight. I told Patrick as much.

"We have the benefit on Sunday," he reminded me. "At the Museum of Fine Arts."

"That's the day before the reading of the will. I can't go."

"I need you there. The governor is coming."

I shouldn't have been surprised. Patrick has social anxiety. He denies it—he thinks it makes him seem weak. But he does. I, on the other hand, am an extrovert. Having me on his arm at these sorts of functions makes everything easier. I didn't mind my role. In all honesty, I loved it: it made me feel purposeful, needed. But, in that moment, I resented it tremendously.

"Wear the silver dress I love so much?"

"Sure," I said.

But I didn't stop eating the ice cream. A minor act of rebellion.

The next morning, I tried on the dress. The zipper wouldn't close. The extra weight wouldn't have made a difference in a different gown—but the silver one was particularly form-fitting. Patrick walked inside my closet and winced.

For a moment I wanted to push him out the window.

"I'll go on a diet," I said.

I expected him to dismiss my suggestion. To point out that I had a closet full of couture. That I could go shopping.

Instead, he said, "You have four days." And then: "And no more pills. You need to stay awake to exercise. I'm going to count how many are in the bottle. If I see one missing, you'll have to explain yourself to me."

"Fine," I said, through gritted teeth.

My diet consisted of starving myself. It was easier than I expected. As it turns out, both overeating and starvation are effective ways to deal with pain—they're both numbing. I subsisted on oxygen and coconut water, which Sophie had taught me to be both filling and a laxative. I laid off the Xanax, reasoning that they wouldn't go well with my empty stomach anyway.

By the day of the party, I was one pound lighter than I was before Nana passed away. Patrick beamed with pride when he saw me wearing his dress of choice. Here's the thing about Patrick: he's generous with his compliments—as long as I follow his rules. That night, he spun me around and said I'd be the most beautiful woman at the party.

I agreed: I looked stunning.

I started feeling dizzy in the middle of the governor's speech. At first, I thought it was because I was bored—the man was very dull. I tried distracting myself with a fairy tale, but I couldn't. That's when I knew something was wrong. I felt lightheaded, and I was both shivering and sweating—a combination that had me alarmed. Patrick and I—along with the senior partners at the firm—were standing close to the stage. I wanted a glass of water. To sit down. I remember looking for chairs nearby.

The next thing I remember is waking up to the sound of my name.

"Julie?" a female voice was saying. "Julie?" She used the American pronunciation.

I opened my eyes. A woman was standing in front of me, her frowning face uncomfortably close to mine. She was wearing a simple black pantsuit and an earpiece.

"Are you her husband?" the woman said.

I thought she was talking to me. Her question made no sense—how could I be my own husband? But then I heard Patrick's voice.

"I am," he said.

"Can you hear me, Julie?" Our eyes met.

"Yes," I said. My throat was dry. "I'm so sorry."

"Don't be sorry," she said. "You fainted. We were worried about you. How are you feeling?"

"Did I interrupt the speech?" I looked around. We were in a different room. Had I been carried here?

"Don't you worry about that," she said.

"I'm really sorry," I said again. I was aware I sounded like a parrot. But I just felt so awful.

"Stop apologizing, silly," the woman said.

"Could I get some water?"

"Right away," the woman said.

I reached out for Patrick's hand as soon as she left. He looked tense, wound up. I felt awful. I knew how embarrassed he must feel, having me faint in the middle of an important speech. Patrick was too self-conscious to be able to laugh it off. I understood that about him. I knew the vulnerable side he didn't share with anyone else.

Seconds later, I had my water. I drank it in one gulp. It was pure relief.

"Thank you," I said. "I'm so sorry."

"Don't you dare apologize to me again," the woman said. "You did nothing wrong."

"How are you feeling, darling?" Patrick asked.

The kindness is his voice lifted my spirits. I felt such gratitude towards him, such love. I knew it wasn't easy for him, being so understanding. Over the years, there'd been countless moments when I'd accidentally embarrassed him in public. He'd turn beet red with the smallest things. If I mispronounced a word. Or accidentally cut in line. If I walked into a door before someone walked out of it. To most people, these are oversights, inconsequential mistakes. But to someone with Patrick's crippling self-awareness, they are catastrophic events.

"I'm better now," I said. "Maybe a little weak."

Patrick decided we should leave early. I told him I was OK to stay, but he wouldn't hear of it. I was touched by his concern. I knew what a big deal these functions were to him. But when we got in the car, his demeanor changed.

"Do you have any idea how embarrassing that was?" he said through gritted teeth.

"Patrick, I fainted. It's not like I did it on purpose." And then, because it needed to be said, "You were the one who wanted me to wear this dress. I haven't had anything solid in days."

"This has nothing to do with dieting. You always do this, slip away into God knows where inside your head. If you'd been paying attention, you wouldn't have fainted."

"You think I fainted because I wasn't paying attention?" I half-laughed, though I wasn't amused. "To what, gravity?"

He sighed heavily. "Grow up, Julie. Get your head out of the clouds."

It's something I'd often heard as a child, too. *Get your head out of the clouds.* It used to hurt me, until Nana confided in me that her parents used to say the same thing to her when she was a kid. *Don't listen to them, Julie,* she used to say. *You can't beat the view from up here.*

But Nana wasn't there anymore. She was gone.

"What were you thinking?" he continued.

"I wasn't. I was passed out."

"In front of *all* my colleagues. They're probably talking about it right now."

"Patrick, these past few days have been hell for me," I began, my tone incredulous. This was a new low, even for him. Had he forgotten that I was mourning the loss of my grandmother? "All I've wanted to do was cry and sleep—"

"Is that what this is about?" He glared at me. "Have you been popping Xanax like some drug addict?"

His words struck me like an open palm across the face. "No," I managed to say.

We went quiet for a few minutes. I kept replaying his comment in my mind, silently seething at his cruelty. *Have you been popping Xanax like a drug addict?* Who says something like that?

After a while—five minutes, maybe more—I heard him clear his throat. I assumed he was about to launch into an apology. Or at least that he'd say something nice. Pay me another compliment.

But that's not what happened.

"That was really embarrassing, Julie," Patrick repeated. "I hope it never happens again."

"Not for me it wasn't." My tone was defensive. "People faint. It happens."

"So why were you constantly apologizing to that woman?" he asked. "People heard you, you know."

"Because I knew you'd be upset," I said. "My first thought when I woke up was 'Patrick is going to be mad at me.' It sucks to see that I was right."

"Of course I'm upset, Julie. You acted like a child in there, fainting like an unprepared girl. And, to make it worse, you had to keep apologizing until the minute we left. You made it seem like I'd be angry at you for fainting. They're probably talking about me right now. Calling me insensitive, cruel."

His words felt like a slap in the face.

In that moment, all I could think was, *That's exactly what they should be saying about you.*

But I kept it to myself.

I remember thinking I'd never be able to tell anyone about our evening because if anyone were to hear about his behavior, they'd tell me to run for the hills. What kind of man reprimands his wife for fainting?

Except now I'm telling Janette everything. I half expect her to get up, drive to Boston, drag Patrick out of the apartment, and slap him senseless. Instead, she reaches over, cups my hand, and threads her fingers through mine.

"I'm sorry that happened." There's a gentleness to her tone. But there's something else, too. A muted impatience. A total lack of surprise.

"He didn't used to be like this," I say. I don't mean it as a defense, but as a statement of fact. Patrick *didn't* used to be this way. He's always been too self-aware for his own good: image-conscious and overly concerned with others' opinions. And he's always been particular about his routine. But, over the years, his fixation on appearances has become pathological. I used to think that the more power he amassed—I met Patrick when he was still an associate, and now he's a senior partner—the more secure he'd become. But the opposite has happened. Lately, his insecurity has bordered on paranoia. It's turning him into a cruel man.

I watch as Janette bites the inside of her cheek. "I have to ask," she begins, her tone tentative, "do you think it's going to get better?"

Silence stretches between us. I don't know how to answer her question.

Not without crying.

CHAPTER ELEVEN

Cassie

Sunday, July 1st

Christina has ordered the quinoa bowl. It looks tasty, but insubstantial.

"Is that all you're eating?" I ask.

We're sitting on the patio at Babette's, a restaurant on Newton Lane that Christina promised would be worth the drive. And by the look of the cinnamon swirl French toast in front of me, she's right.

"Don't mock, Cass," Rachel says. "Not all of us can be born with your metabolism."

"You're both way tinier than me." I'm a magnet for petite people. I feel like a female version of Gulliver when I'm around my friends.

"You're tall." Christina takes a swig of her mimosa. "Weight distribution is on your side."

"You know what? I apologize." I take a bite of my French toast. It tastes even better than it looks. "We shouldn't be talking about food, or our weights."

"Or else the patriarchy wins," Christina adds.

"Exactly." I nod.

"Drink," Rachel says with a smile. "She said 'patriarchy.'"

We all laugh—and drink. Christina's unapologetic feminism is one of her many admirable qualities.

"Cassie, don't keep us in suspense. We both want to know how things are going with your sister." Christina says *sister* like one would say *pet dragon* or *unicorn*.

I roll my eyes—it's rude, but I don't care. Must everything be about Julie?

"Come on." Rachel leans forward. "We're curious. We drove all the way from Boston for this."

"It's been so weird," I say. "She keeps offering me food. Compulsively, I mean."

"That's kind of sweet," Rachel offers. "She's probably missed you."

I definitely don't think this is true. Julie had fourteen years to reach out to me, but she never did. We live in the same city.

"No, it's weird. It's like she's trying to be Nana. Plus, she looks like a Stepford wife." I don't add that this is particularly disconcerting because, as a teenager, Julie had a laid-back, bohemian style. Now she looks like a magazine cutout: glamorous, polished, but ultimately artificial. "It's whatever. She's changed. I've changed. It's been forever."

"But now you're living with her," Christina says. "You two share a history."

"And a house," Rachel adds.

"And a dad," Christina finishes.

The last one is patently false. Not that I'd ever be able to explain it to them.

Julie and I have the same father—biologically speaking. But we didn't have the same parent. From what she's told me—and this was something we discussed at length as kids—her father was a happy person. Flawed, of course. Absent and untrustworthy—but loving and cheerful. A pleasant person.

My father was an altogether different individual.

I did not have an absent father. He traveled a lot *on business*—which I later learned was a lie: he'd been staying at Julie's house. But he was a constant figure in my life. He never missed a music recital or a track meet. He came to parent-teacher conferences and Father's Day events at my school. He also spent every summer with my mom and me at Nana's house—he only stopped after Julie and I met and began coming by ourselves. I do not remember sitting at the dinner table until the early hours of the morning, hungry because I refused to eat until he showed up—which is something Julie had done quite a few times.

What I do remember was his explosive temper. I was terrified of my father.

"We could stop by the house, you know," Rachel says. "Meet her for ourselves. Since you won't tell us anything."

"There's nothing to tell," I say. "We've barely said two words to each other."

"Shouldn't you, I don't know, try to get along?" Rachel asks. Her brown eyes are kind, sincere. I know she means well. But it's a remarkably stupid question.

"You know, the two of you should really drop this. If you don't, I won't be able to tell you my news." I feel my cheeks stretch in a smile.

"Oh, I know that voice." Christina's tone drops a register. "This is about Daniel."

"How did you know?" I ask.

"You've got your Daniel glow." Rachel shoots Christina a warning look. This is not uncommon: Christina is wary of my relationship with Daniel. She's like me: a pessimist. Rachel's more of a romantic.

"I asked him to leave his wife."

Christina is staring at me, her mouth agape.

"That's amazing, Cass." Rachel is grinning, beaming. Sometimes it's nice to have optimistic friends.

"What did he say?" Christina is eyeing me suspiciously.

"He obviously agreed," Rachel tells her. "Look at her smile. She's thrilled. I can't believe you didn't tell us right away."

"You wouldn't shut up about Julie."

"What about your career?" Christina asks.

"I spoke to Claudia. I didn't give her any specifics, but I explained the general situation. She said that as long as we come out with the story first, we should be fine."

"Really?" Christina looks unconvinced.

"I'm not saying it'll be easy," I say. "I'll probably have to go on a bunch of shows and talk about my personal life, but it'll pass. Everything does. The important thing is that Daniel and I will be together."

"Has he spoken to Tatiana?" Christina asks.

"No, he's been here with me." My tone is defensive. They know Daniel is staying at the Surfside Inn for the weekend. "He wanted to join us for brunch, actually."

Christina shrugs. "He could call her."

"He's not ending his marriage over the phone," Rachel says.

"Why not?" Christina asks forcefully. "He keeps telling us his marriage has been over for a long time."

A hush falls on the table. Rachel and I exchange an uneasy look.

"So when *is* he doing it?" Christina asks.

"We didn't set a date, Christina," I say. "And I'd appreciate a little more support."

Christina sucks the air between her teeth but says nothing.

"I'm sure he'll talk to her soon." Rachel places a protective hand on top of mine.

I shoot Rachel a grateful look and take another bite of my food, ignoring the bitter taste that is now in my mouth.

"This is a little off-topic," Rachel begins. I feel myself relaxing. A change of subject is exactly what we need. "Is it weird that your grandmother left her the house?"

"Her as in…Julie?" I ask.

Rachel nods.

"Why would it be weird?" I feel my eyebrows squishing together.

"I don't know." Rachel shrugs. "You were her, and I hate using this word, 'legitimate' granddaughter. Maybe you thought she'd leave the house all to you."

The truth: I never thought of what would happen to the house after Nana passed away. Probably because I never thought of Nana dying. As illogical as it sounds, I thought she'd live forever. If I had given it any real thought, I would've guessed that she'd leave it to my father. Not because he deserved it, but because she was his mother—and mothers love their children despite their flaws. But the idea of her leaving me the entire house would be unthinkable. It makes perfect sense that she split it between Julie and me, fifty-fifty. She loved us equally.

I tell them as much as I eat my last sweet potato fry.

"Would you rather she'd left it to your dad?" Rachel asks. "That way you wouldn't have to spend the summer here with Julie?"

"Absolutely not," I say. Growing up, the Montauk house was my sanctuary. My father has no business inheriting my sanctuary—he was the reason I needed one.

People tend to enjoy my father's company. He comes across as calm, together. He's good at pretending. But he never pretended with my mom and me. At home, he was himself: a temperamental bully.

A memory overtakes me. A family dinner, when I was seven, maybe eight years old. My father asked my mom if she added onions to the stir-fry. My mom slurred something incomprehensible—she was having a particularly bad day. By my count, she'd had at least two extra glasses of whiskey. My father repeated the question. This time, my mom started laughing.

That set him off.

He got up from his seat, pushing his chair back with a crash. He slammed his fists against the table. "Are you laughing at me?" My father was a big man. He looked scary. Threatening.

He began ranting. I was used to his rants.

"There aren't any onions," I said loudly. I had ordered the meal myself. I'd made sure to say no onions.

"And how would you know?" he asked, turning to me. He resented my interruption. His tirades were a twisted sort of therapy for him. A way to purge his demons. To feel better about himself. He required an audience, but it had to be a silent audience.

"Because she ordered it," my mom said.

The rant continued—he accused her of being in a vegetative state. "You don't cook, you don't work. You don't do anything." He went on, spewing vile, odious things. Calling her useless. Lazy.

I knew that sooner or later my mom would interrupt him. She always did.

I was right.

"My money pays for this house. It pays for our life. So if I'm lazy, then you're nothing." Her speech was still garbled, but less so. Their fights had an odd sobering effect on her.

I braced myself for the worst. The money card always made it worse. Our lifestyle was only possible because of my mom's money, which she'd inherited at the age of seventeen. We wouldn't have been able to afford a house in Dover on my father's salary. This bothered my dad tremendously. He was power-hungry, status-obsessed. He felt that life had shortchanged him, sticking him with a middle-management position at a bank. He enjoyed the assumption made by his peers, which was that he was the sole breadwinner in our family and the admiration that came with it. That he seldom talked about his job only upped his stock because it made him seem modest. But whenever my mom reminded him that the real power, a.k.a. the money, lay with her, he'd lose it.

"How dare you talk to me like that?" he roared.

"You better shut up, Stephan. Or our neighbors will find out that you're not the gentleman you pretend to be."

"I don't give a damn about the neighbors," he said. But he did take it down a notch. Because he absolutely did care. She did, too. What they didn't care about was me. "You better show me some respect."

"Or what?"

What he did next was something he'd done many times before. He reached for my mom's china cabinet and began throwing its contents on the ground. Plates. Saucers. Teacups. One by one, they shattered into a million sharp pieces on the hardwood floors.

My mom flung herself at him, yelling for him to stop. The dishes had been in her family for generations. But he didn't stop. Instead, he swatted her like a fly. I heard the familiar thud of her thin, frail body hitting the floor. I raced to her. She hugged me, burying her head in my arms. I looked up. I was prepared to beg my father to stop. But he was already walking away, a satisfied expression on his face. He wanted her to show him respect—and, in his mind, she finally had. To him, fear and respect were one and the same.

Fights like these happened all the time. My father never walked up to my mom and hit her—he saved his initial anger for inanimate objects. But if my mom dared intervene—and she usually did—he'd become physical. He'd throw her on the floor. Pull her hair and toss her against a piece of furniture. One time, he slammed her head against a wall. He never knelt down to check to see if she'd been badly hurt. That was my job. It had been my job for as long as I could remember.

One day, after a heated argument, my father walked into my room. I was curled up in a ball, crying. I'll never forget the words he said to me—or his casual tone. "I know you don't like to see her getting hurt, Cassie, but sometimes your mother needs to be reminded that I'm still the man around here." He seemed to believe his own excuses.

I wish I'd had the presence to point out that being aggressive didn't make him a man. I wish I'd told him that he wasn't just hurting my mom—he was hurting *me*. Witnessing abuse, whether verbal or physical, scars children for life. It's a form of abuse in itself. I was a hyper-vigilant, anxious kid, incapable of kicking back and having fun. Looking out for my mom was my job, my burden. And I knew that wasn't how things were supposed to be. When I went to my friends' houses, it was their moms who looked after them—not the other way around. But that wasn't my reality. There's a term for this role reversal in my profession: parentified child. A child who feels responsible for caring for their parent.

Julie was a parentified child as well, although her mother's excessive reliance on her manifested itself in an altogether different way. We both had to grow up too soon. We both learned how to take care of our mothers before we learned how to take care of ourselves. Maybe this is why we were able to keep our father's secret for so many years: we were used to being burdened by our parents.

But Rachel and Christina don't know about any of this. They know my father and I don't get along. They know that he was verbally abusive. That Julie and I don't speak to each other anymore. That's it. I can't bring myself to share further, to unpack the messiness. It's too traumatic, too painful.

"Let me put it to you this way," I say, looking at my friends. "If I had to, I'd spend a year here in Montauk with Julie to keep my father from getting the house."

Rachel and Christina are both stunned into silence. I don't usually speak with such finality, such anger. That I would about my own father is probably disconcerting to them. Shocking, even. I don't mind.

They don't get it—and that's fine. They don't have to.

CHAPTER TWELVE

Julie

Tuesday, July 3rd

I read somewhere that the sense of smell is closely linked with memory—more than any of the other senses. I didn't believe it at the time. How could a scent be more powerful than hearing a song, or seeing a picture? But now, as I inhale, I understand. The whiff in the air—a blend of olive oil, Mediterranean spices, and nutmeg—is enough to transport me back in time. If I close my eyes, it's almost as though Nana is here, cooking with me.

Almost. Because I'm missing an ingredient.

The problem is, I have no idea which one.

I'm searching Nana's spice cabinet—sniffing each bottle like a deranged dog—when I hear Cassie coming down the stairs. She looks pretty in a pair of white denim shorts and an oversized striped green and white T-shirt. She's holding a book in her hands.

From an early age, the Fire Princess has cultivated the habit of losing herself in stories. One time, the Sky Princess picked up one of the books to read aloud to her, but she kept changing the story, adding a second hero, or altering a sequence of events. The Fire Princess teased the Sky Princess for having too much imagination. Does the Fire Princess remember that day?

"I'm making pasta," I say. "Want some?"

I expect her to say no. It's all she's been saying to me: no. We haven't shared a single meal together. But something passes through her face. Indecision, maybe. I feel a tingle of hope.

"I can open a bottle of wine." We've been living together for almost a week now and I've noticed her drinking a glass in the evenings.

"Sure," she says.

It's not much. But it's a start.

She turns and heads outside. I watch her lie on the hammock and thumb away at her phone.

It makes me feel like a nine-year-old girl again: being in this house, trying to get her attention.

Over the years, I've developed a theory about why Cassie and I didn't get along that first summer. Sisters are either older or younger. Older sisters tend to boss their younger sisters around. Younger sisters learn to share more easily—they've never had their parents all to themselves. The age difference acts as a mold, shaping their relationship. It gives them a *thing*.

When Cassie and I met, we didn't have a thing. We were the same age—my two-week seniority meant nothing. We didn't know how to act around each other, how to navigate our newfound sisterhood.

From the start, I could tell Cassie didn't like me. Sophie had warned me that she wouldn't. Cassie was used to being the only one, the family princess. Unlike me, she hadn't known I existed until very recently. I expected her to pout when Nana developed pictures of me to put up around the house. I expected her to be jealous that she'd have to share her beach house with me. I expected her to be bothered when Sebastian took a liking to me (cats usually like me) and began following me around the house, grazing his soft fur against my legs. But Cassie didn't seem to mind any of that.

Instead, she acted as though I was invisible. The one exception: the bizarre looks she gave me when Nana put me on the phone with Daddy. Since she heard us speak, I'd notice that, on occasion and always when she thought I wasn't looking, she'd stare at me as if I was a riddle she was trying to figure out.

Cassie's behavior aside, I was having the best summer of my life. I was in awe of the house (a whole house just for the summer!), the beach (right in front of the house!), and the throngs of beautiful, glittery people. I loved everything about the Hamptons. Small, Colonial-style shops on Main Street. Day trips to Block Island. Lunch at the Yacht Club followed by strolls down Westlake Marina.

But what I loved the most was Nana.

Nana's love for me was instant. She became my grandmother from the moment we met. As soon as she saw me, she pulled me in a hug. She said she'd been waiting my whole life to meet me. She pointed to my eyes and then to hers and we both smiled: they were the same.

She wanted to know everything about me. We started with my favorites—food, color, subject in school. Did I prefer white meat or dark meat? How did I like my eggs? What kind of music did I listen to? The truth was, I hadn't stopped to consider most of her questions. I hadn't developed tastes of my own yet. It was assumed that I enjoyed what Sophie enjoyed, an expectation that extended to my palate (olives, sharp cheeses, mushrooms) and acoustic predilections (Richard Cocciante and Jean-Jacques Goldman). My mom was French, which meant that I was French. And, in my house, being French meant looking down on all things American, especially when it came to food and pop culture.

Nana changed that.

It was my grandmother who unwittingly encouraged me to look inside myself. To think of what I wanted, what I liked. I don't think she realized what she was doing. To her, she was just asking questions. But in reality, Nana was giving me permission to be a kid. I was worry-free that summer. I didn't worry about making dinner—that was Nana's job, one she seemed to enjoy. I didn't worry about Sophie working late and forgetting to pay a bill or to sign a permission slip for school. I didn't worry about consoling Sophie when my dad canceled plans or forgot an anniversary. All that free time allowed me to discover who I was. I found out how I liked my eggs (scrambled, with goat cheese on the side and diced tomatoes), I listened to new music (I was blessedly free to dance along to the Backstreet Boys and Spice Girls), and I concluded that I didn't much like chicken at all.

And best of all: I developed a sense of style.

Sophie had taught me about clothes—or couture, as she called it. I knew which fabrics didn't go well together. That thin belts worked better with wide waists, and thick belts with small waists. I knew not to mix shades of white without a bold-colored accessory. Useful knowledge, but it had nothing to do with personal style. Sophie's own sense of style was impeccable, of course. Elegant, understated. Except it was a bit too classical for my taste.

Nana had a passion for colors. She'd boldly mix fabrics and prints—rules be damned. Because of her, I fell in love with vintage clothing. I developed an eye for the eccentric. I like to think that I managed to combine the best of my two worlds. I knew all about haute couture—I still loved the classical cuts of Chanel and Prada. But I also grew to appreciate Pucci and Missoni. I knew how to pair vintage designer items (a few of which Sophie was able to secure because of her new job at *Posh*) with my regular clothes. My outfits became fun, unique.

And it was all because of my grandmother—and that first summer we spent together.

Not everything was perfect, though. Cassie still mostly ignored me. By the tail end of summer, I had given up on getting her to like me. It saddened me, having a sister who was a stranger. But I was also used to it.

And then the spider incident happened.

I was lying on the beach when the giant, spindly thing landed on my bare stomach. I shrieked in terror. I'd never even seen a spider that big, let alone touched one. Cassie came to my rescue. She swatted it off while I flapped my arms wildly. That's when she lost her balance—and fell on top of me. Our collective clumsiness and my recent hysteria sent us into a laughing fit. We must've spent ten minutes clutching our bellies, hiccupping.

Her words took me by surprise.

"My mom told me to spy on you," she said, when we stopped laughing.

We were lying on the beach under a large, yellow umbrella that Nana insisted Cassie put up every time because of her fair skin.

"You're doing a really bad job then," I said.

"Because I've been keeping my distance?"

"I don't think spies are supposed to say they are spies."

"I'm not doing it."

"Why not?"

"It doesn't feel right."

"Thanks?" It came out as more of a question than a statement.

"She's super jealous of your mom," Cassie said. "She thinks she's still having an affair with my—with our, father."

I couldn't picture Katherine being jealous of my mom. Katherine was Daddy's wife. She had him *all the time*. It was Sophie who should be jealous—and I was pretty sure she was.

Sophie had warned me not to tell Cassie that she and Daddy were a couple. *If Katherine is stupid enough to believe that all he does when he comes over is see you, then that's her problem.*

"Your mom is really pretty," I said. A lie: Nana's house had several pictures of Katherine—I didn't think she was pretty at all. But that seemed like a mean thing to say, especially when my own mom was so beautiful.

"Thanks," Cassie said, and I could tell by her voice that she was putting her guard up again. That she was going back in her shell.

I'm absolutely certain that what I said next changed the course of our lives. And I only said it because I was desperate to bond with Cassie. I had just learned the wonders of having a grandmother. I wanted a sister, too.

And so I told her my mom's secret. A secret that was not mine to share.

"Your mom's right," I said. "Sophie and our dad? They're a couple."

Cassie suppressed a gasp. She met my gaze and began asking me all sorts of questions. I answered each of them honestly, without knowing whether or not she'd share her newfound information with her mother.

Of all of the questions she asked, this was the strangest one: Did our dad love my mom?

"Of course he does," I said. "He adores her."

Sometimes I wonder if I should've lied. I was used to lying—I had been taught how to from an early age. Maybe Cassie and I wouldn't have grown close.

But at least Katherine would still be alive.

CHAPTER THIRTEEN

Cassie

Tuesday, July 3rd

Despite her new look, Julie hasn't changed. She's still a people-pleaser who tries too hard.

It's Tuesday, day six of our mandatory vacation—an oxymoron if I ever heard one. Julie seems intent on bonding through food. She offers it all: fruit salad, homemade potato chips, yogurt. Elaborate seafood dishes. Beer—at this, I gag. I keep saying no. I'm not an idiot: I know what she's trying to do. Growing up, meals were sacred in this house. It's a huge part of how we bonded. But we're not girls anymore. And she isn't Nana.

Except now she's offering me pasta—with wine. My favorite combination in the world. And I'm hungry. I say yes, but I don't offer to help. I can't cook, anyway.

I step outside, plop on the hammock and take out my phone. Technically, I'm on break, but I can't seem to shake off my habit of checking emails at least a couple of times a day. I scroll down my inbox: the only work email I have is from Alice Dewar. I'm used to getting emails from Alice: she and her husband, Nick, are one of the few couples I treat via Skype. I scan her message. She wants to let me know that they'll need to reschedule their mid-August session because they'll still be at the Sag Harbor house with the rest of the Dewar clan—I know this is painful for Alice.

I hadn't realized that Alice and Nick were summering so close to me—I hope I don't run into them. It's always awkward, running into patients. I write back, assuring her that I'll keep her regular appointment slot, starting in September.

It's a beautiful day—cerulean sky with puffy clouds, a slight breeze. I wish Daniel were here. I miss him. I take a deep breath and let it out slowly. I scan the picturesque setting in front of me. I'm going to note five things. Describe them slowly to myself. A grounding technique, one that helps me stay present. My eyes land on the front door, but then they quickly travel upwards, to the wind chimes that are hanging above me. I blink rapidly and narrow my gaze. It can't be—can it?

I glance inside the house to see if Julie is watching me. Thankfully, she's facing the stove. I get up from the hammock and take a step closer to examine the colorful, handcrafted chimes: driftwood and seashells. I remember when they made it, Julie and Nana. It was one of the first things they did together.

That summer comes rushing back to me.

Julie and Nana hit it off right away. They had a lot in common: an affinity for crafts, a talent for cooking, and a love of storytelling—Nana would tell us tales before bedtime and Julie would jump in, suggesting plot twists and new characters. There were other things, too. They both laughed a lot, loudly. They spoke in superlatives. They were utterly unselfconscious. Free spirits. Nana was thrilled to finally have an artistic, imaginative granddaughter.

Except that's not fair.

The unsettling truth was that Nana didn't stop loving me. She still showered me with attention and affection. Still prepared my favorite dishes—and baked as many cakes as I wanted. Still talked to me about the books I was reading (she was a reader, like me). Still played backgammon with me after dinner or on rainy days (a two-person game, which meant Julie couldn't join).

Still worked on thousand-piece jigsaw puzzles with me for hours (Julie declined Nana's invitation to help us out).

I had expected her love to be divided between Julie and me. Instead, it was doubled. And, for some twisted reason, that made me furious.

Although, in retrospect, it might've been because I was already angry.

Before coming to Montauk, my mom had asked me to befriend Julie. She wanted me to find out whether my father was still involved with Julie's mother. Romantically involved— something I'd never considered myself. By then, I'd had a few conversations about Julie's existence with Nana and my parents, and they all delivered the same speech: years ago, my father made a one-time mistake and from that mistake Julie had been born. But my mom suspected there was more to the story, that my father might still be seeing Sophie. Cheating on her.

I disliked being asked to spy on my half-sister. That's *not* what parents were supposed to do—I knew that because I read so many books about stable, happy families. Books about identical twins living in the Golden State. About friends who founded a babysitting business. These kids all had drama in their worlds, but it all stemmed from their own life events: puberty, first crushes, and tame competition among friends. It did not come from their parents.

Julie assumed I didn't give in to my mom's request because it offended my morals.

The truth: I didn't give in because I was resentful.

I wanted better parents. I deserved better parents.

I made no effort to bond with Julie, an act of defiance against my mother's selfishness. It wasn't easy—I was curious about her, about this girl who was both my half-sister and a complete stranger. I kept my distance, silently sulking at the injustice of having irresponsible parents. I could tell that Julie was hurt by my behavior, but I had no intention of letting my guard down. Of letting her in.

It's been twenty-two years since that first summer.

I force myself to look away from the wind chimes. I sink back into the hammock and open my book, an advance copy of Jane Harper's latest novel, courtesy of my publisher. Noting things won't help keep me present, not in this house. But losing myself in a story just might.

About twenty minutes later, Julie walks out, holding two plates. "Should we eat outside?" she asks. "It's so nice."

"Sure." I do not want to sit at the dining table with her. It's where we used to eat as young girls, the three of us in the corner of the twelve-seat table. I wonder, not for the first time, why Nana was so attached to having such a large table. It's not like we had a big family.

Julie brings out the pasta. I recognize the bowl: colorful, with pictures of green and red peppers and the names of different types of pasta in cursive—fusilli, penne, spaghetti. Nana used it all the time. I wonder if Julie would mind if I asked to keep it. Eventually, we'll have to divide up Nana's things. I shouldn't get ahead of myself—in order for that to happen, I'll have to survive the next three weeks.

I go inside the house to choose the wine: a 2007 Robert Mondavi Cabernet Sauvignon. It's hot, but I don't care. Sun-dried tomatoes call for red wine. I stop short as I'm eyeing the goblets in Nana's cabinet. The question seems inevitable. I pop back outside.

"Two glasses?" I ask, standing in the doorway.

"No, thanks," she says. "I'm having beer." Her tone is chirpy. Everything about her is chirpy.

Beer with pasta. I probably look disgusted. I don't care. I turn around to retrieve the bottle and glass. She waits for me to get back before taking a seat, a wide smile on her face. I do the same, sans smile. It's the first time we're eating together in over a decade.

"What are you reading?" she asks.

I flip the book over so she can read the title.

"Is it good?" She seems unfazed by my curtness.

I bring a forkful of spaghetti to my mouth, mostly to keep from answering her question. And then everything stops—sounds, thoughts. It all melts away.

This is magic. Actual witchcraft.

It's the pasta Nana used to make for us as children. I indulge in another forkful. I'm vaguely aware of a low moaning sound coming from my throat. What's in this? Basil. Chili. Something else, too. I obviously don't know what—I use my oven as storage—but it's *delicious*. From the corner of my eye, I can see Julie watching me.

"Do you like it?" Julie looks pleased with herself.

"Hmm," I say, nodding. This time, I'm not trying to be rude. I just can't stop eating.

"It's Nana's recipe..." she says, her voice trailing off.

A melodic sound interrupts us. It's coming from my phone. Bella's name is flashing on the screen. This is unusual. Bella and I text often (Daniel likes to tease that his sister and I are closer than they are), but she seldom calls.

"I have to get this," I say. I bring it all inside with me: phone, plate, glass of wine, and make my way up to Nana's room.

"Cass, thank God," Bella says, after I pick up. "*She was just here.*"

"Who?"

"Tatiana."

A blast of cold air hits my core. I sit on Nana's four-poster bed. The familiar creaking noise makes my heart beat faster. I'm not sure why. "What was she doing there?"

"She's crazy. She accused me of trying to take her children away from her. She just took off with them. I tried to stop her, but she's their mother. I didn't think there was anything I could do."

"Have you called Daniel?" He's back in Boston already, but he's headed over to Bella's tomorrow to spend the Fourth with the kids. I worry about what this will do to his blood pressure.

"Yeah, he's stressed out of his mind. Jackson made the mistake of telling him Tatiana had crazy eyes." She lets out a sigh. Bella's husband, Jackson, is known for being hyperbolic. Hopefully Daniel remembers this. "Listen, he made me promise I wouldn't say anything to you."

A sense of guilt claws up my throat. It's a feeling I know well. One I dread because it's broken me before. I've made a mess of things. The timing is no coincidence: last night, Daniel asked Tatiana for a divorce. This is her retaliation, taking the kids away from their aunt. It isn't even subtle: she's showing him she'll take them away from him, too.

The scary part is that she isn't wrong: Angie isn't Daniel's daughter, biologically speaking. Daniel has consulted a lawyer: Tatiana could make a case for sole custody of their daughter. It would be harder with Sam, but still not impossible. Tatiana doesn't have a job. She's their primary caregiver.

Do I want to be good or happy? The question my therapist asked me, years ago. I wouldn't know how to answer it now.

"I've made a mess of things," I say. I can feel the tears coming.

"Stop. This is not on you."

"I asked him to leave her."

"My brother is a grown man. He's leaving her because he wants to."

"But the kids—"

"They'll be fine. Kids are resilient."

I'm not sure I agree. Growing up, I was considered to be just that: resilient. People used to compliment me all the time on being responsible, together. They had no idea what I was going through. Children are adept at hiding things. And *resilient* is a nice word for *survivor*.

I don't want Angie and Sam to be survivors, especially not because of me. But I also want to be in Daniel's life—properly, officially—and that means being a part of his kids' lives. At first, it terrified me, the idea of being a stepmother. But something inside me has shifted ever since Daniel had his not-quite heart attack. I've been picturing a life with him, and all that it entails, including his kids. I've begun thinking of us as a proper family. Tatiana will always be their mom (God help them), but I could be something to them, too. A loving adult. A cool stepmom.

I hear one of Bella's terriers barking in the background. "Listen, I have to go. But remember. Not a word of this to my brother."

"He'll tell me himself?" I didn't mean for it to sound like a question.

"He might give you the watered-down version." A sigh from Bella. "He's afraid you'll have second thoughts."

"That's ridiculous." It's beyond ridiculous, actually.

"It's what he told me. He loves you, Cass."

"I love him, too."

We hang up. I immediately try Daniel's cell. I'd never break my promise to Bella, but I need to hear his voice. It goes straight to voicemail. I don't leave a message.

My body is a balloon deflating. I smooth Nana's bedspread with my hand—a watercolor pattern of reds, oranges, and pinks. I eye the plate of spaghetti and the full glass of wine, both sitting atop the carved wood dresser. Five minutes ago, I'd been in a celebratory mood. Daniel had talked to Tatiana. He was moving out. Our lives were about to begin. I was even eating with Julie, albeit silently. Now, I feel disgusted at my own selfishness. A darkness spreads inside my stomach like oil. My happiness is coming at the cost of others'. Tatiana. Sam. Angie. Even Daniel. They'd be better off without me. I deserve to be punished.

Bella's words ring in my ear. *He's afraid you'll have second thoughts.*

I can imagine Daniel saying just that. Bella probably thought they'd bring me some measure of comfort, knowing he's afraid of losing me. But now I'm afraid. I know Daniel. He's passionate and sensitive and kind. He also has a tendency to project his feelings onto others—he does it often. I first noticed this as his therapist. But I've since noticed this as his girlfriend, too. This could be his way of voicing his own fears.

What if he's the one having second thoughts about being with me?

CHAPTER FOURTEEN

Julie

Tuesday, July 3rd

I try calling Dad again. I get his voicemail, full.

This is unsurprising. I've been leaving him messages for days. There's no point in texting. Dad calls when he wants to. It isn't personal, it's just who he is. He's busy, he doesn't like being a slave to his phone. Nana used to say that she'd learn more about him from her holistic therapist than from their sporadic phone calls. Still, I wish he'd pick up. I miss him—now more than ever. Probably because Montauk reminds me of Nana. Probably because of the wall Cassie has erected between us.

I feel needy. I don't like it, but I think it's who I am. It doesn't help that Patrick has been giving me the silent treatment for the last six days. It's the longest we've ever gone without speaking to each other. I wonder how he's faring without me. I try to picture him arriving home at the end of the day to an empty house, rummaging through the kitchen cabinets in search of his almonds, pouring his own Scotch, ordering takeout. There won't be anyone to massage his neck—and Patrick needs his daily neck massages. I feel a tug of guilt for having left him by himself. Could Sophie be right? Could Patrick actually leave me, all because I'm here, and not there?

I stare at my half-eaten plate of pasta. I stopped eating after it became clear Cassie wasn't coming down from Nana's bedroom. Or perhaps I should be thinking of it as Cassie's bedroom?

Cassie hurrying into the house to pick up a phone call made me think of the rumor. I'd seen Sophie do that so many times, interrupt meals because Dad was calling. Being the other woman means settling for crumbs. Sophie used to admit as much when she was blue.

Like I said, my mother is many things, but she's seldom wrong.

And she isn't wrong about Cassie being the reason why I didn't have a dad. Katherine had been trying to get pregnant for years—Dad worried they couldn't. When Sophie announced she was pregnant, he was over the moon. He promised to leave Katherine, which thrilled Sophie. Except, two weeks later, Katherine broke news of her own: she was also expecting.

Dad chose Katherine and Cassie over Sophie and me.

Even before we met, I was envious of Cassie. I wanted her life: a stay-at-home mom, a full-time dad. I wanted to be official, to be seen. And, as Sophie often points out, Cassie had all these things—and she still wasn't happy. Cassie is—and has always been— a critical person. That's a nice way of saying that she's a complainer. She has a habit of zeroing in on other people's flaws, magnifying them. If they aren't up to her standards—and they often aren't—she rejects them. It's probably a trait of highly intelligent people. Cassie was twelve when she diagnosed her mother as an alcoholic suffering from clinical depression. It never occurred to me to diagnose my own mother. I didn't see the point in it—it's not like I'd be able to trade her in for a better model.

At the age of six, I finally worked up the courage to ask Sophie why Dad couldn't tuck me in every night. She winked at me and said she was working on it. That spring, Dad arrived with his bags packed. "I'm moving in," he announced. I was overjoyed. Here was my dad, all to myself.

For three months, we were a real family. They both dropped me off at school in the morning. We had dinner as a family every evening. We went on road trips on the weekend. We even talked about taking a family trip to France, though that didn't happen until many years later, and I didn't go with them. I never saw them argue or fight. Not even once. Sophie was elated, beatific. And I was the happiest kid on earth.

I wanted Sophie to quit her job. To me, it was the natural next step. But it wasn't an option—we needed both their paychecks, she said. Dad made a decent living, but most of their money came from Katherine. Even though I was only six, I understood this—money concerns had always been at the forefront of my mind. And I didn't mind, not really. Some of my classmates' moms worked. Having Dad live with us was enough. More than enough.

Dad left us two days before Memorial Day, 1995. I didn't see him again until the beginning of the fall. Sophie said he'd done the math and it turned out he couldn't leave Katherine, after all. Divorce was expensive. She delivered this news with stoicism, but I could tell that it was a front borne out of pride. On the inside, Sophie was breaking. She loved my dad. I shared her pain, her heartbreak. I also felt—irrationally, unreasonably—betrayed. And I blamed Sophie: she'd promised she was working on it. But Dad had only stayed for a few months. She should've worked harder. Should've found a way to make him want to stay. To make more money.

That was the real culprit: money.

Our lives were constantly being disrupted—made worse—by a lack of money. Money was both a disease and a vaccine: a cure made from its sickness.

I hated money. I also wanted money.

I'm on my third beer when I decide to call Patrick. We haven't had a conversation since I arrived in Montauk. He probably won't pick up. It's Tuesday, he's at work. Everyone else at the firm will have left early, or maybe they didn't go in at all—tomorrow is the Fourth, after all. But Patrick will still be there, toiling away, proving his worth to the world in the only way he knows how: by working harder than everyone else. I admire his work ethic, even if it is rooted in a deep sense of insecurity. I decide I'll leave him a message.

Except I'm wrong. He does pick up.

"Hey, you," I say. My strategy is to be affectionate, warm.

"Where are you?" His tone is polite, formal. Maybe there are other lawyers around him. Maybe he's made his team stay late.

"At Nana's house." I'm staring at my reflection in the antique commode's aged mirror. Immediately, I zero in on what's wrong with my appearance: barefoot, bitten-down nails, hair up in a messy bun. Not to mention the beer I'm drinking. I feel a jolt of panic, but quickly check myself. Patrick can't see me. We're on the phone.

"Are you coming home?"

"Not for another three weeks." I don't add that he knows this already. I finger the seashells around my neck. Patrick wouldn't approve of them, either.

"Your mother said you'd be coming back." I hear him breathing through his nose. "I thought that's why you were calling."

"I'm calling because I miss you." A pause. He doesn't say he misses me, too. "I know that things have been weird between us," I continue. "But I don't want to fight. I know I didn't handle this very well. I shouldn't have left in such a hurry. I was upset because of what happened at the benefit."

"You overreacted." It's something he's said before.

"No," I say. I fight the urge to tell him that it was his behavior that was unacceptable: blaming a fainting spell on me, telling me to get my head out of the clouds, insinuating that I had a pill problem. I resist the impulse to say that his obsession with the image we project is getting out of hand. That it's OK to gain a few pounds or to miss an event. People fall, people faint. People nap. I want to tell him that he doesn't have to be a winner all the time. That we are allowed to be fallible. That he can let go, unwind. Instead, I simply say, "I want to put it behind us."

A pause. "You leaving really hurt me."

"I understand." A lie: I do not. I do not understand Patrick's mind. I know it works differently from my own. I try to be patient, to appreciate that he suffers from anxiety, that he needs a certain level of emotional validation—and that often leads him to act in a controlling way. But it's exhausting.

"Then why are you there?"

"I have to do this," I say. "For me and for my grandmother."

"I told you we could fight the will in court."

"It's not just about the house. It's about fulfilling her last wish. She wanted me to be here."

"That's not acceptable."

"It's just for a month, Patrick. It's not a big deal. And you can come visit."

"You know I can't do that."

The troubling part is that he believes he really can't. Traveling drains him. Anything that takes him away from his routine sends him into an internal spiral. To Patrick, life is a script that must be followed to the letter. He can't forget a line. He can't improvise. He can't handle spontaneity. It's who he is.

Is it possible to love someone but not love who they are?

"Could you at least think about it?" I get up to fetch another beer from the fridge.

"What if we bought the house?" he asks.

I hear the sound of a door closing in the background. The air on the other side of the line is now quieter.

"Patrick, come on."

"It's humiliating to have you out there all summer long."

I feel queasy when I hear him say that. Sometimes I think all of Patrick's life is an exercise to avoid humiliation. "Do you even miss me?" I hear the catch in my voice.

"I want you home."

"Because you miss me?" I insist. "Or because you're worried about how it looks, having me spend the summer away from you? Do you really think anyone cares, Patrick? I can think of two, no, *three* lawyers at your firm whose wives are here for the summer. They join them on the weekends. They allow themselves a little bit of fun every now and then."

"You're being difficult." I don't have to see him to know he's speaking through clenched teeth.

"I'm being honest." A pause. "For the past decade you got to decide how we spent our summers. Can't I have a say just this once? Can't we compromise?"

An impatient exhale on his end. "We'll buy the house." His voice is thin, metallic. "You'll still get to keep it. Just come home. You belong with me."

It's like talking to a child. A rich, entitled brat.

"I don't want to buy the house, I want to inherit it." I take a deep breath. I can feel my skin prickling with frustration. "I want to honor Nana's wishes."

"What's more important: your dead grandmother or your husband?"

I gasp. I can't believe he just said that.

"I'm serious, Julie. I want you here." He delivers these four last words slowly, carefully. They sound like an ultimatum.

I feel something come apart inside me.

"This isn't about you, Patrick," I begin, a wave of indignation crashing in my chest. "This is about me. My childhood home. My grandmother." My voice goes up a notch. I don't care. "If you can't be flexible, then at least be supportive. I'm sick of everything being about you. You, you, you!" My throat hurts. I may have yelled this last bit.

"You're being irrational." His voice is cool, collected. It's infuriating.

"Go to hell, Patrick." I'm screaming. Cassie can probably hear me.

I hear him suck the air through his teeth. "I don't know what's happened to you, Julie. I barely recognize you. First you stuff yourself with junk food and sleep all day. Then you leave our home, after everything I've done for you. I wanted to give you the benefit of the doubt, but I think you've gone off the rails. I'm beginning to think you were better off when you were popping those pills."

"*Popping pills?*" I hear my tone: shocked, horrified. "I took a couple of Xanax because my grandmother had just died!"

"Then do me a favor and take a Xanax now," he says, acidly. "I'd rather have a wife who's asleep all day than hysterical."

I end the call. I don't even think about it. I just do it.

I stare at my phone, slack-jawed. How dare he talk to me like that? My pulse quickens. The living room is now spinning. I take a seat on the rocking chair. A mistake: I need a steadier surface.

A beeping noise floods my mind. A sliver of smoke is coming from the kitchen. I turn around, blinking. I must be imagining things. But, no—I've left the burner on. Smoke has caught on to a cloth potholder. There's a small fire.

A fire. In Nana's kitchen!

I throw the potholder inside the large, farmhouse sink. The alarm won't stop beeping. I climb onto the dining table, using a tea towel to fan out the fire detector.

"What's going on?" Cassie is standing by the stairs. Her face is flushed.

"I must've left the stove on." I have to yell because the alarm is deafening.

"That's not helping." She crouches in front of the cabinet under the sink and takes out a fire extinguisher. How did she know it was there? "Here, let me."

"No, I'll do it." I grab the red tube.

"It's fine," she says, irritated. She climbs on top of the table.

It happens in the blink of an eye: we bump into each other and come stumbling down onto the floor. Cassie goes down first. I land right on top of her, feeling a thud in my leg. I roll off her, groaning in pain.

"Why did you do that?" she says. "I was handling it."

My head is still thumping because of the blaring noise. I'm not interested in another fight, not today. I'm relieved when the fire alarm stops shrieking.

"I just wanted to help," I whisper. Something stirs inside me, something not altogether unpleasant. This tableau we're in, it reminds me of how we became friends in the first place. It's enough to make my heart smile. Maybe this is Nana interfering from above. Maybe this is the push we need to—

"Next time you want to help, just do nothing." Cassie's brittle tone cuts me. I feel the hope inside me begin to evaporate. "You could've burned down the house."

"But I—"

"Just stop, OK? Stop cooking. Stop cleaning. You're not Nana."

What does that mean: I'm not Nana? "I was trying to be nice."

"I know, it's all you can do. *Be nice*." Her face is now red.

"How is that a bad thing?"

She lets out a high-pitched, animalistic grunt. It's possible that my sister has gone mad.

"It's bad enough that I'm stuck in this house with *you*!" Cassie says. "Is it too much to ask that you not burn it to the ground?"

In that moment, a primal nerve explodes inside me. I am a bear that's been poked one too many times. That's been let down

one too many times. By grief. By Patrick. By my silly imagination.
And now by Cassie.

"Maybe you think you can get away with this kind of behavior
because no one else will call you on it. So I'll say it: you're a bitch,
Cassie!"

I don't wait for a response. I race up the stairs, the boldness
that allowed me to stand up to her quickly evaporating.

I don't want her to see me cry.

CHAPTER FIFTEEN

Cassie

Tuesday, July 3rd

This isn't me. I know how to keep my cool, how to control my emotions.

I don't know what made me snap like that. It's true that Julie was massively irresponsible—who forgets to turn off a stove? But I didn't have to come down on her like that.

It occurs to me that I might have scared her off. Maybe she retreated to her room to pack. Maybe she's forfeiting our claim to the house—and it will be *our* claim. The will leaves no room for interpretation: we either both stay here for a month, together, or we both lose the house. I can't let that happen. I swallow the fully formed lump in my throat and go up to her room.

Her door is open. She's sitting on her old bed, hugging her knees. I can tell she expects an apology by the way she meets my gaze. She isn't getting one. I look around: her suitcases are neatly stacked behind the door. She hasn't been packing. I am oddly relieved.

"The fire extinguisher is in the cabinet under the sink," I say, standing by the door. "In case your pyromania strikes again."

"Fine."

The smart move would be to walk away or to defuse the situation. But her stance is making me angrier. She doesn't get to sit there looking like a wounded deer. Not when she was the one who insulted me.

"You've made your point. No need to sulk up here."

"Who says I'm sulking?" It's unfair, how pretty she looks: bright eyes, rosy cheeks, dark, cascading hair. She's even more beautiful when she's hurt—it's something about her vulnerability.

"What else am I supposed to think? You use an awful word to describe me and then you come up here to do God knows what." I don't add that her calling any woman the b-word is an affront against feminism.

"What God? You're an atheist."

I scoff derisively. It's so typical of Julie to assume that time has stood still over the past decade. It doesn't occur to her that I could be an altogether different person. For all she knows, I could've found religion, joined a cult, become a nudist!

OK, the last one would've been fairly obvious by now—we are sharing a house.

"I've watched your interviews." She rubs the back of her neck.

I raise my eyebrows. I don't want to, but I think of Rachel's comment, the one about Julie missing me. Could it be true?

"Just try to be more careful when you cook."

"I'm careful."

"You're obviously not."

"Accidents happen." She turns to face the window. The water is a pale blue, with just a few whitecaps off in the distance.

"This wasn't just any accident. You almost set the house on fire. Nana's house. Full of Nana's things. So I don't care how careful you're being, be *more*."

She won't look me in the eye. It's unnerving. She should be taking responsibility for what she did. She should be apologizing.

"Could you…stop?" She scowls. "I'm tired of being told what to do. I'm not a child."

"You're acting like one." It's true. Responsible adults do not leave the stove on.

Julie scoffs and looks at me with an expression that approximates anger.

"Well?" I continue, undeterred. "Aren't you going to apologize?"

I wait, but she remains silent. There's a tension around her mouth. Her cheeks are now red. Does she really think I'm going to walk away before she recognizes the severity of what she's done?

"Are you even listening?" I say. "Get your head out of the clouds."

"Stop it." She covers her ears.

"Stop what? Trying to talk sense into you?"

She lowers her hands. "I don't need you to talk sense into me."

"If only that were true."

"I don't appreciate you coming into my room to scold me." Her face is blotchy, red. Beads of sweat are gathering at her forehead.

"And I don't appreciate you acting like a child." I pause. "A forgetful, hysterical child."

"Now I'm hysterical again! Just what I needed to hear." What is she talking about? This is the first time I've called her hysterical. But I don't get a chance to ask because she continues, her eyes stormy. "What's next? Are you going to tell me to take a Xanax, too?"

The shock is like falling through ice—cold, painful. I wince.

She takes in my reaction. I know this because her face twists into an expression of understanding. And then horror.

"Cassie, I'm sorry," she says. Gone is the edge in her tone. "I didn't mean it."

I look down at my arm. It's stinging. I see why: I've dug my nails into my skin. I take a deep breath. I'm not letting her get away with such a cruel, cowardly comment.

"I'm sure you didn't," I say. "Just like your mother didn't mean to kill mine." I turn around to leave, slamming the door on my way out.

Miss me? The woman doesn't even like me.

I race down the stairs. I need to leave this place, if only for a few hours. I'm two steps from the landing when I hear something falling on the ground. A picture frame.

I sit on the last step and pick up the photo. The fall has knocked it out of its pretty wooden frame. I turn it around. It's an old one, taken on my sixth or seventh birthday. We're all standing around the dining table—Nana holding me up on her lap, Gramps next to her. My mom is to our right, holding a glass of something in her hand—whiskey maybe?—and my father is to the left, his fist thrust in the air like he's celebrating some type of victory. Earlier that year, he'd left the house for several weeks, possibly months—I don't quite remember now. I didn't know he'd been staying at Julie's house. Back then, I didn't know Julie existed. I remember this day, though. Nana baked me a triple-chocolate cake with marshmallow frosting. White on the outside, black on the inside. I didn't want anyone to eat it. It was too pretty—and it looked delicious.

"I'll bake you another one," Nana had said, cutting a big piece for Gramps. "And I'll give your mom the recipe." I didn't say, "Mom doesn't bake," because I knew it made Nana sad to hear about my parents' lack of domestic bliss.

Nana had kept her promise, baking a total of eight cakes that summer. Eight delicious cakes that I ate over a period of two months—the wonders of a child's metabolism.

I study our tiny faces. I don't look like an anxious kid. My mom doesn't look drunk. My father doesn't seem angry.

We look normal. Happy, even.

A picture may be worth a thousand words, but, in this case, they are all lies.

CHAPTER SIXTEEN

Julie

Tuesday, July 3rd

Her mane is the first thing I see—red, wild. A crown of curls. She's sitting at the bottom of the stairs. I tiptoe down the steps and lower my body next to hers.

"I'm sorry," I whisper. She doesn't meet my gaze. Her body is folded inwards, her hair covering most of her face. I wonder if she's crying. "I'm really sorry."

There's so much more I could say. I could explain how my mind is pathetic, impressionable. How my husband had just said those exact words to me during an argument, that I was chewing them over in my head, festering in anger. I could explain how her comment—*Get your head out of the clouds*—is a huge trigger for me. That I didn't appreciate being treated like a child because that's how Patrick treats me—and I'm tired of it. Maybe if she knew, she'd understand.

But maybe not. I decide against sharing. She doesn't want to hear about my life.

Instead, I offer an apology. Weak, insufficient. But ultimately sincere.

The Fire Princess turns to face the Sky Princess. She is not crying. Instead, she is covered in thorns. Poison ivy shoots out of her eyes. The Sky Princess is scared.

"I don't expect you to forgive me," I say. It isn't true—I am nothing if not expectant. Or maybe hopeful is the word. Hope is not the same as expectation. Hope is fueled by longing, expectation by entitlement.

The silence stretches between us. I shouldn't be surprised. This is Cassie: ice runs through her veins. Maybe she should be the Ice Princess instead. My eyes dart to her hands. She's holding a frame. I recognize it. It used to be hung on the wall above us.

"Let me see that," I say. I reach over, expecting her to flinch. But she lets me take the broken frame.

I get up and make my way to the chest of drawers in the living room, where Nana keeps her arts and crafts supplies. I take out a pair of tweezers and a tube of superglue. It's a relief to have a small, solvable problem. A broken thing I can actually make whole again.

When I'm done, I hold up the frame like a prop.

She finally speaks.

"Pleased with yourself?" She stands up, crossing her arms over her chest.

This is my punishment. My happiness has always bothered her. She's admitted as much, years ago, back when we were children. When we traded stories about our home lives.

"I get it," I say softly, walking back towards the steps where she was sitting a moment before. "You're angry."

"Me? I'm fine. You just said the cruelest possible thing to me. But it doesn't matter because you fixed a picture frame." She marches past me, heading towards the chest of drawers. She picks up the frame. "See? All good now!"

"I didn't mean it." I feel tears welling up in my eyes. My voice quivers.

"Oh, no. Now I've made you upset," she says, in an unkind falsetto. She cocks her head to the side. "Should I break another frame so you can superglue it back together? I'm sure I can find another one with my mom."

When angered, the Fire Princess turns into lightning and wind and thunder. The Sky Princess needs to find a way to defend herself, or she'll be swept away by the tornado, never to be seen again.

"How about we get one of my mother?" I pause, letting the words sink in.

She blinks, confused.

"You can't, can you? She's not up on these walls or on the mantle or anywhere else in this house. Because everyone acted like she didn't exist."

I'm not done.

"Do you know how hard it was for me, seeing how Nana adored your mom? She hated mine, Cassie. Ignoring her was the nicest thing she could do. I loved Nana, but God forbid I bring up Sophie around her. God forbid she catch me writing her a postcard or checking her horoscope. When I was here, I had to forget about her."

"None of that's my fault, Julie." Her nostrils flare.

"And it's not my fault that your mother killed herself." The words leave my mouth without my permission. Sometimes it scares me, how easily I can lie. I should be ashamed of myself. I am.

"Who said it was?"

"You did," I say, taking a step closer. "When you cut me out of your life like a rotten limb."

"My mother had just *died*."

"And then what? It's been fourteen years." Indignation bubbles inside me, spreading like poison. She doesn't know what I did. She doesn't know what I did and yet she still shunned me. Why would she do that? "At some point you have to let go. Isn't that what you're always preaching to your viewers? And yet you're incapable of it. You're such a hypocrite."

"How dare you?" Her tone is low, wounded. A hissing sound.

"How dare I what—stand up for myself? You never expected me to, did you? You think you can go through life bossing people around, poking at their wounds. Well, guess what happens when you do that? People snap. *I* snap."

She lets out a grunt, a low rumble. "Just leave me alone."

"I don't want to leave you alone." I take a step closer to Cassie. She moves back. We're locked in a stare. "And Nana didn't want that, either. It's why she brought us here. Don't you see?" A pause. "Cassie, I'm sorry about what I said. But can't we get along? I'll do anything. Do you want me to beg? I'll do it. Do you want to hit me? Go ahead."

She frowns. "I'm not going to *hit* you."

"I won't hit back." I smile weakly.

"Yeah, because that's what I'm worried about." She scoffs. "I'm twice your size."

"Jamaica Plain versus Dover?" I say. "We both know who'd win."

I see the corners of her mouth twitching, the beginnings of a smile. I want to reach out, take her hand in mine. I want to tell her that it's me, Julie. Her sister. But she slips the mask back on. Returns to her icy self.

"You really think I don't see what you're trying to do?" Her tone is steely. "You feel bad about what you said. And you should. It was below the belt and I'm not going to indulge in your stupid idea just to make you feel better."

And then she turns around, leaves the house, and drives off.

CHAPTER SEVENTEEN

Cassie

Tuesday, July 3rd

I blame the house for my erratic behavior. This used to be my safe space—the one place I got to relax, to let my guard down. But I can't do that now. I can't get sucked back in. It has cost me too much.

I try to stop the memories of my first summer with Julie. I fail.

A few days after Julie arrived, Nana pulled me aside to talk in private.

"I'm still getting used to having two granddaughters," she said, her tone gentle. "It's a big change for all of us. And it's natural to have feelings about any kind of change."

I knew what she was doing. Teachers did it all the time: talked about their feelings to get us to open up about our own. I also knew why she was doing it. I'd been quieter than usual, reserved. Keeping my distance from Julie.

"How are you feeling about your sister?" Nana asked.

"She's nice." It seemed like the polite thing to say.

"I'm always here if you need to talk. You know that, right?"

I nodded. I expected her to tell me that I had to get along with Julie, that a friendship between us wasn't optional. But she never did. Nana seemed to sense I needed space.

That space evaporated when a hairy spider jumped on Julie. After falling and laughing, we found ourselves on the beach, in front of Nana's house, trading secrets. Summer was almost over.

"My mom is Daddy's girlfriend," she told me. "They love each other very much."

I didn't understand why she would share such a monumental secret with me. Looking back, I see that she was desperate to get along. But, at the time, I just thought she was very bad at keeping secrets. Especially after she told me that everyone in her school knew about the affair—and that they were really mean about it. Cruel, even.

I had follow-up questions. Julie seemed eager to answer all of them.

Did her mother and our father sleep in the same room when he came to visit?

Of course. (A small laugh.)

Was our father romantic? Did he surprise her mother with flowers and stuff?

Not really, maybe once or twice.

Did he ever get mad at her mom?

Maybe sometimes? (She seemed unsure.)

Did he ever yell or break things around the house?

No. (Her confusion was palpable.)

Did our father want more children with her mother?

She'd never asked.

Did they do things together? Like go out and stuff?

All the time. To dinner or to the movies. Or dancing.

Had our father lived with her for a few months around three years ago, in the spring?

Yes. It had been the happiest time in Julie's life.

Did our father love her mother?

Of course. (No hesitation.)

I quickly understood what Julie was telling me: they were a family. More than that: a happy family. Any other kid would've freaked out. But not me. I was used to being hurt by my father. The fact that he had been cheating on my mom for a decade was just another bruise in a series of beatings to my heart. I wasn't even surprised, at least not as much as I should be.

But I was torn. Because now I had a big decision to make.

I had to decide whether or not to tell my mom about my father's infidelity.

My third-grade teacher, Ms. Eleanor, had taught us how to make a pros and cons list. It was a habit I quickly—and happily—picked up. I loved the simplicity that came with dividing arguments into two different sides. It all seemed very logical to me—and I loved logic.

And so I made a list. But that didn't help. There were too many variables—another term Ms. Eleanor had taught us.

My mind spiraled with possibilities. If I told my mom, her drinking could get worse—but it could also get better. Maybe she'd finally decide to leave my father—to her, divorce was a sin, but so was adultery. If she did leave, it was possible that she'd find happiness—but what if she didn't? I worried she'd blame me. That she'd move back south, where her parents were from, and make me go with her. What if I never saw Nana again?

I didn't know what to do.

I needed help. And so I asked Nana if we could talk, just the two of us.

We went for a walk on the path that connected the houses along the shore, the lush vegetation that surrounded us providing a comforting sense of privacy. I told her everything.

"What your mother did, asking you to spy on your sister," Nana began, shaking her head. "She shouldn't have put you in that position. A child shouldn't concern herself with her parents."

"I know. But it's what she does. It's what they both do."

At this, Nana frowned. "What do you mean?"

I told her about what went on at my house. About my mom's drinking—there were days when she wouldn't even get out of bed. About my father's temper—he yelled and broke things around the house. About their constant fighting, which sometimes became physical. It was the first time I opened up to an adult—to anyone, really—about my home situation. I'm sure she already knew about some of it—maybe even most of it. But it couldn't have been easy for her, hearing it from me.

I didn't notice I was crying until I felt the salty taste of tears in my mouth.

Nana pulled me into a hug. I felt soothed, comforted. I felt something else, too. Hope. Maybe Nana would be able to do something. She was an adult, she had power.

But being hopeful was a mistake.

"What your mother asked you to do wasn't fair," Nana said. "I can only assume that she wasn't…all there when she decided to do that."

I told her how Julie thought I was lucky because my parents were married, but I didn't feel lucky. I felt like I was living in a world of pretend. My parents pretended to be happy, but they weren't. They pretended to love each other, but they didn't. Sometimes, I wish they'd pretend with me. At least then, I wouldn't know the truth. The truth hurt.

"The universe works in mysterious ways," Nana said. "When your grandfather died, I was devastated. I didn't understand why he had to go, why I was left behind. But if it weren't for his passing, Julie wouldn't be here. It was only when he died that I realized how much I wanted to have both my granddaughters in my life. And now you're both here, friends. Sisters." She smiled. I knew she was thrilled that Julie and I were finally getting along.

"Does that mean I should lie to my mom?"

"It means you should remember that your mom and your dad have a history that predates you. It's not up to you to either make or break their marriage. Your job is to enjoy your summer with your favorite grandmother." She paused to tickle my nose. "And your sister."

I nodded, sniffling. "This is all my father's fault."

I waited for Nana to agree with me. To say that my father's behavior was irresponsible and selfish. That he had created this mess.

"Your father is doing the best he can, Cassie." Her tone wasn't stern, but there was a finality to it. I sensed I shouldn't argue. No matter how much she loved me, she loved my father more. He was her only son, after all.

That's when I understood that revealing my father's secret would mean upsetting Nana. And I didn't think I could handle that.

When I returned to Boston, my mom asked me about Julie. I told her I'd found out nothing. I was a good liar—she believed me. The following year, when it came time for me to go to Montauk again, she asked me to keep my ears open. She didn't say about what. She didn't have to.

I considered, once again, whether I should tell my mom the truth.

Except, by the end of the following summer, Julie and I were best friends. Spending three months in a house with someone who knows the biggest secret you're carrying is a very effective way to bond.

I loved my mom. I didn't want to see her being lied to. But I loved Julie more.

My sister became my person—even more than Nana. With Julie, I could be myself. She was the only person in the world who understood the burden I carried because it was her burden, too. We were both keepers of our father's secret. We understood that if we were to reveal it, we'd lose summers with Nana. We'd lose each other. I opened up to her without reservations or fear of judgment. She didn't have the power to change my parents or improve my home situation, but she never made me feel guilty about being critical of them, about feeling like I deserved better. She never told me my father was doing the best he could. She understood my anger. She validated my emotions. She made me feel seen and safe. For years, she made me feel lucky. I was happy.

And then it all came crashing down.

CHAPTER EIGHTEEN

Julie

Tuesday, July 3rd

It must be a record, fighting with one's husband and sister on the same day.

I peer out the window. It's partly cloudy—the sun occasionally making an appearance. It doesn't look like it'll rain. I decide to go for a walk on the beach.

The first thing I do is take off my shoes. A tactile memory of Montauk: walking barefoot, the sand hot on the arches of my feet. I scurry towards the ocean, relieved when I reach the cool dampness of the shore. If I close my eyes, I can sense Nana walking beside me. Holding my hand.

But when I open my eyes, she's gone.

Maybe Patrick is right. Maybe coming here was a mistake. I've underestimated how lonely I'd feel, being here without Nana. Actually, lonely isn't the word. I feel hollow.

I lower by body onto the sand. This stretch of the beach is empty. It's usually empty, even in the summer. Especially on a cloudy day. I graze the seashell necklace (I haven't taken it off, except to go to sleep) with the tips of my fingers as I consider my next move.

I glance at my phone, wondering if I should text Patrick. I could tell him that he was right: that there's nothing left for me here. That I want to go back home. He'll be pleased, relieved. He'll send a car to pick me up—he wouldn't dream of asking me to take the jitney back to Boston. He'll contest the will in court and win—Patrick always wins. He'll buy out Cassie's share if I ask him to. He's never said no to me, not when it comes to the things that money can buy. It's been this way from the start.

I met Patrick when I was out with Janette at Copley Place, slurping on fruit smoothies, pretending we had enough money to do more than window shop. Earlier that week, a girl from our floor at BU brought home twelve (I repeat, *twelve*) shopping bags from Neiman Marcus, all filled with horrendously expensive things. It was cold outside—April in Boston is always cold—but for a moment it really felt like spring. I watched as she unveiled her finds: a Missoni lightweight scarf, a Donna Karan denim jacket, a Burberry skirt, and, my favorite: a pair of colorful, hip Louis Vuitton espadrilles that looked nothing like the brand's classical shoes. I salivated when I saw those shoes. And even though we couldn't afford them, Janette and I decided to go to Copley Place and try them on. Patrick walked in when I was eyeing my feet in the store's mirror.

I was attracted to him right away. He was handsome, in a charming, slightly older way: tall, with a square jaw, an aquiline nose and seashell ears. His brown hair was beginning to gray. He was dressed in a gray three-piece suit, silk tie, cufflinks and tie clip. But the most impressive thing about him was his confident stance: impeccable posture, hands in his pockets, easy smile. He looked like he belonged.

He complimented my shoes and asked if I'd mind helping him pick out a present for a female colleague at his firm. I'm not an idiot—I knew he was hitting on me. I was very much used to male attention. It didn't often flatter me, but that day it did.

"I'm Patrick Smith," he said.

"Julie Meyers." I shook his hand.

"Julie," he repeated, pronouncing my name correctly. "Are you French?"

"Half," I said. "My mom is French."

He eyed the purple plush cube, the one I'd sat on minutes ago to try the shoes. My BU student ID was there, next to a half-empty Starbucks cup. He asked me what I studied at Boston University and invited me out for *real* coffee. Right then, the saleslady approached me again to ask if I would be buying the espadrilles. I looked down at my feet, feeling my face burn. I'd forgotten I was wearing them. I returned them to her, mumbling something about them being too small. She looked unconvinced. I didn't blame her. I slipped back into my comfortable, but decidedly unglamorous shoes—an old pair of beaded, fleece-lined moccasins by Alma Boots—and said goodbye to Patrick. He hurriedly gave me his business card before I left, but I wasn't about to call him. I left that store assuming I'd never see him again.

A week later, a courier was at my dorm, asking me to sign for a package. I flushed when I noted the emblem. Louis Vuitton. Inside it was a pair of black stilettos with a discreet gilded LV engraved behind the heel. I opened up the card next.

Beautiful shoes for a beautiful woman.
Patrick

They were undeniably gorgeous—even if they were nothing like the trendy, colorful espadrilles I coveted. And they were the right size. I took in the impeccable stitching, the flawless design, the timeless refinement. I was an English major with massive student loans. How long would it be until I could finally afford these shoes myself? I wanted to try them on. To wear them every day of my life.

But there was no way I could keep them. I paid fifteen dollars to return the shoes.

Two days later, another delivery. This time, seven pairs of stilettos by different designers: Chanel, Dior, Manolo Blahnik, Jimmy Choo, Christian Louboutin, Miu Miu, and Louis Vuitton.

I'm not giving up.
P.

I was furious. Who did this man think he was? I had to put a stop to this. I found his business card buried inside my bag and wrote him a curt message asking him to please stop sending me shoes. I was not for sale.

His response was instant: he was sorry to have offended me, he meant no harm. Would I let him take me out to dinner to apologize? I didn't reply.

The next day, a courier arrived to pick up the shoes and deliver me flowers. Tucked inside the bouquet was a card: another apology, another invitation to dinner. All of my friends encouraged me to accept, declaring his behavior to be romantic and gallant. Janette added that I shouldn't turn down free food—she was only half joking.

I did say yes, but I was a nervous mess during the entire meal. It wasn't Patrick's fault—he was behaving like a perfect gentleman—but something about the way he courted me made me retreat into my shell. I'm an extrovert, I know how to be charming, sociable. And Sophie had taught me the art of small talk. But that day, my stomach was in knots. Instead of enjoying the view at Top of the Hub, I was counting the minutes until I could leave. Patrick didn't seem discouraged by my attitude, he kept the conversation going almost singlehandedly. Looking back, I can only imagine the kind of effort that took on his part. Now that I know how anxious he is.

If he hadn't brought up his childhood, we never would've gotten married.

I don't remember how the subject came up, but I do remember it started with him mentioning his half-brothers. At this, my ears pricked up—I thought about Cassie all the time. When I asked him about his family, he opened up. His mom was from Southie, he said. When she was barely eighteen, she fell for a rich, married man from Beacon Hill. Their affair was a brief one, but it lasted long enough for Patrick to be conceived.

"I lived in the same city with the dad I didn't have," Patrick said. There was so much vulnerability in his words, so much pain. He described his fatherless childhood, the taunting from other children who didn't know how cruel their words could be, his anger at his dad for not being there for his mom.

By then, I'd stopped looking at my watch. I'd never met someone who knew what it was like to be invisible, to be the *other* family, the dirty little secret no one talked about openly but that everyone loved to judge. I told him about my dad, about how his anomalous blend of presence and absence had left an imprint on every aspect of my entire life.

"It's the same with me. The way I grew up defined who I am now," he said, quietly. "My ex-wife never understood that."

"You were married?" I felt a tug of disappointment. I didn't want him to have been married. I didn't care if it was premature: by then, I was picturing a future with Patrick, and I didn't want to share my husband, not even with someone who was in the past.

"Yes," he said. "But she never understood me."

But I could, I thought.

I didn't know it then, but I was hooked. Hooked on the idea of building a life that was whole with someone who understood what it was like to be half. Hooked on a fairy tale that I thought was real.

Now, as I'm sitting on the beach only a few feet away from Nana's house, an awareness swims to the front of my mind: I don't know if I believe in the fairy tale anymore. And maybe that's a good thing. Maybe I have to grow up and come to terms with the reality of my life. The reality of my marriage.

I stare at my phone's screen, thinking of the text that I could compose to Patrick. Thinking of what it would mean to go back to Boston, to give up on the idea of mending my relationship with Cassie. To refuse Nana's last wish. To accept my marriage for what it is.

I clutch the necklace again with my left hand, feeling the shells' sharp edges against my skin. I look up at the sky and close my eyes. I ask Nana to send me a sign. I tell her the truth: that I want to honor her wish. I, too, want Cassie and I to find our way back to each other. But I worry Nana underestimated the depth of Cassie's resentment towards me.

When I open my eyes, nothing has changed.

The sun is still fighting to puncture the clouds. The air is still salt-heavy and quiet. And I'm still here, alone. I'm not sure what I expected as a response—a message from a seagull? A strong gust of wind on this otherwise breezeless day? Whatever it was, it doesn't happen.

I lower my gaze towards the horizon and let out a deep breath. I'm about to text Patrick when my eyes land on something in the ocean. Movement. A splashing of water. I squint in its direction, trying to figure out what I'm looking at. It can't be a whale, not this close to shore. Could it be a dolphin? Whatever it is, it's getting closer. Then I see him.

A man.

I watch as he emerges from the water in the exact moment that the sun pierces through the clouds. He's closer to shore now, the waterline just below his chest, receding. Slowly, he's revealed: wide shoulders, strong arms, a perfect six-pack. He's wearing a pair of red shorts that cling ever so slightly to his thighs. He wipes his face with both his hands, rubs his eyes.

Then he looks straight at me. And smiles.

I sit motionless as he makes his way in my direction. I want to look behind me—maybe someone arrived while I was lost inside my mind? But I can't tear my eyes away from him. From this tall, tanned god who emerged from the sea.

"Hi," he says. He's now standing right in front of me, dripping wet.

I place my hand on my forehead like a visor and meet his eyes. They're warm, the color of honey. I'm aware that I'm staring. It's rude. But how can I *not* stare? It's not that he's attractive (though he absolutely is), it's that he's just materialized from the ocean. I've been here for a while. I didn't see anyone at the beach, didn't see anyone go in the water.

"Hi," I finally say. I'm about to get up, but he lowers his body towards the sand.

"Julie. It's you." He's beaming at me, grinning. His teeth are white and straight.

"Ho-how do you know my name?" I seem to have forgotten how to speak.

"I'm Craig," he says. His tone suggests I should know this.

It takes an extra second for my brain to make the connection. Craig. Nana's Craig. Her neighbor. Her friend.

I frown. Nana talked about Craig all the time. She'd often express her gratitude for having met him. She'd say that he was unfailingly kind and helpful around the house. She mentioned he was a great dad. That he was funny and polite.

She never said anything about him being handsome. Let alone unbelievably *hot*.

"I recognize you from your pictures." He runs his hands through his wet hair. Is he aware of how sexy he looks? He must be. He *should* be, even if just for safety reasons. His dimples alone could cause a heart attack. "I've been wondering when we'd run into each other."

"I…I got here last week." I can feel the crease deepening in my forehead. I still can't believe this is Craig. This is the man who installed grab bars and rails in Nana's shower. Who put up motion-sensor lights on the stairs. Who checked on her daily. I'd pictured someone entirely different from the man sitting across from me.

"I'm so glad to finally meet you," he says.

"Me, too." I manage a smile. I can feel my cheeks burning. I must look deranged.

"Is that Bertie's necklace?" he asks.

My hand touches the shells again. "It's mine. I made it when I was a kid. It was here."

"Right, I knew that. Bertie used to wear it." A pause. "She said it made her feel like she was with you."

Right then, I feel it: a rush of air coming from the southeast. It only lasts a few seconds and then the air goes back to being heavy, still. But it was unmistakable.

A gust of wind on an otherwise breezeless day.

CHAPTER NINETEEN

Cassie

Friday, July 6th

I jump when I hear a knock on the door.

"Can I help you?" I ask, from the hammock. I'd been napping. Or trying to, anyway.

The man spins around. "Sorry, didn't see you there." He looks surprised.

I don't point out that this is my house. It makes perfect sense for me to be on the porch. It's his presence that has yet to be explained.

"Are you with the law firm?" I sound annoyed—and I don't care. Exactly how often are these people coming to check on us? It's disruptive and just plain rude.

"I'm Craig." He frowns. "We met a few days ago."

"Right." I remember him now: Nana's handyman. But what is he doing here? I'm about to inquire when Julie appears at the door.

"Oh, hi Craig," she sings. "Come in. Want something to drink?"

I don't mean to, but I get up and follow them inside. Julie looks up at me, confused. This is not an unreasonable reaction—she and I haven't exchanged a single word since Tuesday's showdown. She no longer offers me food or asks inane questions. It's been, quite frankly, a relief.

"Have you met Craig?" She's looking at me like I'm a large animal at the zoo.

"We met the other day," he says.

Julie nods. She stares at me for an extra beat. I offer nothing in return. They're both acting like I'm interrupting something—which is exactly how I know I should stay put. Why is this strange man in our house? I remember how curious he'd been about meeting Julie. He might be a stalker for all I know. A serial killer. A practicing member of scientology.

"Let me grab my bag and we'll head over?" she asks, looking at Craig.

"Sounds good," he says. "I really appreciate this. And I'll be home before dinner, I promise."

I follow her up the stairs. Julie's eyes widen slightly when she sees me go into her room and close the door behind me.

"What's that about?" I ask.

"What do you mean?"

"That man downstairs."

"Craig."

"Whatever his name is." I swat my hand in the air. "What's he doing here? And where are you going with him?"

Her lips curl into a satisfied smile. It's infuriating. "Are you worried about me?"

I don't have an answer to that. No. Yes. Maybe?

"I'm babysitting his kids," she says.

Why is she babysitting a stranger's kids? She can't possibly need the money. Unless—could she and her husband be separated? I never see them talking. He didn't come to the island last weekend and it doesn't seem like he's coming on this one, either.

"I don't like it," I say. "We don't know anything about him."

"He's *Craig*," she enunciates his name like it's supposed to mean something. "Nana's Craig?"

Before I got here, I'd never heard of a Craig—not that I'm admitting as much. It hurts, realizing that she and Nana had been close to the point where Nana would talk to Julie about her handyman.

"What's it to you anyway?" She crosses her arms.

"It doesn't seem safe."

"But Nana loved Craig." A beat. "He took care of her."

I vaguely recall something about a neighbor's two kids. Nana would call them her placeholder great-grandchildren, playfully. At least I think it was playfully. Still, that doesn't mean Julie should go to his house. We don't know if he's trustworthy. What happened to his kids' regular babysitter? It probably hasn't occurred to her to ask. If she quit, then there must've been a reason. What if Craig is some type of creep?

"Nana trusted people too easily," I say. "She wasn't herself towards the end. She got soft." This isn't entirely accurate. At least not that I know of. But I want to be the one who knows about Nana—not the other way around.

"Please don't start." Her tone is touchy, impatient.

"Don't start what?"

"The negativity, the criticism. At least have the decency to spare Nana."

"Excuse me?" I cross my arms. "You don't get to tell me who I can criticize." Not that I'm criticizing Nana. I wouldn't do that. Not now—I miss her too much. But if I wanted to, I could. My entire life, people have told me that I shouldn't be so unhappy, so dissatisfied. That my anger and opinions would rub people the wrong way. I never listened. I understood from an early age that girls are expected to be pleasing, amenable. Amenable people don't challenge the status quo.

And that's simply not me.

"You're right," Julie says. "God forbid you keep an opinion to yourself."

"What's that supposed to mean?"

"Oh, never mind!" She turns around and begins rummaging through a tote bag.

"No, say it." I take a step forward. "You started it. Now finish it."

"Fine." She turns around, her face flush. "You're entitled, judgmental, and you won't let go. You refuse to be happy. You wouldn't know the feeling if it hit you on the head. All you do is pass judgment and complain about everyone in your life. Nobody's good enough for you. No one can live up to your impossible standards."

Her words hit me like a slap in the face. I had no idea she felt this way. I used to think she understood where I was coming from when I was being critical. She used to say she admired my determination, my sense of self-worth. I think of my mother. Of how she couldn't be happy. Am I the same?

Is this why Nana shared parts of her life with Julie and not with me?

But, no. She doesn't get to say these things to me. I won't be attacked. Not like this.

"You think you're better?" I say.

"At least people like me, Cassie."

"They don't *like* you, Julie. They're ogling you. There's a difference."

"You know, for someone who likes to call me shallow you seem awfully focused on my looks." There's a tremor on her lower lip. I've hit a nerve. Good.

"I didn't call you shallow. You just did."

"You think you're better than everyone, don't you?" She clenches her teeth. "Hiding behind your degree, your TV show, telling everyone how to live. Well, guess what, Cassie? You don't see *anyone*. Least of all yourself."

"You're wrong. I see you. Still the same people-pleaser, desperate for everyone to love you even if that means you don't get to be yourself. I'd rather be hard on the people I love than settle for scraps like you do."

I'm talking about our father—and she knows it.

"At least I'm not angry all the time."

"Easy for you to say. I grew up surrounded by anger." And she knows it, too.

"At least you had two parents."

"Two parents? An abusive father and a sick mother?"

"She could've left Dad, Cassie."

"You know she couldn't."

"What I know is that you let them define you."

I bite my lip. My biggest fear in a sentence: that my parents are all I am.

"Look, I get it," she continues. "It was awful having a dad who had another family. Don't you think I know that? I *was* that other family. I barely got to see him. So how do you think I felt hearing you bad-mouth him for all those years when I would've given anything to have him in the house, temper or not?"

"That's because he was someone else around you." He never broke things at her house. Never hit her mother. Never even yelled. She knows this. We've traded enough stories about our father to understand that the father I had wasn't the father she missed.

"That's not my fault!"

"I never said it was."

"Yes, you did." She stabs her index finger in the air. "When you stopped talking to me over something that happened fourteen years ago."

"That something was my mother dying," I feel my throat close up.

"She killed herself, Cassie." She drops her tone to a whisper. "And I'm so sorry she did. I really am. But if you want to be angry with someone, be angry with her. Not us."

"Us?"

"Dad and me."

I scoff. I'm expected to let go of my anger towards a man who abused my mother for years?

"We're your family," she continues. "Everyone needs a family. Even you."

Patently untrue. I don't need a family—at least not a biological one. Daniel. Rachel. Christina. Even my patients. They're all I need. They're my family.

"Spare me the lecture, Julie," I say. "I *have* a family."

"Really? Because, from what I hear, you're seeing a married man with a family of his own."

I feel the air leave my lungs. My jaw falls open.

"It's true," she says, her voice barely a whisper.

My heart flops inside my chest, a fish thrown to land. I can't let her see me like this.

I turn around and walk away.

CHAPTER TWENTY

Julie

Friday, July 6th

Craig is handsome. I knew this already, but it still feels like a surprise every time my eyes land on him. This could be a problem.

"Is everything all right?" he asks, as I make my way down the stairs. "You're red."

I glance at the mirror. I carefully applied my makeup this morning, but he's right: my cheeks are flushed, like I used too much blush. I brush a loose strand of hair out of my face. There are three things wrong with my appearance today: no nail polish, hair in a braid, and now my cheeks are too red. Surprisingly, I don't care. In fact, it feels liberating.

"All good," I say.

The Sky Princess is lying: all is not well in the Kingdom of Montauk. The Fire Princess is under an evil spell, one that has turned her warm heart into ice. She is now the Ice Princess, a malevolent creature who attempted to thrust a frozen stake into the Sky Princess's heart.

We make our way towards his house. It's only a short walk from Nana's, which is less than ideal. Right now, I'd prefer to have an ocean between Cassie and me. I think back to how differently I felt weeks ago, when I arrived in Montauk, how hopeful I'd been that we'd be able to get along. To find our way back to each other. Now, I'm hurt. And more than a little angry, too. Cassie isn't the only sister who can be angry.

Craig's house is cute: stone and whitewashed wood, barn wood beams, a wraparound porch. Inside, there's a cozy lived-in feel—toys scattered around the living room, throw pillows in disarray on the couch, a delicious cookie-dough whiff in the air. I wonder how he can afford to live here when he works at a pub. The property taxes alone are likely to be astronomical. He doesn't strike me as the type with family money.

"Kids," Craig calls out. Thundering footsteps follow.

I see Ben first. He has blowfish cheeks and Craig's eyes. He looks shy and pensive, although that might be because he's wearing round-rimmed glasses. Kiki is behind him, lifting her arms towards Craig, a pleading look in her eyes. She has wispy blond hair that's almost white and she's so petite that Craig barely needs to move a muscle to pick her up.

"This is Ben." Craig places a hand on his son's shoulder. "And this little munchkin is Kiki." He glances at his daughter, who is resting on his shoulder like a cute baby monkey. My heart gives a little squeeze. I want that so badly.

"It's nice to meet you," Kiki says with a big smile.

"It's nice to meet you as well, Kiki." I turn to Ben. "And you, too, Ben."

"Hi." Ben presses his glasses against his face with his index finger.

"Julie is Nana Bertie's granddaughter," Craig says.

"Cool," Kiki's grins. "Did you know her when you were my age? I'm four."

"I met her when I was older."

"My age?" Ben asks curiously. "I'm six and a half."

"I was nine when I met her."

"Wow," Kiki's eyes widen. "You were *old.*"

"Young lady, where are your manners?" Craig lowers her to the ground.

"That's all right." I crouch so that our eyes are level. "Nine is pretty old." I wink. It's been ages since I babysat—the last time was in college, I think—but being around kids has always felt natural to me. Natural and wonderful.

"How old are you now?" Kiki asks.

"A lady never tells," I say. I get closer to her. She smells of strawberry shampoo. Then, in a whisper: "But just between us girls, I'm thirty-one."

"Wow!"

"Shh," I lift my finger against my lips. "It's our secret."

She beams at me. I switch over to Ben. "So, Ben, I hear you like Minecraft."

"Yeah." His eyes shine. "Do you?"

"I've never played it, actually. I was hoping you could show me? Is it true you can build something called a portal?"

He bobs his head eagerly. "It's really easy."

"Time for me to go," Craig says. "You two behave for Julie. I'll be back before dinner." He turns to me. "Do you maybe want to join us? Since you won't let me pay you, maybe I could wow you with my culinary skills."

"You cook?"

"Daddy can't cook!" Kiki giggles.

"Busted." Craig laughs. "But I do a mean takeout. Unless you have plans?"

"No plans," I say. I might not even have a house to go back to. After what happened, I wouldn't put it past Cassie to change the locks on me.

I'm still shaken up. Not because of our argument, but because of what I now know to be true. Sophie is right: Cassie is seeing a married man. It's a stunning revelation. Completely out of character for Cassie. She knows how badly affairs can turn out. We both do.

"It's a date then," Craig says. And now his cheeks are red.

CHAPTER TWENTY-ONE

Cassie

Friday, July 6th

The woman behind the counter has figured out who I am.

Her name is Rhonda—it's on her name tag, pinned in block letters above her left breast. She's grinning at me, maniacally. This isn't the first time someone has made the connection. I'm not a celebrity, far from it. But, on occasion, I am recognized. When this happens, I am expected to be pleasant, charming. Levelheaded, too—I'm known for my sobering advice. Above all, I mustn't act crazy.

Today, this will be a challenge.

I order one scoop of strawberry ice cream. I take a couple of bars labeled Emergency Chocolate—a white cross against a red background and a promise of immediate relief of all my chocolate cravings. A winning marketing campaign.

"It's you, isn't it?" Rhonda says when I'm paying. She doesn't wait for an answer. "Your hair is different, but it's you."

"I'm Cassie," I say.

"I knew it!" A vindicated smile. "I love your show."

"Thank you," I say. It's not my show. I don't bother to point this out.

"I make my husband watch every week. We never miss an episode. It's like couples' counseling for us, but free. He won't admit it, but he loves it."

I laugh in solidarity. It's all people want: to feel like others are on their side. Validation. I wish I could make small talk with her. For the most part, I enjoy meeting fans—especially ones who work here. The Fudge Company is a Southampton landmark. But not today. I overtip and then excuse myself.

Daniel calls me when I'm stepping out of the shop. Main Street is bustling, decked out in red, blue, and white. Apparently, the Fourth is a weeklong event in the Hamptons.

"Are you OK?" he asks, his voice heavy with concern. I'd texted him earlier to tell him that Julie knows about us.

"Not really."

An understatement. The truth: I've been fighting off an anxiety attack. Julie does *not* know about Daniel and me—she can't. There isn't any overlap in our lives. I've checked. I'm thorough. I did my homework. I always do.

Except I must've missed something. Because she knows, somehow.

"How did she find out?" Daniel asks.

"Your guess is as good as mine."

I've been entertaining irrational thoughts. My grandmother had many talents, some that were a bit…witchy. I sound foolish, I know. I'm not suggesting Nana had supernatural powers. But I've witnessed her intuition verge into clairvoyance. Her predictions were famous on the island. Hurricanes. Minor accidents. Sebastian's death.

What if Julie has inherited Nana's abilities?

I don't share this theory with Daniel. He fell in love with a sensible, rational woman. Not some nutjob who believes in magic. Besides, he has enough on his plate.

The only logical explanation: someone has told Julie. Except the only people who know, apart from Daniel and me, are Bella, Christina, and Rachel. And I trust them completely. Tatiana knows, too—obviously. But she wouldn't have said anything.

She's too hung up on appearances. Besides, if she wanted to enact revenge, she'd tell the world—not my half-sister.

"What should we do?" he asks.

It all depends on how Julie knows—and whether or not she's planning on sharing this information. I tell him as much now.

"What if you talked to her?" he asks. "Asked her to keep this to herself?"

"We don't exactly get along." A pause. "I hate this," I say. "And not just for the obvious reasons. I don't like that she knows things about me. Things other people don't."

"It's a violation of your privacy."

That it is—I feel exposed, vulnerable. But it's more than that. Julie and I may be estranged, but for some annoying reason her opinion still matters.

"I don't want her thinking I'm some kind of fraud."

"One more reason to talk to her. Explain our situation."

"I don't think that's an option anymore," I say. "All we do is ignore each other and argue. She's developed a confrontational streak." It's true: the Julie I knew never would've stood up to me like that. If it weren't so upsetting, I'd almost be proud of her.

I go by a gaggle of glittering, beautiful people who look utterly untroubled. This makes sense: they're here out of their own voli-tion. No one is forcing them to spend a month in Montauk. I'm hit with an odd sensation, a déjà vu of sorts. Or maybe it's just an amalgamation of memories: Julie and me, ages nine through seventeen, walking down this very street, ice cream cones in hand. She'd look at window displays—mostly in clothing boutiques— and say that one day she'd have enough money to buy anything in them. It wasn't long before I understood that what she wanted weren't the things themselves—it was the sense of freedom. In many ways, Julie's life was much more carefree than mine. She didn't monitor our father's moods, didn't worry about him breaking things around their house or hitting her mother. But she did worry about making ends meet—her financial situation was considerably different from mine.

At the end of the day, we're both shaped by our traumas.

Although she seems to have escaped hers: this new Julie—sophisticated and moneyed and apparently unafraid of confrontation—can probably buy anything she wants. I wonder if financial freedom is as rewarding as she thought it would be.

"Then maybe it's time to interrupt the cycle by changing the narrative," Daniel suggests. "Seriously, it might do you good. It's obvious you two have a lot of repressed issues to work through. Otherwise you wouldn't be fighting all the time."

"You really need to stop shrinking me."

"I learned from the best." He chuckles.

It's good to hear him laugh. I tell him as much.

"I can't wait to see you," he says.

"Me, too."

A pause. I can hear Daniel thinking on the other end of the line.

"Promise you won't change your mind?" he asks. "Promise you'll still choose happiness?"

His words take me back. Daniel knows about Mia's advice—he knows everything there is to know about me.

It happened on the morning after my first night with Daniel. I'd woken up buoyed by giddiness. Daniel was still asleep next to me, snoring under the tangled sheets. Being with him had been exhilarating. Not just the sex itself, but the experience of giving into emotions that I had fought for so long. We'd spent the entire night talking and making love. I had finally let my guard down. I felt alive. Free.

It wasn't until his phone rang that I allowed myself to fully consider what I'd done.

A baby picture of Angie flooded the screen—wide, trusting eyes, toothless smile—under the word HOME.

Home. As in the house he shared with his wife and kids. Just like the house I used to share with my parents. A structure made of cement, wooden boards, bricks—and lies.

I was the lie in Daniel's life. I was the other woman.

I don't remember putting clothes on, but I did. I also don't remember running to the coffee shop on the corner, but I did that, too. When I got there, I called Mia and begged her for an emergency session. I must've sounded really desperate because she agreed to see me right away.

Mia already knew about Daniel. It had been months since he and I became friends, and I'd spent the last four (maybe even five) sessions discussing him, battling my desire to be with him against the morality of having an affair with a married man. I updated her on our night together.

"You gave in to your feelings," Mia said. Words eerily similar to the ones I'd thought of less than an hour before, when I woke up. But now they sounded different: loaded, selfish. Wrong. "This is a big step for you."

"A step in the wrong direction."

She cocked her head to the side. A non-reply. I was used to this.

"I've been rationalizing it," I continued. "Telling myself that his wife cheated on him first. That he's already asked for a divorce, but she won't give it to him. That's she's using their daughter like a poker chip. That they're not really married. But it doesn't matter. It's still wrong. Being with Daniel is wrong."

"But is it what you want?"

"Does it matter?"

"You tell me," she said. "You've never asked for an emergency session before."

"I've never slept with a married man before, either."

"Is that the only thing that's different about this?"

Now I was confused. I was also beginning to think I was overpaying Mia.

"You have a history of self-deprivation," Mia said.

An understatement: Mia was the one who diagnosed me with severe anxiety disorder (from watching my parents argue) and post-traumatic stress disorder (from my mother's death). The combination of the two had manifested itself in the form of an obsessive-compulsive disorder where I routinely deprived myself of things—big and small—that brought me joy in an attempt to punish myself. A twisted way of dealing with the guilt I carried over my mother's death.

Ever since I was a little girl, I knew I had one job: protecting my mother. And now I'd failed. She was gone, dead. All that was left was pain. And this pain became my companion. A constant reminder of my mom, and of my failure. When it began to recede, I was horrified. I didn't deserve to feel better, to heal. I deserved the hollowness of grief. I missed the pain. And so I found ways to pluck joy out of my life, to experience loss. I stopped reading, which had always been my biggest pleasure. Stopped eating food I enjoyed. In my darkest time, I went four days without eating anything at all. I almost had to be hospitalized. And, of course, I stopped talking to Julie.

"We've talked about how this tendency is connected to feeling of self-blame," she continued. "And now you're blaming yourself for having been intimate with Daniel."

I frowned. Was Mia worried I'd slip back into my old habits? I could understand the concern: keeping my OCD at bay was a daily struggle. But today I had more pressing issues to address. I told her as much.

"What is your goal for today's session?" she asked.

It was a question she often asked—one I usually enjoyed answering. I liked the feeling of control that came with being goal-oriented. But that day I didn't have an answer.

"I'm not sure," I admitted.

"Is it possible you're here to ask for permission?" Mia asked. "To be with Daniel?"

"Too late for that," I said. A lame attempt at a joke.

She indulged me with a kind smile. "You're very skilled at denying yourself what you want, Cassie. Food, hobbies, relationships. Let me ask you this: do you want to deny yourself the chance to be with Daniel?"

My response was automatic. I didn't think about it—not even for a second.

"No," I said. "It's wrong, but I don't want to give him up." I paused, shaking my head. "I can't believe I just said that."

"This is a safe space."

I nodded. I understood that. "But I also want to be a good person."

"And you don't think you can be a good person and be with him?"

"No."

"I'd like to revisit that later. But for now, let's assume that's true. If you want to be a good person and being with Daniel is incompatible with that goal, what makes you want to be with him?"

"He makes me happy."

A simple truth, but one I hadn't articulated before: being with Daniel brought me joy. Unbridled, all-consuming joy. A feeling I hadn't experienced in years.

Mia nodded. "Then, for now, what you have to ask yourself is this: do you want to be good or do you want to be happy?"

When I got back to my apartment, Daniel was still there. He'd been calling me nonstop, worried. At that point he knew all there was to know about me—my childhood, my estranged relationship with my sister, my mental health issues. Daniel is a great listener, it's one of the reasons why we became so close, so fast. He was able to grasp the magnitude of what I'd just done. He understood me. All of me.

I told him I loved him. I told him I chose happiness.

And happiness meant being with him.

At the time, I never thought I'd ask him to leave his wife. Why should he risk losing custody of Angie? If I'm being honest, there was a degree of comfort that came with that. I didn't have to worry about traditional relationship milestones: anniversaries, engagement, marriage, babies. I never wanted any of that, anyway. It was safer that way. Less risky.

Except, now I have asked him to leave his wife. Which is about the riskiest thing I could do.

"Cass?" Daniel says, on the other end of the line.

I shake my head, as if trying to dispel my thoughts.

"Promise you'll still choose happiness?" he asks again.

"I promise," I tell him, using a paper napkin to clean my hand. My ice cream is melting. I'd said those exact words to him last night, when he finally told me about Tatiana's visit to Bella's house. It took every ounce of self-restraint not to bring it up, particularly because we talk on the phone so many times a day. But I'm glad I waited for him to tell me. I'm also glad that Tatiana doesn't seem to have scared the kids—Daniel said she drove them home, where he'd gone to wait for them. He and Tatiana argued, but not in front of Angie and Sam. "I'm not giving up on us," I say. I mean every word, but I'm still scared. I've worked hard for my career. I don't want to lose it.

"What if I talked to her?" Daniel asks. "Is that crazy?"

I'm about to tell him that it most definitely is—I'm not about to let Daniel anywhere near Julie—when something catches my eye. A man, walking in front of me. I can only see his back, but I'm certain I know him. Who was it that said that you can't disguise someone from the back?

My first thought is that he's a colleague. Or maybe a patient. And then it hits me.

It's my father.

CHAPTER TWENTY-TWO

Julie

Friday, July 6th

I know it's been a long time since I last babysat, but I don't remember it being this exhausting. I'm beat. Happy, but beat.

We've spent the afternoon playing. First, at the beach: sand-castles and water monster, Ben and Kiki doused in sunscreen. Then indoors: Kiki taking her shoeless Barbies to the dentist while Ben introduced me to the dizzying world of Minecraft. Ben is an excellent teacher, patient and funny. They seem fine. Better than fine, actually—happy. I am, too. Though I will need twelve hours of sleep tonight.

Now, they're entertaining themselves while I clean up. I don't want Craig to think he's entrusted his children to a slob. Sophie calls me as I'm picking up stray Legos under the couch. I'm not in the mood to talk to her, but it's her third call of the day—and I didn't answer the previous two.

"Oh, good, *chérie*. I was beginning to think you lost your phone."

"*Bonjour*, Sophie," I say. "Did something happen?"

"Do I need a reason to call my daughter?"

The short answer is yes. Sophie needs a reason to do anything, and usually it's a dramatic one. But saying this will only lengthen the phone call.

"Now is not a very good time."

"Are you with Cassie?"

"No."

"Did you find out anything about her boyfriend?"

"I told you," I say, lowering my voice, "I'm not doing that."

"This is important to me, Julie."

"Not giving Cassie another reason to hate me is important to me, too."

A pained sigh from Sophie. "I didn't want to do this, Julie. But I see that I have to." A pause. When she speaks again, her voice is thin and oddly high-pitched. Almost like she's holding back tears. "I'm in trouble here at *Posh*. They're trying to—how do you say it—push me out."

"What are you talking about?" Sophie has been with *Posh* for years. She's very good at what she does.

"It's the new kids. They're all about tech and social media. I'm a dinosaur to them."

"I'm sure that's not true."

"Marketing is nothing like it was when I started. It's a miracle I've lasted this long."

"I'm sorry, Sophie."

"Don't be sorry. Help me. I need to bring in this story. Unless you know some other celebrity who's been shamelessly lying to the world?"

I feel a pulsing sensation in my forehead, the beginning of a migraine. I want to remind Sophie that Cassie kept a secret—Sophie's secret—from her mother for years. But now is not the time to discuss the past. I have two children under my care.

"I'm sorry, Sophie. I have to go."

She manages to get one sentence in before I hang up: "I'm counting on you, Julie."

I grew up under the weighty expectation of those words. Sophie has always counted on me. To cook dinner. Make my own doctor's appointments. Go to the bank. Keep her secrets.

My thoughts are interrupted by a low rumbling sound coming from the family room.

When I walk in, Kiki and Ben are tumbling on the rug.

"It's *not* a laser beam," Kiki screams. "It's a princess stick!"

"It's called a scepter, dummy." He's fighting her off. An easy task since he's double her size.

"What's going on in here?"

They untangle themselves, and then both begin talking at the same time, each voice trying to drown out the other. Slowly, I'm able to piece together the reason behind their disagreement: a purple scepter that Ben tried to use as a sword—a grave offense as far as Kiki is concerned.

"How about we play with something else?" I say.

"No," Kiki says, rubbing her eyes. Her chin is trembling.

"But Morning Dew needs the stick," I say.

Kiki tilts her head to the side. "Who is Morning Dew?"

"The pony," I say. They're both looking at me like I've gone mad. I widen my eyes as if in shock. "You guys don't know the story of Morning Dew, the pony?"

They shake their heads.

"Oh. I thought all kids knew that story. Well, never mind, then. I guess Morning Dew will have to go to another house to play."

"No," Kiki says, grabbing my hand. "Tell us the story."

Ben shoots me suspicious look. Clearly, he won't be so easily convinced.

"The thing is, we all have to hold this." I pick up the scepter. "The way it works is I find out what Morning Dew is doing but only if three people are touching the magical object." I take a seat on the couch.

Ben takes a step closer and places his hand on the scepter. Kiki cuddles up next to me, wrapping her chubby fingers around the other side.

"Oh, I can see her!" A pause. I make sure to frown. "Oh, no. She's going into the Forbidden Forest. Don't do that, Morning Dew." From the corner of my eye, I watch as Ben nestles next to me.

There's a lot I can't do, but this is my specialty. I know how to tell a story. It always starts with a character—in this case, Morning Dew—and then the tale takes on a life of its own, unraveling bit by bit until I reach a happy ending. (Happy endings are non-negotiable.) I use different voices and sprinkle surprise twists. It's something I learned from Nana. Even as an adult, I'd ask her to tell me bedtime stories.

Ben and Kiki are so enrapt by Morning Dew's story that they don't hear Craig walk in. I do, though. Which is why I'm not the least bit surprised when he appears at the doorway, holding two large bags of takeout.

"Can I interest anyone in dinner?" he says.

Kiki and Ben both jump from the couch, yelling *Daddy* in unison as they race towards Craig. Soon, their trio is locked in an embrace. This has always been my catnip: watching families come together in rituals they take for granted. It's a touching scene, but it is also heartbreaking. It hurts to be reminded of what I never had in my past.

Especially when it looks like I'll never have it in my future, either.

CHAPTER TWENTY-THREE

Cassie

Friday, July 6th

My first instinct is to duck. A ridiculous move, but one my body does, nonetheless.

After composing myself, I cross the street and start following him. His gait is unchanged: entitled and indulgent. He's never been shy about taking up space. His hair, which used to be copper like mine, is now faded into a rosy blond, but other than that, he looks the same, at least from afar. I keep a safe distance between us, my eyes glued to his back. This only goes on for a few minutes, less than five. Long enough that I wonder what it is I hope to accomplish by trailing behind him. Answers elude me.

He walks inside Second Nature Market. It's across the street from The Fudge Company, mere steps away from my car. He won't recognize it, of course—he has no idea what I drive. Still, I feel nervous. Unprotected.

I lose him inside the market. It's tiny but crowded. I could go in and look for him, but then he might see me. I don't know how I'd react. We haven't spoken since my mother's funeral. When I do think of him, the images that pop up in my mind are enough to make my heart slip inside my throat. He is red-faced and angry, launching into a tirade, screaming and cursing at my mother. Or else he's towering over her, his large, open palm about to strike her fragile face. In those moments, I'm back to being a child. Back inside the house on Claybrook Road, feeling trapped, cornered. Back under my father's rule. Breathing becomes difficult. Thinking, too. As a psychologist, I know that this is a natural reaction to trauma, but identifying this does not offer me protection. It doesn't even offer me relief.

Moments later, he reappears—carrying a bouquet of yellow flowers. He gets in line to pay, fiddling with his phone as he waits. I should leave, or at least take a few steps back. But I don't want to lose sight of him again.

I don't know what he's doing here, but I know it can't be good. Not for me.

My father's presence is never a good thing.

All that I know about his life for the past fourteen years, I know from Nana. *Knew* from Nana. She insisted on keeping me updated, even though I never asked after him. In a nutshell: he lives in Seattle and is seeing "someone special," a vegetarian who is responsible for his new and improved lifestyle, one that apparently involves leafy greens and yoga. Nana liked to say that he was a changed man. That he missed me. I never believed either claim.

He is obviously here for Julie. I don't know why I didn't think of it right away. It shouldn't bother me, but it does. Their relationship has always bothered me. Not because I had a problem sharing him. Just the opposite, actually—Julie and I didn't share him.

Mom and I were his official family, but Sophie and Julie were his home. Julie used to tell me how she loved waking up to the sound of him humming (he was not a hummer) and singing (he was *definitely* not a singer). He was happy in Jamaica Plain. He probably pretended that Sophie was his wife, and Julie his only daughter. After my mother's funeral, I assumed he'd move in with Sophie. But he never did.

I feel a spike of rage claw its way up my throat. He has no right to be here. Nana didn't leave him anything. I asked Norman-the-lawyer about it, twice. Nana probably reasoned that he didn't need it, not after inheriting my mother's money. It angers me still to think that my father profited from their sham marriage.

A thought occurs to me: if he's here for Julie, then why is she babysitting today?

Unless that was all for show. This makes sense: Julie didn't want to tell me that our father was on the island, so she made up a story about looking after the handyman's children. It probably wouldn't take much to convince Craig to play along.

I watch my father leave the market. He's probably on his way to Julie. An image pops in my mind: Julie squealing in delight, flinging herself in his arms like a child, calling out *Daddy*. It's how I've always pictured them together.

He wouldn't dare show up at the house—would he? If he does, I'll kick him out. I don't care that the house is half hers. I'll call the police if I have to. I'm no longer a kid. He doesn't scare me anymore. Or, rather, he does—but I'm not going to let fear paralyze me. Not anymore. As a child, all I could do was stand helplessly while he raged against my mother. I waited until he turned away to go to her. But now I'll fight back.

I am contemplating how I can keep him from Nana's house when my eyes zoom in on the bouquet he's holding. They're sunflowers. Beautiful, yellow sunflowers.

Julie's favorite flowers.

It takes me an hour to drive to Nana's house. One hour and six minutes, to be precise. It's my own fault. It's both summer and a holiday weekend—cars on the island reproduce like fruit flies. I should've stayed at the house. Or gone elsewhere for ice cream.

I don't notice his car until I pull up on Nana's driveway. I feel a wave of euphoria rush over me as I unbuckle my seatbelt and leap out of the car.

We kiss before we say anything, arms wrapped around each other.

"Surprise," Daniel whispers, as soon as our mouths are unlocked.

"But I just talked to you."

"I was already on the highway. Stuck in traffic."

I pinch his arm. "You're the worst." I'm smiling so much my jaw hurts.

"Want to get out of here?" he asks. "I have a room at the Surfside Inn."

"God, yes." I lean in to kiss him again.

The warmth of his breath sends tingles down my spine. It's both like coming up for air and being deprived of oxygen. My senses at once are muffled and heightened. It's such a high, losing myself in his arms like this. He's a drug. Or love is, anyway. No wonder it's terrified me for so long.

I forget about Julie, about my father. About the stupid sunflowers I saw him buying.

I forget about everything other than us.

CHAPTER TWENTY-FOUR

Julie

Friday, July 6th

After dinner, Craig invites me to have a beer on his porch. He seems unpreoccupied and carefree, the opposite of what I'd expect someone to be after working at a bar all day. Nana used to compliment this about him, his perpetual good mood. She was right: I noticed him whistling as he set the table, then again as he did the dishes. He seems like a happy person.

"Do you have plans for tomorrow?" he asks, smiling.

"I don't, why?" I set my beer on the table next to me. We're sitting on two Adirondack chairs painted an ambiguous shade of yellow. It's possible they used to be orange but by now they've faded—their surfaces are bubbly and flaky.

"We're going to a barbeque if you'd like to join. A late Fourth of July celebration since it fell on Hump Day this year." His tone is casual, cheerful. It doesn't sound like he's just asked me on a date—so why is my stomach doing a somersault?

This is stupid. I'm married. And Craig knows it. He probably just needs help with the kids. Or maybe he feels sorry for me, the loser with no friends and no plans.

"I'd love that," I say.

"Should you run it by your sister?" Craig takes a sip of his beer. I'm about to say no when I catch his playful grin. Instead, I laugh.

"I'm kidding," he says. "She's protective of you. It's sweet."

"I wish," I say, as I watch the sky turn from day to dusk.

"I take it things aren't going well?"

"I mean, you heard us fighting."

A shrug. "Sometimes I feel like Ben and Kiki do nothing but fight."

Cassie and I didn't used to fight that much as children. Probably because we only lived like sisters for three months out of the year. Also because I hero-worshipped Cassie.

"Oh, I know. I had to break one up today."

"Thank you so much for today, by the way. You're so good with them."

"It was my pleasure."

"You have to let me pay you." It's not the first time he's insisted.

"Absolutely not." I shake my head. "You did so much work around the house for Nana. And you never let her pay you."

"That's different."

"Different how?"

A sheepish smile. "I don't know. I liked taking care of Bertie. She was my neighbor. She was…family."

"And I enjoy taking care of Ben and Kiki." I could tell him more. I could tell him that being around children does wonders for my spirit, that it feels both stimulating and comforting, like someone is singing to my soul. But I don't want him to pity my childless state.

"It doesn't feel right." He shakes his head. "You're in Montauk for the summer. You should be out, having fun."

"Trust me: this is me having fun." What else am I supposed to do? Stay at the house, while Cassie treats me like I'm invisible? Spend the day lounging on the beach, consumed by my doubts about my marriage? Go shopping on Main Street to buy stuff I don't need? I don't have friends here. A few of Patrick's friends' wives are on the island—Stephanie and Tricia come to mind—but they're all snobby and boring. I'd much rather spend time with Craig and his kids.

"I can see why Nana loved them so much," I say, hoping to move past the issue.

"They really miss her." He pauses. I'm gutted I never got to give her great-grandchildren. It warms my heart to know that she had Kiki and Ben. "I do, too," he adds.

"I know the feeling…"

"It gets easier," he says, his voice taking on a faraway quality.

"Nana told me about Ann." It's strange, how much I know about Craig's personal life. His wife's battle with cancer. Her death. "I'm sorry for your loss."

"Thank you."

Neither of us say anything for a while. I'm surprised at how comfortable I feel, sharing the silence with him. On paper, it's been an unremarkable day: babysitting, having dinner, drinking a beer out on the porch. But there's such comfort to this simplicity.

"So, that elaborate story you were telling them when I walked in…Kiki told me it was about a pony called Mountain Dew?"

"Morning Dew," I say. "And it wasn't elaborate."

"According to Ben it was, and I quote, 'super awesome'. And he's one tough customer." He gives me an easy smile. "Do you babysit a lot?"

I shake my head. "I do spend an awful lot of time in my head. Daydreaming." I wonder what Craig would think if he knew about my fairy tales. "It's a little silly, I know."

"Sounds to me like you're a storyteller." A pause. "Like your grandmother."

Storyteller. The word lingers in my mouth like hard candy. A positive spin on my escapist tendencies. Decidedly better than airhead or daydreamer. Which is what I've been called all my life. By Sophie, by Patrick. My second-grade teacher's name for me was Space Cadet—though I got called a lot worse by my classmates. I don't like to think about it. It's been years, but the trauma is still fresh on my mind.

If I close my eyes, I can hear the snickers, the whispers. The rumors about my mom replicating like cancerous cells through the school's corridors. It went beyond the fact that my mom was someone's *secret mistress* (their words). Sophie was made out to be all sorts of things. A dominatrix. An ex-porn star. A former French prostitute who had moved to America to service an exclusive clientele. It's a particularly cruel form of bullying, to have classmates speculate—and pass judgment—on your mother's sexuality. It made socializing difficult for me—I scuttled to the library at lunchtime to avoid sitting by myself and engaged in zero extracurricular activities. I also made it a point to wear dark, bland colors. My favorite outfits—the ones Nana bought for me: colorful, unique, flowy—were buried inside my closet until the following summer. I tried my best not to stand out in any way.

I used to fantasize about a fresh start. About moving in with Nana, enrolling in a local Montauk school. Sometimes, I'd tell Cassie about these dreams, which made them even more real. As young girls, we'd corresponded through letters even though we only lived a few hours away. We'd talk on the phone, too—but only when it was safe because we never knew who could be listening in. But by the time we were teenagers, we each had our own private email account. We wrote each other every day. A journal of sorts. I remember one thread that must've lasted months, maybe even a year, where we wrote up an alternative life for the two of us. A life where we could be together every single day. In Montauk. With Nana. In our imaginations, it was summer all year round.

There is so much about Cassie that I miss, but this is what I miss most of all: we used to tell each other everything. Nothing was taboo between us. Nothing was kept a secret. This was particularly relieving for me since I'd been weighed down by secrecy since I could remember. But with Cassie there was none of that. She was always there for me. She made me a priority in her life. There was even the time when she did the unthinkable: came to my home, *Sophie's* home. Forbidden territory.

We were sixteen and I was heartbroken. Aaron, my crush at the time, had invited me to a dance. My first dance! I was over the moon, thrilled. But my happiness was short-lived. As soon as the evening began, Aaron revealed the reason why he'd invited me: it was because he thought I would, in his words, *put out*. All because of the rumors about my mom. When I rebuffed his advances (aggressive advances, I should add), he spat on my face. This is not an expression: the douchebag forcibly ejected saliva from this throat and launched it on my mouth. I was horrified. If he wanted to make me feel like trash (he probably did), he'd succeeded. I called Cassie in tears. She took a cab all the way from her home across the city. It was her first time in my apartment. Her only time. I cried on her shoulder for hours. I asked her to spend the weekend with me. Miraculously, she said yes.

"Do you have to get that?" Craig's voice brings me back to the present.

For a moment, I think he's talking to someone else. I look behind me—maybe Kiki had a bad dream and came down to find her dad. But then I notice him glancing at my phone. Sophie's name is blinking on the screen. Leave it to my mother to interrupt such a peaceful evening.

I ignore her call. From the corner of my eye, I can see Craig raise an eyebrow.

I wonder if he knows who Sophie is. Probably not. What I said to Cassie before had been true: Nana liked to pretend that Sophie didn't exist. I don't think she ever knew how much that hurt me.

"Another one?"

I look at the green bottle, surprised to see it empty. "Why not?" A smile. It's liberating to be able to drink as many beers as I want.

Once he's inside, I make the mistake of checking my phone. One missed call and two texts from Sophie.

Please don't tell me you're ignoring your own mother.

And: *I don't understand why this is a problem. You don't owe her anything.*

I press my lips together, swallowing the absurdity of her claim. Coming from Sophie, it's particularly egregious. I owe Cassie everything. Sophie knows this—she knows the full story, knows what I did.

She knows I killed Katherine.

CHAPTER TWENTY-FIVE

Cassie

Friday, July 6th

The room at the Surfside Inn is pretty, in a storybook sort of way: pale yellow walls, white wicker chair with a baby blue cushion, floral bedspread. The view is spectacular—the Atlantic Ocean in all of its unobstructed glory. But it's all lost on me. Daniel and I have spent an hour under the sheets making love. I'm not with him because of the sex. I know this because I fell in love with him before we even kissed. But it is amazing, the way our bodies react to one another; a skin-on-skin reaction that is intense, animalistic.

We order room service: lobsters, fresh shrimp, corn on the cob. We tell ourselves that it's because we don't want to get out of bed, but really, it's because we can't risk being seen. Even in disguise—big hair, sunglasses, oversized hat—I could still be recognized. My paranoia has spiked since learning that Julie knows about us.

I wait until we're done eating to tell him about seeing my father.

"Do you think he knows, too?" he asks.

I nod, feeling the tears pool in my eyes. My relationship with Daniel is nothing like the one my father had with Sophie. Daniel's marriage has been over for a very long time. Tatiana knows about me. She doesn't care about Daniel—she didn't bother showing up at the hospital after he thought he had a heart attack. But my father won't see it that way. He'll see me as a hypocrite.

"I've been worried about, I don't know, karma," I say.

Daniel lifts his eyebrows. "My skeptical girlfriend believing in karma?"

"It's this stupid, wonderful place," I say. "Nana used to believe in that sort of thing."

It was such a big part of her life, too. Nana used to say that everything happened for a reason. She was never religious, but she was spiritual. She thought life was governed by forces beyond our control. By the poetry and rhythm of the unseen. She claimed she could sense people's energies, see their auras. Julie was blue. I was purple.

Purple is close to black. That's always concerned me.

"I asked you to leave her," I say. "And now all these bad things are happening."

"You're not hurting her," he says. "She doesn't love me."

"I don't disagree, but…if she doesn't love you, why does she hold on to you?"

"I don't know," he says.

I know a lot about Daniel's marriage to Tatiana—more than I'd like to. Which is why not understanding her motivations is so strange to me. I know women who stay in loveless marriages for all sorts of reasons. A lack of financial independence. Deep-seated insecurities brought on by a society that equates marriage with accomplishment. Concern for their kids. But with Tatiana, something has always felt off. Like a piece of the puzzle is missing.

"I do think it was karma that brought us together," Daniel says. "Good karma. We've both been through our fair share of heartbreak. We deserve this."

Deserve. It's such a narcissistic concept. The idea that individuals—specks of dust in an infinite universe—are important enough to be rewarded or punished based on our actions. Life is chaos, and yet we want to believe that it also has meaning, balance. Even without a shred of scientific evidence to support that notion. I'm no exception. I claim to be rational, evidence-based. And yet, here I am, indulging in thoughts about whether all that's happening to me—seeing my father, learning that Julie knows my secret, losing my grandmother—is karmic retribution for falling in love with a married man.

"I love you." Daniel gives me a peck on the lips. He tastes like lemon butter.

I look out the panoramic windows. The sky is lit by the soft glow of twilight.

"Will you come to Nana's with me?" I say. If my father is there, then I want Daniel by my side. Even if he does know about our affair. Everything is better with Daniel.

"I'll go anywhere with you."

When we arrive, the house is empty. I walk over to the refrigerator, expecting to find a note from Julie. It's where Nana left us messages as children. But I don't see one.

"It's still early," Daniel says to me.

"It's nine-thirty." A pause. "What if something's happened to her?"

He suppresses a smile.

"Don't look at me like that," I say. "I'm not worried about her." I'm really not.

"You said she was at the neighbor's?"

"Allegedly." It could all be a cover story to secretly meet with our father.

"We could stop by to check on her."

It's not a bad idea, except I don't want Julie to know I'm at all concerned about her whereabouts. Maybe we could walk by Craig's house, as though we're taking a late-night stroll on the beach. I'm about to suggest this when I hear a sound coming from the porch.

Julie is standing in the doorway, looking like something out of a luxurious summer catalog: ruffled white dress on olive skin, cascading hair, barefoot, not a bead of sweat on her forehead despite the heat.

"Oh," she says, surprised to see us. Her eyes dart from Daniel to me.

My eyes fly to her hands. No sunflowers.

"I didn't know you had company," she says to me. There's a hint of a smile on her lips. Not a trace of the anger she'd shown hours before. Just the opposite—she's glowing.

"We were wondering where you were," Daniel says.

I resist the urge to kick him.

"I'm Julie." I watch her saunter over, extend her hand, and tilt her face in that annoying way she does when she's introducing herself to a man. Helen of Troy could learn a thing or two from Julie.

"Daniel." He shakes her hand. Mercifully, he doesn't look the least bit intoxicated by my siren of a sister. He moves closer to me and wraps his arm around my waist. "Cassie's boyfriend."

Her eyes flick to his left hand. A relief: Daniel doesn't wear a wedding ring.

"It's nice to meet you." A beat. "Well, I'm exhausted." She throws her hands up in the air, wiping her brow theatrically. "Big day. Craig's kids are wonderful, but they're a handful."

"Were you at his place this whole time?" I narrow my eyes at her. I remember Craig saying he'd be home for dinner. And she doesn't look exhausted. She looks happy and carefree.

She nods, smiling. "I'll be in my room if you need me."

I watch her as she sashays to the staircase, humming up the steps. The humming grows into a whistle. She even sings a little. When she's out of sight, I hold a finger to my lips. I wait until I hear the familiar click of the door closing upstairs. As little girls, Julie and I would listen in when Nana was on the phone with our father. Sound carries in this house.

"She seems nice," Daniel says quietly.

Normally this kind of remark would be vexing. Of course she *seems* nice. Beautiful people-pleasers always do. But I can't focus on that, not now.

Now, I'm thinking of the tune she was whistling as she went up the stairs. Cat Steven's 'The First Cut is the Deepest'.

Our father's favorite song.

CHAPTER TWENTY-SIX

Julie

Tuesday, July 17th

Rainy days are when I miss Nana the most. She used to say it symbolized renewal, rebirth. It was also when she'd bring out the Ouija board.

"It sounds crazy, but that thing moved," I say, staring at the cloudy expanse. "That house was a magnet for spirits."

"Maybe it still is," Craig says.

"With Nana gone? I doubt it."

He and I are on his porch—our twelfth evening together, not counting the barbeque that we went to in honor of the Fourth. Once Kiki and Ben are sound asleep, we sneak outside to partake in beers and conversation. Craig doesn't even invite me to stay anymore. It's understood that I will. It feels familiar now, a ritual.

I know how dangerous this is. Nothing has happened: Craig has been a perfect gentleman, but the current that runs between us is strong, enough that I feel like I might spontaneously combust. In my mind, I've been unfaithful. I fantasize about running my hand through his hair, biting his lower lip, feeling his breath on my neck.

Neither of us have brought up Patrick—and I know Craig knows about him. Nana has filled him in on every detail of my life. Nana couldn't stand Patrick. She is probably looking down on me now, unsurprised to see him refusing to answer my calls. About a week ago, after I called him four times in a row, he sent me a two-line message: *Don't bother calling me unless it's to say you're coming back home. You need to understand that actions have consequences.* It hadn't hurt me as much as I expected it to. Being here has fortified me. It's reminded me that there's more to me than my marriage, that my life isn't an empty shell—or, at least, that it doesn't have to be. Maybe I don't have to be married. Maybe I don't have to live by Patrick's suffocating rules. Maybe I can have a baby on my own.

Because that's another thing that's been fortified: my resolve to have a child.

Being around Kiki and Ben has further confirmed that there is nothing I want more in this world than to hold my own little one in my arms, to watch her grow and play and learn. I want it all, not just the good. I want sleepless nights and picky eating and mysteriously sticky hands. I want to read the same story on a loop. I want to answer questions for which answers are either impossible or inappropriate. I want to deal with tantrums: both of the toddler and of the teenage varieties. I want to be the mother I never had. And if I stay with Patrick, that will never happen.

Lately, I've been thinking of staying in Montauk. I could get pregnant on my own, raise a baby in Nana's house. A ludicrous thought—how would I support myself?—but one I entertain, nonetheless.

I'm happier here. I've always been happier here.

And not just because I can eat junk food and drink beer and whistle.

"You remind me of her," Craig says.

"It's the eyes."

"No, it's more than that. It's not something physical. It's how you see the world."

"You've noticed this after less than two weeks?" I feel tears welling up.

"She'd say it, too. How alike you two were." He glances over at me. "Sorry, should I not talk about her?"

"Please do," I say, my voice soft. "I like it. I miss her."

I don't add that my tears aren't just because I miss Nana. It's been difficult, my time at the house. Patrick has frozen me out. Cassie has perfected the art of ignoring me. Dad won't return my calls. If it weren't for Craig—and Kiki and Ben—I'd be miserable.

"I like to think she's looking down on us," I say.

"If she is, she's really happy you're here." A pause. "You and Cassie."

I pull up my feet and hug my legs. "Even though her plan isn't working?"

"It'll get better."

"I don't know about that." In eleven days, we'll both be free to leave the island. I should probably come to terms with the fact that we aren't going to find our way back to each other. It's become clear to me that Nana has underestimated Cassie's stubbornness. She should've made us stay here for at least two months.

"Trust me. Bertie's plan is going to work." There's a confident edge to his voice.

"Do you know something I don't?" I turn my body to face his. He's only a few inches away from me, on his own chair. But I wish he were closer. I wish his arms were around me.

He shrugs. His non-answer should annoy me, but it doesn't. He's so handsome. So kind.

"Did you find it strange that she didn't want a funeral?" he asks.

"I thought it was strange she didn't want a wake. Or a drum circle. She used to say she wanted people to come together to celebrate her death."

"Sounds like Bertie." He chuckles softly.

"Maybe we should do that. Invite her friends and have a ceremony at the beach. Right here." I picture gathering her friends together at night surrounded by tiki torches and flute music. Kiki and Ben could read something. Nana would like that. Then, a thought occurs to me. One I've been curious about for a while now. "Can I ask how you bought this house?"

"It belonged to Ann's parents," he says. "We moved after they passed. I'd just lost my job at the time and it felt right. We both wanted a simpler life. But then she got sick…"

I want to ask more—what did he do before? How could they afford the property taxes? Does he miss his wife?—but don't. Craig is a private person. Our time together has taught me that. One question at a time.

"Are you happy you did?" I ask.

"Absolutely," Craig says. "Poughkeepsie was fine. That's where we lived before. It's where I'm from. But this is my home."

"Nana said you fit right in."

He gives me a winning smile. "Do you have plans for tomorrow?"

I shake my head. "Not unless you count being ignored by Cassie."

"Do you want to come over? I don't have to go into work, and it's supposed to be nice. We could go for a swim. I promised Kiki I'd build her a castle with a moat and a bridge. I don't have to go into work, so if you'd rather not spend the day with us—"

"Spending the day with you is exactly what I want."

I feel my face flush. By "you" I meant the three of them: Kiki, Ben, and Craig. But maybe he thinks I meant only him. I decide not to clarify.

A silence falls between us. I wonder if he'll kiss me. I wonder why he hasn't tried anything yet. He must feel it, too, the electricity between us. It would be wrong, but I want it to happen. Maybe it's because Patrick has been punishing me with silence.

Maybe it's because losing Nana made me realize how precious life is. Maybe it's the beer. I don't know. But I'm ready to throw caution to the wind. I'm ready for him to kiss me.

But he doesn't.

CHAPTER TWENTY-SEVEN

Cassie

Wednesday, July 18th

If I didn't trust my own mind, I'd be convinced that my father was a hallucination.

Since seeing him on Main Street, I've kept tabs on Julie's whereabouts—discreetly, of course. All she does is spend time with the handyman who may or may not be a serial killer but is most definitely obsessed with her. Other than the tune she was whistling, I have no reason to believe she's seen our father.

This has only increased my paranoia. Too much is unknown at this point. My father's exact location. The reason he has flown from Seattle to Montauk. Whether he's even still here—and, if he is, where exactly he's staying. Julie's apparent ignorance of it. Most of all, there's this: how does Julie know about Daniel and me?

I hate that she knows. I hate the way she looked at him when they met. Mischievous, shrewd. Like she was helping us keep our secret. Like we used to do, as children.

I don't want her help. My situation is nothing like our parents' triangular mess.

What I want is to find out how she knows about my most private relationship.

It can't be public knowledge—Claudia would've told me. Rachel and Christina would never say anything. Daniel has checked Tatiana's Facebook account: she and Julie don't have any friends in common. I've run out of leads to chase.

But I haven't given up. There has to be a way to get to the bottom of this.

These are the thoughts running through my head as I'm lounging on the hammock with a paperback. I look up when I hear a warm, raspy voice.

"Cassie? Oh dear, is that you?"

I turn around. For a minute, it's like I'm looking at a ghost.

Is that…Mrs. Bunsen? I haven't seen Nana's friend in so long, but it looks just like her. I slowly make my way out of the hammock. It is her: flowered tunic, big, silver hair, cane.

"Let me help you, Mrs. Bunsen." I hurry down the steps, offering my arm. It occurs to me that Nana climbed these same steps day in and day out in her old age. Craig-the-handyman could've made himself useful and built a ramp. Nana could've paid him in pictures of Julie.

"Oh, thank you dear," Mrs. Bunsen says. "Mandy's on her way."

Mandy. The name is vaguely familiar. Where have I heard it before? But now is not the time to be asking questions. Climbing these steps is a challenge. I'm relieved once we're on the porch. I pull up a chair for her.

"No need to fuss over me, dear. Park me anywhere." She lets out a bubbly laugh. "That's how it feels after we grow old, you know. People park you like a car. In my case, a rather large one."

"This is a nice surprise." I take a seat next to her. "How have you been?"

"All right, I suppose." She pats my leg gently. "I miss Bertie."

"I do, too," I say. I feel a knot in my chest.

"I don't mean to make you sad, dear. She wouldn't have wanted that." She looks around the porch, taking in the salt-heavy air. "This is what she wanted, you and your sister together. Wherever she is, she's happy you're both here."

I resist the urge to point out that Julie and I are sharing a space—nothing else. Nana might've meant well, but she had no right to force a reconciliation between us. In a sense, I'm glad there's no afterlife. If there was, Nana would be hurting. Disappointed to watch me spending my days ignoring Julie. Spying on her.

I can't wait for this month to be over. Only eleven more days to go.

"Don't be sad, Julie."

"I'm Cassie, Mrs. Bunsen." I make it a point to keep my tone gentle, soft, but I feel a familiar thrum of disappointment echo in my chest: Julie is always the one people want to see.

She eyes me curiously, like she thinks I'm playing a prank on her. But then she nods, laughing. "Of course you are. You'll get names confused at my age, too."

I clear my throat. "Can I get you anything? Some coffee or iced tea?"

"Mandy should be here by now. Where is she?"

"Mrs. Bunsen," I begin, enunciating carefully. "Who is Mandy?"

"There she is."

I follow her gaze to see a short, plump woman in a headscarf walking on the beach. I have no idea who she is, but I recognize the woman beside her. Julie.

"I'm confused, Mrs. Bunsen."

"Did Bertie not tell you? She asked Mandy to come. We should've been here days ago, but my back gave out."

Nana asked her to come? Oh, dear. I'm not sure what to do. I don't think I have it in me to explain to her that Nana isn't here anymore.

"Who is Mandy?" I ask again, leaning forward.

"My granddaughter, of course, Julie. Aren't you forgetful? Your grandmother used to tell you about Mandy's predictions all the time."

Of course. Mandy is the meddlesome psychic who gave Nana the harebrained idea to bring Julie and me here after Nana's death. I try to think back to my talks with Nana—had she mentioned that Mandy is Mrs. Bunsen's granddaughter? It's entirely possible she did. I used to tune out when Nana began talking about auras and spirit animals. I hate myself for not having paid more attention. I'll never get to talk to her again.

Mrs. Bunsen's eyes are glued to Julie and her granddaughter. The two of them look like old friends. They probably *are* friends, I realize. Julie visited Nana with some frequency, after all. Julie probably knew Mrs. Bunsen was coming and rudely did not tell me. I feel a jolt of irritation.

Julie and Mandy are strolling at a leisurely pace along the shore. If they had any manners, they'd take the rocky sand path that connects the houses on this part of the beach.

Then it occurs to me to use this time to my advantage.

"Mrs. Bunsen, did Nana talk to you about her plan to bring us here?"

"All the time, dear. You know, Bertie. She never liked the city."

True, but irrelevant. I press on. "Did she say anything about asking our father to come, too?"

"I'll tell you what she did say. She didn't like your husband. I don't think she'd mind me saying so."

"Do you mean Julie's husband?"

"Yes, of course. The lawyer. He isn't good for Julie, my dear. She's too trusting, too sweet. She's not like you. I never understood how that happened. How you became so strong. She was raised by a single mother, she should be more resilient. You were lucky."

I should take offense at this, but instead I press on. No time to waste.

"Did Nana mention bringing my father here?" I ask again.

"Bertie loved that boy. He could do no wrong in her eyes. But me, I'll never forget how he refused to spend time with you two together, no matter how many times she begged him to." She's referring to Nana's pleas that my father come to the island while Julie and I were both here. She insisted it was important that the two of us spend time with him together. Julie and I overheard her on the phone once, her voice an exasperated whisper. *Come for the weekend, Stephan*, she'd say to him. *Surely, Katherine will understand. She can't blame Julie.* But my father never did. He said my mother wouldn't stand for it, but I know better: he had no interest in spending time with Julie and me. It was probably too much for him, seeing his two worlds collide. My father's most frequently used defense mechanism was compartmentalization.

Now that I think about it, it makes sense that her last wish to her son would be for him to honor the request that he never fulfilled while she was alive.

"Did she ask my father to come to the island now? With Julie and me here?"

"Of course she did. She wanted the three of you together. Four, if you count Craig."

What in the world does Craig have to do with any of this?

I don't get a chance to ask. Julie-the-sloth is now making her way up the porch steps. Mandy is right behind her.

"Mrs. Bunsen, I've missed you so much." Julie wraps her arms around her, a gleeful smile on her face. I'm envious of her tan— weeks under the sun have given her skin a gorgeous golden hue.

"My pet. It's so lovely to see you. And so beautiful, you're like a movie star."

I resist the urge to roll my eyes, though I have to admit she looks stunning and somehow younger. Maybe it's the beachy waves (I much prefer them to the sleek, perfectly parted style) and the lip gloss.

"Hi, I'm Cassie." I extend a hand to Mandy, who has smooth, rosy cheeks and an encouraging smile. She looks like a friendly teacher, not a kooky psychic.

"I recognize you from Bertie's pictures." She shakes my hand, smiling with her teeth, which are ultra-white and perfectly straight.

"Can I get you anything?" I ask. "Coffee, water?" I'll play hostess for another five minutes. Then I'll make up an excuse and drive into town. I'd rather be stuck in traffic.

Mandy shakes her head. "No coffee. Caffeine will interfere with the process."

"Process?" I feel the ripples on my forehead.

"Oh, yes, dear," Mrs. Bunsen says. "Mandy is here to look at your chakras."

Of course she is.

CHAPTER TWENTY-EIGHT

Julie

Wednesday, July 18th

Before Mandy and I came inside, Cassie shot me a contemptuous look, one that read *this is all your fault*. For the record: it isn't.

I had no idea Nana had asked Mandy to visit us for a reading. She showed up at Craig's, asking me to come over to Nana's house. Kiki, Ben, and I had been right in the middle of breakfast. It's lucky that Craig wasn't at work because otherwise I wouldn't have been able to come. At least not without Kiki and Ben.

"You're keeping a secret." Mandy's gaze is intense, but not uncomfortable.

I peer behind her shoulder, looking out the large window. Cassie is on the porch with Mrs. Bunsen. I'm surprised that she's still here. I would've thought she'd bolt at the mere mention of the word *chakra*.

"Could we do this upstairs?" I whisper. We're inside, seated at the dining table.

She lowers her voice. "Don't worry, they can't hear us. This is a safe space."

There is no such thing as a safe space. Not when it comes to my secret.

"You feel divided," she continues. "Like a rope being pulled on both sides."

I think of Sophie. She's still insisting that I gather information about Cassie and Daniel. I haven't told her anything, obviously. Though it isn't easy, ignoring her. Especially when her job is on the line. And I've thought about Janette's point, about how an article about Cassie's affair could jumpstart a career for me, maybe even get me a book deal.

But none of it matters. I am not going to be responsible for ruining Cassie's life. Not again.

"I see more than one now," Mandy says. "You have...many secrets."

I swallow a smile. I'm a fan of psychic readings, but they're usually private. The front door is closed, but what if Mandy is wrong? What if Cassie and Mrs. Bunsen can hear us?

"Your secrets are keeping you from your destiny."

I slide my chair closer to hers. "What's my destiny?"

"There is resentment. And bitterness. And so many crossed wires, I can barely see what's ahead," she pauses, looking up. "But there's...something else. Something beautiful and golden. A river." A shadow passes through her face. I hear the wind chimes outside. "But there's blood in the river. A betrayal."

I have to put a stop to this. I place my hand on hers.

"Can I ask you about my marriage?" A convenient interruption. I'd love to hear Mandy's take on my relationship, especially after the fight Patrick and I had last night.

It started with a phone call. One that he initiated—the first time he's called me since I've been here.

"I'm sending a car to pick you up," he said. We had a party to attend—one I couldn't miss. A partner at the firm wrote a book. Everyone was going to be at the launch on Martha's Vineyard.

"I have to spend the night here," I reminded him. I stared down at my bright orange, bitten-down nails and my dirty feet. I thought of how I'd been letting my hair air dry and how I hadn't refilled my eyelash extensions since before I left Boston. I did not look like Patrick's wife.

"The driver will take you back after the party. Did you bring any acceptable dresses with you or should I have Annalise pick a few outfits?"

I'm still unsure what made me react like I did. Maybe it was his tone. His arrogance. The way he seemed to be grooming me, like I was a prize mare. Maybe it was the fact that in all the time I'd been away he hadn't bothered to ask me how I was doing, how I was feeling about being in my dead grandmother's house with my estranged sister after nearly fifteen years of not speaking to each other. I don't know. What I know is that I told him I wasn't going to the party.

"I'm not asking, Julie. I'm informing you that a car will pick you up on Saturday at five." His tone was not unlike the one Craig uses on Kiki and Ben.

"Fine. I'll go with one condition." My voice was barely above a whisper. I was outside on the porch. I didn't want Cassie to overhear us. "You have to come pick me up."

"Why would I do that?"

Because we need to meet halfway. Because I want you to show me you miss *me*—not just my presence at parties. Because I want you to see Nana's house.

But I didn't say any of these things.

Instead, I said, "Because it would make me happy to see you here. You could stay for the weekend. I can make a reservation at a hotel."

"You know I like to go golfing on Sundays."

"Please?" I asked. "Just this once?"

Just this once. I'd said those words before. Brunch with my dad. Janette's birthday party. Dinner at U-Burger. All things I'd asked him to do instead of golfing or working or reading. He always refused. Sometimes it felt like I was married to a robot—and that Patrick was married to his routine.

I knew what his answer would be.

Sure enough, it didn't surprise me.

"How about you go on a shopping spree instead?"

Here's the thing: it's my fault. For years, I said yes. To the shopping spree, to the shiny gifts. I told myself I was lucky. That I couldn't have it all—no one did. It was ridiculous to expect that someone like Patrick—successful, well-connected, generous— would also be sociable and spontaneous.

Except I've changed. Maybe it's being here. Maybe it's the realization that motherhood isn't something that I'm willing to give up on. Or seeing Craig's uncomplicated happiness. Maybe it's just that I've put some distance between us. Whatever the reason, I told Patrick no. And then I hung up. When he called back, I didn't pick up. He called again this morning—three times so far—but I haven't answered. If he hadn't brought up Sophie in a text, I wouldn't have even bothered to text him back. He punished me with silence for days. Now it's my turn.

Now, I'm staring at Mandy, wondering what she'll say. It's possible she'll tell me my marriage is over, that I've made the biggest mistake of my life. Or maybe she'll say I did the right thing, that standing up for myself is just what I needed to clear my aura.

I hold my breath and I wait.

CHAPTER TWENTY-NINE

Cassie

Wednesday, July 18th

I expected props. Crystal ball. Tarot cards. Candles.

Instead, Mandy is motionless, her gray eyes fixed on mine. Almost like she's trying to hypnotize me. It would be spooky if she didn't look so harmless.

"You should know I don't believe in this sort of thing," I say.

"You're here by choice." Her tone is peaceful. She's got the Zen thing down to a T.

She's wrong. I don't have a choice—not really. I'm desperate. I need to know why my father is—was?—on the island. Mandy may have information.

Mrs. Bunsen's words are still echoing in my mind. She became chatty once Julie was inside with Mandy. *Bertie spent hours writing those letters. She wanted to get it just right.* At first, I thought she was referring to letters Nana sent to me—and presumably to Julie as well. Nana resisted the switch to email, flat out refused to buy a computer. But then Mrs. Bunsen said something else. *Bertie went through a lot of trouble to make sure you'd get them after she moved from this life. Your father, too. I teased her about being like that man in the* P.S. I Love You *film. Have you seen it, dear? It's lovely. Her letters are lovely, too. And that turquoise stationery was heavenly.*

It was the stationery detail that stood out to me. Nana used it for special occasions—birthdays, milestones. I tried pressing Mrs. Bunsen for more, but she became conveniently disoriented. I'm not entirely convinced her senility isn't an act. Not that I'd ever come out and say it to her face. I'm not about to accuse an old woman of faking dementia symptoms.

Here's who I will confront, though: Mandy.

I cut right to the chase.

"Your grandmother just told me Nana left letters behind. For Julie and me." I pause, deciding to omit the mention of a letter to my father. "Do you know anything about that?"

To her credit, Mandy doesn't hesitate. "I do."

"So it's true, then? Nana left us letters?"

"I believe so, yes."

"Where?"

"I don't know," she says plainly.

"Do you know who does?"

"My grandmother might. But she's not likely to tell you. Not on purpose, anyway."

"Will you ask her?"

"That's not why I'm here." Her smile is patronizing. Like I'm a child she's indulging. "I'm supposed to be looking at your chakras. They need opening." A pause. "Your grandmother warned me about you."

I feel a tug at my heart. "About my jaded cynicism?"

"She was worried about you."

"About what?"

"She was concerned you were too hard on yourself."

I'm quiet for a moment.

"I have sisters. I get it." Her tone is now more normal person than psychic.

I'm not sure how this has become about having a sister. "What do you think you get?" Although, since we are on the subject of sisters, I wonder if I can ask her how Julie knows about Daniel being married. It irritates me no end that I actually wonder, if only for half a second, if Julie could possibly have psychic powers. (Maybe she and Mandy are holistic partners?) But, of course, if I were to ask that, I'd be confirming the fact that Daniel is, indeed, married. And if I were to do that, then I might as well ask if Daniel is going to leave Tatiana.

Great, now I'm considering asking a psychic for love advice. My life really is a messy cliché.

"Sisters challenge us," Mandy says. "They make us braver and better. They sometimes also make us angry and jealous." She looks at me when she says that last word.

"Nana was concerned that I'm jealous of Julie?"

"Are you?"

Less than five minutes with this woman and this is already all about Julie.

CHAPTER THIRTY

Julie

Wednesday, July 18th

My session with Mandy didn't go at all like I expected.

I followed her instructions: kept my eyes closed, relaxed my shoulders, focused on her voice. I thought she'd guide me through positive visualizations. But she kept bringing up prompts like disappointment, resentment. Failure. And she didn't respond to any of my questions. Instead, she fed me variations of the same line, some crap about how the answers I seek are inside me.

I thought holistic therapy was supposed to be soothing—or at least not depressing. But that session has left me disheartened. More than that: bitter. The way I assume Cassie feels all the time. Right now it seems like a miracle Cassie even *has* a boyfriend—married or not.

She's now up in the attic doing God knows what. I can hear rumblings and the occasional "Darn it!" followed by loud, clunky sounds. Maybe her session with Mandy has left her angry. Angrier.

I call my dad. It goes straight to voicemail, but this time it's not full.

"Hey, Dad, it's me. I just wanted to talk to you. I've been doing a lot of thinking now that I'm here and I wanted to hear your voice. Call me?"

I sound impatient, which isn't fair on him. He's just lost his mother. Still, I need him to call me back. Patrick has given up on texting me once it became clear I wasn't going to answer him. Nana is gone. Cassie is set on snubbing me. I need my dad. I've needed him since I got here, but now I need him even more. A thought has been unfurling inside my mind for the past days, maybe even weeks: I need to leave Patrick. There are many factors that have contributed to this decision. The silence he subjected me to for weeks. The sense of relief I've experienced from not having to constantly monitor my appearance to his specifications. The fact that I've obviously developed a crush on Craig—and happily married women don't go around developing feelings for other men. But most of all, there's this: I want to be a mom.

Except I need someone to walk me through what that would even look like. Someone to tell me that everything will be all right. It can't be Janette—she has too much going on right now with work and, besides, she dislikes Patrick too much. It has to be my dad because, like Sophie, my dad approves of Patrick. *He's a good man, Julie. A good provider.* It's sweet, but it's also a little insulting. Sophie does the same. The underlying message isn't lost on me: I'm lucky to have Patrick. He rescued me from an unmarried life, after all. Rescued. Like a Disney princess, or a three-legged dog.

If I can make my dad see that being with Patrick is antonymous with being happy, then I'll know I'm doing the right thing by asking him for a divorce.

I'm reaching into the fridge to get the pitcher of iced tea when I hear Cassie moving around the attic with renewed energy. What exactly is she doing? It didn't even occur to her to tell me, even though whatever is up in that attic is mine as well.

I feel my skin prickle. No one would ever expect Cassie to need rescuing.

My phone rings. My face flushes when I see my dad's name on the screen.

"Dad?"

"Julie!" his voice booms on the other end of the line.

"Dad, I've been trying to reach you for—"

I hear a whooshing noise coming from the phone, like the wind, only with more personality. "I just got back from fishing. My first time. I know what you're thinking, but it wasn't boring at all."

"That's nice." I don't want to discuss fishing. "Dad, can we talk?"

"Sure, sure." His tone is unsurprisingly cheerful. My father is nothing if not happy.

"I spoke to a psychic today."

His laugh makes me blush.

"She's Nana's holistic therapist. It got me thinking about my marriage. I'm a little, I don't know, confused."

"You're not having problems, are you?" he asks.

"Well, no. Not *problems*, exactly. It's just that I wonder if Patrick and I are compatible—"

"Don't let this place get to you, Julie."

"What do you mean?"

"You know what I mean. This plan your grandmother came up with, it isn't healthy. Your sister isn't a good influence on you. Don't listen to her. Stand by your man."

"Cassie doesn't know about any of this, Dad. And it's been going on for a while now. Before Nana passed away." I pause. "I feel lonely."

"A pretty girl like you, lonely?"

At this, I flush with pride. I love it when he calls me pretty. "It's that Patrick works such long hours—"

"He's a lawyer, Julie. You knew how hard he worked when you married him."

I can't argue with that. Still, that doesn't explain his withdrawal when he's at home.

I step out of the house. I need fresh air.

"It's more than that, Daddy," I say. I go on to explain how controlling Patrick is. I offer a tame example: his insistence that I put on a full face of makeup in the morning, but never any lipstick. I once made the mistake of trying on a red lipstick (I felt certain that he'd like it) and he told me I looked like a whore. Luckily, we were at home because he refused to speak to me until I took it all off.

"So he doesn't like red lipstick."

"Dad, it's a lot more than that." I explain how Patrick insists that I be home on weekends and in the evenings, even though he doesn't seem the least bit interested in interacting with me. I add that he gets upset if I make plans with any of my friends, which is why all of them have given up on me, except for Janette. "It's just that I wonder sometimes. Maybe we don't belong together."

"Who's been filling your head with these ideas?"

"No one. It's just me." Does he think I'm incapable of wanting more, of being critical?

"Tell you what. Why don't I meet you in Boston when you go back? We'll have some nice father-and-daughter time. Patrick and I will go golfing."

I bite my lip. He's not listening to me, but he is offering to fly to Boston to spend time together. I know better than to look a gift horse in the mouth. Part of me wishes he and Sophie were still involved—it would mean I'd see him more often.

"Can we go for brunch, Daddy?" I ask. I decide that I'll tell him about Patrick's stance on babies then. Even if dad doesn't find fault with Patrick's other behaviors, he'll surely be horrified by his refusal to give me children. "Just the two of us?"

"Absolutely. I have to take off now. But we'll talk soon, OK?" I hear background noise. Traffic, maybe. "I love you, Julie."

"I love you, too, Daddy."

I stare at the blue expanse in front of me. It's a cloudless day, one of those perfect summer skies, balmy and clear. When we were little, we used to see rainbows from this very porch, usually towards the end of summer. Nana would tell us to make a wish, as if a rainbow were a shooting star. For the longest time, I thought that was how it worked: you see a rainbow, you make a wish. Cassie wished for something different every time, but I only wanted one thing: more summers with Nana and Cassie, more time in this place where I felt at peace. I wished for more days where I could be a butterfly and not a caterpillar.

"That makes no sense," Cassie once said to me. "You shouldn't waste a wish on something you already have. Ask for something new."

But that never came easily to me. I was comfortable dreaming, not asking. The idea of articulating my wants to other people—even to a rainbow—sent me into a panic. I was lucky to have Nana and Cassie. Asking for more seemed rude, ungrateful. Which is why I kept my wishes to myself, close to my heart.

Until I didn't. Until the day I opened Pandora's box and destroyed my family.

CHAPTER THIRTY-ONE

Cassie

Wednesday, July 18th

Today I learned something new about my grandmother: she was a secret slob.

The attic is disgusting. The contrast with her otherwise immaculate house is staggering. Clearly, her level of neatness was only possible because she stored every last bit of junk in the attic. A box filled with laces (sentimental relics?), the old Ouija board (that thing used to give me the creeps), receipts for dirt she bought for flowerpots. There's an entire corner filled with multicolored beads and string. Beads!

I'm beginning to suspect Nana may have had some hoarding tendencies.

I feel my allergies start to act up as I roam through a stack of boxes. It's possible the letters do not exist—and, if they do, they may not be here—but I'm not giving up until I've searched every square foot of this dusty place.

And the dust isn't even the worst part. That would be the heat. The single, tiny round window offers no relief against the punishing July sun—in fact, it seems to magnify its power. I open it, anyway, hoping for a breeze.

That's when I hear her. Julie, on the phone.

At first, her words get mixed in with the sounds of the beach: waves gently crashing along the Montauk shore, the creepy flecks of insects' wings. But then I hear it.

Can we go for brunch, Daddy? Just the two of us?

Julie is making plans with our father. Just the two of them.

A lump forms in my throat. What exactly is keeping her from telling me he's on the island—is she too dense? Too stupid?

I crane my neck, hoping to hear more, but she's quiet now. They must've hung up.

I feel my blood boil as I finish rummaging through the large, faded blue box that I've left open. There's an envelope inside it—cream white, almost the exact shade of the eggshell white envelope Sophie mailed to my mother on the night she died. This one has nothing of importance: two lists of china and silverware with dots next to some of the items. I think of what was inside the other envelope and I shudder.

My decision not to speak to Julie has haunted me for years. A part of me has always felt it was…unfair. Sophie was the one who sent those pictures to my mother. Julie wasn't at fault.

But now she absolutely is at fault. Her behavior is callous, heartless. Julie thinks nothing of making plans to see our father here in Montauk. No thought to warning me. No concern for my feelings. She knows how much he cost me. She knows why I don't talk to him. Yet they've been meeting in secret, behind my back.

It hurts. The Julie I knew would never do this to me.

I let out a sneeze so powerful it makes my head throb. I should've taken an antihistamine before coming up here. This place will be the death of me.

But I can't stop now. I have to find the letters.

I open a box that seems to contain nothing but old newspapers and magazines. And I do mean old: some are from the nineties. Why would Nana keep these? I brush my fingers over a timeworn

US Weekly. I had no idea Nana was even remotely interested in celebrity gossip. The headlines are predictably foolish.

Revealed: Celebs' Hottest Beauty Secrets

Disowned due to Morality Clause: an Heiress Fights Back!

Hoop, There It Is: The Season's Hottest Trend

This box will be thrown out. I won't even bother asking Julie—she couldn't be bothered to tell me our father is on the island. I'll sort everything into two piles: toss and keep. It'll mostly be toss. I'm thinking of how I can dispose of so much junk when a thought pops in my mind.

My eyes flick back to the magazine: *Disowned due to Morality Clause.*

The words ring in my ear. Is that why my father is here? Could he and Julie be planning on contesting the will? On taking the house from me on the grounds that I am a couples' counselor who is romantically involved with a former patient—a married man?

Would that even be legal?

My head is spinning. I need to get out of here. I need fresh air. I head for the rickety stairs attached to the trapdoor that leads to the second floor. I don't see what happens next. It's possible I slipped. Or tripped. But I feel every inch of the fall until I'm on the ground, my right ankle caught on one of the steps. A *snap*, then a rush of raw pain.

A high-pitched cry rings in my ears. I soon realize it came from me.

"Cassie?" I hear Julie scream.

Within seconds she's standing over me, cupping my head with her hands, her voice tremulous and grating.

"Cassie, oh my God! Are you OK? What happened?"

If I could form a proper sentence, I'd say it was all her. *She* is what happened.

CHAPTER THIRTY-TWO

Julie

Wednesday, July 18th

Cassie's face is twisted in a gruesome, painful expression. Her foot might be broken.

"I'll get Craig." I jump up.

"What? No!" Her voice is a guttural roar. "Take me to the hospital. My car keys are on my nightstand."

"I can't drive."

She looks at me like I'm a unicorn. No—unicorns are special. A troll. A swamp monster.

"How is it possible," she begins, enunciating each word through gritted teeth, "that you don't know how to drive?"

Not all of us got cars when we turned sixteen. Not everyone learns to drive in the idyllic setting of Dover, Massachusetts, where the roads are wide and safe, and traffic is non-existent. In Jamaica Plain, the only way for a sixteen-year-old to have a car is if he'd stolen it.

"I learned enough to get my license, OK? But I've never really driven." I'm stumbling on my own words. I hate that I feel defensive.

"Fine, get Craig." She lets out a testy sigh.

I leave the room feeling wounded. I came to her rescue after she fell off the stairs. She could afford to be a little nicer. I just hope she won't be this rude to Craig.

Except Craig isn't home. I'd forgotten he and the kids are out. Ben wanted to go to Ditch Plains. I would've gone with them if Mrs. Bunsen hadn't shown up. Like an idiot, I'd forgotten.

I've now wasted fifteen minutes dashing to and from his house.

"He isn't home," I tell Cassie. "Should I call an ambulance?" I'm fumbling through my purse trying to find my cell phone. Maybe I can text Craig? How long would it take him to drive back?

"No. No ambulance. Look, just get in the car and drive, OK?" And then, a mutter, "How bad of a driver can you possibly be?"

I swallow, unsure of how to answer.

I help her get up, doing my best to ignore her wincing. I have a feeling it has more to do with me touching her than it does with whatever pain she's experiencing. I'm thankful for my Pilates training—I need a strong core to help hold her down the stairs.

I'm sweating as I turn on the car and reluctantly start to back up on Nana's driveway. Driving has always scared me. There are just too many things to watch out for. If you think about it, cars are like weapons.

"Watch out," Cassie says, at the exact moment I hit the mailbox with the side mirror.

"Shit. Sorry."

I hear her suck in a heap of air. She's clenching her fists in pain or annoyance. Likely both. Does she think I *want* to be driving?

But now is not the time to mull over her ungrateful attitude. Eyes on the highway.

I exhale when we finally arrive at the emergency drop-off of the Southampton Hospital. Within minutes, we're out of the car and in a waiting room so cold it feels like winter. Cassie is filling out a bunch of forms while I pretend to check something on my phone.

"No painkillers," Cassie tells a nurse, as soon as she leads us into a room.

"I'm just here to check on your blood pressure, ma'am." She instructs Cassie to take a seat on the aluminum cot.

Cassie complies but keeps her eyes on the woman in lavender scrubs as if she might surprise her with a needle.

When the doctor arrives, Cassie tells her the same thing. Dr. Adams is a thin woman with a long nose and deep cheekbones who looks like she hasn't slept a day in her life. I fight the urge to open my makeup bag and cover up the blue circles under her eyes.

Dr. Adams raises her eyebrows. "Not even Ibuprofen? Tylenol?"

"That's fine," Cassie says. "Just nothing strong."

Dr. Adams nods somberly, then glances my way. "Is this your friend?"

"I'm her sister," I say at the same time that Cassie slices the air with her hands and says, "No."

Dr. Adams nods. Clearly, our relationship is of no consequence. "We'll need to run some X-rays before I can be sure, maybe an ultrasound, but right now I'd say it's a bad sprain."

"That's good," I say.

Cassie rolls her eyes.

This behavior has got to stop.

Dr. Adams leaves. We're back to waiting, this time for the X-rays.

"You don't have to be here," Cassie says when we're alone.

I look at her, my mouth agape. "Are you planning on driving home?"

"I can take a cab," she mumbles.

"Fine." I reach for her car keys in my purse and stuff them into her hand with a little too much force. I love Cassie, and I can appreciate that she's in pain. But this hostile attitude is completely unacceptable. Enough is enough. "But I'm taking a cab, too."

She shrugs and avoids my gaze.

I'm about to leave when I feel the hooks of indignation forcing me to turn around.

"You know I didn't push you, right?"

"What?" Her face looks like a crumpled-up sheet of paper.

"You're acting like it's my fault you're here."

"Shut up, Julie." Her tone is low, breathy.

Oh, she did not just say that. "Why are you so rude all the time?"

She juts out her chin imperiously. "So what if I am?"

"You're right, so what!" I glare at her. "Why should you be polite?"

"Cut the act, Julie." Her look nearly chokes me. "I'm not falling for it."

I blink. "Not falling for what?"

"I know, OK?" she narrows her eyes at me. "I know what you've been hiding."

My legs feel watery. Could she really know? I feel sirens blaring inside my head. I need to get out of here. I can't face her. Not if she knows what I did. But then she speaks again.

"I know about you and our father."

And then she looks away.

CHAPTER THIRTY-THREE

Cassie

Wednesday, July 18th

When Dante Alighieri wrote about the nine circles of hell in the *Divine Comedy* he forgot about one. It comes right after Treachery. It's bright and white—a deceitful detail, one that people associate with heaven—filled with the rhythmic sounds of oxygen machines and the quiet beeps of electronic devices. It tricks you into letting your guard down, fools you into thinking that you're safe. That's how *evil* it is.

The tenth circle of hell is called a hospital.

Nurses. Doctors. Staff. All of them wearing uniforms, some with name tags and caps and special equipment around their necks. To some—those who don't know better—this is a comforting sight. It means that *things are going to be OK*. It means an army of people are here to help you. To keep you safe.

To me, it's the opposite. It's despair.

I avoid hospitals like the plague. But when I do come, I'm on high alert. I pay attention to everything that's said to me, take note of every medication prescribed. I even record my conversations with the doctors.

I can handle being at a hospital to support my loved ones. I was there for Daniel when he had his not-quite heart attack. And when Christina had appendicitis.

But I cannot be here as a patient. Not when all I have is Julie.

Never mind that she's too focused on herself to pay attention to anything of consequence—the nurse who checked my blood pressure could've sedated me and she wouldn't have noticed—or that she can't drive. The worst part is putting up with her wounded-bird routine. Typical Julie: making everything about her.

Thank God the doctor is a no-nonsense woman. The last thing I need is an inexperienced, pimple-faced idiot who spends his time drooling over Julie.

Why is this room so small? My thoughts are jumbled. I'm hyperventilating. I don't want to be here. My ankle is fine. Except it's not. I knew it wasn't when the words *take me to the hospital* came out of my mouth.

I am trying my best to stay calm, to steady myself, but how can I when Julie is being narcissistic, saying this isn't her fault? As if I've accused her of twisting my ankle with her bare hands. I want to scream at her. But I don't. She is so self-absorbed. I'm not spelling it out for her.

But she presses on, calls me impolite. And I snap, revealing what I know about her and our father. A jolt of fear flashes through her eyes, but it only lasts a second. Soon, she's performing again. Pretending.

"What are you talking about?" She stares at me blankly. Her acting skills are impressive. "What about dad?"

"Just shut up. The last thing I want is to deal with the two of you here."

A startled look. I expect her to turn around and leave. But then she frowns, confused. She throws her designer purse on a metal chair and walks over to me. Now, her hand is on my forehead.

"What are you doing?"

"I think you hit your head or something." Her tone is soft.

I swat her hand away. "I didn't hit my head."

"You must've hit something. You're not making any sense. Dad isn't here, Cassie."

"Christ, how long are you going to keep this up?" My breathing is labored, my head throbbing. But I can't stop now. "I heard you talking to him earlier. And I saw him here. I know he's on the island."

"What are—" But she doesn't get to finish her sentence because a nurse walks in. My eyes dart to his name tag—*Jenkins*. He looks efficient. Short, African-American, buzz cut, sensible shoes, no smile (happy people are inefficient people).

"Miss Meyers, we need to get you into X-ray."

I nod. Another nurse is behind him with a wheelchair. I hate those almost as much as I hate hospitals. I shut my eyes, just for a second, just so I don't lose it. I will *not* think of that night.

I see Julie gripping her fingers into the fabric of the bed. I see it happening: her brain finally rotating its cogs. She understands. In a second, her face is flooded with pity.

"Cassie," she whispers. "I'm sorry. I should've known…"

"Is everything OK?" the nurse asks.

"Everything's fine," I tell Nurse Jenkins.

"Can I come with her?" Julie asks, looking at Nurse Jenkins with watery eyes.

If she starts crying, I'll punch her in the face.

Nurse Jenkins nods, then helps me into the wheelchair. I have to give him credit for not staring at Julie like a panting dog.

"It's fine," I tell her.

"Please. I want to come. I didn't realize. I'm an idiot."

I'm not about to disagree with that.

Our eyes meet. It's all spelled out on her face. The sympathy, the sadness.

She remembers that day as clearly as I do.

CHAPTER THIRTY-FOUR

Julie

It was supposed to be a happy day. I was Cassie's first call on the Tuesday she got the letter.

"I got in!" she cried on the other end of the line. There was no need to specify where she got in—and not just because we spoke in the shorthand of sisters. It was The Dream.

We were both going to Boston University.

"Sophie is saying I'll have to live at home," I told her. It had been two days since Sophie had relayed this bit of information to me. I had cried and cursed—but I hadn't told anyone yet, not even Cassie. It felt wrong to tell her before I knew if she'd been accepted to BU. Besides, I didn't want to make it real. I have no idea why I chose that moment to break the news. Cassie's moment.

She asked me why. The obvious answer didn't even occur to her. It never did.

"Boarding is too expensive."

"Can't you talk to our father?"

It was a subject that roamed around us like dust motes sparkling in the sunlight, barely visible but always there. Katherine's family came from money. Most of what Cassie had—the colonial house on Dover, the flashy cars, the trust fund—came from her mother. Daddy made a nice living, but he also had his own expensive tastes. I'd gotten into BU on a scholarship. Not a full ride, but enough that it helped. Dad and Sophie had set aside some money for me, too. But the bulk of my tuition would be coming from student loans.

"He's already helping out with tuition."

"Shoot," she muttered. "I can try to—"

"No." I knew what she was going to offer, and I didn't want it. Cassie wouldn't have access to her trust fund until she was twenty-one. I really didn't want her going to her mother, making up some story about why she needed thousands of dollars.

"We could ask Nana?"

"Maybe," I said. But I knew I wouldn't. I didn't want to be the charity case. I had to fix this myself. "I'm looking into taking more loans."

The Dream was BU mostly because of Cassie. If it were up to me, we'd go to the opposite coast, to California or Oregon—far away from Sophie. But Cassie refused. She needed to be close to her mother. Katherine's mental health was precarious. I knew how much this conflicted Cassie: she resented her mother for not being able to take care of herself, but at the same time she felt a parent-like responsibility towards her.

Like I said: it was supposed to be a happy day. But I was in a funk.

"We'll figure something out," Cassie said. "It's The Dream."

It was. We came up with The Dream as children. It was simple: Cassie and I would go to the same school. Any good school in Boston would do. We'd finally get to share the same space year-round, like proper sisters. I am not exaggerating when I say that it's what kept me going all through high school.

"What do you say we celebrate on Thursday? I can meet you in the city. We'll go to Stephanie's." Cassie was so happy, she sounded like a bird chirping.

"Maybe." I knew I sounded like a big baby.

"Come on, Jul. We'll figure something out. You'll still get to go."

I was about to agree when I heard Katherine's voice in the background.

"Hold on, Mom," Cassie called out to her. "I'm on the phone with Mimi."

Mimi was my alias. If Katherine wanted to know where Cassie was going when she was out with me, she'd say Mimi. Mimi and Cassie were very good friends.

I heard Katherine mumble something to Cassie.

"I'd better go," Cassie said. "Don't let this get to you. It'll all work out. It always does." She hung up.

I was mad at Cassie. It was completely irrational of me, but I was devastated. The idea of living with Sophie during my college years sounded as appealing as being dropped into a pot of water and being slowly boiled to death. I expected more sympathy from Cassie. We didn't have the same mom, but she'd always understood what it feels like to want—no, to *need*—to move out. Being stuck with Sophie for another four years, maybe more, meant that everything would continue to be about her. Her house. Her rules. Her life.

It was all Katherine's fault. If Katherine weren't so intent on staying married to Dad even though *she didn't love him*, none of our problems would exist. My mom would be married to my dad. Cassie would probably come live with us—Katherine was *not* fit to be a single parent. Nana would have to welcome my mom into the family. Katherine was responsible for everything that was wrong with my life. Katherine and her stupid money. The money she used to control our dad.

I crawled into bed to take a nap. For once, I didn't tell myself to snap out of it. Didn't force myself to be cheery and optimistic. It felt freeing, allowing myself to indulge in my own resentment for a while. I'd spent far too long using other people—Sophie, my dad, Cassie, even Nana—as my emotional barometers. If they were happy, then I was happy.

Well, I wasn't happy.

I was happy *for Cassie*, of course. Happy she got into BU and that we'd be able to go to the same school. But if I had to live at home, then, no—I wasn't going to be happy. I was going to be upset. I was going to sulk. Like any normal teenager.

Looking back, that's what undid me: allowing myself to feel. My heart took over—my brain was replaced as the driver. And hearts are irrational, fickle things.

That's when Sophie called. She'd forgotten to pay the phone bill. Again. Could I do it? It wasn't really a question. When I stormed into her room to find the stupid paper with the stupid barcode so I could go to the stupid bank and pay the stupid bill, I wasn't just sad or angry. I was done.

The first picture I saw on Sophie's nightstand was of my dad looking at her as she smiled to the camera. Her lips were slightly parted, caught in the moment before her smile turned into a grin. Her dark hair was loose against the wind. She looked so happy, at ease. And Dad looked like what he was: a man in love. Anyone who saw that picture would immediately understand they belonged together. That their love was real. Meant to be. I was the fruit of that love—of the passion I knew they shared.

It wasn't fair that Katherine got to have Dad as a proper husband while Sophie had to settle for a life of sneaking around. Sophie made him happier than Katherine ever could. I knew that because all Cassie talked about was her parents' unhappy marriage. She sometimes contemplated telling Katherine about Dad and Sophie—but she was afraid her mother would hate her.

It was such a waste. If Katherine knew about Sophie, she'd kick Dad out of the house. He'd be upset, but only for a minute. He'd move in with Sophie and they'd find a way to pay for room and board in college, because if there's one thing those two loved, it was being alone. As their daughter, I was constantly being asked to "go to the store" because they wanted the place for themselves.

The idea hit me like a virus: taking up all the space, eating away any trace of common sense and restraint inside me. It happened when I was going through Sophie's desk, looking for the bill, and accidentally knocked off her memory box. It was heart-shaped and red, filled with pictures of our family. There must have been at least one hundred snapshots of us throughout the years. I bent over to scoop them up, happy faces staring at me.

Me as a little girl on Daddy's shoulders, feeding the ducks at the park. Dad and Sophie posing in front of the Eiffel Tower. The three of us at the aquarium. Dad and me at Cheers on Government Center—Sophie had taken the picture. Dozens of snapshots of holidays, most of them—all of them, I think—celebrated on the wrong day: Christmas on the twenty-sixth, Easter one full week before. All so Dad could be there with us. We looked so freaking *happy*.

The smiling faces on those pictures made me even angrier. Like being drunk, only I'd consumed fury—not alcohol. I wanted this happiness to be known, to be acknowledged. The three of us, we were a *family*.

I yanked an envelope from Sophie's drawer, wrote down Katherine's name and address on it, my grip on the pen so strong it almost dug its way through the envelope. I grabbed a handful of pictures, stuffed them inside the envelope, and stormed out the house, fueled by my determination not to be invisible anymore.

I don't remember if I stopped by the post office before or after the bank.

Two days later, Katherine was dead.

CHAPTER THIRTY-FIVE

Cassie

My mom was already dead when the paramedics burst into our house.

She was found lying on the living room floor next to an empty bottle of pills she'd taken hours before, but they still took her to the hospital. It was protocol.

I'd been out since early in the morning—I left my house before my mother was up. After school, I went to the mall with some friends, and then I met up with Julie. My father called me when we were at my favorite restaurant, Stephanie's, on Newbury Street. It was our celebratory dinner. I remember Julie being worried about money to pay for room and board. I was, too. It seems like such a small thing now.

At first, my brain didn't register what my father was saying. *Come to the hospital. It's your mother.*

When I told Julie what happened, she froze. I had to do it all by myself: get up, call a server, pay the bill. All while Julie stared at me with an expression of dread. I was used to being the one in charge, but I needed her then. I needed her to step up. She only got up when I shook her—literally. We got in a cab and rushed to the hospital.

When we got there, Julie was asked to wait at reception. Only family was allowed inside, a nurse explained. It says a lot about my mental state that I didn't pick a fight with the nurse, that I didn't set him straight, telling him that Julie was *absolutely* family, even if she wasn't related to my mom. I saw my father sitting on the floor outside a room. His knees were bent, his head was almost between his legs, a version of the fetal position that made his large frame seem shrunken to the point of irrelevance. The doctor came out of nowhere and told us they'd done everything they could. My mom had taken too many pills. Strong pills. They'd been in her system too long. At first, I didn't understand that he'd meant on purpose. I kept asking him how many pills she took—she always took more than normal anyway. Surely there was something they could do. But then he explained that it was an entire bottle. And I knew: she had done it on purpose. She'd wanted to die.

I screamed, loudly. I also lunged at my father, asking what he'd done to make her want to take her own life. I remember someone grabbing me—nurses, maybe security—but not before I managed to scratch my father's cheek. His sobbing face now had an ugly red mark.

"He did this," I yelled. "He killed her."

They had to restrain me. I was put on a wheelchair and hurried away from my father, the grieving widower. I felt powerless, lost. I remember thinking this is how I'd feel for the rest of my life: trapped in a never-ending darkness. To this day, I can't see an empty wheelchair coming my way without my heart hammering inside my chest.

A social worker came to see me—a patronizing idiot. He kept saying it was only natural to look for someone to blame, but that the doctors were certain of their assessment: it had been a suicide.

But I knew better. I knew my father had done something to make her take those pills.

Eventually, they allowed Julie to see me. She wasn't related to my mother, so they hadn't filled her in on what happened. I told her everything, including how they had whisked me away on a wheelchair like I was some mental case.

"Cassie, I'm so sorry," she'd said, holding me in her arms, somehow managing to fold my gangly figure into her petite chest. "I never thought this would happen."

I didn't, either. I knew my mother was sick, but I never thought she was suicidal.

"Oh, Jul, what am I going to do?" My voice meek—grief squeezed my vocal cords.

I needed her to tell me that we'd get through this. That it was all going to be all right. It's funny how when tragedy strikes you want to hear those words, even though that's when they're the least true.

But Julie never said what I needed to hear. She was stunned, paralyzed to a freakish degree, almost like she'd just found out that *her* mom was dead. She didn't leave my side, but her presence did little to alleviate my pain. I knew she meant well, but she was too sensitive to be helpful in a crisis, too horrified by death, I suppose. When I told her to go home, she didn't refuse. I decided to go home, too—I didn't want to be around my father, and he had to stay behind at the hospital to take care of paperwork. I was even considering packing a bag and going to Julie's apartment. I'd rather be around Sophie than my father.

I saw the envelope as soon as I walked into the living room, torn open, dozens of pictures spilled on the floor. If I close my eyes, I can practically see the smiling shots of the family my father had in the city, so close—and yet so far—from our pretend idyllic suburban life. It's a tactile memory: my fingers can almost feel the glossy paper of frozen moments that proved that Sophie was more than a one-night stand. More than Julie's mother. Sophie was my father's second wife.

That was what my mother saw before she died.

Then I found her note. It was on my nightstand, under a duck-shaped crystal paperweight she'd given me when I turned fourteen. It had belonged to her mother. Next to it stood an empty orange bottle: Xanax, 2mg.

> I expected this from your father but I didn't expect this from you.

Beside the note was a picture of Julie and me, smiling inside Sophie's home.

I'd only been there once, on the day after that awful boy had assaulted Julie. Julie's eyes were red and puffy from crying, but I'd managed to make her laugh and her mother had taken a picture of us. Sophie had seemed so nice, normal. In my mind, she had been an exotic creature: half woman, half enchantress. Seeing her in her home had broken that spell. She wasn't exactly a regular mom—regular mothers do not offer cocktails to their daughter's friends. But she was a good one. That had been a surprise.

I never went there again. It felt wrong, somehow. But I liked seeing Julie's home.

That was what my mother had seen before she died. My betrayal.

How could I keep Julie in my life after that?

I know that the sins of the mother do not—or at least should not—pass on to the daughter. But how could I exchange words, be in the same room, share smiles, engage in any kind of interaction with someone who was related to the woman who gave my mom ammunition to take her own life? It was impossible. I could never forgive Sophie, which meant that I could never forgive Julie.

That day, eight years after gaining a sister, I lost her. Forever.

CHAPTER THIRTY-SIX

Julie

Wednesday, July 18th

We're on Old Town Road. I'm driving, but I'm too overwhelmed to be scared.

"Do you want to talk about it?" I ask.

I don't get a response, verbal or otherwise. Cassie sits motionless, staring out the window even though there's nothing to see but well-pruned trees and cookie-cutter houses with American flags waving in the breeze.

For once, I deserve her silence. I should've realized we were inside a hospital, should've anticipated how triggering that would be for her.

"I'm an idiot, Cassie," I say again. I've said this multiple times already, though if there's ever been a time to reiterate one's own idiocy it's when you fail to make the connection that your sister's mother died in a hospital. "I'm *really* sorry."

I see her shrugging from the corner of my eye. At least it's a reaction. People think I'm sweet. I hear it all the time: *Julie, you're such a sweet girl.* It's the silence. Being quiet makes people assume I don't feel the sorts of feelings that a *sweet girl* shouldn't. Rage. Jealousy. Resentment. But I'm only human. I was upset before—angry that Cassie was being rude to me. That anger kept me from realizing that Cassie was hurting, too.

My mind takes me back to a day, shortly after Katherine's death, when I was so consumed by guilt that I came to Montauk and announced to Nana that I was placing my life in her hands. I confessed right there on the spot—it was the most difficult thing I've ever done. With the exception of losing Cassie, nothing was more terrifying than the thought of Nana hating me. But I pushed through the fear and told her everything. Nana had done a very poor job of disguising her shock, but she was firm in her opinion that I should not, under any circumstance, tell Cassie. Not right then, anyway.

"But she'll know," I had told Nana. "When she sees me, she'll know I'm hiding something."

Back then, I still thought Cassie was just taking some time to herself. I had no idea she'd cut me off from her life for good. And neither did Nana.

"We'll tell her eventually. When the time is right. But if you tell her now…" Nana paused and shook her head sadly. "She just lost her mother. She can't lose you, too."

"But she thinks my mom did it," I said.

"Better that she be angry with your mother than with you. You're her sister."

The message was clear: in Nana's world, my mom was expendable. I knew that already, but it still hurt.

I've always wondered if I would have confessed if Cassie hadn't cut me out of her life. Part of me likes to think I would've done the right thing: come clean. But deep down I know better. I would've been too afraid of losing her. I've always been afraid of losing her—ironic, given how things unfolded.

But now is not the time to think about me. I need to focus on Cassie. She's wounded, physically (her ankle) and emotionally (memories of the hospital). Also, I'm worried she hit her head, despite her insistence that she hasn't.

"Will you consider getting your head checked later on?" I've looked up signs of a concussion on my phone, but I don't want to tell her that. The only thing she dislikes more than doctors are wannabe doctors.

"Why do you keep asking me that?"

"Do you remember what you said about me and Dad?"

"Of course I do," she snaps. "Are you telling me it's all in my head? I saw him."

"Where did you see him?" My tone is patronizing. I can't help it.

"On Main Street. About two weeks ago."

I frown. I expected her to say at the hospital.

Wait—has she really seen Dad?

"Of course I have," she tells me when I ask her.

"Did you talk to him?"

She lets out a snort that tells me the idea of speaking to our dad is preposterous.

"But you're sure it was him?"

She narrows her eyes at me, studying me like the psychologist that she is. "You really expect me to believe you don't know he's here? I heard you on the phone today."

I pause at a stop sign and look both ways even though no cars are coming. Intersections are the scariest part about driving. "I talked to him on the phone, yes."

"And he wasn't here? In Montauk?" Her tone is a challenge.

"Of course not. He'd tell me if he were. He hasn't been here in years."

I ignore the voice that's asking me if he really would tell me. He's my dad. He's not mushy and sentimental, but he wouldn't hide from me.

"Whatever." She wiggles in her seat, wincing in pain. I'm glad that her ankle isn't broken—the ultrasound revealed it to be a high-grade ligament tear—but I still wish she'd accepted the painkillers.

"Why would I keep something like that from you?"

"I have no idea. But you're obviously hiding *something*."

I feel a cold rush down my spine. "I'm pulling over."

I find a shoulder off Hampton Road that looks quiet enough. I expect her to protest, to demand I take her home, but she just stares at me blankly.

"To the best of my knowledge, Dad isn't here. I'll call him if you want." I pick up my phone and thumb my way to his contact.

She doesn't stop me when I call him on speaker. It goes to voicemail after five rings.

"Hi, Daddy, it's me," I pause when I see her roll her eyes. "Just wanted to say that I loved talking to you earlier today and that I'm happy to hear that you enjoyed fishing. I hope things are good in Seattle." I give Cassie a knowing look. "And that we can meet up in Boston when summer is over, like we discussed."

She scoffs when I say I love him and hang up.

"It's not my fault it went to voicemail. You know how Dad is."

"Mercifully, I'm beginning to forget," she mumbles.

"He isn't here. You saw someone else."

"I know what I saw," she tells me.

"Why would he be here and not tell me?"

She draws in her breath and then releases it heavily before saying "Why does he do any of the things he does?"

"I'm not lying to you." I look her straight in the eye even though she is avoiding my gaze.

"Fine," she says. "Then why did he buy your favorite flowers? And why were you humming his favorite song? And—" she pauses and looks at me in disgust. "Never mind."

I blink rapidly as her questions hit me like angry bullets. "OK," I say, holding my palms up. "I have no clue what flowers you're talking about and what song was I even humming? I don't even *know* Dad's favorite song."

She stares at me, no doubt hoping that if she engulfs me with enough silence I'll cave and tell her everything. Well, there isn't anything to tell. Not about Dad, anyway.

"My life is none of your business," she says all of a sudden.

OK, it's official. She hit her head and is losing it.

"I know that," I say, slowly. "Would you like me to try Dad again?" I hold up my phone.

"No," she says. A moment later, she hesitates, like she's reconsidering. But she doesn't say anything else.

"Fine." I turn the car back on, hoping she'll stop me so we can actually talk about what happened.

But hope is futile.

This is Cassie: master bottler of emotions. Angry silence is her comfort zone.

CHAPTER THIRTY-SEVEN

Cassie

Wednesday, July 18th

It's not my fault she's too stupid to password-protect her phone.

The idea came to me when she offered to call our father for the second time. I watched her unlock her phone with a faint swipe of a finger—nothing more. No password required, no touch ID. Like I said: a genius.

It's almost too easy to snatch her phone. She is staring fixatedly at the road, her neck as stiff as steel.

"I don't want to argue anymore." The words spill out of my mouth quickly. Too quickly. "I'd like to clear the air between us. Maybe we could start over."

The naked relief in her eyes is almost too much to bear.

"Watch the road." I look away.

"Sorry," she says, tightening her grip on the steering wheel. And then: "I want that, too."

"OK. Can we go by King Kullen? If I'm going to be on bed rest, I need chocolate."

She shoots me a surprised look. Did I sound too eager? "Sure."

If our father's intention really is to steal my share of the house, I don't think she's in on it. Julie is many things—dishonest isn't one of them. He must not have told her about his plan. He must've asked her to keep quiet about him being on the island for some other reason.

Minutes later, she pulls up in front of the market. I act as though I'm getting out of my seat, but then I wince, a bit too theatrically. Thankfully, Julie does not seem to notice my subpar performance.

"Maybe I should go." She looks at me expectantly.

"Would you mind?"

She flashes me a grateful smile. I almost feel guilty. Almost. Now is not the time to be sentimental. I need to focus on the task at hand, to find out what she knows. I take out a pen from my bag and begin jotting down a lengthy shopping list.

I hand her the prescription and ask if she'd mind picking up a few other things for me, too. "Emergency essentials," I say. "I wrote them down on the back."

She does what I knew she'd do: agrees readily, one step away from clapping her seal hands in delight. I lock the car as soon as she leaves.

Let the snooping begin.

First things first: her texts. A thread with someone called P is top of the list—she's been ignoring their calls, whoever they are. I scroll up.

Today 7:31 A.M.
I spoke with your mother. She agrees this behavior is completely unacceptable. You are to return to Boston right now.

Today 7:41 A.M.
Do you hear me?

Today 7:59 A.M.
Answer me.

Today 8:01 A.M.
Please don't talk to my mother about me

Today 8:02 A.M.
What else am I supposed to do when my wife is acting like a lunatic? Is this all for a baby? Or because of the day you fainted?

Today 8:02 A.M.
How am I acting like a lunatic?

Today 8:04 A.M.
You hung up on me yesterday. You've been ignoring my calls. Do you expect me to go to Tammy's book launch by myself? What's this about?

Today 8:05 A.M.
This is about wanting ME back. I'm feeling like myself again.

Today 8:06 A.M.
Are you saying you're not yourself with me?

Today 8:10 A.M.
How can I be?

Today 8:11 A.M.
You tell me what to wear, what to eat, how to act. You don't want me to be anything other than your wife. Not even a mom. Do you have any idea how it feels, being married to someone who doesn't want children with you?

Today 8:12 A.M.
You've lost your mind.

> *Today 8:13 A.M.*
> *No, I may have found it.*
> *And I'm not blaming you. I let you change me.*

Today 8:14 A.M.
What are you saying?

> *Today 8:15 A.M.*
> *I'm saying I want more out of my life.*
> *I want a baby. And an occupation of my own.*

Today 8:17 A.M.
I didn't see you complaining when I took you out of your working-class neighborhood and brought you to Beacon Hill.

Today 8:25 A.M.
You better be really sure about what you're doing.

> *Today 8:26 A.M.*
> *Do you even miss me?*
> *Or are you just angry I came here*
> *even though you told me not to?*

Today 8:27 A.M.
I won't dignify that with an answer.

> *Today 8:28 A.M.*
> *You just did*

Today 8:29 A.M.
Don't expect me to be here when you come to your senses.

Today 8:45 A.M.
I just called you. Pick up.

Today 9:15 A.M.
Pick up the phone.

Today 9:48 A.M.
Don't bother calling me back. I'm done with you.

Today 1:36 P.M.
Why aren't you taking my calls?

P is Patrick, her husband. He seems awful—though I know better than to jump to conclusions based on a few texts. Besides, if he could see Julie and Craig making eyes at each other he'd be devastated. I wonder, not for the first time, why Patrick hasn't been to the island on weekends.

I scan their earlier messages. There aren't a lot of them. Nothing about me, let alone my relationship with Daniel. And nothing about our father, either.

Time to move on to other threads. Her contact list seems to be made up mostly of single letters: J, N, L. One of them catches my eye: Tricia the B. Is that intentional? It's certainly amusing. Then I see it: Sophie. Julie and her mom exchange *a lot* of messages. The most recent one alone is so long it takes up the entire screen. I scroll up.

I stop when I see my name.

Today 8:15 A.M.
Please stop talking to Patrick about me.
You're only making him angrier.

Today 8:55 A.M.
Did you get the information on Cassie?

Today 8:59 A.M.
Are you blackmailing me??????

Today 9:09 A.M.
Don't be dramatic. I asked you a simple question. How is that blackmail?

Today 9:12 A.M.
Because I asked you a question and you brought up the Cassie thing

Today 9:20 A.M.
I brought it up because people here are getting impatient. Tell Patrick why you really went there and he will understand and forgive you. He may even visit you.

Today 9:22 A.M.
I am not here to spy on Cassie!!! LET IT GO

Today 9:24 A.M.
Are you really going to choose her over your own mother? Do you want me to lose my job?

Today 9:25 A.M.
Just tell me if it's true or not. Does she have a boyfriend? Is he married? If you get me his name, I'll find out the rest.

Today 9:30 A.M.
No boyfriend. Not even dating anyone.

Today 9:31 A.M.
Are you sure?

> *Today 9:41 A.M.*
> *100%. I know what someone who's*
> *having an affair looks like, remember?*

Today 9:42 A.M.
Maybe she's good at hiding.

> *Today 9:43 A.M.*
> *I live with her. Her girlfriends came to town and talked*
> *about girls' night out, being single, etc.*
> *She's also never on her phone.*

Today 11:12 A.M.
If you're lying to me, I'll find out. It may take a while but
I will. If there's a story, someone is going to come out with
it and then I'll be out of a job and what good will that
do? You should think about your actions, think about your
priorities. You're burning bridges, Julie. Burning them with
your husband and with your own mother. Is that really the
kind of person you want to be? Who will you have left if
you don't have Patrick or me? What will you do without
your husband? Women like you can't be on your own. Trust
me, I know.

So it was Sophie.

CHAPTER THIRTY-EIGHT

Julie

Wednesday, July 18th

It's like being inside one of my fairy tales.

An evil spell has been broken. Well, maybe not broken. But her heart has definitely started to melt. She asked if we could start over. Then she asked for help. I know how hard that is for her. It's what she struggles with: showing vulnerability. It feels incredible, miraculous.

It feels like magic.

The Ice Princess has planted a seed of hope in the Sky Princess's heart.

Should she go back to being the Fire Princess?

I'm scanning the shelves for Double Stuf Oreos—I resent the deliberate misspelling, but Cassie has been very specific in her requests—when I hear familiar voices chatting animatedly down the aisle.

I turn around and I see them. Kiki and Ben.

"Julie!" They run towards me. A cuddly bear hug comes next.

"This is the best surprise," I say.

"Hey, stranger," Craig says, a warm smile on his face. "Are you following us?"

"Hey," I say. I don't know how to greet him. A handshake seems too formal, a hug too affectionate.

"We went to Ditch Plains. I'm learning how to surf," Ben says. He looks adorable in a pair of yellow shorts and a blue T-shirt that says: IF HISTORY REPEATS ITSELF, I'M GETTING A DINOSAUR.

"That's amazing, Ben!"

"Julie, will you come home with us?" Kiki asks. "We need to finish the you-know-what." She gives me a conspicuous wink.

"Kiki!" Ben exclaims, shushing her.

"What are you three hiding?" Craig asks.

"It's a birthday surprise for you, Daddy!" Kiki says.

"All right, we've already said too much," I say. Poor Ben is looking like he might have a seizure—he doesn't want to ruin the surprise.

"You came all the way here for groceries?" Craig asks me.

I tell him about Cassie's sprained ankle. And about my driving debacle.

"That's too bad," he says. "An injury in the middle of summer."

"Does that mean you can't come back with us?" Ben looks at me with his big eyes.

"Of course I can," I tell him. "I just need to get Cassie home first. Make sure she has everything she needs."

Craig lifts his eyebrows in surprise.

"We're starting over," I say. "Clearing the air between us." I borrow Cassie's words.

"Was this because of Mandy's reading?"

"You did know she was coming," I say, grinning.

"I was sworn to secrecy," he says. And then: "I'm happy you two are working it out." His tone is warm, sincere. I can tell he's genuinely happy for me. Probably happy for Nana, too. This is what she wanted.

"I'll fill you in later."

"Dad says we can watch a movie," Ben announces.

"*Frozen 2!*" Kiki exclaims.

"No!" Ben puts his hands on his waist. "We said *Sonic*."

"Julie likes *Frozen*," Kiki says.

"She prefers *Sonic*," Ben counters.

"No fighting. Or Julie won't want to hang out with us," Craig says.

Kiki, ever the diplomat, changes the subject. "Julie, how come there aren't any movies about your stories?"

"I don't know, honey. I'll call Hollywood and find out."

"Will you tell us another one tonight?" Ben asks.

"Of course," I say.

"I should record your stories, so I don't have to do movie-night mediation," Craig says. "We should go. You'll stop by after you go home?"

"Deal." I smile when I hear him refer to Nana's house as home.

Ben and Kiki lean in to give me kisses. They're so loving, so affectionate.

As I wave goodbye, I have to bite the inside of my cheek.

Otherwise my smile might break my jaw.

CHAPTER THIRTY-NINE

Cassie

Wednesday, July 18th

I go through it all. Emails, pictures, messages.

I no longer have a credible reason to be snooping. I already know it was Sophie. I should've known: Sophie is a shameless gossip with a faulty moral compass. At least Julie has lied to cover for me. This realization comes as a relief, but not as a surprise. Julie is gullible and careless, but she isn't cruel. And I've found no evidence that Julie has seen our father on the island.

Still, I read it all. I'm like a hungry Pac-Man devouring pellets of information on her phone. My curiosity is not a want—it's a need. I need to know more. I force my brain to shut down, to process the phone's contents later. Right now, my mission is to gather data. I know I'm crossing a line. A significant one. This is a major invasion of her privacy. But it's also a window into Julie's world. I can't *not* look. I don't think I realized how curious I was about her life until now.

It's astounding how much of our lives are on our phones.

Most of it has nothing to do with Daniel and me. Dozens of pictures of two kids, probably Craig's, grinning for the camera. A list of random names separated into two columns: boy and girl. I check her social media: Facebook, Instagram. I find nothing but articles she shared and scenic pictures of Boston. Emails: from designer brands (promotions), from Tricia the B (discussing a fundraiser), from Norman-the-lawyer (checking in on us—I got them, too).

But some of it does: a lengthy text exchange with Janette, listing reasons why Julie should investigate Sophie's claim and then write a story exposing me as a marriage counselor who is dating a married man. Julie keeps telling her no. I read it all, hungrily, quickly.

And then I see it. The stories.

It would be impossible to read all of them. But I know what they are, I remember how she began making them up when we were just kids. In grad school, I learned that this tendency had a name—absorption, a trait that's highly correlated to fantasy-prone personality—and that it isn't altogether uncommon. Has she been weaving stories since then? I want to know what they're about. I find myself trying to grasp the basic plot of the most recent one.

It's about two sisters who've lost each other—and their powers—because of an evil curse. All they have from their former magical life is a sun stone that was broken in two: each sister wears her half around her neck. The curse is broken when they meet on Fort Pond Bay at sunset, notice their matching medallions, and bring the two pieces together.

I gasp when I read the last paragraph.

> Of course, it was never about the sun stone. The two sisters' strength—their powers—lay in their unity. Together, they became whole. They became magic.

It's a more poetic version of what Nana used to say. I first heard it during the summer I met Julie, back when I still referred to her as my half-sister. Nana would correct me every time. *There are no halves in families,* she'd say. *Only wholes that, when brought together, make magic. You two are stronger together.*

Nana was a very special woman. Sensitive but strong. Intuitive but rational. Maybe she really was the best of Julie and me in one person.

I scan some of the shorter stories. They're fantasies, of course. But the story about the sun stone was obviously about Nana—and me. By that logic, these other tales—about a king who controls his queen like a doll, about a fairy who longs for a baby but has been cursed—hold a grain of truth, as well.

My chest is aching—guilt, no doubt. I'm spying on a woman who has shown me nothing but kindness. But there's something else stirring inside me. A deep sadness. Julie's life seems so lonely, so utterly hopeless.

I look up from the phone. And then my heart stops.

Julie is standing outside the car, staring at me, mouth agape.

CHAPTER FORTY

Julie

Wednesday, July 18th

"Are you *kidding* me?" I say. "You were going through my phone?"

Cassie rolls the window down. "Let me explain."

"Explain?" I drop my shopping bags. A box of cookies falls on the asphalt. I don't care. I open my palm. "Give it back."

She complies.

That's when I realize what she'd been doing before.

"That's why you asked me to stop here," I say. "So you could snoop. You *planned* this." The nonsensical questions, the strange way she was acting, pretending to have seen Dad. The peace offering, the fresh start. All lies.

The Ice Princess takes off her mask. Underneath her creamy, freckled skin is an evil witch: moss green, covered in blisters and scabs. She isn't a princess at all. The spell can't be broken. She is forever changed, forever cursed.

I've been such a fool. Why did I think we could go back to the way we used to be?

"I'm sorry," she says.

"Why?" I ask. "Why do this?"

She exhales deeply. "Because of what you said about…my relationship. With Daniel. About him being married. I needed to know how you knew." To her credit, she looks ashamed. But I know better than to believe her. It's all an act. Again.

So that's what this is about. She's afraid for her own reputation. She thinks I'll sell her story to the tabloids. Call her on national television and out her. Expose her on social media. That's the kind of person she thinks I am: dirty, deceiving. A traitor.

And she doesn't even know. She doesn't even know my secret.

"You're a psycho," I say, through gritted teeth. I think of the contents of my phone. The personal, sensitive information in there. I feel vulnerable, exposed. "You had no right."

"I deserve that." She looks wounded. And then: "I read your messages to your mom. Thank you. For keeping my secret."

I feel my face burn. How much has she read? Those were private exchanges.

And I wonder if she realizes she's just revealed that Daniel really is married.

"You could have just asked me."

"I didn't think I could trust you." A pause. "I was wrong. I'm really sorry, Jul."

I feel a pull inside my chest. *Jul.* She's the only one who's ever called me that.

"How could you, Cassie?" I say, under my breath. I throw her car keys inside the car. They land on the floor, where I know she'll have a hard time reaching, but I don't care. She begins to say something, but I hold up my palm like a stop sign. "Figure out a way to drive yourself home," I say. "I'm done with you."

And I walk away.

CHAPTER FORTY-ONE

Cassie

Wednesday, July 18th

I could have lied. I realize that now.

I could've said that her phone rang, and I picked it up.

No, that wouldn't work—I wasn't holding it against my ear.

Maybe I could've said that Norman-the-lawyer's app started beeping. That I unlocked her phone to check that everything was OK, to protect our inheritance. Or that I was admiring her screensaver. Anything would've been better than the truth, than admitting to such a massive invasion of her privacy.

Still, a part of me is relieved. Maybe I didn't lie because I can't. Not anymore.

My phone buzzes. I look down, hoping it's either Daniel (I've texted him, but he's in a meeting) or Triple A (I've called them and was informed I'd have to wait an hour for a tow truck). But no, it's just another email from Claudia. The subject reads *Good Morning America*. I can't think about work, not now. I wish I were back at Nana's.

I didn't expect Julie to leave me here. Not that I don't deserve it.

I know I've been distant towards her since we got here. Unkind, even. But what was I supposed to do—act like we haven't been estranged for the past fourteen years? That wouldn't have made any sense. It's been too long. People move on. People change.

Except Julie hasn't changed. She's still loyal. Still kind.

Even though I've done nothing to deserve it.

Even though all those years ago I chose to sever contact with both my father and Julie.

When it comes to my father, I have zero regrets. He's an abusive, narcissistic man who tormented my mother and, by extension, me. But with Julie it was different. For the longest time, I *missed* her. Learning to live without her was almost like learning to live without a limb. Sometimes, in the beginning, I'd pick up the phone to call her. I once dialed her number. But I never actually made the call. And not only because I felt guilty or because I wanted to punish myself.

I never reached out because a part of me thought she was better off.

Seeing her here confirmed my theory. From the outside, she looked like she had achieved everything she had ever wanted: a stable marriage, financial freedom. A charmed life. A happy life.

But now I think of those stories, the ones on her phone. Every single one of them had a heartbroken, disillusioned heroine. Could she really be that lonely?

Could she really miss me?

CHAPTER FORTY-TWO

Julie

Wednesday, July 18th

Craig holds out his hand when I walk in, a sheepish smile on his face. He's looking into my eyes with an expression of delight. The hand is obviously meant for me, though I don't know why. He's never done this before. Maybe I'm dreaming.

I take his hand. It's electric, it's familiar. For a moment, I forget that Cassie has hurt me. I forget about everything except for his touch, his warmth. If this is what it feels like to hold his hand, it's possible I'll go up in flames when we share our first kiss.

When?

He leads me into the family room. We sit on the couch. The door is open. Kiki and Ben are in the living room, playing with Legos. This shouldn't feel romantic, but it does.

"I have something for you. But you have to promise you won't be mad at me." He's smiling bashfully, but there's a hint of worry in his eyes, too.

"I could never," I say. This is true.

He reaches behind the blue cushion. I watch him take out an envelope.

"This is from your grandmother."

I can feel my face falling, my eyebrows furrowing. I see him register my confusion.

He continues, "She asked me to give this to you and Cassie once you started getting along. I didn't think it would take this long, to be honest."

I hesitate for a moment. It isn't true that Cassie and I are getting along. I still haven't told Craig about her tricking me. Feeling curious, I take the turquoise-blue envelope. It's good quality stock; thick, buttery.

"All this time you've…kept this from me?"

"Bertie made me promise. I keep my promises. This was months ago, when she changed her will. Neither of us expected her to pass away so soon after that. But you know how she was. She liked being prepared."

Like Cassie, I think. She and Nana were both planners: organized, efficient.

"It broke her heart, knowing that you two were estranged."

"I know." My finger grazes the sealed flap as I take in the full weight of his statement. Craig doesn't know this yet, but Nana's heart is still broken.

"She wanted you and Cassie to open it together."

It occurs to me that this might not be possible now. I haven't told him about Cassie's stunt with my phone, about the fact that I left her stranded in the middle of a parking lot. If I do, will he try to take the letter back?

"Have you read it?" I ask.

"No." He shakes his head. "I don't think anyone has, except Bertie."

"Then I need to read it first."

"Why?"

Because Nana knew my secret. Because it's possible she wrote about it in this letter—not likely, but possible. And because Cassie can never find out.

"Do you know why Cassie and I don't talk to each other?"

"I know what Bertie told me," he says. "It happened after Cassie's mom found out that your dad and your mom were... together. She killed herself, didn't she? Cassie didn't handle it very well. Bertie said she became distant with her...with everyone."

"Katherine found out about the affair," I say. "But it was more than that. She found out Cassie knew. Someone sent her pictures of my mom and my dad throughout the years, at my house. Pictures that showed we were a family, too. And in one of those pictures, Cassie was at my apartment with me. You could even see a little bit of my mom because she was standing in front of a mirror. Katherine had no idea we were even friends."

"How could she not know?"

"We were both good liars," I say. "We had to be. Or else we couldn't have been sisters. Katherine wouldn't have understood. She was really sick."

"She had to be, to do what she did." He pauses. "Did your mom send the pictures?"

"No," I say. A one-two punch: first relief, then dread. I know I have to tell him. I knew it the second I held the envelope from Nana.

It's not the answer he expected. I can tell he's trying to hide his surprise.

I take a deep breath. Once I confess, it'll all be different. He'll never again cup his hand in mine. We won't share our first kiss. He probably won't want me to babysit his children again. Still, I have to come clean. I might be angry at her, but I'd still rather lose him than Cassie. I'd rather lose anyone than Cassie. "I did."

He frowns, searching my face for signs of misunderstanding.

"I sent those pictures," I say again. "And my grandmother knew. So if she wrote about it, Cassie can't see it."

A silence falls between us. I lower my head, my eyes on the rug. I can't bear to see the look on his face, whatever it is.

CHAPTER FORTY-THREE

Julie

Wednesday, July 18th

Cassie is waiting for me when I walk in the house.

"Jul, I crossed a line." She pulls herself up from the couch and takes lumbering steps towards me. "And I want you to know that I'm really sorry for—"

I lift an open palm. "What exactly did you do? Read my messages? My emails?"

"I read everything," she whispers, looking at her bandaged foot. I follow her gaze.

Does she expect me to feel sorry for her because she's injured? Well, I don't. Though I do want to ask if she's used the ointment I bought at the store. Her ankle does not look good—it's swollen and bruised. She should also take Advil. But I can't think about that now—I'm supposed to be upset with her. I *am* upset with her.

What does she mean by *everything*? Since leaving her at the parking lot, I've looked over my phone, trying to imagine what she now thinks of me. My life is a mess—and it shows. My mother is blackmailing me. My husband is emotionally unavailable and controlling.

And then, it hits me. My stories.

"Did you look through my notes?" I ask.

She nods quietly, pain and pity dancing behind her eyes. She really has read everything.

My face burns hot—I'm no longer angry, just embarrassed. It's like I told Craig: I don't have the right to be angry. I killed her mother.

Craig disagrees—he says I was just a kid when it happened, only seventeen, that I didn't mean to cause Katherine's death. That it was a foolish impulse, one for which I should forgive myself. He encouraged me to come clean, to tell Cassie everything. He's convinced that she'll find it in her heart to forgive me. I hadn't expected him to be so understanding. He really is kindness personified. But while I appreciate his words, I don't agree with them. There's no way Cassie will ever forgive me.

Which is why Cassie can't ever find out. And she won't. Craig and I steamed the letter open. It was his idea.

"Can we sit?" she asks.

I pick the armchair. She flops down on the couch, elevating her right ankle like the doctor recommended. I make a mental note to find Nana's ice pack.

"I made a mistake," she says.

"It's not just that you went through my phone. You lied to me."

"I know. But that's not the mistake I mean." She takes a deep breath. "I made a mistake when I told you I didn't want you in my life. Jul, I…I was in a dark place. A really dark place. It lasted a long time—years. I kept finding ways to punish myself because I blamed myself for my mom's death. And not being your sister, that was the biggest punishment of all. I've been in therapy because of it for years. I'm not making excuses, just offering context."

I swallow. She's saying all the things I've dreamed of hearing for the past fourteen years.

"I knew I was hurting *me* when I chose to stay away," she continues. "But I didn't think of how I was hurting you. All I can say for myself is that I'm a selfish idiot. You defended me, lied to your mom to protect me, wrote these beautiful stories about two girls and a magic necklace. And I repaid you by being awful."

I don't understand why she's getting up until she moves closer to me. Her hand is grazing my cheek, catching the tears that are falling. I hadn't noticed I was crying. I don't want her to see me like this. She's seen too much already.

"I'm so sorry." She cups my hand. I have orange nail polish on. Kiki and I applied it together. It's smudged and streaky—and I love it. "Please don't cry." The softness in her voice cracks something inside me. I thought this side of hers was gone. I thought she'd been hardened beyond recognition.

"I feel embarrassed. What you read, it was…really personal."

"I know. I had no right. I'm more sorry than you'll ever know."

That's not true. Regret is a stalker, following me wherever I go.

"Once I started, I couldn't stop," she says. "You became real to me again. I'd forced myself to think of you as a concept, not a person. You became the guilt I felt, the pain. The anger. But then I saw your phone and…I don't know. I saw my sister again."

I search her eyes. An alarm goes off in my mind—she sounds sincere, but she could be playing me again. I think back to what I told Craig: we're both good liars. We had to be.

But then it happens.

I look at Cassie and I see me. I see Nana. I see our summers together, our shared secrets, our childhood. I see us growing up, becoming young women, making plans to tackle the world, both of us unafraid because we had each other.

Her eyes. My eyes. They're finally open, almost like she lifted an additional lizard-like membrane. A protective layer. This is why she pretended not to see me. Why she yelled at me. It was fear. With Cassie, anger is a shield she puts up when she's afraid.

"Can we get past this?" she asks. "I want us to be…us again."

A slight nod from me. But I'm afraid, too.

"Yeah?" There's doubt in her tone. Uncertainty. It is very strange to hear Cassie uncertain about anything. "I understand if you need time," she says. "I don't expect us to, I don't know, braid each other's hair and play twenty-one questions."

Another nod from me. Though the truth is, I'd like that. There's so much I want to know. What's it like to be famous? Does she love her job as much as she seems to? How did she and Daniel meet? Why hasn't he left his wife? Is it because she doesn't want to get married? *Does* she still not want to get married? Who are her friends? What has she been up to?

Most of all, there's this: Has she missed me?

"What I'm trying to say," she continues, "is that I'd like to work on repairing our relationship. I want to prove Nana right in bringing us here, to put the past behind us. Start over as sisters with a clean slate."

A clean slate. A do-over. It's all I ever wanted. But it always felt like a dream.

"I want that, too," I say. A cowardly move, accepting her offer. She doesn't have all the facts, doesn't know the full story.

She moves in to hug me—and I let her. This is wrong. Spineless. I'm a wicked, despicable person for not telling her the whole truth.

But it's Cassie—my sister, my flesh and blood. My best friend.

I can deal with being wicked and despicable, as long as she's in my life.

And so I hug her back. I hear her low laugh, and then my own. When we part, she's doing something I haven't seen her do ever since she got here: she's smiling. I am, too—smiling and crying, feeling both relieved and terrified.

"There's something else," she says. "I really did see our father."

Wait—what?

"When?" I ask.

"Almost two weeks ago. Near The Fudge Company." A pause, she tilts her head. "He was buying sunflowers."

"Are you sure it was him?"

"Positive." She nods. "I thought the flowers were for you. They're your favorite."

They are, though I haven't gotten sunflowers in ages. Patrick always gives me roses or orchids. And I never buy flowers for myself. It's one of the things Sophie taught me.

"If Dad's here, then he didn't tell me." I don't add that I don't think he'd do that. She's probably mistaken. It's the downside of being so confident: it never occurs to Cassie that she could genuinely be wrong.

"I believe you," she says. There isn't a hint of skepticism in her tone. "But I know what I saw. And that was the same day that you got home singing his favorite song."

"I don't even know Dad's favorite song." I knew Cassie was a naturally suspicious person, but I had no idea she was this paranoid. And it's strange that she remembers Dad's favorite song. Maybe she imagined the whole thing.

"'The First Cut is the Deepest'," she says. "By Cat Stevens?"

A memory floats up. She's right: I *was* singing the song. I remember feeling overjoyed that I got to sing, to whistle.

"You remember," she says, reading me.

"Yeah." I nod slowly. "I was humming it because..." I stop myself.

"Because?" She narrows her eyes at me.

It's not just the song I remember. I remember where I heard it, too. It was on the day I started babysitting. The day Craig and I shared our first beers on the porch. The day he called me a storyteller.

"I heard it from Craig," I say. "He was singing it when he got home. He said he heard it from a friend he'd just seen."

CHAPTER FORTY-FOUR

Cassie

Wednesday, July 18th

Dear Cassie and Julie,

If you're reading this then it means that I've crossed over the rainbow bridge (Cassie, kindly stop rolling your eyes, just because you're an atheist doesn't mean we all have to be) and met my maker. It also means that my plan to bring you to the Hamptons for one final summer is working. Didn't see that one coming from your old grandmother, did you? Turns out I'm quite the master strategist! You both got your smarts from me, of course.

I'm predicting that you will receive this before the end of your first week at the house. I had the privilege of watching the two of you get to know each other as friends and as sisters. I saw the bond you forged and believe with every fiber in me that, while it may have gotten rusty with time, it is too strong to be broken.

Life is a beautiful but arduous journey. It tests us time and time again, until the very last day. It's filled with sorrow and disappointment, but, for the lucky ones, it is also filled with hope and joy. I believe the lucky ones are those who get to walk through life with a companion.

Sometimes this person is a spouse, like with your grandfather and me. Sometimes it's a friend. But more often than you'd expect, that person is a sibling.

Know that wherever I am—personally, I am rooting for a magical land with unlimited marrons glacés and port wine!—I am happy to know that you two have moved in the right direction.

Love,
Nana

P.S. Don't be mad at Craig. I asked him to keep this until he saw that you two showed signs of getting closer.

P.P.S. Julie, have the two of you fallen in love yet?

The letter is insulting. I say as much to Julie now.

"I thought it was sweet," Julie says, dabbing her eyes.

"It's manipulative, withholding information from us like that." I feel a sting, like the prick of a needle, only it covers my entire body. "Losing Nana was hard enough. I would've killed to have gotten this letter when I heard the news. To know that I'd still hear from her, in a sense." That's the thing about being an atheist: when someone is gone, they're gone. I know there is no afterlife with unlimited marrons glacés and port wine. I know I'll never see Nana again.

"You're not wrong," Julie says. "But wasn't it manipulative of her to bring us here?"

"Your point?"

A shrug. "Nana knows what she's doing."

I feel my shoulders drop. "I don't like it."

"Of course you don't." She smiles. "You love being in control. The irony is that you get that from Nana."

I can't argue with that. But even if I could, I don't want to. Ever since our hug, I've felt a dam breaking inside me. Feelings I'd kept sealed for over a decade rushed into my heart. I've missed her so much—I can't believe it took me this long to admit it. I don't want us to argue ever again. "So now what? We wait until the next one? Or do we get a clue, like in a treasure hunt?"

"Craig didn't say anything about other letters." She's pointed this out before.

"Mrs. Bunsen was very specific about there being letters. Plural." I've filled Julie in on my conversation with Mrs. Bunsen and my subsequent reading with Mandy. It was nice, telling her about it. I'd forgotten how much I missed sharing my life with her. I love Christina and Rachel, but it's different with Julie. She saw me grow up. Saw me becoming a fully formed person. It's been years—my fault, of course—but talking to her feels natural, like returning to my native country.

"Mrs. Bunsen has a touch of dementia," Julie says. She's chewing on a celery stick, her jaw making a satisfying crunching noise as she chews.

"Well, we have to ask Craig about it," I say. "If there are more letters, I want them now. Besides, don't you want to ask him about the song?" I certainly do. I've been suspicious about Craig from the start.

"It's a popular song."

I'm fairly certain it is *not* a popular song. I only know it because of how often my father listened to it on the old stereo system we had. I like the song—and not just because of its melody. Hearing it meant my father wasn't in a foul mood. It meant he probably wouldn't break anything that day.

"Craig clearly knows more than he's telling us."

"What would we even ask him?"

"'Have you seen our father?' and 'Are there other letters from Nana?'"

"What if waited a few days?" Her tone is pleading.

"What's this really about?" I ask. "Why don't you want to talk to him?" I soften my tone.

Julie chews on her bottom lip, her eyes darting. I know this look. I've seen it before.

"You like him," I say. It's not a question.

"I think I do." Her cheeks are now pink. "Please don't think less of me."

"Why would I think less of you?"

"I'm married."

"My boyfriend is married." I lower my gaze.

She leans in. "So what's the story there?"

"You first." There's so much I want to know, especially after reading her messages to her husband. I know her, but I also don't. I've missed fourteen years of her life. It would be easy to obsess over it, to spiral. But I force myself to stay present. And positive. Clean slate.

"Nothing's happened with Craig. But I think about it. More often than I should," she says. "I love my husband, but I'm not happy—Actually, I don't know if that's true. I don't know if I still love him."

I let the silence settle between us. She should share at her own pace.

"He's a good provider," she continues. "And he can be fun when we're out with other people. He's just very set in his ways. He's older than me, that could be it. And he's very…controlling. Maybe that word is harsh. I don't know. But he has these rules for how things should be…for how *I* should be. And if I don't follow them he retreats into silence. He doesn't scream at me or anything. There's no violence. But it still hurts. I feel lonely. And suffocated. It wasn't always this way. I mean, he was always very strict, but in the beginning…I don't know, I haven't really figured out if I had more patience, or if he had fewer rules." She sighs.

I rub my chin, thinking back to the messages I read on her phone. My invasion of her privacy has allowed me a small glimpse into her marriage—and from what I've seen it does not look good. I'd never say as much to Julie, not without listening to her first, but Patrick seems both unstable and tyrannical.

Julie must pick up on something in my face because she adds, quickly, "It's not all bad. As long as I do everything his way, he's very kind to me. And he tells me I'm beautiful all the time." A pause. "I know it sounds, I don't know, superficial. But it's nice to hear. It's nice to be wanted."

I wince. I did accuse her of being superficial, didn't I? Or something similar.

"I get it," I say. "And I'm sorry I said you were superficial."

"It was more of an implication."

"I'm sorry for implying, then. In fact, I'd like to apologize for the way I've been treating you. I was holding on to my anger. I guess I felt I had to. Or I'd crack."

"I know," she says. And I can tell that she really does. "I'm glad you cracked."

I am, too.

CHAPTER FORTY-FIVE

Julie

Thursday, July 19th

We've reached a compromise: catching up first, confronting Craig second.

I feel relieved—and not just because I'm bubbling with curiosity about her life. I'm hoping that by the time we're done sharing, Craig will have given us the other letters. If they exist at all. I'm not looking forward to an argument between him and Cassie. I pity anyone who has to go up against my sister.

"I called her back," Cassie tells me. "Claudia."

I now know who Claudia is—her publicist. Minutes ago, I didn't have this information. It feels exhilarating, being on the inside again. A little odd, too. Especially given the setting. We're sunbathing on the stretch of beach in front of Nana's house. Well, I'm sunbathing. Cassie is hidden under the yellow umbrella. We're on the exact spot we used to come to as kids, closer to the beach grass that surrounds the property.

"What did she want?" Claudia had called Cassie. This, apparently, was unusual. Claudia much prefers emails or the occasional text.

"To discuss a timeline for 'the reveal'. That's what she's calling it. 'The reveal'." Cassie flicks her sunglasses to the top of her head.

She's squinting, even though she's under the shade. "I told her someone at *Posh* knows. That they're investigating."

I feel a knot at the pit of my stomach. I wish I could help. Wish I could convince Sophie to back off. But I don't have that kind of power. Sophie will do whatever she wants—she always has. I just hope she never finds out the whole truth: that Daniel used to be Cassie's patient. That would give more fuel to the story.

"She thinks we should negotiate an exclusive with them," Cassie says. "Sooner rather than later."

This is something I hadn't expected. "Are you considering it?"

"Absolutely not. It would be like giving into blackmail. Besides, we're not ready to come out with the news yet. Daniel needs to talk to Angie. His situation is complicated."

Affairs are always complicated. Especially when there are children involved.

"And did you decide on a timeline?" I ask.

She shrugs, then sits up on the towel, propping herself up by her elbows.

I glance at her ankle. It's still bruised, though it's a lot less swollen than yesterday. I'll remind her to rub some more gel on later.

"What's wrong?" I get up and move closer to her, under the shade.

"It's something Claudia said. She asked me if I was sure he's really leaving her."

"Hasn't he told Tatiana already?"

"But he hasn't packed up and left." She meets my gaze. There's a shadow of sorts passing through her face. Not sadness, not exactly. But concern. Real concern.

Inside the Fire Princess was a deep, dark well. A reservoir where she kept her emotions safely hidden from the outside world. Outsiders assumed the Fire Princess maintained the well because she was cold-hearted. But the Sky Princess knew the truth: the Fire Princess hid her emotions out of fear.

"I didn't know that was bothering you," I say.

"It wasn't. At least it wasn't until now." She pauses. "Claudia kept saying I had to be sure he is committed to me. She says people will forgive anything if it's in the name of true love. But if Daniel goes back to Tatiana—or worse, doesn't even leave her in the first place—then my career is over."

"It's her job to ask these questions, though, right?"

"I guess. It still got me thinking though. It's been weeks since Daniel told Tatiana, but he hasn't moved out."

"Have you asked him why?"

"No," she says. She doesn't say that it's because she's too scared to hear his answer. She doesn't have to. "I wish she'd leave."

"Maybe she will."

"Maybe. I don't know. At this point, I think it's a game to her."

This could be true. Some people are messed up in the head like that. But it's not likely. "In my experience, people struggle with divorce for one simple reason: it's an admission of failure. Marriage is supposed to be forever."

"Is that why you're still with Patrick?"

I consider her question for a moment. The silence between us feels comfortable, safe. Cassie has always been a good listener. Why am I still with Patrick? Whenever I try to answer that question, my mind takes me back to our first date. To him telling me about his childhood. About his dad.

"I felt a connection to Patrick from the start," I begin. "His mom was kind of like my mom. His dad had another family, only Patrick had it a lot worse than I did. He only met them at his dad's funeral."

A quiet nod from Cassie. She understands. It's what defines us, our shared paternal experience. Shared, yet entirely different. Like a book that was split in half and we each got a chunk.

"I used to think that because we had this huge thing in common we'd automatically work, you know? We complemented each other—or at least I thought we did. I was younger, I was more comfortable letting him take the lead. We've never had a partnership, not in the sense of being equals. It didn't use to bother me, though." A thought occurs to me, one I hadn't been able to articulate until recently. "In fact, I liked it."

Cassie nods like she's already figured this out. Which she probably has—she analyzes couples for a living, after all. Counsels them.

"It's not like I harbored some secret desire to be controlled," I continue. "But it was a relief. For as long as I can remember, I've had this sense of being on the outside, like everyone around me got an instruction manual for life, but I didn't. Which meant that I had to watch people to figure out what was expected of me. And with Patrick I didn't have to do any of the work. He'd tell me. How to dress, what to eat, how to behave myself. He had an answer for everything."

"So what changed?"

"I don't know exactly. Something happened to me at that party." I've told her about the benefit, about my fainting spell. "I've always known how much he cared about what people thought. He embarrasses easily. But that day, I felt scared." I blink back tears. "And there's the bigger issue. He doesn't want to have kids with me."

Cassie bites her lower lip. "Did you talk about starting a family before you got married?"

"Not really. I just assumed, which is pretty dumb, I guess." I feel the blood rising to my face. I remember I didn't bring up the subject of kids when we were dating because I didn't want to seem too eager. Sophie had taught me that men perceive eagerness as desperation. "Anyway, two days before our wedding I actually made a comment about our future child, something small, I can't remember what, and he just casually corrected me. Said he wasn't going to have any more kids."

Cassie scrunches up her face. "Feels like something he could've told you sooner."

"It's why I decided not to change my name. I told him that if we ever had kids I would happily become Julie Smith. But until then, I was keeping Meyers. I thought it would piss him off, but he didn't seem to mind. All of his friends refer to me as Julie Smith, anyway. When we get invitations, they read Mr. and Mrs. Patrick Smith." I brush a stray hair from my face, exhaling slowly. "And in a sense it's what I've always wanted, to be a Mrs., to be official."

Silence falls between us again. I watch as Cassie's mind turns. She's used to this, used to hearing about people's marriages. Though this must feel different, more intimate.

"I have to ask," Cassie begins, slowly. "Are there daddy issues at play here?"

Coming from Cassie, it's a loaded question.

"Do you miss him?" I ask.

"Our father?" She scoffs. "Not at all."

"Dad has his flaws," I say. "But he's still our dad, Cass."

"He's a bully." There's a finality to her tone. It's always struck me as both impressive and frightening, how easily she passes judgment on him.

"You're harder on him than you are on anyone else." I pause, looking at the horizon in front of us. "We've all made mistakes. Even Nana. She kept the truth about you having a sister for nine years. Your mom—and I'm sorry to bring her up because she's in heaven and all—but, she drank and, well, she wasn't much of a mom. But it's like you save all your rage for Dad. I get that he wasn't the dad you wanted. But he's the dad we have."

"I never understood that logic. So he has a monopoly on being our father. Does that mean I'm supposed to settle for whatever I can get?" She says this quickly, like it's a counterpoint she's offered before. But then she stops, like she's turning something over in her mind, her eyes glued to a seagull that's close to the water. "And it's not about him being the father I wanted. It's about respect. Our father has never respected me. Not when I was a child, and not now. He was different with you."

I was also different with him. But of course I won't say this. It wouldn't be a fair comment, anyway. Our family—famil*ies*, depending on how you look at it—is too nuanced, too complex.

"Do you feel like *you* have daddy issues?" I ask.

She seems to consider this for a moment. "I have issues with our father. But not daddy issues, no. That's not what my relationship with Daniel is about. He's…my person." She pauses, a smile forming on her lips. It's like she's glowing. "I love him. So, so much."

I nod. This must be true, or else she wouldn't be considering breaking her no-marriage rule for him. I just hope he actually leaves his wife.

"I'm happy you found him," I say.

"Me, too," she says.

"How did that happen, by the way?" I turn on my side, propping my head on my elbow. "How did you two meet? The second time."

And then she tells me.

CHAPTER FORTY-SIX

Cassie

Thursday, July 19th

My story with Daniel is complicated. And not just for the obvious reasons.

"Daniel was a good thing, a great thing, that came from something terrible," I say. "Do you know how you use your fairy tales as coping mechanisms?"

Julie nods, smiling. I catch something else in her expression, too. A slight wince. Probably, she's thinking of how I invaded her privacy and read so many of her stories. I know she's forgiven me—my sister isn't the sort to hold a grudge—but she's still hurting. Every once in a while, when she thinks I'm not paying attention, she'll steal a glance in my direction, and I see it: the shame dancing behind her eyes. It pains me to see that my invasion of her privacy has affected her so much. I wish I could take it back. Or maybe I don't—if I hadn't done that, we wouldn't be here now.

"I had my own coping mechanisms," I continue. "Except mine were destructive. When my mom died, the pain was unlike anything I'd ever felt before. Sharp and twisted, like someone was ripping me from the inside out. I had trouble breathing. Literally. My chest ached like there was something physically weighing down on it. It's *all* I felt, too. All my other senses were numb. I wasn't hungry or even sleepy. I had no energy, no will to do anything."

"I'm so sorry, Cassie," she says. Her voice is a whisper. She's giving me the look again—pure agony, almost as if she blames herself for my pain. A ludicrous notion. She isn't responsible for her mother's actions any more than I am responsible for our father's.

"It's not your fault," I say. She needs to know that I don't blame her for what her mother did. Even when I shunned her from my life, it was never about blaming her. That wouldn't be fair.

I turn on my side, meeting her gaze. I'm surprised at how much I want to tell her this story. All of it. She might be the only one who'll understand, especially now that we've both lost Nana.

"All I felt was loss. It's like I *became* loss. Became empty. But after a few weeks, the pain began to change. It didn't hurt any less, but it became familiar to me. My body learned to handle it and soon I began craving normal things. Eating out with my friends, chocolate. A glass of wine."

"You're the only teenager who loved wine."

"All thanks to Nana's unorthodox ways," I say. On the summer we turned fifteen, Nana began to occasionally allow us one glass of wine with dinner. People are often horrified when I point this out. Personally, I'm all for it—it's not like I was binge drinking.

"So you started feeling better."

"But feeling better felt disloyal. I wanted to hold on to the pain. It was the only thing I had left of hers." I feel my eyes well up with tears. There's a reason I don't often talk about my mom: it's too messy, too emotional. It throws me off balance, makes me lose control.

"You felt guilty?"

"It was more than that. It was about *needing* the pain. It made me feel in control. Gave me power. Think about it. After she died, I was finally able to tell our father to get the hell away from me. I stopped trying to please him." I pause when I see the confusion in her eyes. "You're not the only one who wanted to please him, believe me. I put up a tough front, but I just wanted him to love me. I wanted him to want to be with Mom and me like he wanted to be with you and Sophie."

She nods, quietly. She looks surprised. She shouldn't be. All children have a primal desire to please their parents. Even the ones who pretend not to care. Especially the ones who pretend not to care.

"After my mom died, I decided I'd had enough of his behavior. He was still doing it, too. Breaking things around the house. Cursing. Raging against my mother for not being there. He'd actually call out her name as if she could hear him. It was almost like he needed her to still be afraid of him, even in death because that was power to him: fear." I wince, thinking of those dark days right after my mother's suicide. Looking back, I can see that my father was hurting. That he was trapped in a cycle of abuse—one where he was the abuser. He is a sick man. I've been aware of this for quite some time. But it's not my job to cure him. "I decided I wouldn't put up with it anymore. I'd no longer be an audience to his displays of rage. But it wasn't easy. It hurt, telling him I didn't want him in my life. But the pain, it made me feel…" I pause, searching for the right word.

"Relieved?" she asks softly.

"Alive," I say. "I started equating pain with life, which sounds so messed up, I know. But after a while that pain receded, too. Or calcified. And then I felt empty again. I felt like something was missing. So I began finding ways to hurt myself."

"What did you do?" Her lips part ever so slightly, fear written across her face.

"Not in the way you're thinking," I say. "I began depriving myself of things. Food, for example. I'd barely eat, and I when I did eat, it would only be things I hated. Sleep, too. I'd set up my alarm for four in the morning and force myself to stay awake. Smaller things as well, like shows I liked or books I wanted to read. I wouldn't allow myself to do any of it. I had to do it in such a way that it wouldn't affect school and eventually work. I was still functioning. Highly functioning, actually. I look back and I'm not sure how I pulled it off for so many years: on the outside, I had a normal life, I hit milestones like everyone else. But secretly I was creating a sort of living death for myself, finding ways to keep the pain alive. People would look at me and they'd see that I had lost weight, that I had dark circles under my eyes. They assumed it was from stress. They had no idea it was deliberate."

She squeezes my hand. "I'm so sorry you had to go through that."

"I finally went to therapy," I say, thinking of Mia. Christina and Rachel were instrumental in getting me to seek help. They were the only ones who knew that something was seriously wrong with me—that it wasn't just a case of being busy or stressed. I'd been to therapy before, with a counselor with a leveled voice and earnest eyebrows. It hadn't been by choice: therapists need to go to therapy as a part of their training. But I never let my guard down on those sessions. It wasn't until Mia that I truly opened up to another professional. "And my therapist helped me understand what I was doing. And how to stop."

"Did you ever date?" she asks. "During this time?"

"A little," I say. "But none of my relationships lasted. You'd think that not wanting to get married would attract men, at least the ones who are afraid of commitment, but all my exes actually hated that—"

"Which just proves that people only want what they can't have."

"Or maybe it's because they could tell I was broken."

We're both quiet for a moment, letting my words sink in. I'm not exaggerating—I did feel broken. Like an integral part of me was missing. I take in the sounds around us. The squawk of a seagull. The roar of the ocean. The low hum of cars on the highway. There is something comforting about this place, a cocoon-like element to it. Maybe it's the sea air with its medicinal properties. Maybe it's the isolation that comes with being on an island. Or maybe it's the connection to my childhood, to Nana and to Julie.

"But it was different with Daniel?" Julie asks.

"I was in a better place when we ran into each other. It had been a year since I had last seen him and Tatiana. I was taking a wine course." It's something my therapist had suggested. She thought I was ready for an indulgence.

"Let me guess: he was in your class?" She's now grinning, her face lit up. Love stories are like catnip for Julie. They were for Nana, too.

I nod. "He was there with a friend, but his friend flaked out after the first day, so he began sitting next to me. He was friendly, but I kept my distance. He was a former patient after all."

"Were you attracted to him?"

"Yes and no. I thought he was handsome, but I didn't think of him like that. Like I said: he was a former patient. I don't really know how it began, to be honest. The wine helped. Not because it gave me a buzz, but because he loves wine as much as I do. So we enjoyed learning together. We only saw each other in class. At first, anyway."

"Did you know he was still married?"

"I never asked. He hadn't mentioned Tatiana, not once. I assumed they weren't because he wasn't wearing a wedding ring and because he was taking a class by himself. But then one day I heard him on the phone with her. They were arguing, but I could tell from the conversation that they were still together."

"Were you disappointed?"

"Yes." A pause. "But also relieved. He was fun to be around, but I also wasn't looking for a relationship. Especially not with a former patient. And *definitely* not with one who was still married."

"What made you change your mind?"

"On the last day of the course he asked me out to dinner. As friends. I agreed."

"Weren't you worried that somebody would recognize you?" she asks.

"Like in public? God, no. It's not like I'm a host on *The View*. Besides, it was just dinner. I wasn't doing anything wrong."

"Plus, you look really different on TV."

"I know," I laugh. "You wouldn't believe the amount of prep that goes into a ten-minute segment."

"So, you went out on a date and fell in love?"

"Not exactly. But I did have a lot of fun. He's easy to talk to. We have a lot in common. And he didn't make a move on me or anything. I actually thought he wanted to be just friends. It felt…easy. Being with him felt easy." I smile, remembering the night we went out for Italian food in the North End. We didn't kiss or hold hands, but it felt so intimate.

"Did he talk about Tatiana?"

"Never. He did talk about his kids a lot. He's a great dad. A few months into our friendship, I started noticing that he looked at me differently. At first, I thought I was being self-absorbed. You know, conflating friendship with romance. But then he flat out told me he had feelings for me." I still remember everything he said, word for word.

"And you?"

"I told him I was flattered, but that I didn't date. We agreed to stay friends."

"Until?" She inches closer to me, her eyes widening in expectation.

"Until one day we were grabbing dinner and it started raining. Pouring, actually. He wouldn't let me take the T back home, insisted on dropping me off. When we got to my building, I thanked him and was about to race out of his car so I wouldn't be too soaked. But he got out through his side at the same time. And when I opened the door, I accidentally slammed it on his face."

"Ouch!" Julie laughs.

"I felt horrible. He was soaked and his nose was bleeding. I thought I'd broken it or something. Anyway, I invited him inside so I could at least have a look at the damage I caused."

"And then you kissed?" She has that dreamy expression in her eyes.

"We did," I say. My cheeks are warm. "It was clumsy and awkward, but it was also kind of perfect. I knew I loved him. I'd loved him for some time, but I chose to ignore it."

"You felt he was the one," Julie says.

"I knew he was the one," I say. And I still do.

Which is why I'm terrified. Because while I know that Daniel loves me, he still hasn't left Tatiana. I think back to brunch at Babette's with Christina and Rachel. I'd been completely and unequivocally sure that Daniel would be packing his things within the week.

But that hasn't happened yet. He's still at home, living with his wife.

CHAPTER FORTY-SEVEN

Cassie

Friday, July 20th

I tell Daniel everything—it's how our relationship works. But now, I'm holding back. I'm beating around the bush, discussing Julie's marriage when I should be asking him about his.

"He sounds like a sociopath," Daniel says, in a hushed tone. He scoops popcorn with his right hand.

"Julie is at Craig's," I say, pinching his arm playfully. "You don't have to whisper."

We're on the porch, splayed on the canopy daybed, drinking Prosecco (a Nino Franco Grave di Stecca brut) and eating junk food (popcorn, Twizzlers, Reese's peanut butter cups). Daniel has assured me he's been eating healthy all week, so I'm OK with a little indulgence. Daniel took the day off work so we could have the weekend together—or part of it, anyway. Tomorrow morning, he'll head over to Bella's to spend time with Angie and Sam, who've been back at their aunt's since yesterday. It's drizzling outside, but it isn't cold. The perfect day to stay in. Except a question is rattling inside my mind, one that I can't seem to work up the courage to ask him—Why hasn't Daniel left his wife?

"And I doubt it," I continue. "Actual sociopaths are rare."

"But she seems really unhappy?"

"She does." An understatement. Julie seems woeful, miserable. "When she talks about him, it's like she's recounting a traumatic experience."

"So why is she still with him?"

The perfect segue. I take a deep breath. "You tell me. Why are you still with Tatiana?" My voice quivers at the end, betraying my nerves.

He frowns. "Where's this coming from?"

"You said you'd leave."

"I did," he says, rubbing his finger on my chin. "I will. But you know it's complicated, right? It's different when you have kids."

A silence falls between us, one that does not feel comfortable.

"I was going to wait until tonight to talk to you about this," he says, looking down. Is he averting my eyes? "But Tatiana and I talked about our situation. About telling Angie."

"You did?" I feel my stomach lurch. "How did that go?"

"Really well, actually." A pause. "I think we reached a compromise. She agrees it's best to wait until Angie is older to tell her I'm not her biological father."

This I did not expect. Daniel's communication with Tatiana oscillates between hostile and non-existent. I think back to the day I saw her at the hospital, how belligerent she acted towards me. It's strange to imagine Tatiana being reasonable, conciliatory. Especially now that Daniel is leaving her.

"That's great," I say.

"Yeah." He smiles. "I was relieved. Angie is still too young to understand. Tatiana also agreed to joint custody."

Now I'm shocked. It's possible my jaw is on the floor.

"But there's a catch," he continues, his smile slipping. He meets my gaze. "She wants us to stay married a little while longer."

"No." A knee-jerk reaction. But one I do not regret. "You told her no, right?"

"Hear me out," he says. "Remember Ava?"

I do—by name only. Ava is their next-door neighbor and Tatiana's best friend. Or at least that's how Tatiana used to refer to her during our sessions. Their relationship didn't seem friendly at all. It seemed toxic and competitive, one always trying to show up the other.

"Ava's having a party in Nantucket on Labor Day. Tatiana wants us to go with the kids, as a family unit. It's the first time Ava's asked her to help plan the party. You know what a big deal that is for her."

"And you agreed?" I ask. "To go with her?"

"It's just a party, Cass. After that, I can leave."

"Why can't you leave now and still go to the party?"

"Tatiana doesn't want Ava to know we're splitting until after the party. You know how she is."

This is the most challenging aspect of my relationship with Daniel: I *do* know how she is. And I hate that I know.

"The way I see it, it's a small price to pay to keep Angie feeling safe and happy."

"This is a stunt, Daniel." I narrow my eyes at him. "She's manipulating you. Trying to buy time."

"Cass, come on." He squeezes my hand. I pull it away. I've never done this before. Not that I remember. "I don't think that's what this is. Why would she want to keep me around? She doesn't love me. She hasn't loved me for a very long time."

This is something I've said before. To Rachel, to Christina. Recently, to Julie. Most of all, to myself. Tatiana does not love Daniel. I repeat the words like a mantra, an incantation. I told myself that, if Tatiana actually loved Daniel, I'd know it. She used to be my patient, after all. And I remember confronting her at the hospital, assuring her that all she had to do was tell me she loved him, and I'd step aside. She didn't. To me, that was one more piece of evidence to support my theory.

Except now I'm not so sure.

Tatiana is status-obsessed. I can see how a party at Ava's would trigger a certain kind of anxiety in her. She'll want everything go to smoothly, to project a certain image. Having Daniel by her side would certainly help. Married women in her world have more social cache than unmarried ones—the patriarchy has kept that bias alive and well. Still, this is too much. The lengths to which she is going to stay in this marriage are extreme. Even for Tatiana.

A thought occurs to me. One that Julie pointed out. I was telling her about Tatiana, specifically about how she knows about me—and doesn't seem to care. And Julie asked me if I was certain of her indifference. *Sometimes people hide their feelings from everyone, including themselves. Sophie was like that.*

What if Tatiana's indifference is an act? What if she's still in love with him—and is too proud to admit it?

I feel a sense of panic spreading inside me like spilled oil. With it, comes questions. A sense of insecurity, of doubt. I'm not good at doubt. I never have been.

I know that my situation with Daniel is complicated. But I never thought I was being fooled—whether by him or by myself. Or by Tatiana. I've prided myself on maintaining a clear-eyed perspective on our circumstances, on the parts that make up our relationship. And, to me, a huge chunk of it was this: Daniel and I love each other. We've been together for nearly a year and a half and in this time, I've never had any reason to doubt his love for me—and only me. But now, I'm not so sure.

Because the facts remain as follows: I've asked him to leave her—and he hasn't. Which means there's something I'm overlooking. Something I'm not seeing.

The question is: what?

CHAPTER FORTY-EIGHT

Julie

Saturday, July 21st

I bring an extra beer back to the couch. This turns out to be a grave mistake.

"Do you prefer wine?" I ask. Disgust is written across Cassie's face. Like beer is revolting, offensive. "If you do, you need to be specific. I'm clueless when it comes to wine." What pairs well with tears?

Cassie shakes her head, sniffling. The box of tissues next to her is almost empty. Only yesterday it was full.

I'm trying not to let it show, but I'm freaked out. Cassie isn't a crier. I am—crying is a cathartic experience for me, a way of weeding out undesirable emotions. But Cassie's default reaction is anger. It's always been anger. Her tears scare me.

I'm reminded of the day she lost her mother.

A long time ago, the Fire Princess was under a salty, lachrymating waterfall. On that day, the heavens covered all the land with a gray veil. The woodlands became a fog forest, the evergreen became a savannah, and the mountains bowed before the Fire Princess, in respect for her mourning.

"Can I make you something to eat?" I take a seat on the end of the couch.

"I can't even think about food," she says, hugging one of the pillows.

I hear a knock on the front door. It's the same pudgy man who stopped by on the first week, coming to check on us. I want to tell him to leave us alone. Can't they can check their fancy GPS system instead of bothering us?

"I'll deal with him," I say.

"If he needs to see me, tell him to come inside. I'm not getting up."

"OK, Rudolph," I say, squeezing her nose.

In two minutes, I take care of business: yes, Cassie and I are home. Yes, we're adhering to the terms of the will. Kindly get lost because my sister is crying. I don't actually say this last part, of course. But the man does see Cassie curled up on the couch sniffling and quickly mumbles something about not needing to come in to do an inspection.

"I'm here. You can let it all out," I say, when I plop back on the couch.

"I'm just feeling insecure." She sniffles and rests her head on my lap. I stroke her hair, thinking of all the times I saw Sophie crying over my dad. "I convinced myself that Daniel loves me for real. That what we have is different. That it's not like every other affair." She pauses, sighing. "It's life's biggest trap: thinking that we're the exception. And I fell for it. I thought he loved me."

"That may very well be true."

"Do you really believe that?"

I believe it's possible. Not all affairs are created equal. But I can't possibly know if she and Daniel are the real thing or not. I barely know him—and I'm also not the best person to ask. Seeing Sophie with Dad scarred me. Not to mention that my own marriage is a disaster. I'm in no position to give anyone love advice.

"From what you've told me, you two have a solid relationship," I say.

"I've always thought so."

Could she think he's leading her on? I'm afraid to even posit this question. But I know I have to. It's the difference between a sister and a friend: a sister goes there. Sisters are each other's keepers. "Do you think he still loves her?" It's the question that used to torment Sophie.

"I have no idea what to think anymore. I was so sure, Jul. So sure." She blinks rapidly. "But I need to be logical about this. He hasn't left her and he's buying into some stupid story about staying with her for a party? Come on. That makes no sense."

"Do you trust him?" I ask.

"I do." She nods quickly. An unthinking reaction. "I've been turning it over in my mind. Considering all angles. But when I tune everything out and listen to my gut, the answer is yes, I trust him. One hundred percent. Maybe that makes me an idiot, but I do. I really do." She looks at me, the crease between her eyes deepening. "But something doesn't add up. Something's fishy about this whole thing. I don't know what, which means it could be anything, which means that I'm going to overthink this thing to the death."

"I'm sorry, Cass."

We're both quiet for a while. I stroke her flaming hair. She's stopped crying. Her brain is working overtime. I can tell. I can see the wheels turning.

"Nine times out of ten, cheating isn't about the other person," she says. "It's about the main relationship."

"Meaning?"

"Meaning it's a symptom of a larger problem within the marriage. The other person is just a stand-in. A way to scratch the itch but not the *cause* of the itch."

I'm quiet for a moment. I can't argue with what she's saying. In my experience, affairs *do* end badly for the other woman.

I jump when the phone rings. It's such a foreign sound, the actual ring of a landline.

Cassie looks at me quizzically. Nana's number hasn't rung a single time since we've been here. I assumed it was disconnected, actually.

I stretch my arm, not wanting to move from the couch since Cassie is resting her head on my lap.

"Hello?" I say, holding the white, cordless phone to my ear.

"Is this Cassie Meyers?" The voice is chilling, steely.

"No, this is her sister."

"Could you put Cassie on?"

"May I ask who's calling?" I feel a frown bury its way into my forehead.

"Tell her it's Tatiana."

My free hand flies to my mouth to conceal a gasp. Cassie picks up on my shock, lifts her head. She looks at me quizzically.

"It's Tatiana," I mouth.

Cassie blinks repeatedly, her expression now panicked. Then she reaches for the phone, swallowing. "Hello?"

I search the phone for a speaker button but find none. I'll have to wait.

"How did you get this number?" Cassie asks. A pause, and then: "What do you want, Tatiana?" Her tone is impatient. Another stretch of silence. "I already knew that. If that's why you're calling, then—" She stops. I'm pretty sure she's now holding her breath. "What are you talking about?"

Anxiety is building up inside me. My mind is trying to escape, to wander into a fairy tale. But I concentrate on staying present. Cassie needs me.

"Tatiana, do me a favor and don't call me anymore," Cassie says in a firm tone.

Cassie slams the phone down. It's a tactile experience that's missing with cell phones, being able to hang up on the other person with actual force. A button is no substitute.

"What did she want?" I ask.

Cassie lowers her head. For a moment, I worry she doesn't want to tell me. But then she looks up, brushing her red hair out of her face. She's crying—again.

"She told me that Daniel is seeing someone else." A pause. "Another woman."

CHAPTER FORTY-NINE

Cassie

Saturday, July 21st

The smart thing to do is nothing—for now. Impulse control is what prevents bad decisions. I need to take a step back, assess the situation. Tatiana is likely lying. She has to be. Still, her voice lurks in my mind like a bad dream.

There's something you should know, Cassie. Daniel is a cheater. You're not the first mistress he's ever had and I'm sure you won't be the last. Years ago he was seeing a woman named Jill. Don't say I didn't warn you when you find out he's cheating on you.

Jill. Daniel has never mentioned a Jill. At least I don't think he has.

"Are you ready?" Julie's voice shakes me out of a stupor.

"Yes," I say. "Let's go."

She frowns, no doubt taking in my shell-shocked expression. "Are you sure this is a good idea?" she asks.

"I need to get out of the house," I say. And I don't want to get in a car with Julie behind the wheel. Not right now. Going to Craig's house seems like a pleasantly innocuous activity. Useful, too—I've been wanting to get to know the man with whom my sister is infatuated.

We walk along the sandy path that connects the houses, our feet crunching over stray twigs. I'm still wearing my Havaianas—

it feels safer because of my ankle. But Julie is barefoot, wearing a pair of white, linen belted shorts and a matching shirt. She looks lovely, of course. But I miss her old look: peasant skirts, a crown of flowers on her head, minimal makeup. At least her hair looks more beachy and less coiffed. And she's wearing the funky seashell necklace she and Nana made together.

"Promise me you'll be honest?" she asks. "About Craig?"

"You know I will." And then: "What is it about him that you like so much?"

"I'm not sure."

"You've been having dinner with him every day for two weeks. You say you two spend time together after the kids go to bed. You know him quite well, I'd say."

"When I'm with him it's like I'm not *on*. I don't overthink or worry about saying the wrong thing. It feels easy. Right."

"Easy is good," I say. It really is—it speaks to feeling comfortable around someone. "Let me ask you this: if your marriage weren't going through a rough patch, would you still be interested in Craig?"

"I think so?" She looks up for a moment at the clear, blue sky. I wonder if she misses Patrick. I sense the answer is no. They've spoken once since their argument: she texted him to let him know she's all right, but all he did was tell her that they'd talk when she got back to Boston. And yet she's still bubbly and happy, still filled with that rosy glow. It's possible she doesn't love him anymore.

"What about his kids?" I ask.

"What about them?"

"How much of this is you loving the idea of an instant family?"

"I don't think that's it," she says. "Though I do love seeing Craig with his kids. He's great with them, you'll see. They're very lucky."

"He's lucky, too," I remind her. "They seem like good kids."

She lifts her shoulders. "A good dad is a rare thing."

"I'm not sure that's true, actually." I pause. "I feel like we got shortchanged."

She stops for a moment. I do the same. I wonder if she's going to pick up a seashell from the ground, or a pretty stone. She used to do that a lot as a kid. But instead she just looks at me and says, "It's weird. You had him full-time, but you don't talk to him. All I got was scraps and I have a relationship with him."

I want to tell her that she didn't get scraps. But that might not be a fair thing to say. Still, what I got wasn't any better. She knows this.

"Why do you think that is?" I ask her.

"Because I prefer something over nothing."

"That right there," I begin, "is the root of your problem. I've heard you describe this unfulfilling marriage to a domineering man, but your conclusion always seems to be 'but maybe that's OK' or 'what do I know about a marriage?' or 'no relationship is perfect'. It's like you'll take whatever you can get. But that's no way to live. I'm not telling you to leave Patrick, that's something only you can decide. And I'm not telling you to go for it with Craig, either. In fact, I don't think you should jump into a new relationship if you do decide to leave Patrick. Here's what I am telling you, though: find out what makes you happy. Not what you *think* will make you happy. Not what makes you happy given what's available. But what really makes you happy. And don't settle for anything less."

Julie is silent for a moment. I wonder if she'll ask if that's how I live my life. It's not—obviously. It's a lot easier to preach than it is to actually live by my words. I think about the years I spent punishing myself for my mom's death.

"Thank you for that," she says softly. She leans in to give me a hug.

We share a comfortable silence as we make our way to Craig's house. It's smaller than Nana's, with a low-pitched roof that gives it an appealing ranch-style look. I admire the potted hedges flanking the front door, the small herb garden. Craig must have a green thumb like Nana.

"Remember, you promised not to ask him about Dad or any letters," she says.

"I know, I know."

When we're at the front door, Julie reaches for the doorknob. Apparently, she's beyond the ringing-the-doorbell stage.

But the front door opens before Julie can get to it.

"Hi," a woman says.

I've never seen this person before—I'd remember. She's wearing all white: crochet cropped top and long skirt. It's a good color on her, she's tanned and toned and very healthy-looking. Her earrings are much too frilly for my taste, but they match her rakish look. Her hair is golden and long, probably the longest hair I've ever seen. There's something unsettling about her. She's stunning, of course. But that's not it. She looks familiar. I can feel a thought forming in the back of my mind, but it goes away as quickly as it arrived.

"You must be Julie," she purrs, moving in for a hug. She pronounces Julie's name correctly—with a soft *j*. No one does this unless they've met her. Or heard of her.

I watch Julie awkwardly hug her back, a puzzled expression on her face.

"I'm Cassie Meyers." I extend my hand. I do not enjoy embracing strangers.

"Oh my gosh! Where are my manners? I'm Elle." She has a faint southern accent, which always reminds me of my mother.

"Who?" Julie blurts out.

I feel my lips curling into a smile. This is a side of Julie's that I'd missed the most: the way she speaks first and thinks second. It's refreshing, candid.

"I didn't know you were coming over," Elle drawls. "This is such a nice surprise. Oh dear, what's wrong with your foot?"

"It's just a sprain," I say.

"Are we interrupting something?" Julie cranes her neck.

"Not at all! Come in, come in," Elle seems oblivious to Julie's hostility.

Craig's house looks untidy in a way that gives it a homey feel. Nana's house has always kept its pied-à-terre look to it, even after it became her primary residence.

"Julie! Julie!" Two high-pitched voices—and two adorable children—come barreling into the living room. The smallest one—she goes by Kiki, I believe—jumps and latches on to Julie. She's wearing a pair of pink cotton shorts and a matching pink shirt with a drawing of a large, glittery purple unicorn.

"You're quite the flyer," I say, smiling at her. Seeing a little girl makes me think of Angie, and then Daniel. I miss him. I need to talk to him once I've sorted out my feelings about Tatiana's phone call.

The boy—Ben, I think—is wearing a Spider-Man costume. "Are you Julie's sister?" he asks, adjusting his glasses.

"I am," I say.

"I'm Ben." He grins. "This is my sister, Kiki."

"It's nice to meet you." I crouch down to shake their hands.

"How are my two little monsters behaving?" Julie asks, looking at the two of them. She's studying Elle through the corner of her eye. Her face is burning red.

"Jul," Craig says, coming down the stairs. He is wearing a white T-shirt and a pair of blue-striped shorts. I envy his tan almost as much as I envy Julie's. Why can't redheads tan?

"Hey." Julie's tone is warm, but it's also questioning. It says: *Who is this beautiful woman in your house?*

"Hi, Craig."

"Hi, Cassie. This is a nice surprise."

"Um, Cassie and I just wanted to, we, uh…" Julie stammers, looking at Elle.

"I asked to stop by," I interrupt. Julie shoots me a grateful look. "I wanted to meet your kids." I hope I sound convincing.

"Do you want to play with us?" Ben asks.

"Of course I do."

"Do you know how to tell stories as good as Julie?" Kiki asks.

"I'm afraid not," I say.

"I've heard so much about your famous stories, Julie," Elle says. Julie blinks at her. It's possible she's sneering.

Craig seems oblivious to all this. Basic awareness is clearly not his strong suit.

"Craig, I'm heading off," Elle sings. "Walk me to my car?"

Craig follows Elle, a dopey smile on his face. I want to smack him on the head with the plastic shovel that's lying on the foyer floor.

"Do you guys want to go upstairs and grab some props for a story?" Julie says.

"Yes!" the kids answer in unison. They turn and begin running up the stairs.

"No running indoors," she calls out. Then, to me, "Who the hell was that?"

I don't have a chance to answer. Elle and Craig walk back inside.

"Jul, would you mind staying with the kids for a few minutes?" Craig asks. "I'm going to follow Elle to, um, her place. I'll be back in an hour."

"Sure," Julie says, a plastic smile on her face.

"Thanks."

"It so lovely to finally meet you two," Elle says. "I hope we see each other again soon. Oh," she pauses and looks at Julie. "Will I see you tonight?"

"Not tonight," Craig answers curtly before Julie can say anything.

"Oh, too bad," she says.

They leave again.

"What was that?" Julie whispers. "Did you see how she was all over him?" She doesn't give me a chance to answer. "And did you notice how she made a point of saying they were going to meet tonight? Who does that? Do you think they're dating?"

"I didn't pick up on romantic vibes between them," I say. It's the truth. Frankly, the only disturbing thing about Elle is how oddly familiar she looks. I still can't put my finger on what it is about her that I recognize. "Let's not jump to conclusions."

"But how could it be anything else? She's gorgeous and flirty."

And then it hits me. Elle looks like Julie.

It isn't a physical resemblance. It's more her style, the way she carries herself. Elle looks like Julie used to back when we were teenagers and she wore flowing skirts and beaded necklaces. Her summer style, she called it. Because she only got to wear the outfits she loved when we were in Montauk.

Julie really is Craig's type. At least the Julie she used to be.

CHAPTER FIFTY

Julie

Monday, July 23rd

The living-room floor is covered in plastic tarp. It looks like a carnival float, speckled in glitter and paint. Clean-up will take at least an hour. But it'll be worth it. Ben and Kiki look thrilled, proud of their art. I love seeing them like this.

"I think it's ready." Ben grins.

The three of us examine the giant poster: messy and beautiful.

"We should add a puppy," Kiki says. "Elle has an English bullfrog called Chunky Monkey. Maybe we could get a picture of him and put it on the beach where we went?"

"Bull*dog*," Ben corrects her, rolling his eyes. "But he wasn't there that day."

The Sky Princess has resisted the urge to ask the two adorable munchkins about the origins of Horrible Hurricane Elle for three whole days. The handsome knight hasn't said anything about her, almost as though the tall, leggy blond was never here. They continue to spend their evenings together, lost in laughter and conversation—at least on the outside. The Sky Princess has suffered in silence.

But now I have to say something.

"Does Elle come here often?" I ask, trying to sound casual.

Ben shrugs.

Kiki singsongs, "Only since Nana Bertie passed away. I want to meet her dog. I've only seen pictures of him on her phone."

"Is she a summer person?"

"She's from Washington."

"Kiki." Ben nudges her.

"Ops!" Kiki covers her mouth. "I forgot."

"What did you forget?" A lump forms in my throat. I don't like this.

"We're not supposed to say," Ben whispers, his head lowered.

"What aren't you supposed to say?"

Another shrug from Ben.

"Daddy says we can't tell you yet," Kiki offers.

"Can't tell me what?"

"About Elle and—" Ben stops himself abruptly.

I feel my heart clench inside my chest. Ben had been about to say *about Elle and Dad.* I'm sure of it. They really are a couple. I've spent the past three days thinking of reasons why Elle was at the house, why she'd clearly heard of me while I'd never heard of her. Maybe she's dating a friend of Craig's. Maybe they work together at the pub. Maybe she's his cousin. But Occam's razor applies: the simplest answer is most often correct. Elle is his girlfriend. Craig has asked his children not to bring her up because he can tell I've developed a sophomoric crush on him. And he feels sorry for me. Poor Julie. Unhappily married, grieving the loss of her grandmother. I mistook pity for interest.

Patrick is right. I'm a silly girl who lives inside my own mind, feeding off ridiculous fairy tales. I'm not a grown-up. I don't understand relationships. I never will.

And yet.

The Sky Princess is thinking of the day when the handsome knight brushed his hand on her cheek. She is reliving the dinners they shared with his children, where she was included as a member of the family. Her mind is transporting her back to the moment when he handed her an envelope and she shared her deepest secret with him. Instead of judgment, he offered her comfort and cooperation. And when they held hands, the air was filled with sparks.

How could I have imagined all that? It doesn't make any sense. And if they really are dating, then why does Craig ask me to stay for dinner every evening? And why do we spend time together, just the two of us, on his porch, lost in easy conversation?

"Julie?" Kiki's voice interrupts my raging thoughts. "Please don't be mad at us." Her face could melt steel: innocent, sweet. I hope Elle loves them as much as I do.

"I'm not mad at you, baby. Or you, Ben," I say, turning to him. "I could never be mad at you guys. You're the best kids in the world."

"Promise you won't tell Dad?" Ben asks solemnly.

"I promise."

I'm smiling. I have to be—they need reassurance right now. But on the inside, I'm fighting back tears. My body is quivering slightly. I feel heartbroken. Over a guy I've never even kissed. How pathetic am I?

Crying in front of them is not an option. So I take a page from Sophie's book. When she wanted to be alone—in her case, to spend time with my dad—she put me in front of the TV.

"How about we watch a movie?" I say cheerfully.

"Yes!" Ben says, his eyes gleeful. "Can we watch *The Lego Movie*?"

"Great choice," I say. "I'll set it up and go make us some popcorn."

In a few minutes, they're on the couch in the family room, hypnotized by the colorful little men dancing on the screen. I hurry out of there. I need to be alone. I go up the stairs, walking into the only door I've never opened before.

I sit on the floor, tears running down my face. My breath is ragged in my throat, my chest is heaving. I'm trembling. It's a feeling I know well. I call them emotional earthquakes because it feels like my body is rumbling from the sheer force of my feelings.

This one only lasts a few minutes. I focus on my breathing, willing my body to stay strong. I blink away the last of the tears as my eyes adjust to the room. Craig's room.

I walk towards the nightstand and pick up the only framed photograph. It's Ann, smiling adoringly at the baby she's holding. I can't tell whether it's Kiki or Ben. She has that new-mother glow. I've always wanted that glow. Other than the frame, the room is unremarkable, with scant signs of everyday life—a desk with stacked papers and an uncapped pen, a mug with the remains of what I am assuming is coffee, an unmade bed.

I study Ann's face. She's beautiful, serene. It's a peculiar thing: I love her children so much, and yet I know very little about her.

What I do know: her grandfather was a fisherman on the island, as was her dad. Her family has been in Montauk for five generations. Six, with Kiki and Ben. It's so unfair that she isn't here, that she has to miss out on so much. Ben's first wave on Ditch Plains. Kiki's first lobster roll. Ann has never seen Kiki on a boat. She won't get to hear Ben tell her about his first crush. It's revolting. Nonsensical. Ann deserves to be here. Kiki and Ben deserve a mother.

But maybe Hurricane Elle loves them. Craig is probably devoted to her—she seemed so confident of his affection. Not the least bit fazed by my presence. Their relationship is probably serious. The real deal. But when do they even meet? I've been hanging out with Craig—and his kids—for weeks now. Maybe she works nights? Or could she work at Holly's? Could he be with her now? The possibilities are maddeningly endless.

I wish he'd told me about her. Spared me the humiliation, the heartbreak.

Because my heart is breaking. It sounds dramatic, but it's also true. Maybe it's because he's handsome. Maybe it's because

Nana used to talk about Craig with such affection—and then there was the postscript in her letter. Maybe it's because he's such a sensitive, dedicated father. Whatever the reason, I have feelings for him. Real feelings. Unreciprocated feelings. Feelings that are very different than the ones I have for Patrick—or had for Patrick before they faded. Because what I said to Cassie is true: being around Craig feels easy. And being around Patrick has always been difficult, even when it was less so. I didn't use to mind difficult—maybe because that's all I've ever been exposed to. But now I've seen how different things can be. Platonic or not, my time with Craig has given me a glimpse of another way to live. One where I can relax and be myself.

I look around the room for signs of Elle. If they're in a committed relationship, there must be something of hers here. A drawer with her clothes. A novel she left behind. A sexy negligee under the pillow. Or worse, a pair of pajamas—pajamas imply the comfort of familiarity.

I take a step closer to Craig's nightstand. It's simple, modular: brown wood, two drawers. I am snooping. There's no other word for it.

I open the bottom drawer first. It's like looking inside the drawer of someone's desk at work. Scattered pens and folders. A box of paper clips. A stapler. Boring, impersonal items.

And then I see it. The bright color. Nana's curvy penmanship.

I count three turquoise envelopes in total. One says, *To my granddaughters, Cassie and Julie.* The other two say *Craig* and *Stephan Meyers.*

Dad.

CHAPTER FIFTY-ONE

Cassie

Monday, July 23rd

Christina is asking me if Daniel is worth it. A dumb question—and she knows it.

I am settled in Nana's rocking chair, staring at the ceiling. I've done nothing but mope today. I'm blaming my indolence on my sprained ankle. Really, the culprit is my heart.

"Yes," I say. "Of course he is."

On my phone's screen, I see her nodding. "Why?"

"Because I love him." I look down and catch my reflection in Nana's gilded, antique mirror. It looks darker somehow, less shiny. I have no idea how to clean it. I look unpleasantly unkempt. Frizzy hair (I blame the humidity), dark circles under my eyes (insomnia), and red burn marks on my shoulders and left arm (the sun).

"You also love your career," she says. A statement both obvious and unhelpful.

"Your point?"

"My point is that you've both agreed to take risks in order to be together. You with your career, Daniel with his daughter. You've done your part by talking to Claudia. What about him?"

"He talked to Tatiana," I say, adjusting my earbuds.

"And was summarily convinced to preserve the happy marriage charade for another seven weeks because of some party."

Christina's logic is irritating. Also, *summarily* is a stupid word.

"What are you saying?" I ask, looking her in the eye.

"Daniel is stalling," she says. "And you know it."

"You don't know that." And then, in a quieter tone, "You can't."

"You're right. I can't. But that's what it seems like. I think you should convey to him in no uncertain terms that you are not comfortable waiting until after Labor Day to be together. And if he doesn't understand, then I think you should consider ending things with him."

"I can't."

"Why not?"

Because I love him. Because he's my person. Because what we share is different, once-in-a-lifetime. Magical. I used to think that didn't exist, but it does. Since Daniel left on Saturday morning, I've been analyzing every aspect of our relationship. I was objective about it, too. I took a step back, assumed nothing. Contemplated our time together. He loves me. I love him. I still think there's something I'm missing, but whatever it is it's not about how much we love each other.

"He's not lying about his feelings," I say. "We're together all the time. He knows everything about me, I know everything about him. I know he loves me. I'm closer to him than I ever was to anyone. Even Julie, and she and I were inseparable when we were younger."

"What does she think of all of this?" Christina's tone is impatient. I'm glad I haven't told her about Tatiana's phone call, about the woman named Jill. I'm beginning to think I shouldn't have told her about Ava's party.

You're not the first mistress he's had and I'm sure you won't be his last.

It has to be a lie. I was their therapist—I would've known if he'd been unfaithful. But no—I know that's not true. My patients don't always tell me everything. For whatever reason—trust issues, denial, a misplaced sense of embarrassment—people often tuck away bits of information from their therapist.

"Let me guess: she agrees with me," Christina says.

"No," I say. "She knows it's complicated."

"Of course she does. She's seen firsthand how messy these things can get. You *both* have. That's what baffles me about your situation, Cass. Never in a million years would I have pegged you for the type to get involved with a married guy."

"I love you, Tina. But we've had this conversation before."

"I know, I know. But you worked things out with your sister. That's progress. I thought maybe you'd come to your senses about Daniel, too. It's time to move on with your life."

"Daniel and I have made progress." I feel my skin prickle in irritation. "He asked Tatiana for a divorce."

"Is he still living with her?"

"You know he is."

"Then that's not progress."

I let out a heavy sigh. This isn't a productive conversation. We're talking in circles. I tell her I have to go. She doesn't argue with me. Tells me to take care and we hang up. We haven't argued, not exactly, but there's an unacknowledged tension in the air.

Wine. What I need is a glass of wine (or two). I scan my eyes through Nana's cellar. There's a Gewürztraminer I've had my eye on since I got here, chilled at precisely 45 degrees. But maybe I should wait until Julie gets home. She may think she prefers beer, but that's only because she hasn't found the right wine for her palate. Julie's palate favors sweet with a hint of citrus: lychee, grapefruit. She'll appreciate the Gewürztraminer.

Thinking of my sister makes me consider Christina's question—what *does* Julie think of my relationship with Daniel? I don't think she's ever told me, not explicitly.

Christina has shared her opinion: in her mind, my relationship with Daniel is a cry for help. Sophie cast a formidable shadow in my parents' marriage. She was invisible, but powerful. And I grew up watching her wield this power. My mom's drinking. My father's "business trips". Julie's existence kept a secret from me for nine years. This was all because of Sophie—directly or indirectly. All because my father loved her. Christina's theory is that I've chosen to be the other woman because, in a twisted way, I crave power. *It's either that or you're a masochist*, she once told me. *Why would you knowingly set yourself up for heartbreak?*

Christina is one of the most intelligent people I know. And it's not that I can't see the logic in her thinking—I can. But she's wrong. My relationship with Daniel isn't informed by my child-hood trauma. Just the opposite. I grew up feeling both neglected and trapped. Daniel is my safety blanket, my oxygen. I have no legal claim to him. No ring, no marriage certificate. And yet he's mine. And I'm his. I know this in my bones. I know this, even now. I'm swimming in doubt and insecurity—but not about how much I love him or how much he loves me.

At the end of the day, isn't that all that matters?

These are the thoughts circulating my mind when Julie's name pops up on my phone. "Hey," I say, picking up.

"You have to come over." Her tone is low, urgent.

"What happened?" I ask.

"Just come. There's something you have to see."

CHAPTER FIFTY-TWO

Julie

Monday, July 23rd

There's one letter I have to steam open before calling Cassie. The one for Dad.

Dad doesn't know that the pictures sent to Katherine came from me. He assumed it was Sophie, and she never corrected him. It cost her, too. I'm sure she and Dad would still be together if she hadn't taken the blame for me.

I still have nightmares about that night.

It began with an email from Cassie saying she never wanted to see me again. No explanation, no apology. My reaction still surprises me: I raced to her house. Well, raced is too optimistic a word. It took me nearly two hours to get there—I had to get on a train and then on a bus. As a part of my dad's invisible family, I'd never been to the house on Claybrook Road before, had never been anywhere near the old-monied suburbs that was Dover, Massachusetts—but I knew the address by heart. I used to daydream about living there, about sharing a room with Cassie. In my fantasy, Katherine was gone. Not necessarily dead. Just gone. Peacefully. Definitively.

The house was something out of a storybook. Arched entryway flanked by white columns, a red double door, two chimneys. Inside, it had every feature I fantasized about—warm, wood-paneled living room, gourmet kitchen, a sprawling staircase—and some that were beyond my wildest dreams—a gym, a theater room, *five* bedrooms.

Cassie wasn't there: she'd already packed her bags and left. I never knew where to. (Nana had said she was safe but wouldn't divulge any details.)

I talked to Dad about Cassie's decision. I was sure he'd be on my side, that he'd help me convince her to let me back in. I've always been his favorite. I was wrong.

"She doesn't want to see you," he'd said. It was the first time he'd spoken to me in such a callous tone. The first time he didn't sprinkle his sentences with *ma petite*. I tried to be understanding of his grief, but his words cut deep inside me. I was used to having an absent father, not a cold one.

"Please, Dad?" I asked. "I just need to talk to her."

"She doesn't want to see you," he repeated, more harshly this time. "Sophie killed her mother."

I did not correct him, did not take responsibility for what I'd done.

Later, it occurred to me that his characterization was grossly unfair. The pictures hadn't killed Katherine—the affair had. And that was on him, not on Sophie. Sophie wasn't the one with the official family. The one who insisted that their relationship be kept a secret. That was all Dad. But at the time I'd been so wrapped up in my own sense of guilt that I did not point this out. I'm not sure I would have even if I'd realized his hypocrisy at the time.

I spent the next few days in a fog of guilt and dread. I felt like it was only a matter of time until my secret was revealed. Until I was unmasked as a monster. I missed Cassie—I kept having conversations with her in my mind, kept dreaming about her showing up at my apartment and embracing me—but in a sense, every day I spent apart from her was a relief. It meant she hadn't found out. I knew that she'd confront me when she did.

And I knew that whatever fury she directed my way would be well-deserved.

My dad showed up at our apartment two weeks later. He was there for Sophie.

"You bitch," he said. "What the fuck were you thinking sending her those pictures?"

It was the first time I saw my dad use that kind of language with my mom. He'd always been so gentle before, so caring. It made me think of the fights Cassie had witnessed as a child, and how terrifying it must've been for her.

Sophie seemed unafraid.

"Whatever happened was your fault, Stephan." She slammed the door on his face.

I knew the toll that took on her. I knew how much she loved him.

Still, she did not let it show. She held her head up high and moved on with her life. Everyone did. Dad moved to Seattle. Cassie followed her dream of becoming a psychologist. Even I moved on—on the outside, anyway. I went to college, I got married.

But now, as I hold Nana's letter to Dad, I realize that a part of me is still seventeen years old, stuck in that nightmare, filled with dread.

CHAPTER FIFTY-THREE

Cassie

Monday, July 23rd

Our father is in Montauk. The letter proves it.

"It doesn't actually prove anything." Julie looks at me with big, sugary eyes.

"Nana says so herself," I say, stabbing a finger on the blue paper. Nana's words sit under my fingernail: *Now that you are here, you must guide the girls through this arduous journey. They need their father.* "She makes reference to another letter. One he obviously already got or else it would be inside Craig's drawer."

Julie chews on her lip. "Maybe he's still on his way."

"I saw him." My tone is harsher than I intended. I have no sympathy for my father, but I do feel for Julie. I understand why she doesn't want to come to terms with him being on the island: it means he could've seen her if he'd wanted to. "Maybe Nana asked him to give us space," I offer.

"You don't believe that."

"You're right, I don't. I think he's a selfish jerk who hasn't told you he's here because he doesn't think of anyone but himself."

"Volume," she says, whispering, jutting her chin towards the family room. The kids are inside watching some movie. I can hear the telltale sound effects of cartoons. We're in Craig's kitchen, which is small but cozy, with blue walls and white backsplashes.

"Sorry." I shoot her an apologetic look. I blame Craig for this mess—not his kids.

As if she can read my mind, she asks, "But if Craig knows he's here, why hasn't he told me?"

I have no idea. What I do know is this: when Craig gets home, I'm making him tell us everything. I've waited this long out of respect for Julie, but no more. But I'm not about to say this now. It'll just add to her anxiety.

"They're dating," she says. "Craig and Elle."

I feel my expression softening. "You asked him?"

"Ben let it slip." Her tone is barely audible.

"Oh, Jul." I lean in to give her a hug. "I'm sorry."

"I feel so stupid," she says, her head buried in my neck. "It doesn't even make sense that I'm this upset. It's not like we're together."

I pull away from our embrace to meet her gaze. "Feelings are feelings. They're not bound by logic." It's something I often say to my patients. It's liberating, in a way. To accept that the emotions you experience aren't right or wrong—they just are.

I want to add that Craig is an idiot. Julie is perfect: kind, gentle, creative. Not to mention stunning. Elle might be attractive—and she is; very attractive—but Julie is the most beautiful woman in the world. Plus, she's a genuinely good person. Too good, in fact. Too forgiving. Too understanding.

I shouldn't complain. I'm lucky she forgave me.

"I just hope she loves them," she says, leaning her elbows against the countertop.

"Who?"

"Ben and Kiki." Her eyes are glued to the eggshell white ceramic tiles on the kitchen floor.

"Oh, honey," I say. Now my heart is breaking. "I know you don't want to hear this right now, but maybe this is for the best."

"You're right," she says. "I don't want to hear that."

I smile. "Fair enough."

But then she frowns and adds, "Remember when you told me to find out what makes me happy?"

I nod.

"Craig would've made me happy, I think. God, how stupid am I for thinking that?"

"Not stupid. Nana agreed, remember?" I don't add that I'm upset with Nana for planting this seed in Julie's heart to begin with. Leave it up to her to play Cupid from beyond the grave.

"But now I'm wondering how she even knew that?"

I shrug. "She knew both of you well?"

"Maybe," she says. "Can someone know you when you don't know yourself?" A pause, she looks up and then blinks back tears. "Because I feel like I don't know myself."

"Most people don't." I squeeze her hand. "And that's OK. Better than OK, actually. It's what makes life worth living. Finding out who we are."

"You said I used to be more like Elle, at least my clothes were. Look at me now." She pauses, glances down at her green silk blouse and slacks. "I look like a Stepford wife."

"Not entirely. You have a flower in your hair." I gesture to the daisy sitting prettily next to her pearl earrings.

"I grabbed it on the way here." A sad smile spreads across her face. "It was lying on the beach, closer to the bushes. It felt like such a shame to just leave it there. It was so…beautiful."

"You used to do that when we were girls."

"I did?"

"You don't remember?"

"No." She's silent for a moment. "I guess I had to erase so much of who I was to make room for the person Patrick wanted me to be."

"Maybe being here is allowing you to reclaim that person, then."

"It wouldn't be the first time," she says. "I used to think of it as the Nana-effect, but maybe it's the Montauk-effect."

"Maybe it's you and me. What Nana taught us. What we taught ourselves, too."

"I like that," she says.

"I do, too."

CHAPTER FIFTY-FOUR

Julie

Monday, July 23rd

The voices coming from the foyer are getting louder. Or Cassie's voice is, anyway. She's confronting Craig. I want no part in it, which is why I'm sitting on the couch in between Kiki and Ben. They're both still entranced by the TV, but if Cassie raises her tone even a little bit more they'll be able to hear her. I look for the remote, but I can't find it.

I get up from the couch and manually turn up the volume. My ears prick up when I hear my name. I step out of the family room. Craig and Cassie can't see me from where I'm standing. I can't see them, either. But I can make out what they're saying.

"You don't know the kind of man he is," Cassie is saying. "The kind of father he was."

"You're right. I don't. But I knew Bertie. And I plan on respecting her wishes." A pause. "I'm sorry you're upset. I really am." His tone is sincere, but unwavering.

I feel a pang in my chest. I'm grateful Kiki and Ben are oblivious to the drama. And, incidentally, I'm beginning to understand why so many parents rely on a TV.

"He scared us constantly, he cursed and yelled and broke things around the house. He made me watch, too. Do you want to know why? He once told me, when I was still a child. It's so he wouldn't hit her. That was his explanation. He smashed a vase so he wouldn't smash her head. Except sometimes he did, too. If she tried to stop him, he'd smack her to the ground. My mom was a tiny thing. You've met my father, you've seen his size."

I feel something cut inside me. Cassie isn't saying anything I don't already know, but it's different, somehow, hearing her condense Dad's behavior like that. Maybe it's because we're adults now. Maybe it's the way she's saying it: there's no inflection in her voice, no emotion. It's disturbing.

I wonder, not for the first time, why Dad was so different with Sophie and me. Why were we spared his temper? Is it because he spent less time with us? Could it be that his feelings for Sophie turned him into a loving man when he was around us? Or is it something else, something darker and more complex about his nature as a person?

I know Craig is talking, but I can't make out what he's saying. I eye Kiki and Ben nervously. I don't want them listening in on this. But they're smiling gleefully at the TV.

"That's because she's a better person that I am," Cassie says. "Do you want to know what Nana used to say? That she isn't meant for this world. That she is an angel walking among humans. It's true. She forgives him because she's too good."

I decide to come out of hiding.

The Sky Princess takes in the scene before her. The front door to the knight's house is still open. The Fire Princess is standing in front of him, her height so imposing that she's nearly his size. Her arms are crossed, and her left eyebrow is curved upward, the classic defiant stare of the Fire Princess. Her bright mane is covering part of her face; she is like a lioness staring down its prey.

My imagination is playing tricks on me: I see Craig's face light up when I walk into the room. I really am a dreamer. Maybe I should ask Mandy to recommend a spiritual cleanse to free me of delusional thoughts.

"Take us to see him, Craig," I say. I do my best to look at him without longing.

"I will, Jul." Craig nods. There it is again: the jolt of energy that comes when he says my name. I need to snap out of it. I need to stop equating pity with love. "We'll go tomorrow, the three of us," he continues, looking at Cassie and me.

"No." Cassie's tone is firm, resolute. "We're going now. And you're not letting him know we're coming."

"What if he isn't at the hotel?" Craig asks.

"I'll take my chances." Cassie gestures commandingly towards the door.

CHAPTER FIFTY-FIVE

Cassie

Monday, July 23rd

We've been driving for ten minutes. The kids are with us, which could be a problem. Conversations with my father tend to get heated—the last thing I want to do is scare two innocent children. But their presence can't be helped, I suppose. It's not like we could've left them at the house by themselves.

"When did he get here?" I glance at Craig, who is driving.

Julie claimed to prefer the backseat to be close to Kiki and Ben, but unless Craig is a total dimwit, he's figured out that she knows about him and Elle. I'm still shocked that the two of them are an item—I was certain Craig was enamored of Julie. It makes me wonder what else I'm wrong about. Hopefully not Daniel.

"I'll take you to him, but that's it," Craig says. "I'm not getting involved in this."

"You're already involved," I say.

He doesn't disagree—how could he? He doesn't answer my question, either.

We spend the rest of the ride in silence. Julie is telling the kids a story. I'm not paying attention to the details, but Ben and Kiki seem engrossed in the tale.

We pull up to the Southampton Inn on Hill Street, a small Tudor-style construction with a pretty garden at the entrance.

"Give me a minute," Craig says.

"What for?" I ask.

"The night manager is a friend of mine. She can keep an eye on Kiki and Ben, so they don't have to come up with us."

"Fine."

I peek at Julie, but she doesn't meet my eye. She's lost in her story—and so are the kids.

I follow Craig into the lobby. It's a charming space, artfully decorated with antiques. The night manager turns out to be a sweet-looking woman with pale lips and bangs falling into her eyes. She happily agrees to look after his kids.

We make our way up the stairs to the second floor. Craig leads us to room 201. He stops at the door and eyes me as if to say, *I'm done here*. Fine by me.

I rap my knuckles against the door.

"Who is it?"

It's him. I'm sure of it. I used to be an expert on his voice—its rhythm and intonation. A skill that allowed me to anticipate a shift in his temper, to prepare for his rage. Right now he's in a good mood. That won't last.

His face falls when he opens the door.

"Girls?" His eyes dart frantically between Julie and me. Then they move over to Craig. His face is a series of question marks. We look alike, my father and me: red hair, freckles dotting our round-shaped faces, long-limbed. I never liked that. Now that I'm looking at him up close, I see the signs of aging: the lines around his mouth are pronounced, his skin is thinning, his neck is sagging. But he's still a fit, imposing man.

"What are you doing here?" he asks.

I push past him, not bothering to be invited. He doesn't protest.

"Your grandmother, she wanted me to be here," he continues, as if a question has been asked. He's still standing by the door, holding it open. Craig and Julie are outside, looking uncomfortable. The suite is gorgeous: spacious and luxurious.

"You're not welcome here," I tell him.

"Oh?" Two letters. Barely a word. And yet I hear it, the shift. The drop in his tone. The challenge in his pitch. He's annoyed now. "You own the Hamptons now?"

This is the father I know. From the corner of my eye, I see Julie stiffen.

I gesture for Julie and Craig to come inside. My father closes the door behind them.

"If you're thinking of challenging the will, you'll lose," I say. "The house is ours."

A beat. He narrows his eyes at me. "Is that why you think I'm here?"

"I have no idea why you're here."

"I'm here for you." The words sound rehearsed.

I scoff. "When have you ever been there for me?"

A pause. I watch him swallow, then rub his temples. He hates being questioned. He always has. He's just moved over from annoyance to frustration.

"Cassie, let's not start with the drama." The edge in his voice is sharper.

"Your gaslighting won't work," I say. "I see you for what you are. A spoiled man-child who bullied my mom for years. I read Nana's letter to you." I don't explain that the letter I read is the one he hasn't gotten yet. "She was delusional to think that Julie and I needed you here."

The upside of finding Nana's letter to my father: I learned that she saw him—the *real* him—after all. In her letter, she urges him to step up, to finally be the father Julie and I deserve. She all but calls him a lousy parent. I think back with astonishment to the number of times Nana counseled me to be patient, reminded me that he was doing his best. I thought she was blind, that the generational gap we shared meant that she was incapable of understanding the gravity of his behavior. But, no—she was just being loyal to her son. And protecting me, too. She felt that I needed a father—any father—and that accepting mine would be better than rebelling against him. She tolerated his behavior—she thought she was powerless to stop it—but she didn't condone it.

"Cassie, I'm not in the mood for one of your self-righteous lectures." He squeezes his eyes shut for a moment. I recognize another escalation coming. Sure enough, he twists his jaw in a disgusted half-smile and adds, "You're right about your grand-mother's will being bullshit. The house should've gone to me. *I'm* her son, whether you like it or not."

"And yet she still didn't leave you the house." I feel my cheeks burning. "Because she knew the kind of man you were. The kind of man who hurt his wife. I can only imagine how disappointed she must've been in you."

He swallows. "I never touched your mother."

"Right. She just fell a lot." I shake my head. "You do know I work with couples for a living, right? I spend all day learning about people's marriages. If any of the men I treat acted like you, I'd tell his wife to leave him."

"Your mother wanted to be with me."

"You think I don't remember you telling her that she was unlovable? That no one else would want her? You said all those things even though you didn't want her. You only wanted her money."

I don't realize what I've said until I see his reaction: the way he clenches his jaw, squares his shoulder. His eyes burn with rage. I've done what my mother used to do before he went off on one of his tirades: I've played the money card. Playing the money card is unforgivable. It makes him feel emasculated, weak.

"That's enough," he says, seething.

I decide to press on. "We all know it's true. You could yell and you could smash things, but you couldn't pay for our lifestyle. She controlled the money, which meant that she controlled you."

"You watch your mouth, Cassie!" His voice is louder now, his tone menacing. He takes a step towards me. I can tell that he means it to be intimidating. He's a tall guy. I get my height from him as well.

Blood swooshes in my ears. I force myself to stay put, to keep my eyes on his. I don't want him to know he still scares me. "You couldn't stand the hold she had over you, and so you did the only thing you know how to do: you terrorized her. You drove her to drink and pop pills. She self-destructed because of you."

"You don't know what you're talking about!" His neck veins are jumping up like pieces of rope.

"Oh, but I do. I watched your fights. I iced her bruises. I put up with you coming into my room and telling me she was killing your spirit, as if that made it OK for you to hurt her. You thanked me for not telling her that Sophie was still in the picture, remember?"

"So that's what this is about," he says, snidely. His forehead creases. "You feel guilty because you know you could've told her about Sophie. You could've stopped her from finding out the way she did."

His words slap me on the face. How dare he? "I was a child," I say, through gritted teeth. And then, because I can no longer keep this bottled up inside me: "Do you have any idea what living like that did to me? How messed up I am because of you? All my life I've had to carry this darkness inside me. It touches everything I do. It consumes me." I stop when I sense my eyes burning. I can't cry. A part of me wishes he could see the years I spent hurting myself. I was attached to pain, to agony. It's all I knew.

"Enough with the goddam victim drama, Cassie." He's huffing now, his face red. "Or you'll end up like your mother."

"Stop yelling!" Julie's voice cuts between us.

We both stare at her as if we've just remembered she's there. Craig is looking at her, too, his face heavy with concern. She should leave. This is too much for her, watching me go up against our father. Julie loves him. I don't know why, but she does. He spent years keeping her a secret. He made her countless promises he never kept. When he was at their house, he spent more time with her mom than with her. And yet she still loves him.

"Why didn't you tell me you were here?" She's looking at our father. Her voice is a whisper.

"I wanted to, *ma petite*." He clears his throat. I watch him release air through his mouth. I can tell he's making an effort to sound calmer, to become the dad Julie knows him to be: loving and gentle.

I feel a tug in my mind, a memory: my mom, my father, and I driving to church on Sunday mornings. More often than not, they argued on the way there, but as soon as we parked the car, he'd take a deep breath, check his reflection in the rearview mirror, and soften his facial features into his public persona: genial, charming. He literally needed to see a different man in the mirror before becoming the person our friends and neighbors knew and loved. He enjoyed being admired by others as a *nice guy*. A family man. Successful, polite, friendly—so that's the show he put on.

That's when I see it: to my father, people are mirrors. The reflection he saw when he faced my mom and me wasn't to his liking. But now, watching him look at Julie, I see that what she reflects back at him is the man he wants to be.

And just like that, I understand. I understand that my father was different with Julie because she validated his every emotion. Because she was grateful to have him. I was the opposite of grateful. No, I was worse than that: I was vociferously critical of him. I harbored an unapologetic contempt toward him—and he could tell. I felt cheated for not having a proper family, a sentiment that was exacerbated by the fact that my peers—teachers, classmates, neighbors—were under the impression that I did have just that.

This dissonance was at the heart of my frustrations: if only people knew the pressure I was under. The magnitude of the secrets I was expected to keep: the depths of my mother's drinking, my father's temper, his ongoing infidelity. But they had no idea. I was very skilled at keeping it all under wraps, at leading a double life. It made me anxious and guarded and distrustful. But I did it.

Is it any wonder I was critical?

Being critical of my parents was an act of resistance. A way to remind myself that what went on in my house was not OK. That I deserved more. That it wasn't my fault.

Except it came with a price.

If I hadn't been critical, if I had played along and validated my father's emotions, he might've loved me just as much as he loves Julie. He would be regarding both of us with affection right now. Not just her.

"I really missed you," Julie is still talking to our father. "I kept leaving you all those messages."

"I was going to call you back."

"When?" Her chin quivers.

He moves closer to her. "Soon, *ma petite*. I was just about to."

She stares at him for several seconds. Her eyes are twitching, as if reacting to flashes of light that no one else can see. When she finally speaks, she's no longer whispering. "You owe us an apology."

"What?" My father looks surprised.

"Cassie's right. She's messed up because of you." Julie's voice is low and a little cracked. "We both are. It affected us, Daddy, having to keep your secret for all those years. We were just kids. It was too much pressure, thinking that one little slip could ruin everything." She blinks back tears. "You owe us an apology."

Now it's his turn to be silent, his eyes glued to hers. I know the magnitude of what she's asking: our father doesn't apologize. I don't have a single memory of him saying *I'm sorry*. He sees it as a sign of weakness. But if anyone can get him to do it, it's Julie.

"This isn't you, *ma petite*," he says softly. It is not lost on me that he hasn't apologized. "You're not…bitter."

"I am." She sniffles. "I've just kept it inside because I was too afraid to say anything. Just like I do with…" She pauses and shakes her head. I know she's thinking of Patrick, drawing parallels between the two men in her life.

My father turns to me. "Is this what you've been doing? Filling up her head with this nonsense?"

I don't get a chance to answer. I'm interrupted by the sound of the door opening.

"Babe, you'll never guess what I found!" a bubbly voice exclaims.

I look up to see Elle, looking carefree in a white crochet dress, holding about half a dozen shopping bags.

My father steps away from Julie.

"Oh! I'm sorry. I didn't know you girls were coming over today," she says, looking between Cassie and me. And then, to my father: "You should have told me, babe."

"Honey, now isn't really the best time," my father says. He's further modulating his tone, trying to compose himself.

Babe? Honey? There's a ringing in my ears.

"Excuse me," I say, darting my gaze between my father and Elle. "You two are together?"

"Oh my gosh, yes!" Elle singsongs. "I'm your dad's girlfriend. I wanted to tell you the other day, but I knew he'd want to be there when we officially met." She's smiling from ear to ear, obviously unable to read the tension in the room. "I've wanted to meet you for so long, but we had to keep putting it off. But now here we are!" She drops her bags and claps her hands like a seal. "Oh, the two girls that my boo raised, all by himself. Let me tell you, I would have killed to have a dad like yours."

My father's face turns beet red. I don't need to be told what's going on. I see it. More performance on his part. More lies. This time, with Elle. I try to catch Julie's eye, but she isn't looking in my direction. She's blinking rapidly, as if she's just woken up from a confusing dream.

"Elle, I don't know what he's told you," I begin. "But my father terrorized my mother and me for years. He hurt her. She killed herself because of what he did. My advice to you is to run far, far away. Before he does to you what he did to her." I stop when I see Elle's mouth hanging open. And then I turn to my father. "And you? You're dating someone young enough to be your daughter? Actually, let me amend that. You're dating someone who even looks like your daughter." I give him a once-over. "You're pathetic."

Elle blinks, confused.

But before I can tell her that she's basically a blond version of what Julie looked like growing up, I notice Julie walking to the other side of the room, where Craig is standing, his eyes still fixated on her.

Of course. If Elle and my father are a couple—Mr. Mid-life Crisis meets Miss Daddy Issues—then Craig is single.

Julie whispers something to him. The chemistry between them is buzzing, kinetic. For a moment, I wonder if they're actually going to kiss in the middle of this overcrowded hotel suite. They don't—obviously. But they do stare at each other, dreamy grins on their faces.

My father looks confused. "What the…?"

"Stay out of it," I tell him.

He stares at me for a beat and then flicks his eyes back to Julie and Craig. "Oh, I see what's going on here," he says, sneering. And then, under his breath, "A slut just like her mother."

The shift on Craig's expression is instant. He looks up at my father, his face twisted in disgust, antagonism. He walks across the room slowly.

And then Craig punches him in the face.

CHAPTER FIFTY-SIX

Julie

Monday, July 23rd

Our first kiss is everything I thought it would be. Soft lips and hot breath. Tickle of tongues. His strong hands around my waist. My fingers laced around his neck, grazing his hair. A tingle that starts in my stomach and reaches every extremity in my body. A feeling of electrifying weightlessness, of overdue surrender.

"I've wanted to do this since the moment I saw you on the beach," Craig murmurs, when our lips part slightly.

"That makes two of us." I open my eyes to meet his gaze. Our foreheads touch and we both grin.

It's our evening ritual—catching up on the porch with beers—but it's also not. Because today we're not sitting side by side on the Adirondack chairs. I'm curled up on his lap, staring into his honeyed eyes, his thumb and index fingers holding my chin. We kiss some more.

"I'm so glad you're not dating Elle," I say, laughing. The absurdity of my assumptions are coming back to me. It's been an eventful day: finding the letters (I've confessed my snooping to Craig), seeing Dad, finding out that Elle is his girlfriend.

He chuckles. "I still don't know what gave you that idea."

"She was here," I say. "Looking gorgeous and, I don't know, *at home*. And she talked about maybe seeing you in the evening."

"I told you, she came over to return my fishing rods and to borrow a surfboard. Elle was learning how to surf, like Ben." I think back to my phone call with Dad (hadn't he mentioned he'd gone fishing?) and to what Ben accidentally told me, about him and Elle catching waves at Ditch Plains. I wonder if my dad was learning how to surf, too. But I don't ask because if I bring him up then we might end up talking about what happened at the hotel—and I'm not ready for that. I've said as much to Craig. "And as for our evening plans, she and your dad asked me out to dinner, but I said no because I wanted to spend time with you." He shakes his head. "If I'd known you thought we were together…"

"This should teach you not to keep anything from me." I pinch his stomach through his shirt. His abs feel like warm marble.

"I was following orders. Bertie left me very specific instructions. She said she'd haunt me if I didn't keep my promise."

I feel my mouth stretch into a smile. I can picture Nana making that threat.

"You promise there are no more letters?" I ask.

"Scout's honor." He gives me a winning smile.

Cassie and I still have to read Nana's last letter to us, the one we never opened because we were too busy being shocked over the fact that Dad was on the island and that Craig knew about it. Craig explained that he would've given it to us on the very last day. Cassie and I agreed to wait until then. It feels right.

"You sure you don't want to stay over?" he asks. "The kids are never up before seven."

"I didn't take you for a rule breaker." I feel a buzz of excitement.

"Bertie would understand." He gives me a magnetic grin.

I tip my head back, laughing. I don't disagree—Nana really would understand. And there are ways around the rules. I could leave my phone back at the house. Cassie would cover for me if someone came over to check on us. But I should go home, at least for tonight. I should be with Cassie.

"Soon," I say.

"See you tomorrow?"

I give him another kiss. He tastes like sea salt and beer.

"I won't go into work," he says. "We'll spend the day together."

I can barely contain my excitement. We won't be able to kiss in front of the kids—it's too soon, we don't know where this is headed—but I'll get to spend the whole day with him knowing that he likes me as much as I like him. The thought is enough to sustain me until sunrise.

And to give me the nerve to talk to Patrick.

Back at the house, Cassie is slicing tomatoes we bought at the farmers' market. There's an open bottle of wine next to her. The label reads Stag's Leap Cabernet Sauvignon.

"We're celebrating," she says, when I walk in. "I'm making bruschetta. It's the only thing I know how to make."

"I like bruschetta. What are we celebrating?" I ask.

"You and Craig." She shoots me a smile. "And Craig punching our father. I wasn't sure about him before, but now he's my favorite person in the world. Top ten, anyway."

I study her expression for a trace of reservation, of hesitation. But none is there. Cassie's feelings for Dad really are black and white: he is a bad father, she wants nothing to do with him. I understand where she's coming from. I'm hurt, too. What he said was cruel, but I know he didn't mean it—he was probably just being protective of Patrick. Men are often tribal like that, irrational and impulsive when they get jealous. And part of me still hopes he'll apologize. I know he loves me—loves *us*—in his own way. I don't want to give up on him. Cassie gave up on me for years. I know how that feels.

"Don't keep me in suspense," she says, handing me a glass of wine. I take it even though I plan on grabbing a beer from the fridge. "How was it with Craig?"

"It was…everything." I feel my cheeks expanding. It's been a long time since I've felt this way about a guy. Come to think of it, this might be unprecedented. It's not like I dated a lot before marrying Patrick—and with him it was always more about safety than passion.

"That's great, Jul," Cassie says. "I'm happy for you."

I am, too. But I'm also mindful of my situation: I'm still married.

"Is it all right if I call Patrick before we eat?" I ask. "I don't want to put this off any longer."

"Go ahead, there's no rush." She begins to mince garlic, humming to herself.

Once I'm in my room, I close the door and call Patrick. He picks up after three rings.

"Hi, it's me," I say.

"Yes?" His tone is tense, but I can hear the undercurrent of expectation in his voice. He thinks I am calling to apologize. Unreservedly, too.

"There's something I have to say."

"All right."

The Sky Princess is about to leave the king. She's thought about doing this dozens of times before, speaking the words into the wind, not daring to say them when anyone was around, but feeling the need to utter them anyway, so at least someone—the trees, the skies, the universe—would know how she felt. In her heart, she never thought she'd have the strength to say them to him.

"I want a divorce. I'm sorry to be so blunt about it, but I know how you appreciate brevity."

A loud sigh on the other end of the line. I recognize that sound: he's annoyed. It's 9:30 p.m., which is when he unwinds. He was probably watching a documentary on Netflix. Or reading a book, usually a political one. I'm interrupting sacred time. If I were there, I'd be nervously checking my appearance (I would *not* pass a body scan right now) or else fixing him a Scotch.

"You're clearly not yourself. I spoke to your mother about this. We agree we should forgive you for going away. Your behavior was irrational, but I suppose that was to be expected. You've just lost your grandmother."

I swallow my irritation. "Patrick, I'm leaving you. I hope we can do this amicably."

A beat. "Is this about me not picking you up for the party?"

"No."

Another sigh. "What is it then? Why the drama?" He sounds displeased, but calm. Patrick is always calm. He's incapable of raising his voice, of losing control.

There is so much I could say. Objective reasons: his behavior at the benefit, his refusal to have a child with me, his fixation on controlling me. But it isn't about any of these things, not really. It's about him not wanting to be happy. Because that's what I've realized: Patrick has no interest in happiness. He's ambitious and driven and brilliant. He's generous, quick to compliment me, skilled at making me feel safe. But what he wants out of life is easily measured. Money. Awards. To become name partner. He has no interest in slowing down, in living in the moment. No desire to explore the unknown together or to listen to me tell a story. To him, I'm not a storyteller. I'm a prop. A beautiful, cherished prop.

But I don't say any of this. What would be the point?

"I want a divorce. I've made up my mind."

"Are you expecting to get half of what I have? Because that's not happening."

"I don't want anything."

"You don't—" He stops short. "OK, now I *know* this is a joke."

"This is not a joke. I want nothing."

"Good. Because that's what you'll get."

And then he hangs up the phone.

I place a hand to my heart. I feel my chest rise and fall as I take a long, deep breath. Despite my conviction, I had expected to feel mournful over the end of my marriage. Instead, I am experiencing a sense of weightlessness, of calm. A taste of something sweet in my mouth. A pleasant buzzing from head to toe.

Freedom.

CHAPTER FIFTY-SEVEN

Cassie

Monday, July 23rd

It's a simple affair, bruschetta. Diced tomatoes simmered with a mix of minced garlic and onions, olive oil, basil, and a sliced loaf of Italian bread. It pairs wonderfully with red wine (my favorite) and can be served as both party and comfort food (today it's both). It's not an impressive dish—but it's delicious and easy.

My phone pings as I'm setting the table. A text from Daniel: a heart emoji with a question mark. Shorthand for *how are you feeling?* I text him back: two hearts. Code for *all good.* Not a lie—I feel liberated after confronting my father (and watching him get punched). But not the whole truth, either. Tatiana's words are still nagging at me. I don't think it's true, I really don't. But I still want to ask Daniel about it—about Jill, if she even exists. Just not over the phone. Certain things need to be done in person.

"I did it," Julie says.

For a moment, I think she's referring to her look. She's changed into a long, gauzy turquoise skirt and a white crop top. She looks young—younger, anyway. Like she's seventeen again. Her face is different, too. Fresh and luminous, more so than usual. I notice she's not wearing any makeup.

"You look great."

She blushes, looking down. "It's from Nana's closet. The skirt." She looks at me expectantly, as if seeking permission. "Is that weird?"

"Why would it be weird?" And then: "Come, eat."

She eyes the plate of bruschetta, picks one up and takes a bite. "This is good," she says, her mouth still full. She chews slowly. "I asked him for a divorce." She delivers this matter-of-factly.

"How are you feeling about it?"

A shrug. "Fine, I guess. It was less momentous than I expected."

"What were you expecting?"

"I don't know. That he'd put up a fight? He didn't. Anyway, I'm relieved." She takes a sip of the wine and makes a face. "I don't like this."

"You're incorrigible." I roll my eyes. "There's beer in the fridge."

A smile. Then another bite of the bruschetta. She makes her way to the refrigerator, takes out a green bottle, opens it against the counter. "He hung up on me."

"I'm sorry." I take a seat at the table. It should feel too big for the two of us, but it doesn't. Julie joins me, beer in hand.

"And told me I wasn't getting any of his money."

"Did you sign a prenup?"

"I don't think so."

"Then I'm pretty sure you're entitled to something."

"I don't want anything."

"Are you sure?" This is surprising. I'm not suggesting that Patrick's finances were the reason Julie married him, but it had to be a factor. Money is always a factor in relationships. People only like to pretend that it's not because it sounds unromantic.

"I'm going to get a job," she says. "Any job."

It's something we've discussed, albeit briefly, her finding a job. She's excited about it. I am, too—excited for her, that is. I'm also worried. In a sense, it's like she's only now growing up. Paying one's bills is an essential part of adulthood.

She continues, "I thought about asking for alimony, but it would make me feel, I don't know, like a child. Which I think was sort of the problem in our marriage. In a strange way, he was like a parent to me: deciding what I could wear, what I could eat. If I take his money, I'll still be dependent on him. I'll still feel like a child."

"Can I help?" I offer. I've been mulling this over in my mind: I've always had more economic privilege than Julie. As a kid, I was powerless to do anything about it. But I'm not a kid anymore. And I've been financially independent since my mom passed away—her death meant that the trust I'd get when I turned twenty-one kicked in when I was seventeen. I explain this to Julie now. "It would be a gift. Not a loan."

She looks touched. "Thank you," she says. "But I couldn't. I'm going to figure this out on my own. I have a few ideas. I don't need much. I thought I did. I thought it would bring me happiness, having a feeling of plenty. But it didn't. I guess I'm still figuring out what makes me happy."

"Cheers to that," I say, lifting my wine glass. We clink, bottle to goblet.

"And to Nana," she says. "For bringing us here."

"To Nana," I say. "Even when she's wrong, she's right."

She sips her beer. "What does that mean?"

"Our father," I begin. "It was wishful thinking on her part, expecting us to come together as a family. That I'd forgive him, anyway. But, in a weird way, I'm glad he came. I needed to say those things to him. I needed to get it off my chest. It felt... cathartic."

Julie tilts her head to the side. There's a sadness in her eyes.

"I know you love him," I say. I almost add, *And that's OK*, but I don't. It's true, obviously. She doesn't need my permission, my blessing.

"Sometimes I wish I didn't," she says, softly.

"I'm not judging you. You know that, right?"

"I know." She sighs, looks down at her beer bottle. I watch her run her thumb over the label. "And, just so you know, I'm not blind to his faults. My relationship with him is different from yours, but it's still not great. I feel like I'm always calling him, not the other way around. And even when we do talk, he doesn't listen to me as much as he should. He needs to be better." She looks up at me. "If he apologized, would you forgive him?"

It's a senseless question. Our father does not apologize. She knows this. But I'll indulge the hypothetical. I owe her as much.

"I like to think that I would," I say. "For my own peace of mind. But I wouldn't want him in my life."

A shadow passes through her face. She's worried about something. What?

"You do know I have no problem with him being in your life, right?" I add.

"I know." She's peeling off the beer label. "I mean, I think I know. I want to believe that. But I worry. Not just about Dad. I worry there won't be space in your life for me when we leave this place. You've got so much going on. Your practice, the show. Your friends. You and Daniel might start a new phase in your relationship, and then you'll be a stepmom. What do I have?" She puts the bottle down and looks around, as if there's an answer waiting for her in Nana's living room.

It occurs to me that Julie spent her childhood waiting for our father to show up. Because he didn't live with her, she only got him in intervals. As an adult, she's still waiting. Except now she's waiting for him to be better, to give her the steadying love she's been craving since she was a little girl. It was the opposite for me. I spent my childhood looking forward to his so-called business trips. His absence meant that there was no shouting, no destruction. All I had to worry about was making sure my mom didn't drink too much. This is why I am comforted by his absence now. And why it's so difficult for Julie to accept it.

"You have me. And yourself. Your creativity, your curiosity. There will always be room for you in my life." I pause, gathering my thoughts. "In fact, there's been a Julie-shaped hole that's been empty until now. Which is my fault, I know."

She cups my hand. "Not your fault. Never say that." A flash of something passes through her eyes: an emotion I can't quite place. A variation of fear.

"The point is that I'll always have room for you." I graze Nana's long reclaimed wood table with my hands. "As much room as this giant table."

She smiles. "I love this giant table."

"I do, too." Pretty soon we'll have to talk next steps. What to do with the house. With the furniture. With Nana's belongings. But not yet. "I've always wondered why she had such a massive table. We've never had a big family."

"She wanted one," Julie says.

"She told you that?"

"I asked her. Years ago. She said she had a dream where we were all around the table with our husbands and grandchildren. There was someone in every seat."

"That's a lot of grandchildren." The table seats twelve.

Julie gives me a funny look. I know what she's thinking. Nana's dream probably included our father, too. Only a mother could hope to such a degree. Although Julie does, too—and she's his daughter. Maybe it's about how big their hearts are.

"I don't understand why you love our father," I say. I've told her about the realization that hit me when we were at his hotel room, about why he was so different as a father to two daughters born only two weeks apart. "I never have, and, frankly, I never will. I get that he's different with you, that he didn't do the things he did to me and my mom, but he was still a lousy father." I place two open palms on my chest. "In *my* opinion. Which is irrelevant, I know. What I'm trying to say is that I don't need to understand something in order to respect it. You do you. Have him in your life, if that's what you want. Forgive him, love him. That's your business. And you can talk to me about him if you want. For you, I'll listen." I almost add, *I'd do anything for you*, but I don't because it sounds dramatic. Still, it's true. It's what sisters do for each other: everything.

She looks at me uneasily, chewing on her bottom lip. "He hasn't reached out."

And he probably won't. I wish she didn't care. Not because I want our father to be punished, but because I want Julie to be spared.

"He did get punched in the face." I try not to smile. Try and fail. "He deserved it."

"Yeah he did." A pause. "Also, my conversation with Elle probably didn't help."

Elle flagged me in the hotel lobby after I left my father on the floor, both his hands cupping his bloody nose. She grabbed my hand and asked me to explain what I meant when I said that my father had terrorized my mother and me. I did not sugarcoat it for her—she has every right to know the kind of man she's dating. Especially given how young she is. They could have a child together. I shudder at the thought.

"I'm not calling him," Julie says. "This time, he has to call me."

"Good for you," I say. I don't add that she shouldn't hold her breath. It would sound cruel, even if I don't mean it to. She says she misses him, but I don't think that's true. She misses the idea of a father. She always has. We both always have. Except there's no point in waiting for someone who doesn't exist.

I, for one, will be glad to never see our father again.

CHAPTER FIFTY-EIGHT

Julie

Thursday, July 26th

After dinner, Kiki and Ben unveil the poster.

"What's this?" Craig asks, peering at the giant map of Montauk.

"Your birthday surprise, Daddy!" Kiki says. Her grin is almost as big as the poster she's holding. And it's a massive poster.

"Do you like it?" Ben beams.

"I love it." Craig takes a step closer and studies the map. The kids drew it themselves, marking his favorite local spots with balloons. Next to Ditch Plains Ben wrote, *This is were my Dad taut me to serf.* Next to Nana's house, Kiki asked me to write in purple, *Nana Bertie's house.* And under that, in blue, *And Julie's.* I followed her instructions very carefully.

"There's more," I say, walking into the kitchen. I come back with the cake: triple chocolate with crushed Oreos lit up by a single candle. We all sing 'Happy Birthday'. I gleefully indulge in not one, but two slices. It's liberating, knowing I'll never fit into my silver dress again—and that I'll never have to run an appearance checklist in front of the mirror.

We finish off the evening with a movie—*Frozen 2*. It's Craig's birthday, but somehow Kiki still got to pick. Ben is a good sport about it and doesn't complain. He even sings along with Olaf (his favorite) and puts up with Kiki and I singing along with Elsa (our favorite). There's a moment when I look around the family room and I think, I couldn't be happier.

And then, when the kids aren't looking, Craig squeezes my hand and gives me a mischievous wink. And just like that I'm proven wrong.

Craig walks onto the porch holding two champagne flutes filled to the brim.

"Surprise," he says, handing me a glass.

"But it's your birthday."

"It's also our three-day anniversary." He takes a seat next to me. "I wanted to do something special."

I giggle. "This is so sweet." And it is. Even if, much to Sophie's horror, I can't stand champagne. My personal theory is that no one really likes it—they just say they do because it's seen as fancy or whatever. I take a whiff of the golden liquid inside the flute.

"It's Heineken," he says, giving me a knowing look. "Your favorite."

"Oh, thank God." I laugh, toying with the seashells dangling from my neck.

"Come here," he says, raising his right arm.

I look up at the second floor. "Are they asleep?"

"Like two rocks."

I nestle in the crook of his arm. "This is my favorite place in the world."

"Mine, too," he says, his eyes on the view.

I wasn't referring to Montauk—I meant in his arms. There's something about being held by him that feels both exhilarating and comforting. But I don't correct him.

"Tomorrow's the twenty-seventh," he says, stroking my hair. "One month since you arrived."

I nod quietly. I don't want to think about it too much. I'm scared of what's waiting for me back in Boston. Packing up my things. Moving in with Janette, at least for a while— she's gotten me an interview as a receptionist at a law firm. Filing for divorce. These are all steps I'm choosing to take. Steps that will lead me to where I want to go. But I wish there was a way to skip them, to be done with them with a magical snap of a finger. To be in the *after* side of my recent decision.

"Would you consider staying longer?" he asks.

"I would love that." It's the truth: I would. "But I have to go back and figure out what to do with my life." It can't be summer forever.

That's what my next story will be about—a place where it's summer forever. Kiki and Ben will love it. I'll be a storyteller to them via FaceTime.

I can feel Craig holding his breath. His chest has stopped moving. "I need to tell you something, but you can't freak out."

"What?" I get up and meet his gaze.

"I'm falling in love with you." He says it without hesitation, without fear. A deep-water dive executed with mastery and confidence.

"I am, too."

His face lights up. He pulls me into a kiss, gentle at first, but then hungry, intense. He wraps his arms around me, his hands working their way down my back. My entire body tingles at his touch.

I pull away reluctantly, mindful of Kiki and Ben's presence above us.

"The kids," I whisper.

"I love them, but this is the first time I wish they were at sleepaway camp."

"I'd miss them during the day. Maybe someone can come up with a sleepover-only camp."

"When can you spend the night? I'll arrange for a sleepover at a friend's house."

"Saturday?" I say. It's when Daniel is coming. It's also when we'll officially be allowed to leave the house.

"Done," he says, pulling me in for another kiss. "Who knows? Maybe I'll convince you to stay, if only a little longer."

"I could be persuaded to stay for an extra day or two." It's getting dark now, twilight turning into night. Soon, the sky will be covered in stars.

"How about for the rest of your life?"

His words catch me off guard. I look at him curiously. I'm expecting a goofy smile, but instead his eyes are locked with mine, a question mark on his face.

"You're not serious."

"I am," he says. "I know it's soon. But I'm ready. I'm in love with you, Julie."

"But we've only known each other for a month." Less than that, actually.

"And we've spent every day together since. By choice." A pause. "And what does it matter how long it's been? When you know, you know. And I know. I love you. My children love you. You love them. I don't care if that sounds crazy. It's true." A pause. He kisses my hand. "I'll wait. Years, if I have to. But just know that I'm all in."

I stare at him, wondering what to say. I want to tell him that I feel it, too. The rush, the certainty. I also want forever with him. But I'm afraid. I can't deep-dive like he can—I need to inch my way into the water.

"I get that you're still married," he continues. "And I respect that. I know that you could go back to Boston and decide to stay with him—"

"That won't happen." I shake my head.

It's the truth. Whether or not Craig is in my future, Patrick is a part of my past.

"I worry because I can't give you the life he can." There's a catch in his voice.

"If you told me you could, I'd be out of here. I don't want that life anymore. I want something real." I exhale. "We can't move too fast because of the kids."

"OK." A slow nod, the beginning of a smile.

"And because of me, too. I feel like I need to be whole before I can be with you."

"Whole?" he asks.

"I feel like a part of me is missing."

"You mean there's more?" He registers my frown and continues, "You're nurturing and kind. You're generous with your time and talents. You're patient with *everyone*, whether it's Mrs. Bunsen or me or my kids or your sister. You're creative—the most creative person I've ever met. You see the world in a way that no one else can, full of color and light and poetry. You have the biggest heart. You've been through so much and yet you resent no one. You say you're not whole, but I can't imagine what's missing."

I let his words sink in. They're a cool glass of water—and I didn't realize how thirsty I was. No one's ever described me like that before.

"Is that how you see me?"

"Jul, don't you see?" he begins, softly. "That's how the world sees you."

I feel my eyes well up with tears. I can't believe that anyone—let alone someone as wonderful as Craig—sees me like that. The person he's describing is magical, special. And I've never been special. Not to my dad. Not to Sophie. And certainly not to Patrick.

But then I remember Nana. Nana, who knew me at my worst, and still loved me. Who never made me feel like the other granddaughter. Who helped me come into my own. For years, Nana was both my safe harbor and my wind. Mine and Cassie's.

Cassie. I'm special to her, too.

"I'm getting there," I say, mostly to myself. "I need something of my own though. Not just a job. A career."

Craig nods like this is all very reasonable. And it is—I know that. I'm just not used to this level of validation. I've been with Patrick for too long.

"You have all the time in the world to figure out what to do," he says.

"Actually, I think I might already know."

I lean in to tell him.

CHAPTER FIFTY-NINE

Cassie

Friday, July 27th

We're calling it The Last Friday. And it is: our last Friday in Montauk. As of tomorrow, we'll be free to leave Nana's house. All we have to do is spend one final night here. Together.

"I'm a little sad," Julie says, taking a sip of lemonade. "Are you sad?"

"More than a little." Though I don't get why. It'll be a relief to know that we've fulfilled our obligation, to be able to have people over, to sleep wherever we want. Not that I have any other place to go on the island. Julie does, of course. She'll probably go over to Craig's tomorrow and spend the night.

"Would you stay an extra few days?" she asks. I can tell by her tone that she's thinking of doing just that. She should, if that's what she wants. The house will soon be ours. Officially.

"It depends on Daniel." This shouldn't irritate me, but it does. A lot about my life feels dependent on Daniel lately. I don't like it.

"How are you feeling about tomorrow?" she asks.

Tomorrow is when Daniel arrives. He's staying for the weekend. We'll talk, I'll ask him about Jill. Hopefully, he'll tell me that Tatiana is a liar. Hopefully, I'll believe him.

"I'm dreading it, to be honest. I've had this sick feeling in the pit of my stomach ever since she called." Daniel and I talk every day, but I've managed to refrain from bringing it up. I'm proud of my self-control—and more than a little relieved to finally deal with this in person tomorrow.

"That's understandable." Her tone is soft, tender.

"I don't know." I crinkle my nose. "A month ago, I wouldn't have cared. I would've been sure she was lying."

"And now?"

"Now, I feel plagued by doubt and it's eating away at me."

"You're used to certainty."

"I am." I take a deep breath. "But at least I'm certain about what I want."

"Which is?"

"He needs to leave her. Now. I'm not waiting."

"An ultimatum? Are you sure?" There's a note of apprehension in her voice. It's upsetting. Does she think he'll choose her? "Labor Day is a little over a month away."

"And what if she asks him to stay until Thanksgiving? Because Ava or whoever is having a Turkey-Day feast. And then Christmas? Where does it end?" The real question is this: when do I get to be his priority?

"Your phone," Julie says.

"What?" I shoot her a confused look.

She juts her chin towards my phone. It's buzzing. I hadn't even noticed. It's Daniel.

"I'm going to take this inside," I say, getting up from the daybed. It's as comfortable as a cloud. "Hey, when did Nana get this, do you know?" I ask, pointing to the daybed.

"About five years ago."

"I love it."

Inside, I answer the phone.

"Guess who's on his way to you?" he says.

"You are not," I say, feeling a smile at the corner of my mouth. "Are you really?"

"Don't worry, I have a room for tonight. I know I'm not allowed to stay over yet." I can hear him smile. "But I'll be there in time for dinner."

A beat. Julie and I had made dinner plans at the Barracuda Bar. A few gray clouds have started to form in the sky, but I'm hoping it'll be nothing more than a short burst of summer rain. We want to sit outside.

"Cass?" he asks.

"Sorry, I'm here. Julie and I made plans for dinner. But we'll make it a double date. Craig will come." Assuming he can get a babysitter, that is. "What about the kids?" I remember Daniel telling me that Tatiana was spending the weekend in Nantucket with Ava to plan for the party. "Weren't you going to drop them off at Bella's tomorrow on your way here?"

"She picked them up today." And then: "I thought you'd be happy with the surprise."

"I am," I say. I'm also a little nervous.

I open the fridge. I wasn't going to eat before our outing, but I need a snack. I take out a half-eaten jar of peanut butter. I'll have that with leftover bruschetta bread. Maybe some bananas, too.

"Good. Because I can't wait to see you."

"Me, too."

We hang up. I feel a flurry of nerves in my stomach. I decide to forfeit the bread and eat the peanut butter straight out of the jar. Upon further inspection, there's at least two-quarters left.

I'm not sure how long I stay like this: standing dumbly in Nana's kitchen, compulsively stuffing my face. But by the time Julie walks into the house, I've finished the jar.

CHAPTER SIXTY

Julie

Friday, July 27th

It is not impossible that Cassie is pregnant. Even if she seems to think it is.

"It's something I ate." She's hugs the toilet, sweat beads gathering at her forehead.

"But we ate the same things." I'm trying to hold on to her unruly mane. "And I feel fine." This is something I'm particularly thankful for. No one likes getting sick, but I have a particular aversion to throwing up.

"Peanut butter."

"What?"

"I had peanut butter." She looks up at me from the bathroom floor.

"When did you buy peanut butter?"

"I thought you did."

"I don't like peanut butter." It's one of the few tics of Sophie that she's managed to successfully pass on to me. She'd sooner eat sand. "It must've been left behind by Nana."

Cassie groans. "I thought it tasted funny."

"Then why'd you eat it?"

"I had to eat something," she says. Her voice is a plea. "I'm a stress eater, you know that. When Daniel called to say he was coming, it made me think of asking him about Jill, and the ultimatum. I'm feeling insecure."

An insecure Cassie: the personification of an oxymoron.

"You'll be fine," I remind her. "Even if it is true, even if he has seen someone before, you know he loves you. That counts for something." This much is true: Cassie might not realize it, but she talks about Daniel with the ease of someone who is confident in their lover's adoration. What I don't add is that the same was true of Sophie. She had reason to be, too—I grew up around their love. But some men simply don't leave their wives.

"Will you check on Daniel?"

"He's fine." He's downstairs, waiting. I say make him wait. He's making Cassie wait because of some stupid Labor Day party. "But we're obviously not going out."

"Yes we are," she protests. "Chocolate Martinis at the Barracuda Bar." She raises her fist in a pathetic attempt at enthusiasm.

"It's raining. The Barracuda Bar is probably closed." I put my palm on her forehead. "And the only thing you'll be drinking tonight is tea."

She groans but doesn't press the matter. Which is definitive proof that she is sick.

"Do you want me to get him?" I ask. He'll have to go to his hotel eventually, he can't stay the night, but they can at least hang out for a little while.

"Would you go?"

"Go where?"

"Out," she says. "With Daniel."

"And leave you here?" My voice goes up an octave. "Why on earth would we do that?"

"The plan," Cassie mumbles.

Ah, yes. The plan. Earlier today, when she told me Daniel was joining us tonight, Cassie asked me to observe how Daniel acts around her. "I hate that I'm second-guessing myself," she'd said.

"But I need an outsider's perspective. Just watch him with me. See if you think he loves me and only me. If he's the kind of man who would have, you know, *other* other women."

"How can I observe you two together when you're not there?" I ask.

"You know men. It's your superpower."

"Do I need to remind you of my failed marriage?"

"Please?" she asks. "Craig isn't joining us until later, is he?"

She knows he's not. He's joining us for late-night drinks once the kids are in bed. He trusts the sitter, but she's never tucked them in before. They need their dad.

"I'm not going to be able to tell you much," I say now.

"Come on, Jul. Do it for me."

"If you can convince him to go out, then I will."

"Challenge accepted," she says. And then she lifts herself from the bathroom floor and proceeds to brush her teeth.

Daniel is hard to convince. He suggests we order in. I wholeheartedly agree.

"Can you two just go?" Cassie asks. She's lying on the sectional couch. "I need to sleep it off and I won't be able to do that with you here."

"We're not leaving you," he says. I appreciate that his tone seems to suggest that her plan is ridiculous. He reaches for her hand. The gesture is tender, heartwarming.

"Craig is right next door. And he's coming over later," Cassie says. "Please? It'll help me get better."

"I don't want to go without you." He looks at me. "And I'm sure neither does Julie."

"Agreed," I say. "I can cook. What are you in the mood for?"

"We don't have anything," Cassie says, giving me some serious side-eye. "At least pick something up."

"Are you even hungry?" he asks.

"I will be after a nap. It's out of my system. I just need to rest now. And that way I won't feel bad that you're stuck inside because of me. It's a compromise."

"It's raining. We're supposed to stay inside."

"It's barely drizzling," Cassie says.

As if on cue, we hear thunder. I know that Cassie wants a second opinion, but this is ridiculous. And it's most certainly *not* drizzling.

"I'll go. Julie can keep you company," he says. Daniel is a tough negotiator. Maybe Cassie has found her match.

"You're both going or I'll be mad." She crosses her arms in front of her chest and pouts. That seals it. She wins.

I shouldn't be surprised.

The Westlake Fish House isn't packed, but it is busy. An overworked server hurriedly informs us that there's a forty-minute wait on all takeout orders.

"Minimum," he adds, for emphasis. "It's the rain. People order in."

"Want to go someplace else?" Daniel asks me. His tone is casual, friendly.

"I don't mind," I say. We'll be waiting wherever we go.

We place our orders, take a seat by the bar, and each order two beers—I'm happy Daniel is not a wine bully like Cassie. They're playing *Bossa Nova* in the background, a song I recognize because it's one Patrick likes. It's funny how I think of him but don't miss him.

Daniel asks about Cassie right away. Predictable questions (What was she like as a child? How did it work, our relationship as summer sisters?), but also deeper, more thoughtful questions (Do I feel like she'll be OK after the conversation with Dad? Is there anything we'd like to do to honor Nana's life now that she's gone?). He expresses happiness about us having mended our friendship and regret that he'll never get to meet Nana. He talks about Cassie with a mixture of awe and pride. And yet he seems to see her—all of her. Past the armor, the tough exterior. By the time the server lets us know that our food should be coming out shortly, I realize two things:

He hasn't uttered a single sentence that wasn't about Cassie.

And I've never seen a man more in love with his girlfriend. (I'm sticking to *girlfriend*. I hate all the other terms.)

I text Cassie when he excuses himself to go to the restroom.

> *Today 8:46 P.M.*
> *He loves you. I have no doubt.*

Today 8:46 P.M.
Are you sure????

> *Today 8:47 P.M.*
> *You're the one who said I have a superpower, remember?*

Today 8:47 P.M.
Thank you, thank you, thank you! I AM SO HAPPY!

On the drive back home, I decide to act like a normal sister-in-law, which is to say: grill him mercilessly about his intentions with Cassie.

"We have something else in common other than Cassie," I say.

"What?" he asks.

"We're both in bad marriages."

After a month with the Fire Princess, the Sky Princess has mastered the art of direct confrontation.

"True." A sad smile.

"I asked Patrick for a divorce," I tell him. I don't add that since then I've been experiencing equal parts fear and excitement. And something else, too. I've felt…liberated.

"Cassie mentioned that." This is yet another sign of how close they are: they tell each other everything. Or at least she does. "How did he take it?"

"Not well. But it had to be done. I'm hiring a lawyer when I get back."

"He's a lawyer, right?"

"Yep."

"Ouch. Divorcing a lawyer can't be easy."

"Do you have one?"

"Do I have what?"

"A lawyer."

A pause. And then: "You don't have kids, do you?"

"No." It's my least favorite question in the world. Even more than, *What do you do for a living?* It brings me a small amount of comfort to know there's a chance that maybe one day Kiki and Ben will be my children.

I need to stop making plans though. I'm no longer a Charlotte. I'm a Carrie.

If Cassie were here, she'd tell me that I'm not a character from *Sex and the City*. I'm Julie—and that's better than anyone else.

"It's complicated when there are children involved," he says.

I don't disagree. I know about the situation with his daughter, although I've forgotten her name now. Not that I'd bring that up.

"I never thought I'd get divorced," I say.

"Does anyone?"

"Some people are more open to the idea. I was very much till-death-do-us-part."

It's what I told myself when things got tough with Patrick. When I worried that I'd made a mistake. I had to hold on to the idea of a real family as something indestructible. Something different from the scattered pieces I had as a kid.

I'm about to offer to refer him to my lawyer when I hear a loud, screeching sound, followed by a crashing noise coming from a distance. I can't pinpoint its exact origin, but it sounds like it happened up ahead. Close to us.

"Was that a car?" Daniel asks me.

"I think so?" I don't drive, but I know that accidents are that much more common when it's raining. Especially now that's it's dark.

"That was loud. No one's walking away from that."

I feel a hollow shiver run through my body as he says that. I close my eyes and send a silent prayer to whoever was in that accident. *Please, God, let them be OK.*

CHAPTER SIXTY-ONE

Cassie

Friday, July 27th

The encouragement brought by Julie's text only lasts a second.

As soon as I put my phone down, I see him: a lone, soaked figure on Nana's porch. My father. It's dark outside, but the lights are on in the living room, which is how I know he can see me, too, through the glass windows. Our eyes lock.

I make my way to the door, swallowing my fear. I have no reason to be afraid. Still, I shiver as I open it and hear the wind chimes tinkling urgently. Their music is different against the rainy background.

"Cassie," he says. "Is Julie here?" He's wetter than I'd expect. Like he walked all the way over here without an umbrella. Which would be impossible, of course. I peer behind him. An unfamiliar car is in the driveway. I'm not sure how I didn't hear him arriving, probably because of the rain.

"No," I say. "What do you want?"

"This is my house, too."

"No, it isn't."

"It will be. I'm contesting the will."

I scoff, shaking my head. I wish Julie were here to hear him say this so casually, like he's within his rights. I knew he was up to something. Why else would he have come? It certainly wasn't to respect Nana's wishes.

"On what grounds?"

"Funny thing about New York law, a will can be contested for pretty much any reason." A pause. I doubt that's true. Still, I feel a lump forming in my throat. "Your grandmother wasn't herself towards the end. Why else would she have overlooked her only son?"

"I thought we covered that when we last spoke. You were a disappointment to her."

"I don't think that's how a judge will see it. I have more than enough evidence to the contrary." He tilts his head to the side. "Of course, we could come to an agreement. Avoid the litigation."

I let out a low laugh. "Yeah, that's not happening. Nana's will was perfectly clear and Julie and I have done our part. As of tomorrow, this place will be ours."

I begin to close the door, but he blocks it with his foot. I push, but he does, too—and I'm no match for him. He steps forward and I step back, a sick tango. He's inside the house now.

"I think you should hear me out," he says. "Unless you want the world to find out that Miss Couple's Therapist is sneaking around with a married guy."

It feels like all the air has left the room. I struggle to hold myself upright. To breathe.

"Sophie told me everything," he continues. "I should thank you for that, by the way. I wouldn't have called her if you and your sister hadn't made such a big deal about how *messed up* you are. Tell me: does he have kids? Not that I'm judging: I know how *complicated* these things can be." He stares at me for an extra beat, his mouth open in a perverse grin. I can't bring myself to say anything. My mind is spinning uncontrollably. "Fine, don't tell me. I've already contacted a private investigator. I'll know soon enough."

"Leave," I say, my heart thumping against my ribcage.

"Here's how this is going to work. We'll sell the house. You and Julie can keep half the money. If you think about it, you'll see that I'm being generous here."

I stare into his eyes. The Meyer emerald green, like mine and Julie's. Like Nana's. But on him, the color looks off, like it's infected. Eyes of a sick man. Because that's what he is. I take a deep breath and steady myself. He's not going to push me around. Not anymore.

"I don't know what you're talking about," I begin.

"Save it, Cassie—"

I raise my hand. "But even if I did, I'd never give in to you. I don't care what you do. You think you know something?" I grit my teeth and stare at him. "Do your worst. I'm not scared of you anymore."

I see him clench his fists and for a split second I think that he actually might hurt me. But I'm not going to be ruled by fear. I'm not going to back down. He's taken so much from me already. He's not taking this house.

"Fine." He sneers. "I'll keep it all to myself then. I'll probably sell it." He cranes his neck, as if appraising the house.

"What's wrong, are you short on cash?" I ask. "Couldn't find another rich woman to exploit now that you're old and balding?"

He isn't balding—but he is vain.

"Or maybe I'll keep it and let your sister visit." He runs his tongue against his inner cheek. "She's a lot nicer."

"We agree on that much."

"You know, I understand why your grandmother was able to forgive her. She was always soft, and God knows she never liked Katherine." He tilts his head. "What I don't understand is how you were able to get over it."

"What are you talking about?" I feel my forehead crease.

He raises his eyebrows, a smile spreading on his lips. "Ah, so you didn't read the letter after all."

"What letter?"

"The letter your grandmother left me. If you'd read it, you'd know what your sister did."

"What are you talking about?"

He stares at me intently. "Julie was the one who sent those pictures to your mom."

"That's ridiculous," I say. My voice is only a whisper. I feel queasy, weak. "Sophie sent those pictures." I expect a lot from my father. Selfishness. Greed. All manners of cowardly behavior. But I didn't expect this. This is a new low, even for him.

"I thought so, too. I only found out it was Julie weeks after your mom died." He looks to the side. "Do you want to know how? It was her handwriting. On the envelope. By then Sophie wouldn't take me back."

I blink. Once, then twice. "Julie would never do that."

"Maybe you should ask her."

I picture telling Julie what our father has said about her. She'll be devastated, I'm sure. But maybe it'll be good, in the long run. Maybe she'll finally take off her rose-colored glasses and come to grips with who he really is.

"Leave," I say again.

He gives out an ugly laughter, turns around, and marches out the door.

I watch as he gets inside the car. I want him off my property. How dare he say these things about Julie? Is he that desperate for money—has he blown through my mom's inheritance? Or is it out of spite, because he resents Julie and me being back in each other's lives? I've always suspected he loved our estrangement. Unhappy people want everyone else to be unhappy, too. It's something Nana used to say.

Except something is still bothering me. Something he said. *So you didn't read the letter after all.* I'd told him I read Nana's letter to him. Back in his hotel room. I didn't specify that it was the one he hadn't received.

I hear a low rumble of an engine. I'm not sure what makes me step outside, but I do. I stare into his car. I can't see him, but I can feel his presence. The twisted thing that lives inside him.

"Wait," I shout. I hurry down the porch steps, in the rain, to his car. Pain shoots up my ankle. I'm about to knock on the window, but he lowers it.

"Prove it," I say. My breath is ragged in my throat. "Show me the letter."

"Get in," he says.

"I'm not getting in a car with you."

"Then follow me in yours." He rolls his eyes. I look at my ankle, still swollen. There's no way I can drive. "Do you want to read it or not?"

It's a stupid move. Not just getting into a car with my father—but indulging his lunacy. He's bluffing. He has to be. But something's been nagging at me. A memory, a feeling, lodged inside my brain. I can't let this go.

I get in the car.

We're on Old Montauk Highway by the time I realize that I left my phone behind. Julie and Daniel are probably heading back. What will they think when they arrive at the house and don't see me? I know Daniel's number by heart. I could call him from the hotel. Or I could ask Elle to use her phone. I'm not about to ask to use my father's.

"Where's your girlfriend?" I ask. We've been driving in silence until now. The only noise is coming from the windshield wiper, rubbery and busy.

"Elle left." His voice is steely, cold. And then: "Because of what you said to her."

Now it makes sense, why he came all the way here. Why he's making up these lies.

"Good for her," I say.

"It's for the best," he says. "Who knows? Now that Sophie and I are talking again…" He taps the steering wheel with the tip of his fingers. "We've always gotten along well, her and me." A wave of nausea hits me, a familiar response when hearing my dad talk about Sophie. "Maybe this time you two can get along," he continues, a smirk on his face. "Now that you know it's not her fault your mom's dead."

"I don't *know* anything."

"Sure you do." He clicks his tongue. "Admit it, Cassie. A part of you has always known. Why else would you have stopped speaking to Julie like that?"

He glances at me expectantly. I turn away.

"The more you think about it, the more it'll make sense," he continues, as I stare out the window. I can barely see anything because the rain is coming down harder now. "An impulsive move like that? That's classic Julie." I hear him suck in air through his teeth. "I feel bad for her, always have. She's always been so hard on herself. It's why I never told her I knew about what she'd done."

I feel my eyes sting. I hate that he can still make me want to cry after so many years.

That's when I feel it, the pop of a memory. I think back to that day, to the dinner we had on Newbury Street. Julie had been acting strangely quiet. Almost like she was nervous. I remember how I had to shake her into action. How guilty she looked at the hospital. She was in shock.

I relive our past month together. The look she gets on her face when I mention my mom. I thought it was sadness. A feeling of misplaced guilt because of her mother's actions. Shame over me reading her stories on her phone.

But no—it's remorse.

It was Julie.

Julie is the reason my mother is dead.

A knife blade slicing through my chest: that's what it feels like. Sharp, cutting pain.

But…why? Julie kept our father's affair a secret for years. Why would she do that when we were so close to living our dream of going off to college together?

I turn to face my father. He's looking right at me. I feel a salty taste in my mouth. I hadn't realized I'd been crying.

"Stop the car," I manage to say. There's a ringing in my ear. A continuous, high-pitched shriek.

"Relax, we're almost there."

"Stop the car!" I repeat.

"Jesus, shut up." He looks at me. "I can't just pull over in the middle of a highway."

I want to yell back at him, but I can't. My heart is beating too fast, like it jumped out of its usual spot in my chest and is now trying to free itself from my body. I remind myself to breathe because I seem to be forgetting and end up gasping for air after a few seconds of holding my breath. I use my right hand to clutch my chest.

"Cassie?" I hear him say. "Jesus, Cassie." I look up and meet his eyes. We stare at each other for a beat. I wonder if I'm having a heart attack. I don't want him to be the last person I see.

Another blaring noise pierces through my brain. Louder this time. Like a honk.

My father turns to face the road. Headlights flood our view. "Shit!" he yells.

He hits the brakes, but the car begins to swerve uncontrollably, screeching like it's trying to stick to the asphalt to save its life. We crash.

And then it all goes dark.

CHAPTER SIXTY-TWO

Julie

Friday, July 27th

It happens in a rush.

Frantic flashes of red flood the otherwise dark road. Men in blue run towards the car. The smell of rubber and gasoline overpowers the salt-heavy air.

I lunge forward: I need to get her out of the car. But something holds me back. I'm a butterfly trapped by a spider.

I can see. I can smell. I can feel.

But I can't hear.

I can't hear the cry coming from my throat. Or the sound of the paramedics yanking the car door open. I can't hear Daniel, who's kneeling down on the floor, his face twisted in pain, in horror. All I hear is a steady, machine-like ring deep inside my skull.

And then she's out of the car, motionless in a stranger's arms. Her tall, Amazonian figure, invincible and unbreakable, reduced to a cloth doll. Her eyes are closed. Her arm is twisted in a way that looks both painful and unnatural. If she's dead, then I want to be dead, too. I don't want to exist in a world without my sister. I can't.

Someone spins me around. Dad.

He is now in front of me, looking agitated, flustered. His lips are moving.

That's the last thing I remember.

A familiar voice is saying my name. I feel my eyelids fluttering. Wherever I am, the lights are too bright. And it's cold.

"Jul?" This is a voice I recognize. Craig.

I touch my forehead. My hands feel like ice.

"How are you feeling?"

"Am I hurt?" I search my brain for a memory, but I'm drawing a blank.

"You're OK," Craig says, frowning with concern. "Don't push yourself."

"Shouldn't the doctor have gotten back to us by now?" says the other voice. I can place it this time. It's Daniel.

Slowly, I begin to remember. Daniel and I were driving back to Nana's, takeout food in hand. We were chatting about something—what was it? My divorce. That's right, I was trying to get information for Cassie.

And then it hits me.

Cassie. Dad. The accident.

Daniel was the one who suggested we call 911. The crash had been loud, the agonizing sound of tires screeching on asphalt. We'd been curious when we drove past it. Fixated on the twisted allure of an accident scene. We stopped when we saw Dad standing outside the car, his hands on top of his head. I shouted to Daniel to pull over. Panic rippled through my veins when I understood that Cassie was inside the car.

But why would Cassie have been in a car with Dad?

I grab Craig's arm. "Where's Cassie?" I sit up, ignoring the ache in the back of my head. I take in my surroundings: I'm in a hospital bed, wearing a coat over my dress. I run my fingers through the unfamiliar garment. It's soft, fleece-like.

"She's going to be OK," Craig says.

"We don't know that," Daniel says. His tone is altogether different. Steely, almost angry. He looks different, too. Like he's aged ten years.

"Can I see her?" My mouth feels dry. I need water. Lots of it.

Daniel and Craig exchange a look. Something passes between them. Concern, certainly. But something else, too. Daniel's lips are pressed into a thin line, his jaw tense. They're keeping something from me. Something about Cassie.

"What's going on?" My tone is pleading. My eyes dart between them.

Craig holds my hand. "Your father went to the house to see Cassie. He said some things…" He shakes his head somberly.

"What things?" I'm agitated now. "Wait, is Dad in the hospital, too?"

"He told her you were the one who sent her mother those pictures when…" Craig's voice trails off. He doesn't finish his sentence—he doesn't have to. When we were teenagers. When Katherine killed herself.

But, no. That can't be right. Dad doesn't know it was me. He thinks it was Sophie.

"He's here. He'll be fine," Daniel says. "Not that I give a damn." And then, under his breath: "Bastard."

I feel my heart stop, like all the air in the room has gone. And I can't breathe.

"Why would she…?" I clutch the side of the bed. I can't bring myself to finish my sentence. The room is spinning. I swallow. My mouth is dry, cottony. "Why was she in the car with him?"

"He didn't tell us," Craig says.

"You talked to him?" I ask.

Craig nods. He's about to say something when Daniel interrupts, "Want to know what he's worried about? Getting sued. Started talking to me about how she wasn't wearing a seatbelt and that's on her." He twists his face in an expression of disgust. "No wonder Cassie hates him."

"Cassie knows it was me?" I sound like a mouse.

"She does," Craig's voice is barely a whisper.

I remember that Daniel is in the room and cover my mouth with my hand. A reflex. But it's an unnecessary one now. My secret has been revealed. I force myself to look my sister's boyfriend in the eyes. Daniel looks tired, but not angry. "I'm so sorry."

"You were just a kid," Craig offers. I notice that Daniel doesn't agree.

It doesn't make any sense. How did my father find out?

"We don't know," Daniel says. I'd been saying the words out loud, without realizing it. "We don't know anything."

This is all my fault. Cassie's accident is all my fault.

"Can I see her?" I look at Daniel.

He shakes his head. "The doctor is supposed to come by to give us an update."

"Who's her doctor?" I ask.

"Lockhart," Daniel replies. "She's supposed to be good."

"What did she say?" I want to know everything.

"For now, we don't know. She's in a medically-induced coma," Craig begins. I cover my mouth. I can't feel my fingers. Craig continues, "It's common in trauma cases—"

"She hit her head," Daniel interrupts. "There's swelling. They don't know if she'll be OK, we won't know that until she wakes up. All we know for now is that her arm is broken but we can't be sure of other injuries. They ran some tests, but we don't have the results yet."

"Jul, she could be totally fine," Craig whispers. "We need to have faith."

I'm flooded with a feeling that is both unbearable and familiar. Despair. The first time I felt it was all those years ago, on the night Katherine died. When I begged God to turn back time. To take back my mistake. To spare Cassie the loss of her mother.

I meet Craig's eyes. He looks heartbroken, which is strangely comforting. Maybe it's because I know his heart is breaking for me. I'm thankful he's here. That's when a thought occurs to me.

"How did you know I was here?" I ask him. "And where are Kiki and Ben?"

"He called your phone," Daniel says. "I answered."

Craig nods. "I came right away. Kiki and Ben are with a friend. They're all right."

I'm glad they're not at the hospital. Kids should never have to come to a hospital.

"I need to see her." I look at Craig. "I can't live without her."

Craig nods, blinking back tears. "Give me a minute. I'll be back."

Daniel and I sit in silence: him on a chair, me on the bed. I want to beg him for forgiveness, but I know I can't. I don't deserve forgiveness.

When Craig comes back, he's with a short, stocky woman with big brown eyes. Kind eyes. She's wearing scrubs.

"My name is Andrea," she says. "I'm Craig's friend and nurse here." She lowers her tone. "Are you feeling better? You fainted."

"I have low blood sugar. I'm fine now." Not an outright lie: physically, I feel fine. I stand up as if to illustrate my point.

She tilts her head and then gives me a slow nod. "I can take you to see your sister. But that's all you can do, OK? See her."

"I promise." I feel a wave of gratitude. "Thank you. Thank you so much."

"Follow me," she says.

Andrea takes me down a long, white corridor of identical doors. She stops in front of a door marked 312. She's reaching for the door handle when I put a hand on her arm.

"Will she be able to see me?" I ask.

Andrea shakes her head. "I'm sorry," she says. Her tone is gentle. "But your dad is doing well. He's right down the hall."

I can't think about Dad right now. My mind is on Cassie. "She really dislikes hospitals," I say. "Like, a lot."

Andrea nods. "Her husband explained that to me. We made a note on her file."

We step inside.

Cassie is lying on the bed. Her eyes are closed. Her left arm is in a sling. I notice a small cut on her lower lip, but other than that she looks peaceful. Like she's asleep.

Nana would want me to burn sage in her room. To mix garlic, ginseng and gingko and apply it to her cut. She'd make Cassie tea. Chamomile, probably, and hold it in front of her nose so at least she would inhale some of the herb's medicinal power.

The spirit of the Queen Mother hears the distress call coming from the Sky Princess. The Fire Princess is hurt. She needs to hurry. The Queen Mother allows her spirit to descend into the room, where she quietly sprinkles tiny, lilac-scented particles of love—the most powerful medicine in all of the universes. The Fire Princess inhales the magic particles and is cured.

Nothing. Cassie's eyes are still closed.

It only takes me a few minutes to find Dad's room.

"*Ma petite*," he says, when he sees me in the doorway. His tone is gentle, calm. There's a white strip around his nose. I can tell it's badly bruised and swollen. "I'm so glad to see you."

"Daddy." It sounds like a sigh. I feel the tears in my eyes spring up as I take a seat on the corner of his bed. It's firm and cold—the air-conditioning vent is directly above me. The room is nice, though. Or nice enough: spacious and wide, with a flat-screen TV, and a narrow couch with thin, blue cushions that probably emit air when someone sits on it.

"Shh, it's OK." His tone is soothing. There's a reproduction of Monet's *Water Lilies* behind his bed. That's probably meant to be soothing, too. "It'll be all right. Everything will be all right."

"What if she doesn't wake up?" The words come out in between sobs. My hands are covering my face. I can hear the ticking of a wall clock.

"She will," he tells me. "Cassie is very strong."

At this, my heart swells. It's nice to hear him say that about her. For a moment, I wonder if maybe this accident happened so we could all get along. But then I remember what he did. I look up and meet his gaze.

"Daddy, did you tell Cassie I sent Katherine those pictures?"

He swallows. "I didn't mean to," he says, his head hanging heavy. He's so pale, he's nearly matching the room's white walls.

I feel more tears coming. I want to be angry at him, but I'm not. I'm not even upset. Right now, all my emotions are directed towards one thing and one thing only: Cassie. I want her to wake up. I want her to be well. Even if that means she'll hate me forever. I wipe away my tears and take a deep breath.

"I'm glad you're here," he says.

I nod. I'm about to tell him that I have to go—I want to be alone—but he continues.

"There's something I wanted to talk to you about. You and Cassie first got here on June twenty-seventh. Is that right?"

I frown. "Yeah," I say. "I think so."

"Then you need to go home."

"Why?"

"To make sure you won't lose the house."

I blink. "Daddy, now isn't really the time to be worried about—"

"I know about Cassie's affair. Sophie told me everything."

"Sophie?" My head feels heavy and fragile, like a balloon that's been filled with too much water and it's about to burst. "Dad, what are you talking about?"

"Don't you see? The house can be ours. You'll go back to spend your final night there. That way you get half. Cassie won't get a thing—it's clear she'll be here all night. So, come tomorrow, you'll be the only one with a legitimate claim to your grandmother's house."

I'm about to tell him that's not how it works, that Cassie and I both need to be at Nana's, when I feel a spike of something. Irritation. "What do you mean, I'll get half?"

"I'll take Cassie's half. We'll split it fifty-fifty. Cassie won't contest it. Not if I promise her I won't say anything about her affair."

I can feel my mouth hanging open. "You're proposing that we blackmail Cassie and cheat her out of her inheritance?" I deliver these words slowly, incredulously.

"She doesn't need the money, Julie. She has her trust fund."

"I can't do this anymore." The words leave my mouth without my permission, but as soon as I hear them, I recognize their truth. "Dad, we don't know if Cassie will *wake up*. Or how she'll feel even if she does."

"*Ma petite*." He looks confused. He puts a hand on his chest. "It wasn't my fault."

I feel a catch in my throat. "Your daughter is in the hospital and you're worried about property." I don't phrase it as a question because it's not. I can't ignore it anymore: he's showing me who he is. He's been showing me who he is for a long time now.

"You're looking at this the wrong way, *ma petite*." He drops his shoulder. "I'm just looking out for you. Like I've done for all these years. I've always known that you sent those pictures. I never talked to you about it because I didn't want you to feel bad. I love you. You're my good girl."

I close my eyes for a moment. I feel stricken. When I open them again, my gaze lands on Monet's swirls of yellow and green. I remember the day I learned about impressionism in school, about how, up close, the brushstrokes looked broken and ugly. That's what I'm seeing now: someone broken and ugly.

"We don't have to talk about it now," he says. "We're all in shock. It's been a long night. Did I tell you my car was totaled?"

His car. At this, I shake my head. "I don't think I can be your daughter anymore."

His lips part slightly. He looks like I just slapped him across the face. "What?"

"I'm sorry," I say, even though I'm not. "You're not good for me."

"Jul—"

"No," I say, holding up an open palm. "You've said enough. Please stop." I force myself to take a deep breath. "You won't be contesting the will. You'll lose if you do. I guarantee it. We received letters from Nana, too. She did not have nice things to say about you, Dad."

And with that, I walk away. I half expect him to call out my name, but he doesn't.

Maybe he's in shock. Maybe he never cared about me. Maybe it's something else.

Whatever it is, I put it—and him—behind me.

I've said all I have to say. I've said goodbye.

CHAPTER SIXTY-THREE

Julie

Saturday, July 28th

I've been thinking about our phone calls.

It feels like a lifetime ago. And, technologically speaking, it was. This was before cell phones, before instant messaging and caller ID—at least for me. Sophie didn't believe in spending money to find out who was on the other end of the line. It was a hidden part of our lives, like everything else we shared in the months in between summers. We had a system in place to reach each other: simple and effective. Cassie would call my house, the landline—this was back when landlines were a thing. She'd let it ring twice. If I was home (I usually was), if I could talk (I usually could), I'd call her back.

Sophie knew about our system. She once asked me what we talked about for so long. A fair question: we did spend entire afternoons with our ears glued to our phones. She dropped hints that Cassie should just *call like a normal person*. The implication had been clear: there was no need for secrecy at our home. What Sophie failed to grasp was that the secrecy wasn't for her sake—it was for Katherine's. It was not unreasonable to assume Katherine knew our number. Cassie didn't want her mother checking the phone bill, counting dozens of calls to Sophie's number. She'd assume they were from our dad.

We had a secret to protect, together. Until we didn't. Until I traded that secret for another one—this one wholly mine. A darker, shameful secret born out of spite and envy.

A secret that could cost Cassie her life.

"Do you blame me?" I ask.

Daniel looks up at me. His eyes are red and swollen. We've been sitting in a pair of blue chairs for over twelve hours. It's morning, has been morning for a while. We haven't said a word to each other, or to anyone else other than the doctor, who was here hours ago. We were told to go home. Promised a phone call when she woke up. We both refused.

"No." His voice is hoarse.

"You should."

"I did when I first heard. Now I just…" He lets out a heavy sigh as his shoulders drop. He has the look of a defeated man. "I just want her to be OK."

"I do, too."

He doesn't say anything back. Why would he?

"She'll be really glad you're here," I say. "When she wakes up." *When*. It's all I have for now: hope. It isn't lost on me that I am waiting for someone who doesn't want to see me. At least I'll have the memories of this past month to keep me going. It's not much, but it's something.

"You want to know who I blame?" He looks up at me.

"Who?" I ask. I expect him to say my dad. He's been discharged. Andrea told me. He didn't try to find me, which is a relief. I've already called Sophie and told her all about his plan to try to take our inheritance away. To her credit, she's agreed not to take his calls until I'm back in Boston and her and I can have a proper conversation. I'll need to establish better boundaries with Sophie. She also promised to stop spreading the rumor that Cassie is seeing a married man—I insisted it was *not* true and suggested that if she wasn't careful, she could face a defamation suit.

"Myself," Daniel says.

"Oh, Daniel, whatever for?"

"I should've talked to her when I had the chance. I knew she was upset about something. She was weird over the phone. Distant. It's why I decided to surprise her, show up a day earlier."

"To tell her you left Tatiana?"

Daniel shakes his head. "No. To get her to understand why I need more time."

"She wouldn't," I say. Cassie knows what she wants—and doesn't settle for anything else. It makes her stubborn and difficult and really, really picky. But it also makes her strong. The strongest person I know.

"Do you know about my daughter?" Daniel asks.

"I do."

Daniel nods like he expected this. "So you understand how complicated my situation is. I could lose her. Not just legally. Tatiana could make my daughter feel like I'm not her dad."

I consider this for a moment. I may not have children of my own, but I've wanted them for as long as I can remember. I can feel it in my bones, the love I have stored for my future kids. A love more powerful than anything else. Like the love Nana felt for us.

"Then you should never leave," I say.

"But I will," he says, his tone insistent. "I just need time. Tatiana has promised me an amicable divorce. I just have to wait until Labor Day."

"The party in Nantucket," I say. "I know."

A sad smile from Daniel. "She told you everything."

"We're sisters."

"No, I didn't mean it in a bad way. I'm glad she did. She's usually so guarded, so private. I'm glad she has you again."

Had—past tense. She'll never have me in her life again. Not after this. But now is not the time. This isn't about me.

"She thinks Tatiana is stalling," I say. "And I don't know your wife, but I agree." I pause to consider what I'm about to say next. If Cassie would want me to. I feel like she would. "She called Cassie."

Daniel looks at me. "Who did?"

"Tatiana. She called Nana's house."

"Why didn't Cassie tell me?" he's whispering now, his mouth slack.

"Tatiana said you'd had an affair before. She said she was calling to warn Cassie. The timing was awful, too. Cassie was upset because you'd just told her about the party. And Cassie was going to tell you, but she wanted to do it in person."

"She doesn't believe Tatiana, does she?"

"She doesn't know what to believe." And then: "She has doubts."

"About me?" A flash of panic in his eyes.

"Yes."

"But she knows how much I love her."

"But it's hard to believe that when you're still living with your wife. It's been hard on her, Daniel. Really hard. She's never had doubts before. The way she talked about how much she loved you was so…all-consuming. She described your relationship to me like a marriage. A happy marriage, stable and comfortable and loving. But then you blindsided her with this decision. She didn't know if you were having second thoughts or if there was something else she was missing."

Daniel runs an open palm through his face, shaking his head. "I had no idea," he says, under his breath. "I really messed up." He sighs heavily. "I take it all back, Julie. I'll leave Tatiana now. This very second. I just need Cassie to be OK."

An idea occurs to me. One that will make Cassie's day when she wakes up. Something I can do for her, even if she never knows about it.

"Do you mean it?" I ask.

"I do." He says it with conviction.

"Then come with me."

Daniel's fingers are steady as he makes the call. I'm sitting next to him, holding my phone on my open palm. Recording.

"Hello?" Tatiana's voice on the other end of the line is sated, sleepy.

"It's me," he says. "We need to talk."

"I'm busy. What do you want?"

"I'll be brief. I can't wait until Labor Day to file for divorce. I'm really sorry. But it's something I have to do now. I hope you can understand."

Her sigh is impatient. "I wasn't really asking, Daniel."

"I'm going to file for divorce on Monday. I hope we can do this amicably. For the sake of our children."

"And Angie? Are you going to tell her you're not her dad, too?" There's a sinister calm in her voice.

"Tatiana, please don't do this. I'm her dad. I love her. All I want is for us to get along. Our marriage has been over for a very long time. There's no sense in dragging this out. I want us to get along. Co-parent our children together."

"I don't know what's gotten into you, but let me be clear: you can either wait until after Labor Day or I will drive up to Angie right now and tell her that her daddy isn't really her daddy. I'll tell her you're leaving us because she's a bastard. Your call."

I cover my mouth to muffle the sound of my gasp.

Daniel seems wounded, but unsurprised. I watch him take a deep breath. "You'll be hurting our daughter if you do that."

"No. *You'll* be hurting her. Look. Feel free to fuck around with Cassie. I don't give a damn what you do, as long as you're discreet. But I am not going to be humiliated in front of my friends."

"This is blackmail, Tatiana."

"And I'm supposed to care because…?"

"Because I'm recording this."

A beat. And then another. I make a spinning motion with my hands, urging him to go on. We anticipated she'd go silent when he told her about the recording. We practiced.

"This conversation is being recorded. If you purposefully inflict psychological harm on our child, I will show this to a judge and ask for sole custody. For Angie's protection."

"You can't record someone without their consent. It's illegal."

Daniel's face turns white. This we did not prepare for.

"I-I don't…" he stammers.

Tatiana snickers.

"That isn't true," I say. "New York State only requires one-party consent. Daniel, do you consent?"

Daniel shoots me a panicked look. I motion for him to say yes.

"I do." He clears his throat.

"Then this recording is legal and admissible in court," I say.

"Who is this?" Tatiana demands, her voice low.

"This is one of Mr. O'Riley's attorneys." I try to remember how Patrick sounds when he's in a conference call: an eerie blend of threatening and calm. Much like Tatiana, come to think of it.

"It's up to you, Tatiana," Daniel says. "You can either agree to an amicable divorce or have this used against you in a court of law. Your call."

"You'll be hearing from my lawyer," she retorts, and then the line goes dead.

Daniel exhales loudly, like he's been holding his breath all along.

"That was…" he pauses and looks at me. "How did you know to say that?"

I don't want to tell him that I saw it on TV, on a rerun of *The Good Wife*. Especially since that show takes place in Illinois—not New York.

"Do you think it worked?" I ask.

"Maybe? She sounded scared." A pause. He gives me a tired smile. "But even if it didn't, I have that recording. I'll show Angie if I have to."

I send a silent prayer to Nana that Angie never has to listen to that.

"Craig?" Daniel says.

I shake my head, confused. What about Craig? And then I follow Daniel's eyes. Craig is standing at the door, looking at me expectantly.

"You came back," I say. Yesterday he had to leave to relieve his friend who had been babysitting Kiki and Ben.

"I just got here. Mrs. Bunsen and Mandy came over to look after the kids," he says, hurriedly. "Jul, I ran into Andrea outside. She was looking for you." He swallows. "Cassie woke up."

Daniel and I both jump to our feet. The three of us rush to room 312. I stop outside the door, grabbing Daniel's arm. "I can't go in. I don't want to upset her."

Daniel nods somberly. He doesn't tell me I'm wrong.

"Tell her I love her," I say. "Tell her I love her more than anything in this world."

"I will," he promises.

And then he goes in.

CHAPTER SIXTY-FOUR

Cassie

Saturday, July 28th

My bare feet beat on the white ceramic floors, seconds ticking on a clock.

Thump, thump, thump.

I breathe in the cool air. My mouth is dry. My eyes scan the hallways, sterile and white. But I don't see her. I don't know where she is.

I keep running. Thump, thump, thump.

In a room: my father. He's talking to a man with a stethoscope around his neck, a doctor. My father's face is red. Everything in this room is red. He's shouting. Cursing. Calling out my mother's name. Why would he do that—doesn't he know she's dead? I don't stop to ask. I need to find her.

Thump, thump, thump.

Another room: Daniel is inside. Seated at a table across an empty seat. His loneliness is palpable, the room covered in shades of blue. His eyes are searching for me. He misses me, I can feel it. But I don't go in.

Thump, thump, thump.

A third room: my office, a deep shade of green. An empty distressed leather armchair. A chesterfield couch. A divan. A coffee table with books and a box of tissues. The room is calling me, urging me to step inside. I ignore it.

Thump, thump, thump.

One more room: bright yellow, sunny. I peer inside. It seems to be empty, its only presence a bright, beautiful energy. I hear my name. I know that voice. I look closer. I see her inside. Nana, sitting alone at the dining table that seats twelve. She sees me, too, and opens her arms. Come, her eyes say. I want to. But can't. Not until I find her.

Thump, thump, thump.

I go by rooms of all colors. More rooms than I can count. I see Christina and Rachel. I see my agent, Sam. My publicist, Claudia. My patients, dozens of them. Elana, the host for East Coast Coffee.

And then I see her.

I don't recognize this room, but I'm sure it's her. She's standing next to a bed, silent. Maybe this is her bedroom back in Boston. Her eyes are dreamy and sad, like she's trapped inside an unhappy fairy tale. But that makes no sense—her fairy tales are meant to beautify, to add color and purpose to the gritty messiness of the world. I open the door and walk in, calling out her name. But she doesn't turn around.

Julie, I say again.

Nothing. It's like I'm not there.

I walk closer, reaching for her shoulder, but something makes me stop. I look down at the bed, following her gaze.

It's me. Julie is looking at me.

I look around the room. It's not a bedroom at all. It's a hospital room.

I'm in a hospital room.

I need to wake up.

The hospital room smells like bleach. My eyelids feel heavy, like I drank too much wine before going to sleep. Someone is looking at me, a round-faced woman with large brown eyes. She's pointing something bright into my eyes, repeating my name.

"Please stop," I manage to say. My mouth feels like it's been stuffed with cotton.

"Do you know where you are?" she says, squinting at me. She lowers the pointer.

"Where's Jul?" I ask.

The corners of her eyes lift in a smile. "Can you tell me your name?" Her tone is mild, slow. Almost insultingly slow.

I can't have that.

"My name is Cassie Meyers," I say. "I'm in the hospital. I was in a car accident and I'm assuming my arm was hurt because it's immobilized. Thank you for your concern, but, as you can see, I'm feeling fine. I need to see my sister."

Another smile, wider this time. "You're as tough as they said. I'll get her for you."

"OK," I agree. I look at her name tag. "Thank you, Nurse Rollins."

"Call me Andrea."

I close my eyes, just for a moment. But I feel myself sinking with fatigue. I let go.

"Cass?" Daniel's voice wakes me up.

I open my eyes. "Daniel."

He's standing next to my bed, an expression of concern.

"Hey." He reaches for my hand. "You had me worried. How are you feeling?"

I glance at the door. "Where's Jul?"

"Right outside. She really wanted to come in, but she's…" A pause. "What do you remember from last night?"

"I remember everything," I say. And I do. I was stupid and reckless, getting in that car with my father. Letting him get to me like that. "It all happened so fast. I couldn't find her earlier today. I was going crazy thinking I'd lost her again." I gasp at the speed of my words. I feel nervous, agitated. I need to see Julie.

"Cass, slow down," he says. "What do you mean, earlier today? You just woke up."

"I meant earlier, when I was dreaming." I force myself to take a breath. "I know I've been here since the accident. I know my father came to the house and tried to blackmail me. I know I got in the car with him. I know why, too. I know Julie sent my mother those pictures."

"Your dad tried to *blackmail* you?" He looks horrified, but not entirely surprised.

"Sophie told him about us. About her suspicions, anyway. He said he'd hire a private detective. I told him to do his worst." I catch my breath. I'm struggling to talk. "Is he here? In the hospital?"

"He was, but not anymore."

"Good." Another pause, another breath. "I'm totally fine, Daniel, I promise. And I love that you're here, but I need to see Jul."

"OK, I'll go get her. Can I just say one thing first?"

"Of course."

"I love you. More than the entire world. More than I ever thought I could love anyone. You never have to doubt that."

"I know you love me," I say, looking into his eyes. "And I love you. And I want to be with you. But only if it's for real. I can't stop loving you, Daniel. But I also can't wait."

"You don't have to. I've left Tatiana. I called her today. Julie helped me—"

"Julie helped you? How?"

"It's a long story. But it's done. I already texted Bella. Jackson is taking the kids to the aquarium. She's going to the house to pack up my things right now."

I try to sit up on the bed. "Your sister is packing your things?" This doesn't sound like Daniel at all. He's so self-sufficient. I'm sure Angie and Sam will have a great time with their Uncle Jackson at the aquarium, but why couldn't this wait?

"We have to do it now. Tatiana's in Nantucket. If I wait, Tatiana might go back and throw my things out." He notices me moving and helps me sit up a bit.

"But how will she know what to pack? Don't you want to do it?"

"I'm not leaving your side. Not for work, or to get my things, or for any other reason. I'm staying here until you can leave Montauk. We can call Claudia if you want. Tell her it's official. Tell her we're ready for, what was she calling it? The reveal?"

I let his words sink in, a feeling of warmth spreading across my chest.

"You're really mine?" I ask.

"One hundred percent." He leans in and gives me a peck on the mouth. "I love you."

"I love you, too," I say. "Now please get Jul."

He makes his way to the door and whispers something. I hear a gasp and then I see her rush inside. She's looking at me with our eyes, hope and fear written all over them.

"I'm going to hug you now," she says, tears streaming down her face.

"Be gentle, OK?" My entire body aches.

She leans over and whispers in my ear, "I'm so sorry. I'm so, so sorry."

"Jul?" I say, breaking away from her embrace.

She wipes her face, meeting my gaze.

"I'm not upset. I was shocked, yes. And I thought I was angry with you. But I'm not. I had this dream. I couldn't find you. I knew you had sent the pictures and you were gone, and I kept running down this long hallway because I couldn't let you go. I'm not making any sense, I'm sorry. Jul, I know you didn't mean to hurt my mom."

Her sobs come in waves. "I've caused you so much pain, Cassie." She covers her face with her hands. "I'm so sorry."

I think of my mother as I hear that word: *pain*. Living was so very difficult for her, maybe because my father never loved her like she loved him, or maybe because it's who she was. I wish she'd gotten help when she was still with us. I wish I could go back in time and find a way to get her into intensive therapy. I wish I could've saved her.

For her sake—and for mine.

Maybe then I wouldn't be this way: hardened, anxious. Terrified of being vulnerable.

"*She* caused me pain," I say. "It's all she knew. She'd been in pain her whole life. She didn't know what do to with herself, Jul. She was sick. She decided to go. But it wasn't because of you or those pictures. It's never one thing. If it hadn't been for the pictures, something else would have triggered that. Maybe even us going to the same school after graduation."

"I should have told you sooner. I was such a coward."

"I get it now, Jul," I say, thinking of how long it took for me to sort through my emotions. The years I spent hurting myself on purpose. "It took a major accident for me to fully grasp all of it, but I get it now. It doesn't matter how my mom died. She died. I can't hold on to anger or pain or guilt because it's pointless. And it's not who I want to be."

She's still crying. I use my good arm to reach out to her.

"Stop crying, OK? You're my sister. You're my family. You and Nana were the two constants in my life, my two rocks. We only just lost her. I can't lose you, too. I love you. And I'm not mad. I wouldn't have the right to be, but that's never stopped me before." I shoot her a sad smile. "I love you and I want to put all of this behind us."

"Oh, thank God!" she says and leans in to hug me again.

"Thank Nana," I whisper to her. "I know I do."

EPILOGUE

Cassie

One year later

We did it: Nana's dining table is finally full.

Craig walks in the front door holding two large bags. He spots Julie standing by the stove, her back turned to him. Then he looks at me, his face a question.

I nod quickly, quietly. All good, my eyes say. Julie doesn't suspect a thing.

"Four orders of garlic bread, six mini crème brûlées, and six mini apple pies," he says. He glances at the table I'm setting, using Nana's special-occasions china. "Why aren't we eating outside?"

"Do we really need twelve desserts?" I ask.

"Yes," Julie says, from the kitchen. "We won't fit outside."

"Bertie's porch is huge," Craig says, placing the takeout bags on the island.

"When are you going to start calling it our porch?" I say.

"Never," Julie says. "This is Nana's house. It will always be Nana's house."

"All right, but you should know that Sam and Angie are outside calling it their house," Daniel says with a grin.

"And of course we need twelve desserts," Craig says. "There's eleven of us."

Julie nods. "The twelfth can be in Nana's honor."

"And I can eat it," Craig says. "You know, in her honor."

"Nice try." Julie gives his arm a squeeze. He wraps his hand around her waist, pulling her in for a kiss.

"Go," she says, swatting him with a tea towel. "Or I'll ruin the pasta."

Craig lifts his hand in surrender and steps away from the kitchen. On the way out, he winks at me. How can he be so calm? *I'm* nervous—and I'm not the one getting down on one knee.

I lift my left hand, admiring the plain gold band Daniel and I exchanged on our wedding day, less than six months ago, at City Hall. I keep waiting for this giddy I'm-actually-married-to-Daniel feeling to go away—but I don't think it will. I suspect Julie will feel the same way when she says yes to Craig's proposal. And she will say yes. For a while, Craig had been worried there. I don't blame him—he knows about her first marriage, after all. But that's all in the past. Julie's in a good place. She has been for some time now.

I feel a glow of pride thinking of how far she's come. There are things I expected: she and Craig continue to be in love, she's happy in her new career. But there are the things I didn't, too: Julie confronted Sophie, shamed her for asking her to spy on me, for threatening to expose me. For sharing her suspicions with our father. I wasn't there for it, but I can imagine her delivering her speech with her special blend of strength and sensibility. She made it clear to Sophie that our father wasn't welcome in her life anymore. I still expected Sophie to get back together with him, but according to Julie that hasn't happened. In fact, Sophie is seeing someone else. Some big shot at *Posh*.

It's been a little over a year since Julie and I were compelled to come to Montauk. I'd been broken when I arrived. I see that now. But this place healed me—Nana healed me. The very things that I'd shunned are now paramount to my happiness. I'm married to the love of my life. I'm a stepmother to two brilliant, witty kids.

And the biggest one of them all: I have my sister again. My life feels whole, complete.

"Where are you?" Julie asks. The two of us are alone in the kitchen now. "It's like you're doing my fairy tale thing."

"I was thinking about last year. About how much things have changed."

"It's pretty trippy, isn't it?" She shoots me a smile. "Pass me the garlic bread? A lot may have changed, but you still can't cook. Or even heat up bread."

I open up the bags, eyeing the Holly's logo. I remember how surprised we both were when we found out Craig actually *owned* Holly's. He assumed we knew—or at least that Julie did. But for some reason, Nana never told her. The pub is named after Ann—her name was Holly Ann. I don't know how I'd feel if Daniel owned a business named after the woman he once loved, but Julie doesn't seem to mind it at all. It's a delightfully odd thing, witnessing her newfound confidence.

I sneak a peek at the pasta Julie is cooking. The kitchen smells like Nana again.

"Did you find the missing ingredient?" I ask.

"I did."

"Aren't you going to tell me what it is?"

"Maybe," Julie says. But she leaves it at that.

At seven, all of us are sitting around the table. Julie and Craig, along with Ben and Kiki. Daniel and me, with Angie and Sam. And Bella and Jackson, their newborn in his arms. Our family, together.

"OK, I'll admit," Bella says, her mouth half-full of spaghetti. "At first I thought it was a little weird, pasta in the summer. But this is better than barbequing." She turns to Julie. "This is amazing."

"Thank you," Julie says. "It's Nana's recipe."

"It includes a secret ingredient she won't tell us." I look at Bella. "And we'll barbeque tomorrow. We have the whole weekend to celebrate."

"Cheers to that," Jackson says, lifting his bottle of beer. Sadly, his taste buds are a lost cause—like Julie's.

"Aunt Julie, when is your next book going to come out?" Angie asks.

"Cassie says it's soon," Sam says.

"I had to," I lean in and whisper to Julie. "She wouldn't stop asking."

Julie giggles. "It's in the works, sweetie."

"We can tell you what the story is about," Kiki says.

"Julie reads them to us first and we give our ideas and stuff," Ben says. "She calls us cauthors."

"Co-authors, honey," Julie says.

"Wow!" Angie's eyes go wide.

"That's so cool!" Sam says.

Julie's children's books are a monumental success. She started out small, writing kid-friendly fairy tales on Instagram. Her following began to grow, until one day it exploded. I showed it to my agent, who passed it on to Stacey, the kid lit agent at Bees. After that, everything moved quickly: Stacey signed Julie, submitted her work to a few houses, and got Julie a two-book deal with an impressive advance. *The Twin Princesses: The Curse of the Fire Princess* was an instant bestseller. Julie is turning it into a series, with the two princesses tackling a different adventure in every book. Hurricane Elle is going to be included in the next one. Now, Julie is the famous sister—I quit the show about six months ago. I've been focusing on my private practice ever since, which is a much better fit for me.

"You can help us if you want," Ben offers Sam.

"Awesome!" Sam's mouth is half full, so it sounds more like *awjum.*

They're cute together, the kids. Maybe that's what Julie's next series could be about: four cousins. Although by then they might be five. I quietly touch my belly, giddy with the possibility. Julie is the only one who knows so far. I don't want to tell Daniel until I'm sure—he's been wanting a baby ever since we got married. Maybe I'll get Angie and Sam to tell him. That would be sweet. I'm sure Tatiana wouldn't mind. She's off in Ibiza or wherever else with what's-his-name.

I chuckle, thinking back to the day when Bella went to Daniel's old house to pack up his things and caught Tatiana in bed with none other than Ava's husband. Bella had been shocked (Tatiana was supposed to be in Nantucket) but not too shocked to take a picture of the two of them naked and contorted like pretzels (I admit it: I peeked at the picture). After that, everything made sense to me: Tatiana didn't want Daniel to leave her before the Labor Day party because she didn't want Ava's husband to think she'd been dumped. They were planning on running away together. And they did. She seems happy—at least that's the impression I get when I see her pictures on Facebook. She's even sort of nice to me now. Civil, anyway.

I steal a glance at Bella, who's talking to Julie, the two of them tilting their heads back and laughing. I owe my family's peace of mind to her good judgment. Thanks to the picture she took, Tatiana has agreed not to say anything to Angie about Daniel not being her biological father. Daniel and I will talk to her when the time is right. I'm thinking that might happen soon. She's still young, but she's sensitive and extraordinarily smart. She understands, for example, that Julie is my half-sister, and that I'm her stepmom. But she also understands that the prefixes are silly—Nana would be proud of her.

"You look happy," Daniel says, putting an arm around me.

"I am." I give him a peck on the lips.

I look around the table again, glad to be together like this.

*

At sunset, Julie and I go outside. Just the two of us.

We make our way down the beach, holding hands, until we feel the waves brushing against our feet.

"I think she would've wanted this," Julie says.

"It *is* her ocean."

"The Atlantic Ocean?"

"This spot right here, anyway. She would've been happy we kept the house."

"And that it's full of kids."

"Especially since two of them are Craig's kids."

"Maybe three," she touches her stomach, a sheepish smile on her face. If we were on the other side of the island, we'd be able to see the sun lowering itself into the azure water. But I like the sky better like this: endlessly tinted in magenta and yellow and orange, without a central player.

"You, too?" I feel a rush of excitement. "Why didn't you tell me?"

"I was going to wait until after Craig's proposal tonight to tell you."

I feel my face fall. "You know about the proposal?"

"Oh, please. You two are the worst secret keepers. Also, I found the ring on his nightstand." She giggles as a gust of wind catches her hair. "I still snoop sometimes. Just kidding."

"He'll be crushed. The kids are helping, they wrote a song."

"Don't worry, I'll still act surprised. Promise."

"Can you imagine if they're two girls?" My voice is a squeak.

"Summer sisters like us."

"Sisters," I say. "Lucky them."

"Lucky us."

"Yeah, all thanks to this lady." I pat the urn gently.

"Ready?" she asks me.

I nod. "Let's do this."

I open the urn, slowly removing the plastic bag with her ashes. We recite the poem together, Nana's favorite, as we spread her remains in the water.

Lucky us, I think again.

A LETTER FROM CECILIA

Dear reader,

I am so grateful that you have chosen to read *The Sunset Sisters*. If you enjoyed it and want to keep up to date with all my latest releases, just sign up at the following link. Your email address will never be shared and you can unsubscribe at any time.

www.bookouture.com/cecilia-lyra

I want you to know how much I appreciate having you as a reader. If reading a novel is visiting, perhaps even inhabiting, another's world, then surely writing one is creating that world. While readers are guests, authors are hosts. All my life, I've been a guest. And now, here I am, hosting. What this means, in practical terms, is that I'm a ball of nerves. Even as a write this letter, I am eager to know if you've identified with Cassie or Julie—or maybe both. I am curious about what you thought of Nana's efforts to bring them together. I am speculating as to your first impressions of Daniel and Craig. As it turns out, being the host of a make-believe world is quite anxiety-inducing! But it is also the highest of honors. Because while this story is fiction, the emotions in it are real, which means that, as you made your way through *The Sunset Sisters*, you were making your way through my heart. And so, to you, my guest, I say this: Thank you for coming. I am so very lucky to have spent this time with you. I do hope you have enjoyed your stay.

And if you'd like to leave a review, please know that you will be making my day. Finally, if you'd like to share your thoughts with me or ask me any questions, I'm always happy to chat via my Goodreads page, Twitter account, Facebook author page, and Instagram.

Thank you again.
Cecilia Lyra

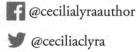

@cecilialyraauthor

@ceciliaclyra

@cecilia_lyra_author

Cecilia Lyra

ACKNOWLEDGMENTS

My infinite, heartfelt thanks to:

My agent, Sam Hiyate, for your continuous faith and encouragement, and to the entire TRF family for welcoming me with open arms. Special thanks to Emily Bozik and Terri Brunsting for notes, and to Michaela Stephen for audio work.

Rich Green, for taking a chance on me even though I was rendered speechless during our first meeting. It's not every day I meet a god-maker.

The entire team at Bookouture for treating me like a bestselling author before I'd sold a single book, especially my brilliant editor, Emily Gowers, for your fresh perspective, genius ideas, and thoughtful, detailed feedback on every line in this novel; Kim Nash for being a publicity rock star; Jade Craddock for copyediting; Shirley Khan for proofreading; Alex Crow and Hannah Deuce for all things marketing; Mumtaz Mustafa for design; Alexandra Holmes, Kelsie Marsden, and Ramesh Kumar for production; and Chris Lucraft and Marina Valles for distribution. I am very grateful to the talented Elsie Roth for giving voice to Cassie and Julie in the audiobook version of this novel under the expert guidance of Alexandra Holmes and Leodora Darlington, as well as everyone at The Audiobook Producers. Thank you, also, to my fellow Bookouture authors. I am so lucky to be a part of such a supportive community.

My teachers, for dedicating your lives to the most important work in the world.

The CBC online novel-writing course, particularly Lisa O'Donnell for being a phenomenal author and the world's best writing instructor, and my peers Edward Hamlin, Jane Harper, Zoe Lea, Fiona Armstrong, Clare Maddox, Alison Bird, Emma Wilkes, Jessica, Kevin Smith, Rhian Jones, Sophie Neville, Dennis Bailey, and Adrian Casey.

The formidable authors whose spellbinding works keep me up at night. It was my love of reading that made me want to be an author, and for that I will forever be in your debt.

Every single reader who picked up this book and traveled to Montauk with Cassie and Julie: if authors are storytellers, then readers are storykeepers; thank you for keeping my story. I am truly honored.

Those who dedicate their lives to books: teachers, librarians, reviewers, bookstagrammers, book bloggers, book club founders and hosts, you are the whisperers of magic.

The beautiful Montauk, and its fiercely loyal residents: I am sorry for any mistake I made or liberty I took in the making of this novel. My imagination is often impertinent, and my memory can be fallible, but my love is always true.

My incredible friends: I am lucky to have too many to name, but special thanks to those who helped me through this journey, especially Clarisse Hughes, for beta reading an early draft of this novel and for patiently answering my incessant texts at inappropriate hours up until the very end; Julie Marquis, whose breathtaking beauty and grace was the physical inspiration for Julie and who generously answered my questions on all things *française*; Shelby Waters, whose talent for hair is rivaled only by her sensitivity with hearts; Kim Noble, for never letting me give up; D.S. for sharing your experiences with post-traumatic stress disorder; and M.T. for answering my never-ending questions about couples counseling with diligence and compassion.

My Wine Club family: thank you for the champagne-infused evenings, laugh-out-loud texts, and lake-side adventures. Special thanks to Kailey and Sarah D., whose belief in me was a continuous source of comfort and courage, and to Colleen for making Nicholas and Charlotte, and for being the kind of friend whose name I call out when I don't know what to do. Thank you to Gary and Lois for the wise words.

My wonderful family: Chris and Rapha, for making my childhood sweeter; Aunt Claudia, for being unfailingly gentle and kind; my mother-in-law, Ana, for being my confidant and cheerleader, and for raising the most amazing man in the world; my brother-in-law, Rafael, for beta reading an early draft of this novel and for our leisurely Baba walks; my goddaughter, Chloe, for being equal parts fearless and compassionate; Cynthia, for loving me as I am; my godson, Dudu, my Leib Moshe, for his infectious smile; and Mari, for making us a family.

My grandmother, who is proof that a hard life does not equal a hard heart: thank you for your quiet strength and generous spirit. Thank you for seeing me. I really do hope you are in a magical land with unlimited marrons glacés and port wine.

My dad, whose epic imagination taught me to love stories, and who never said "no" to buying me a single book as a child, often resulting in me purchasing entire bookshelves. Whenever I write, you are with me.

My mom, for late-night incantations, morning octopus kisses, and for being stronger than all of the monsters under my bed. Thank you for giving me, as you put it, the greatest gift in the world: a sister.

Anna, for giving me the privilege of being your sister. Thank you for building a world with me. Thank you for being my first reader. Most of all, thank you for being my Baby Dino.

Babaganoush, who cannot read, but who was with me, often on my lap, as I wrote every word in this book. Thank you for being my forever baby.

Most of all, my husband, Bruno, without whom this book would not exist. Thank you for being everything I always dreamed of and never thought existed. My life begins and ends with you. You are my story. Thank you for making all of my dreams come true.

CPSIA information can be obtained
at www.ICGtesting.com
Printed in the USA
LVHW051508070720
659996LV00004B/687